A BOD
FOR CH

BY
DONNA YOUNG

AND

THE MAN FROM NOWHERE

BY
RACHEL LEE

"Are you telling me you've never had sex before?"

Her eyes flew open. "Jordan, I—"

"Be quiet." His hands shook as he grabbed her by the shoulders and pulled her off the bed and into him.

He smelled of shaving cream and soap. Spicy, masculine. She gave in to the urge to lean closer, to inhale deeper.

"Regina," Jordan murmured her name like a curse. His eyes drilled into hers, so clear, so sharp. The urge to protect speared his royal blood, cutting him clean to the bone.

Santa's bell rang down the block, breaking Jordan's concentration. He let go and she fell back onto the bed. "What you're asking for isn't going to happen, sweetheart."

But all through that wintry night, he never once left her side.

A BODYGUARD FOR CHRISTMAS

BY
DONNA YOUNG

All the characters in this book have no existence outside the imagination of the author, and have no relation whatsoever to anyone bearing the same name or names. They are not even distantly inspired by any individual known or unknown to the author, and all the incidents are pure invention.

First published in Great Britain 2010
Harlequin Mills & Boon Limited,
Eton House, 18-24 Paradise Road, Richmond, Surrey TW9 1SR

ISBN: 978 0 263 88280 3

46-1210

Harlequin Mills & Boon policy is to use papers that are natural, renewable and recyclable products and made from wood grown in sustainable forests. The logging and manufacturing processes conform to the legal environmental regulations of the country of origin.

Printed and bound in Spain
by Litografia Rosés S.A., Barcelona

Donna Young, an incurable romantic, lives in beautiful Northern California with her husband and two children.

To Ray & Geri, Steve & Debbye, Mike & Sheila, Terry & Janice, Trish & Ed, Matt & Robbie. For your humor, love and immense support,
I love you guys!

Chapter One

Timothy Severs was wired.

Cocaine-wired.

The shock sent his heart into overdrive, pumping blood until it sizzled and snapped in his veins. A high-pitched hum set his teeth grinding, his muscles twitching.

A split second later, euphoria hit. And with it, the rush of confidence, the heightened senses, the understanding he could live forever.

Ironic really, considering his plans for the day.

Using his finger, he rubbed the excess white powder over his gums, then clicked his tongue against the numbness.

He could have done the line in his apartment before coming to work that morning. But the prospect of snorting coke under Big Brother's eye added a sharp, seductive edge to his buzz.

Unhurried, he flipped the latch open and stepped out of the bathroom stall. A quick glance told him he was alone.

With a laugh, he leaned over the sink and adjusted his tie in front of the beveled mirror. He was not an attractive man, with glazed, bulging eyes of watery blue and a receding hairline. Small, red splotches appeared on his pale, slightly pitted skin, betraying his drug habit, which he tried to hide beneath a thin layer of makeup.

He washed his hands, ignoring the slight tremor in his fingers when he grabbed a nearby paper towel. Well, his reputation was about to change.

The only child of David Severs, a prominent Supreme Court Justice, Timothy had been expected to continue the tradition of law in his family. But a drug bust and the accidental overdose of an underage girl—the daughter of a senator—in his dorm room, created a scandal that even his family's connections couldn't cover up.

But with his father's help, Timothy eventually secured an assignment as junior aide to an obscure British attaché. He should be grateful, his father lectured. After all, Timothy had thrown away a promising future. And for what? His father demanded. Sex? Drugs?

Nothing wrong with either, Timothy mused. After a final check in the mirror, more for vanity than necessity, he opened the restroom door and stepped into the hallway.

"Mr. Severs?"

Timothy jumped, slightly startled by the hand on his shoulder. He turned, noting the marine's uniform more than the man wearing it. With short cropped hair and flat, heavy-boned features, the soldier stood a good six inches over Timothy's five-nine frame.

"Yes?" Timothy demanded, taking a deliberate moment to scan the battle-scarred lines and leathery skin before dismissing the man to look at the name badge on the soldier's chest. "Cooper."

The soldier's eyebrow rose. "I was instructed to tell you that your new chair has arrived," Cooper said quietly, but a sickle-shaped scar on his cheek flexed with the tightening of his jaw.

The chair. Excitement caught in Timothy's chest, but he managed to keep his features schooled. "Good," he replied, his tone arrogant. With a dismissive wave, he continued down the hallway to his office.

The other staff called him the Fish behind his back. He heard their smirks, saw the women's features before they could hide their repulsion.

Even the British Ambassador, Sir Christopher Beck, couldn't always conceal his distaste.

Only one person ever understood him, appreciated his talents. And sadly, that one person would never witness his moment of triumph.

When Timothy reached his office, he closed the door and carefully turned the lock. The room wasn't the smallest in the British Embassy, but it certainly was the ugliest. No family pictures hung on the wall or sat on his desk. No plants—artificial or living—cluttered the corners.

He required nothing more than a small metal desk with a computer to do his job. And now behind it, the high-back, leather swivel chair.

For a moment he ran his fingers over the seat, enjoying the cool smoothness, recognizing the top quality of the grain. He let out a small laugh and flung himself into the chair, sending it spinning.

Finally, dizziness forced him to stop. He folded his arms on the desk and leaned forward until the room tilted back into place.

Smugness swelled inside him, riding high on the back of the cocaine. He jerked his desk drawer open and grabbed a pair of scissors. He stood and with shallow slashes, he hacked at the leather until it shredded beneath the blades.

"Come to daddy," he gasped, out of breath from the exertion. Murky drops of sweat and makeup rolled down his face. He wiped away the trickle from his cheek, ignoring the tan smear against his suit sleeve.

Underneath the shredded leather lay a slim, flat clay brick of C-4 wrapped in wax paper. With shaky hands, he picked it up, enjoying the weight of its power. He opened his briefcase and placed the plastic explosive inside. From a nearby drawer, he pulled out the electronic detonator.

Delta had ordered him to use a timer, but the power behind being the human detonator was too seductive to resist. Practically giddy, he inserted the detonator into the clay and punched the code into his cell phone.

Delta had assured Timothy that his identity would be protected. But Timothy understood that if Delta's plans went awry, Timothy would be the fall guy.

A glance at his watch told him he had less than an hour before his meeting with Ambassador Beck.

Plenty of time. He set his phone down on the desk

and pulled a small foil-wrapped package from his pocket, along with a razor and straw. He shook the packet out and used the razor to create a long, perfect white rail of powder.

Slowly, he guided one end of the straw to his nose and leaned toward the cocaine. "Here's to a very promising future, Dad," he murmured, his lips tightening with derision. He pressed his finger against his free nostril and inhaled.

Chapter Two

Two weeks later

The storm struck downtown Baltimore with icy contempt. Slapping and spitting, the gusts of sleet battered the red brick buildings trimmed with Christmas cheer. White lights, wreaths and ruby-red bows were left tattered on the near deserted streets.

From a darkened doorway, the man called Beck watched a pseudo-Santa scurry from his coin bucket into a nearby diner.

Smart chap, he thought with derision. *Smarter than me.*

The frigid air burned like acid in Beck's nostrils. Bits of ice pelted his face, each with the snap and sting of a whip. But the storm couldn't match the rage inside the man. A rage that, if freed, would have set the snow and sky on fire.

But for now, it blazed inside until his eyes burned a blue inferno, and the heat hardened his heart into a heavy stone.

As if to taunt him, church bells tolled—their clang muffled, but their warning clear. Saturday evening services had ended.

Beck stepped back farther into the doorway, letting his black jeans and leather jacket blend with the inky shadows.

He was English aristocracy by birth. A fact that meant little in the modern world—much less in his world. Still, lineage reinforced the long, lean lines of his body, the hard set of his broad shoulders.

As an added precaution, he pulled a dark ski cap from his pocket and slipped it over his head. His light brown hair had enough blond threaded through to draw more than a casual glance.

But it was the nobility of his features that made most glances become outright stares. The pale, blue eyes set deep beneath a broad forehead. The high, prominent cheek bones cut lean into the square jaw that only hinted of a cleft chin. A hard mouth that over the years tended to smirk with the disdain of his ancestors, rather than soften in humor—or compassion.

Beck was born with the proverbial silver spoon. One that corroded long before he'd ever become a man.

Up the street the church bells ceased clanging, leaving in their wake the hum of conversation.

Most people, the smart ones in his opinion, stayed indoors. Others—the more devout, maybe—braved the elements in huddled groups of two and three, searching for their cars through knee-high drifts.

As people drew closer the hum morphed into a spattering of laughter and a few verses of "We Wish You a

Merry Christmas" from those caught up in the spirit of the season.

Cheery buggers.

Beck made note of some nearby pedestrians—a handful with their heads down, their arms hugging their coats close—making their way past the bookstore across the street.

The bookstore he'd been observing for the last hour.

Menlow Books.

Owner, Regina Menlow. Single. American. Age, twenty-eight. Graduated Princeton.

Not exactly a second-class education, he thought with derision. Although, from her file, Regina Menlow used a trust fund left by her deceased parents for most of the tuition and then worked her way through college for the balance.

She had lived off campus, kept to herself. No friends.

Only one estranged aunt for family. Aida Pullman.

An image flashed through Beck's mind. The only photograph from Miss Menlow's file—a driver's license picture.

Her brown hair had been tied back into a long, glossy tail that lay over one shoulder. Shorter hair fringed her heart-shaped face, framed big green eyes that flashed impatience just as the camera clicked. The same impatience that showed in the generous slant of her mouth, the inevitable lift of one delicate brow.

It was safe to assume that Miss Menlow had a temper.

But was she capable of treason?

Beck caught a faint flicker of light in the bookstore's

display window. A silent warning pricked at the back of his neck. He straightened from the doorway, his stance turning predatory.

The sounds of the evening faded into a fuzzy void. His ears strained to hear a cry of fear or pain, while his eyes narrowed on the lighted glass and beyond.

The dim glow flashed, bursting into a frenzy of orange hues that spread from the front door to the front display window.

Fire.

Suddenly, a man—a silhouette really—slipped from the side alley by the store.

Rage worked its way up the back of Beck's throat, forcing him to take short, frigid breaths through his mouth. He palmed his pistol, thought about shooting the man, only to disregard the idea because of the people still on the street.

The shadows shifted back and forth until the fire outlined the intruder's features—caught the slide of the man's hand, the bulge of the book shoved under his overcoat.

"Come on," Beck urged, his words clipped. Shifting toward the doorway steps, he willed Regina Menlow to appear in her doorway. "Get the hell out of there, damn it."

Inside the store, the flames shimmered, growing in height behind the door's window. In his mind, Beck visualized the blaze greedily consuming the dry kindling of books and wooden shelves.

Seconds sped by. The intruder slipped around a nearby

corner, kicking over Santa's bucket in his haste. The coins scattered, making little sound on the snow-covered sidewalk.

Beck willed himself to follow the man, then cursed himself when his legs wouldn't obey.

Swearing again, he hit the wall with the side of his fist. After taking one last glance at the corner, he pulled his cap from his head, ripped a hole in the top and created a tube.

He raced across the street, yanking the tube over his face while he ran, until the material covered his mouth and nose.

The heat blasted him before he hit the sidewalk. He didn't waste time on Menlow's door, the glass having already turned black with smoke. Instead, he heaved the coin bucket through the display window. Alarms punched the night, but he barely registered the noise. He jumped over the broken glass, shoved books and shelves to the side and slid to the floor.

Quickly, he pictured the blueprint of the store in his mind. If she was as smart as her file claimed, she'd be in the loft upstairs or the office in the back.

Beck glanced up. Flames licked the ceiling, then spread in a bloom of crimson and orange—the loft above already engulfed. If she was upstairs, she was already dead.

He started toward the office.

Smoke and heat choked the air. Fire fed off the books, turning the shelves into blazing walls of hell. Cinders stung his eyes, pierced the cloth until the heavy weight of ash coated his throat and lungs.

He coughed in convulsive fits, battling the heat for oxygen.

He heard it then. An echo of his cough. Haggard, rough. Muffled.

Beck discovered her under a desk in the back office, her body clenched in a tight ball. Grudgingly, he gave her credit for having enough sense to crawl out of harm's way.

When he reached her, he realized she hadn't found safety easily. Her hands and feet were bound in duct tape, her mouth covered with the same. He carefully removed the tape from her mouth, making it easier for her to breathe. When she coughed, he fought the relief that rolled through him. Quickly, he shrugged out of his jacket and draped it over her head. He lifted her into his arms, cradling her face to his shoulder.

The office held no other exit or windows, forcing Beck back through the flames. Dread raked his gut as he fought through the inferno. Hot sparks burned his neck, smoked his clothes.

Five steps from the front, a crack of thunder exploded over his head. He charged the broken display seconds before the ceiling crashed at his heels. Beck dove out onto the sidewalk and rolled, hitting the snow packed cement with his back, cushioning the woman against his chest.

For a moment he could do no more than drag in oxygen to his lungs, ignoring the raw burn in his throat. Tears filled his eyes, setting off a thousand needle pricks beneath the lids.

With an impatient hand he wiped the blurriness away

and shoved the woman down beside him. He placed two fingers to the side of her neck. A flutter of her pulse beat against the pressure, reassuring him she lived.

The urge to protect speared through him, cutting him clean to the bone.

The feeling was familiar. Controllable. A person didn't do what he did for a living without dealing with the instinct now and again.

Beck grabbed his switch blade from his pant pocket, and within moments sliced through the tape that bound her. Gently, he peeled it back, not wanting to mar the skin beneath the adhesive.

She was a little thing, he noted. The top of her head not even coming to his shoulder. Her hair was dark and shoulder length now, the color masked by the low light of the evening. According to the file, her eyes were hazel. But the file didn't mention the pale skin—now smudged with ash and blood—the sprinkle of freckles across her nose, or the slender line of her neck.

Blood thickened in his veins, slowed the flow to his brain. It was the only excuse, he thought, for the sharp tug of attraction that pulled at the deepest part of his gut.

The wind blew a strand of hair across her cheek. With a gentle hand he brushed it away.

At his touch, her eyes fluttered opened. The irises were more mossy than hazel beneath heavy lids. Huge, somber eyes that drew on him.

"Chris?"

His father's name hit him—a slap that stung worse than wind and ice.

He shouldn't have been surprised. After all, he looked like his father and this, of course, was his father's mistress.

"No." Anger ripped through him, forcing him to tighten his jaw. Grief edged his temper.

"Chris?" A frown creased her brows, but she said nothing more as her eyes closed once again.

Like father, like son. How many times had he heard that in his lifetime?

Jordan Beck swore in disgust even as he picked her up, cradled her in his arms.

Instantly, a hand grabbed his arm.

"Shouldn't you wait for the ambulance? We've called them." A couple stood next to him, both bundled against the cold, like two misplaced Eskimos, in pea-green parkas.

Jordan dismissed the cell phone the man Eskimo waved in his face with a mitted hand.

"She's my fiancée," he replied instead, adopting an American accent. A British one would be remembered later. He tugged his shoulder free and stepped quickly into the street before the man could react. "I'll take her to the hospital myself."

For a split second, he almost gave in to the temptation to leave her and follow the street where the attacker escaped.

And if the guy had a partner waiting in the crowd for another opportunity to murder her?

He'd given his word to protect her. And she wouldn't be protected well by the police.

Sirens sounded in the distance. The eerie sound blended with the crackle of the fire, the howling of the wind.

Even on snow-packed streets, it wouldn't take them long to reach the fire.

"You'd better be bloody worth it," Jordan muttered as he reached the car, opened the door and shoved the woman onto the front seat. "Or I'll kill you myself."

Chapter Three

Smoke and tape choked her screams, smothered the oxygen she so desperately needed. The flames licked her skin—jagged knives that sliced a downward swipe, flaying a path through skin and nerves.

Suffocating, Regina struck out with her hands, defending herself against the swipe of blades, the bogged down fog that surrounded her.

"Wake up, damn you. Before you hurt yourself."

Chris.

Relief flooded through her, intensifying the burning in her throat. But when she tried lifting her eyelids, they remained stubborn and heavy.

A string of curses floated above her head, then suddenly the weight was gone and in its place a cool rush of air.

Slowly, her eyes fluttered open. Light burst, bringing tears that stung under the lids. Regina looked down, waiting for her vision to adjust and for the first time, she realized her arms refused to move.

"So you're finally awake?"

It took effort to turn her head. Chris Beck stood next to the bed, holding a wet washcloth in one hand.

"Well? Are you okay?"

Regina blinked. No, not Chris.

This man wasn't her friend. She noted sharp cheekbones, the hard line of his mouth, the rigid set of his jaw.

What did Chris say about his son?

The man had no give.

"I asked if you were okay."

"No, I'm Regina." She glanced down for the first time, taking in the tan cotton slacks and gray cardigan with a scooped-neck tee beneath. All smudged with ash, all reeking of smoke. "Do I look okay?"

"You look like hell."

No humor, either.

She almost sighed. Almost. But when her gaze met his, she actually forgot to.

The eyes were the same. Chris's and Jordan's. Both pale blue, cut laser-sharp with specks of silver that flashed little bolts of lightning-edged emotion. Pleasure, sadness, anger, impatience. It didn't matter which, the intensity never diminished.

Harnessed, yes. Controlled, certainly. But never diluted.

"I guess this pretty much defines 'in the nick of time,' doesn't it, Jordan?"

"Yes—" He stopped, surprise flashed in the blue eyes, just before they narrowed.

Regina bet not many caught this man off guard. A huge dose of satisfaction eased some of the frustration—and admittedly, a small bit of fear—stewing in her belly.

"You know who I am?"

She grimaced more from the pounding pain in her head, than his reaction. Know him? She wondered what the man would do if she told him the truth.

Instead, she settled for another truth. "Chris carried your picture in his wallet. You were younger and in uniform. You'd just received your Royal Air Force pilot's wings."

"Considering our relationship, it's hard to believe he carried a picture of me around anywhere."

"He was proud of you." Slowly, she eased up on one elbow. Her gaze skimmed over his jeans and sweater, noting the anger that rode the hard-lined muscles beneath.

"You're taller than Chris. Leaner, too." Regina spoke without thought. Something she tended to do. A habit people developed when they spent most of their time alone.

"I'm not here to be compared to my father, Miss Menlow. In or out of bed."

"Bed?" Confused, she frowned. The sledgehammers in her head had scrambled her brain more than she'd thought. "You think Chris and I were lovers?"

"Weren't you?"

"This is my hard-earned tax dollars at work?" Annoyed, she brushed her hair back over her shoulder. "Your father collected books. First editions. I sold books. First editions. It's really quite simple. Even for a government man like yourself."

"My father told you quite a lot, it seems." His tone was flat with disbelief. "What was in the book?"

"Book?" She froze, remembering. "Your father's journal. Do you have it?"

"No," Jordan replied. "The guy who attacked you left with it. I wasn't able to follow him."

"He grabbed me from behind and shoved a gun at my head." She rubbed her right temple, remembering. "I don't know how he broke in. I had already closed up. Maybe a window in my loft. Although I usually keep both locked."

"If he was a professional, a locked window wouldn't have stopped him."

"He demanded the journal and I told him where to find it. He must have hit me with the pistol right after because I don't remember anything until I came to in the office. I saw the fire and managed to roll under the desk." Automatically her fingers went to her head and she winced when she found the top of her skull tender. "I honestly didn't expect to survive. Thank you."

"Just your tax dollars at work," he commented wryly.

Her head jerked up, her mouth tilted in self-deprecation. "I deserved that. I'm sorry. I guess my only excuse is that I'm not at my best right now."

The apology caught Jordan off guard. She had surprised him for the third time in less than three hours. The fact that she crawled under the desk, then knew he worked for the government and now the apology.

His gaze skimmed over the dark chestnut hair, liking the way the thick waves drifted over the graceful line of her neck, drawing his eye to the delicate spot just above her shoulder.

But it was her eyes—big, somber, moss-green. Pools of liquid that swallowed a man whole.

"I cleaned the wound. The bruise is minor." He sat on the side of the bed. When she continued to probe the cut, he pulled her hand away. "Stop playing with it or you'll make it bleed again."

"I'm sorry." Her fingers fluttered beneath his, just for a moment before she tugged them away.

Nerves?

"What did your intruder look like, Miss Menlow?"

"Regina," she corrected him automatically. Slowly, she sat up and drew her knees to her chest.

The woman intrigued him. She was soft, feminine, intelligent. She stirred something he hadn't experienced in a long time. Desire. Interest.

Another surprise.

"He was football-player big. Linebacker size. Cool, mercenary type. Six-two. Dark brown hair. Crew cut. Dark brown eyes. His features were flat. Almost like his face had been pressed by glass."

"Identifying marks?"

"No tattoos that I saw, but he wore a black corduroy coat. So if he had any on his arms, they were covered. He had a scar, though. A crescent one. Right here." She stroked the side of her left cheek. "But he didn't escape with anything important."

"What do you mean?"

"I mean he doesn't have the journal. I made a fake after I read the original. I gave the fake to him."

"Where is the original?"

"In my loft. Under the sink in my bathroom." She wrapped her arms around her knees, bracing herself. "How bad was the fire?"

"The bathroom, along with the rest of your loft crashed into the store just after we escaped."

Her forehead dropped to her knees. Everything gone. Not that she owned much. But there were photographs, small treasures her parents had left for her. The letter Chris had given her.

The pain wasn't sharp, but a dull throb just under her heart. Or maybe she'd just gotten used to it over the years and didn't notice the sharp edges anymore.

"Did you read my father's journal?"

"Yes." Actually, she'd read it front to back, twice, before she'd been satisfied she'd committed it to memory. "Chris sent it with a letter. He told me to read it then wait for you to contact me. He said you'd know what to do."

"His message told me to find you. To protect you until I could decipher the information he'd given you. I had no idea the information was a book until tonight." He walked over to the window, split the curtain apart barely an inch and peered out. "When I saw Scarface walk out of the store with it. I just knew."

"You watched him?" Regina asked. "How long were you outside the store?"

The curtain dropped back into place as he turned back to her. "Not long. I decided to wait for you to lock up. I didn't want any interruptions."

"So you preferred to wait in a snowstorm rather than

a warm office while I dealt with my customers? Which I didn't have," she rationalized, frowning. "That doesn't make sense. Now if you were to tell me I was under surveillance, that you wanted to make sure I was legitimate before you approached me..."

He ignored her comment, simply because it hit too close to the truth. "The only lead we have now is the guy who left you for dead."

"Not necessarily." She shook her head, only to stop mid-motion, dizzy. "How well did you know your father, Jordan?"

"Bloody well," Jordan responded, smoothly. "The question is, how well did you know him, Miss Menlow?"

"Bloody well," she quipped in a perfect British accent, mimicking him. "Or at least I thought I did."

"Well enough to sleep with?"

With his temper, came hers. "Do I look like the mistress type?" She snapped the question back, expecting the epiphany to dawn on him any moment.

His eyes raked over her, and Regina's cheek's flushed when the blue eyes lingered over her breasts, then her face.

"Yes," Jordan drawled; the deep timbre of his voice set her trembling, but not from temper or fear, she realized. "You do."

"Well, I'm not." The fact that she managed to look down her nose at him surprised them both. "I was his friend." She scooted to the edge of the bed. Her muscles protested with some aches and stiffness, forcing her to move slower than her anger demanded. But once her feet touched the floor, knowing she could run if needed gave her a sense of bravado.

"You're lying," Jordan bit out the words. "And you're not very good at it."

"I'm not lying. Because you're right, I'm not good at it." She turned away, not wanting to deal with the contempt that flashed in his eyes. Instead, she studied her surroundings, cringing.

Roses spattered on the wallpaper all four sides of the room—their image faded until the flowers were no more than red splotches on the walls. The only thing that broke the dizzying monotony was the black lacquered bed and matching nightstand, both scuffed and cigarette scarred.

"Where are we, anyway?" A shag carpet—crimson and orange-speckled—covered the floor, its traffic pattern worn bald from the door, to the bathroom, to the bed.

"We're in downtown D.C."

"I must have been out of it quite a while."

"Almost two hours."

"No wonder I'm dizzy." On the nightstand, she saw the matches. "The Carltonesque? That's catchy," she murmured, suddenly grateful for the scent of her smoke-filled clothes. "Your father never brought me here, that's for sure. Of course, if I had been his mistress, I would have insisted. Can't beat a place that comes with a scarlet shag carpet and matching velveteen bedspread." She plucked at the bedding to prove her point.

"If you're trying to convince me, lady, that you're telling the truth, you're going about it the wrong way."

"I'm not trying to convince you of anything, Jordan." His attitude, his problem. Not hers.

He raised an eyebrow.

"I already told you the truth and I don't have the energy to defend myself." The pounding in her head picked up its tempo. "Could I get some aspirin?"

"I don't have any."

"Then your accusations are going to have to wait five minutes." Regina sat cross-legged on the bed. She raised her right arm and bent her elbow. She found the pressure point two fingers above her elbow and pressed with her thumb.

"You have a bump on your head, not on your arm."

With her eyes closed, she slowly turned her head from one side to the other. "I know that. But it isn't the skull that hurts so much as the muscles at the neck that have tightened to fend off the pain," she explained patiently, before returning to a simple form of meditation breathing.

"So holding your elbow will heal your neck—"

"Shh," she ordered, only to regret the action when another jab of pain hit her head.

"Are you trying to annoy me?" he snapped.

"No, but if I'm succeeding, I'll consider it a bonus. After all, you annoyed me first," she pointed out.

"Of all the bloody—"

"Can you stop yelling? Please?"

"I wasn't." But his voice softened to a dangerous growl.

She let her hands drop to her lap and sighed. "What I'm trying to do is get rid of my head and neck pain. I need to think clearer. If I try to deal with you right now, my headache will only get worse and that won't do either of us any good."

"So your answer is yoga?"

"No, my answer is aspirin, but since there isn't any I have to make do. And this isn't yoga. It's acupressure. I read this remedy in a book—"

"You read it in a book?" His opinion was short, pithy.

"The concept shouldn't be much of a reach, even for a slow thinker like you," she remarked. "Own a bookstore. Surrounded by books. Love books," she added, then once again closed her eyes and continued the pressure. "Plethora of information, if you can read."

Suddenly, she opened one eye again. "You can read, right?"

"Yes."

She grunted, shutting her eyelid once more. "Then you're lucky. Many can't."

"Let me guess, you're into causes, too?"

Regina ignored him. Something that wasn't easy to do. After a full minute, one she was sure he spent staring at her back, he decided to give her the five minutes.

Unhurried, he stretched out on the bed behind her.

His weight threw her back into him. Every time she scooted forward, she'd fall back again. After a few minutes, she gave up.

"Headache gone?" he asked and folded his arms behind his head. He seemed relaxed, but she wasn't fooled. The man was angry. Not enraged, but annoyed enough to keep his jaw tight.

"No." Regina decided to retreat, if only to give her

some space to think. She stood, then walked to the far side of the room—which wasn't more than five feet—and sat in the straight-back chair. The movement only seemed to increase the pressure in her head.

She noticed the gray coin box on the headboard. "Does the bed vibrate?"

He glanced at the box. "It appears so."

"Really?" For a brief second, she debated on trying it out, to see if it would help ease her neck ache. But she didn't have money. When she glanced at Jordan, he shook his head.

"Fine."

"I'll make a deal with you," Jordan said, the hard line of his mouth slipped into an easy smile. "I'll massage your neck while you talk to me about my father's journal."

"It would be easier just to get me some aspirin," she said, more than a little disgruntled. The last thing she wanted was close proximity right now.

"Not at this time of night," Jordan explained. "It's either the massage or nothing."

He moved to the edge of the bed, placed his feet on the floor and opened his knees. "Right here," he said and pointed in front of him.

For a moment she was tempted. "No, thanks."

"Suit yourself."

Instead, she leaned over and placed her forehead in her hands. The throbbing increased until nausea twisted her stomach into knots. She was being truthful; she couldn't think straight with sledgehammers battering her skull. But it was ridiculous to sit there and let the headache turn into a migraine.

"This is such a bad decision." She crossed over and settled into the vee between his thighs. "All right, but just for the record, I wanted you to get me some aspirin."

"Just for the record, I wouldn't trust you not to take off on me as soon as I get you out the door."

"I wouldn't do that," Regina said softly. "I want to help Chris. The journal implicates him as a terrorist."

"You said you looked at the journal. What do you remember reading?"

"He and at least four others were planning some kind of threat. One that involved killing millions."

"Ridiculous. My old man would never have betrayed his country." His thumbs worked the muscles at the back of her neck, lighting little fires along her nerve endings.

"Who were the others?"

"I don't know," she answered. "Chris addressed most of them by code names. Alpha, Beta, Charlie, Delta and Echo. I'm not sure what Chris's code name was."

"Why didn't you let the authorities know?"

"His letter told me to trust no one but you. The journal implied his accomplices held positions high in our government. Chris had connections everywhere," she said, then tilted her head to the side, allowing him more access to the muscles, and nearly groaned when he found a sensitive spot beneath her ear.

"If that's the truth, why didn't he just send the book to me?" he snapped.

The man was full of contradictions. Gentle hands, raging temper. "He had his reasons."

"Which were?"

Not wanting to lie, she ignored the question, hoping to put him off for a while longer. "I think at some point, Chris might have changed his mind about following through on his plans. One of the last entries indicated that one of his colleagues had grown suspicious."

"That narrows the field," Jordan said sarcastically. "My father had a lot of enemies. And even more colleagues."

"Because he was an MI6 agent?"

"Did he mention that in the journal?"

"No."

Jordan grabbed her chin with his finger and brought her face around so he could see her. "He told you he was MI6?"

"Yes."

"He must have trusted you," he admitted. It actually impressed the hell out of him. Chris Beck trusted very few. "He told you I was an operative also."

"Yes. I knew you would be there no matter what kind of falling out the two of you had," Regina said quietly. "The journal said it had been almost two years since he last saw you."

"That long?" Jordan stiffened but otherwise showed no reaction. He hadn't thought so, but honestly couldn't remember. So much had happened in between.

"I received the package a few days after your father was killed. He must have known his life was in danger."

"You said *most* were code names. What did you mean?"

"With one entry he used initials. R.L. A person who supplied him with the weapons. An arms dealer of some kind."

"Why didn't he assign him a code name?"

She frowned. "R.L. was only mentioned once. For all I know, it could've been a mistake, or he assigned R.L. a code name later on in the book. Three of the names didn't appear until after he mentioned R.L."

"Did he mention the type of weapons? Guns? Biochemical? Explosives?" His fingers slipped to the front and skimmed her throat while his thumbs rubbed the back of her neck just at the base of her skull.

"No. It could be any one of them or all of them."

"Okay, Regina. Now the million-dollar question." Jordan's fingers tightened, cutting off enough of her air to get her attention. "Why did my father send you his journal? And if it's not the truth, I just might snap your beautiful little neck."

Chapter Four

"I have an…ability," Regina whispered. She closed her eyes against the tears. From embarrassment more than fear. Jordan wouldn't hurt her, otherwise, Chris would have never trusted him to help her. If she couldn't put her faith in Jordan, she'd put her faith in the belief that Chris had known what he was doing.

"By ability, you mean a talent." It was a statement, but when she tried to shake her head in disagreement, he tightened his grip.

"I don't consider it a talent," she whispered, fighting back the humiliation that came with being different. "I read something, one time—technical manuals, contracts, books, newspapers—anything with words. And it's committed to memory."

For a long moment he didn't say anything, but his fingers didn't loosen, either.

"Chris wanted you to memorize the journal," Jordan stated. "But he must have known he would put you in danger."

"Yes," she said, "But he also sent you to protect me."

"How many pages were in the journal?"

"Almost a hundred."

"That would've taken someone what, a few days of hard studying, to memorize," Jordan commented. "How long did it take you?"

"A little over two hours, but I read it twice to make sure I'd committed it to memory."

Jordan loosened his hands and shifted sideways so he could look at her profile. "Two hours?"

"I can't recite it to you, my head hurts too much."

"That doesn't tell me why I should believe you're not involved with the people who killed him."

Startled, she stiffened and tried to look at Jordan but he held her fast. "I thought a cocaine addict killed him?"

"That's the official story. But we both know there was more to it." Slowly, one of his thumbs stroked the nape of her neck.

A shiver made its way up her spine. But lord help her, it was from anticipation, rather than fear.

"Chris never told me he was the British Ambassador to the United States. I had no idea until after he died and his photograph was flashed all over the news."

"That's hard to believe, considering you read so much."

"I haven't reached the section on the modern politics of the United Kingdom, yet."

"He told you he was British intelligence."

"The point is, he didn't tell me about his job, but he did tell me something once in confidence. Something about you. You were six. And it was a few weeks before

Christmas. Chris said he was in Bangladesh at the time. Your mother mailed him a letter you'd written to Santa. One you had asked her to mail to the North Pole."

Jordan's hand dropped from her. He hadn't thought about that letter in ages.

"He gave it to me a few weeks ago. At the same time he told me he was MI6. He'd carried the letter in his wallet all these years."

Regina saw Jordan's jaw working, the muscle flexing.

"Do you still have it?"

She shook her head. "It was in my jewelry box on my dresser." She didn't admit she took it out and read it almost every night.

"You know it word for word, don't you?"

"Yes," she said quietly. "Dear Santa Claus, I went to get our tree today. Mother was busy, so I went with our chauffeur, Stephen. I saw so many kids with their parents. They all laughed together. It made my chest hurt. I've been good this year. Desperately good. So I'm asking just this once. Could you send my papa home for Christmas? Sincerely, Jordan Beck."

Headache or not, she remembered every aspect of that letter. The painstakingly perfect lettering. The carefully folded creases.

"He never came."

"He received the letter a week after Christmas," Regina said. "And carried it in his wallet ever since."

The silence was deafening, heavy.

"I'm sorry, Jordan. I didn't mention it to be intrusive—"

"You didn't intrude. It was a long time ago. I'd forgotten about the incident actually until you'd mentioned the letter."

Suddenly, he stood in one fluid movement, putting distance between them. "If you're well enough, we need to talk to a friend of mine. I'll get you some aspirin on the way."

That was it, no explanation, no apology. "Now?" She glanced at the nightstand. "It's after ten. And we smell like we've been barbecued."

"He'll still be awake. And he's smelled worse," Jordan replied flatly.

"THE LIGHTS ARE OFF," Regina whispered as they stepped out of Jordan's car in front of a three-story Victorian house. Extinguished Christmas lights draped well-groomed hedges. The occasional bulb poked out from spots in the snow and a big plastic Santa with a bag full of toys stood smiling in the front lawn. The scent of neighboring chimneys filled the air. An ache squeezed her chest, catching her off guard.

"What's the matter?"

"Nothing," she said, then waved it off. His face set in the hard line she'd learned to identify with his stubbornness.

"It's just that this is what I always pictured Christmas to be. The lights, the fireplaces, the tree in the window. The silly, plastic North Poles littering the lawn." Embarrassed, she climbed the porch stairs, grateful when Jordan said nothing.

"Are you sure—"

"They're awake, Regina."

The storm had broken, leaving the sweet scent of new snow, along with the chill of more to come. Regina hugged herself tighter in Jordan's leather jacket.

Jordan wasn't wearing more than his crew neck sweater and jeans, but the biting wind didn't seem to bother him.

He pushed the doorbell, then paused only a moment before he pounded on the door a few times for good measure.

"Well, if they were sleeping, they're up now," Regina muttered.

"I told you—"

The porch light flipped on seconds before the door swung open.

"Jordan." Ian MacAlister took the couple in with a quick glance. "You do realize what time it is."

"I need your help, Ian."

Regina noted the naked chest, the unbuttoned jeans and bare feet before Jordan grabbed her hand and tugged her with him into the house.

"You know damn well you have my help anytime you need it." Ian shut the door behind them. No one would call Ian MacAlister ugly. Light brown hair, cropped military short, accented his broad features and laser blue eyes. "Next time, just give me a call when you're on your way."

"We woke you up." Regina glared at Jordan. "I'm sorry, Mr. MacAlister, but Jordan insisted on coming over tonight."

"You can stop glowering at me, Regina. We didn't wake him up," Jordan snapped. "They were probably—"

"We were just getting comfortable," Ian cut off Jordan. The fact that he'd been roused from his bed while making love to Lara wasn't the point. And it wasn't like his friend to be so blunt.

"Sorry, Ian." Jordan dragged a hand through his hair. "It's been a long day."

If he didn't know his friend better, Ian would have sworn Jordan was…frazzled.

Ian covered his surprise with a dry cough. "It's not me who'll need the apology. You didn't wake us, but you could have woken Clara. If that's the case, you'll have Lara to deal with."

Ian took in the soiled clothes, the freshly ripped hole in Jordan's jeans. The oversized leather jacket on Regina.

"You both smell like you've been cleaning chimneys."

"We have good reason." The tight, military stance Jordan took spoke volumes. Whatever brought his friend here was anything but good.

Jordan glanced around. "Where's Lara?"

Always cautious, Ian walked to the wall unit and punched in the system code. "Lara is in the baby's room, checking on her. She'll be down in a minute. Why?" He thought about calling Lara, but knew if he woke the baby, he'd pay hell for it later. Life or death, his daughter was teething and for the first time in almost a week, Lara had gotten her down at a reasonable hour.

"I need your help. And hers. I have to locate an arms dealer in Labyrinth's computer files."

At one time both men worked for Labyrinth, a black ops division of the government. A year earlier, before Ian had retired after marrying Lara.

Jordan walked to the base of the circular staircase and looked up. "How long does it take to check a baby?"

"Have one yourself and you'll find out," Ian commented, drawing a chuckle from the woman.

Regina was mildly attractive in an unusual way. The soft cloud of brown hair, the small figure beneath the oversized coat. Light cardigan and slacks peaked out from the coat—their style shapeless on what he assumed was a petite figure.

Then suddenly, her eyes met his. Big, solemn—almost sleepy—hazel eyes. Ian froze, startled. Bedroom eyes. He let out a long, silent whistle.

Nothing mild about this woman at all, Ian corrected himself. She was beautiful.

"Why not use your own security to access the files?" Ian asked, keeping his gaze on the woman, more for the enjoyment than curiosity. He'd find out who she was soon enough.

She raised one delicate eyebrow. *You think so?*

Ian laughed, knowing he hadn't spoken the words out loud.

Beautiful and clever.

"Let's just say I retired, prematurely," Jordan said, joining them once again.

"So your security's been revoked," Ian commented, breaking eye contact with the woman to question his friend. "By whom? Cain?"

"He and I disagreed about Chris's death," Jordan remarked. "That's part of the reason why I need the files. As an instructor, Lara still has access to the Labyrinth databases, right?"

"Yes," Ian replied slowly. "Everything except Cain's personal files."

"I'll need her to keep this quiet."

"From whom?"

"President Mercer."

"You don't want your investigation getting back to him," Ian murmured, understanding. Lara was Jon Mercer's daughter. "You know she won't tell him if you ask her not to, Jordan. She loves you like a brother. But knowing what it might possibly do to her relationship with her father, are you willing to put her in that position?"

"I wouldn't ask her if it wasn't a life-and-death matter."

"Does it have anything to do with the fact that you both look and smell like you've been to a fire?" Ian asked, rubbing the side of his nose.

"Someone torched Regina's place today. With her tied up in it."

"And you are Regina," Ian stated, his mouth twitching.

"Yes," she said, inclining her head in a short salute. "Regina Menlow."

"So what does your attempted murder have to do with Chris Beck?"

"I was his mistress."

"Bloody hell," Jordan snapped, exasperated.

"You were?" Ian ignored his friend.

"Not really, but Jordan seems to think so. I figured I'd get it out there first. Doesn't hurt so much when I say it."

"Honest, aren't you?" And tough, he thought.

"Painfully."

"Painful for whom?" Ian glanced at Jordan, saw the flash of male frustration—the kind that came from fighting the inevitable.

Interesting.

Regina's lips curved in amusement. "Believe it or not, more often for me. Jordan just happens to be the exception right now."

"Are you quite done?"

"Quite done." Regina mimicked Jordan's accent before turning to his friend.

She held out her hand and shook Ian's. "It's a pleasure, Mr. MacAlister. Chris was quite a fan of your family's whiskey. And of your family."

"Please, call me Ian. Chris was a favorite of ours, too," Ian acknowledged warmly, liking the woman instantly. He had a habit—a rather accurate one actually—of summing up a person's worth in a matter of seconds after meeting them. Ian decided on the spot that if Regina Menlow were gold, she'd be worth quite a small fortune on her integrity alone. "And I think the pleasure will be all mine, Regina."

"Ian," Jordan warned, understanding his friend and the statement. "You can let go of her hand, now."

He turned on Regina when Ian let her go. "I should have locked you in the motel room."

"Motel?" Ian frowned. "Where are you staying?"

"Some seedy place downtown," Regina replied, crossing her arms in what Ian determined was a deliberate attempt to show no fear. Too bad the deep swallow gave her away.

"We're staying at the Carltonesque," Jordan answered, his frustration becoming palpable.

"You're kidding?" Ian let out a low whistle. "Isn't that the place we busted that Mafia drug—"

"It's fine. And that bust happened years ago. It's under new management." Jordan glared at Regina. The blast of it almost had her stepping back. Almost.

Instead, temper stiffened her spine. She hadn't lived all those years with her Aunt Aida without learning how to defend herself. "Jordan's right, seedy seems harsh. After all, it has a vibrating bed. We haven't tried it out yet, but..." She punctuated the sentence with a shrug.

"Are you finished?" Jordan's back teeth slammed together, forcing his jaw muscles into overdrive.

"Really?" Ian rocked back on his heels and grinned, thoroughly enjoying his friend's discomfort, Regina noted.

"It beats your current living situation," Jordan remarked. "Or did you forget your place is now nothing more than a pile of charred books?"

"I haven't forgotten." Regina's chin went up, daring him to take another swipe. "Nor have I forgotten you saved my life. But that doesn't give you the right to belittle it now."

"Until I'm sure who is after you, you're staying with me," Jordan ordered.

"If Miss Menlow needs a place to stay, we have a

guest room," Ian offered, swallowing a laugh. "I can keep her safe here."

"It's not funny," Jordan bit out.

Regina turned to Ian. "Thank you, but that won't be necessary—"

Jordan cut her off. "She'll stay with me."

Regina tried again. "Of course, I appreciate the offer but—"

"I'm not going to place your family in harm's way, Ian."

Regina placed her hands on her hips. "I can talk for myself, Jordan."

He snorted. "What do you think is going to happen when your friend finds out the book he grabbed isn't my father's journal?"

"I know he'll try to find me. I'm not stupid. In fact, I graduated top in my class at Princeton."

"In what?" Ian asked, curious.

"Not covert operations," Jordan answered, deliberately provoking her. "She has a master's in English literature. But she never finished her doctorate."

Regina gasped, enraged. "How do you know?" She narrowed her eyes. "You have a file on me, don't you?"

"I suspected you of murdering my father, or at least sleeping with him. Of course, I'm going to have a file on you, sweetheart."

"Don't call me sweetheart," she snapped, hating how he turned an endearment into a derogatory pet name.

"Scarface won't take a chance that the book was not destroyed in the fire."

"Scarface?" Ian asked, trying to keep up.

Both Regina and Jordan said, "Later," in unison.

"I know they're out there now," she told Jordan. "I won't be so easy to find."

"Have you ever gone into hiding before?" Ian asked. He thought about stepping between the couple, until he caught Jordan's glare. Ian decided he liked his teeth more.

"Of course not." She dismissed the thought with a frown. "But I've read books on the subject. Many written by retired military or government officials. Some even by people who have managed to create new identities."

Ian's mouth twitched. "You've read books."

"Seems Miss Menlow gets all her life experiences through books," Jordan drawled. "Well, almost all."

A flush crept over her cheeks. "You don't have to be rude."

"I'm only beginning, *sweetheart.*"

Chapter Five

Jordan took a step forward, purposely invading Regina's space, forcing her neck back to see his face.

Startled, Ian stared at his friend. Jordan had never used brute force against someone weaker. It wasn't in his nature.

Regina slapped her hand against Jordan's chest, as if it would keep him in place if he decided to charge. "You don't intimidate me, Jordan."

"You're not going anywhere. If I have to tie you down—"

"You just try it."

Ian almost laughed when Regina actually pushed her sleeves up to her elbows.

Regina didn't notice Ian's reaction, her full focus was on the man before her. "I've really had it with your bullying."

"Sweetheart," he threatened, his tone low and mean. "You haven't seen anything—"

"Am I interrupting something?" Lara MacAlister

asked from the stairway. Her voice was soft enough to make the couple realize they had been shouting.

Ian's wife seemed to float down the remaining few steps, her long red hair swaying against her shoulders. Class, Regina thought instantly, watching the woman descend in a tailored, emerald green velour robe.

"Not at all. Your timing is impeccable, darling." Ian met his wife at the base of the steps and draped his arm across her back.

Lara handed him a sweatshirt she'd been carrying and kissed his cheek. "I thought it might be too chilly down here." She eyed Jordan and Regina, her deep green cat eyes glittering with curiosity. "I guess I was mistaken. Looks like things have been heating up."

Ian's gaze caught his wife's and held it just a second longer than necessary before his mouth slid into an easy smile.

"Darling, I'd like you to meet, Miss Regina Menlow." Ian pulled the sweatshirt over his head. "She's Chris Beck's—"

"Mistress." Regina shook Lara's hand, still smarting from the last exchange with Jordan.

"Will you stop saying that?" he snapped.

"You first," she replied, her eyes narrowing.

Lara frowned. "I must have missed something—"

"I'll explain it to you later," Ian said, enjoying his friend's discomfort. "But if this woman was Chris's mistress, I'll change Clara's diapers for a whole year."

"Really?" Lara asked, surprised. She looked at Regina. "Sure there isn't any chance…a kiss on the cheek perhaps? Holding hands?" Lara's lips tilted into a tired smile. "I really could use the break."

"Chris loved his wife," Regina emphasized, then turned to Jordan. "He might not have spoken about her often, but when he did it was with complete respect."

The blue eyes turned arctic. "Leave my mother out of this," he ordered before turning to Lara. "Hi ya, Red."

The woman walked right into his arms and gave him a hug. "It's been a while, handsome."

Regina would've admired the woman's courage if it hadn't been for the jealousy that snaked up her spine.

Or the hurt that stabbed at her chest when Jordan grabbed Lara closer and lifted her into a tighter hug. "Missed you, too." He kissed her forehead.

"Careful, friend," Ian warned good-naturedly. "You're holding more than one there."

Slowly, Jordan let Lara slip to the ground. "You're pregnant again?"

"One month." She patted her flat stomach. "So you can't do too much damage yet. We just found out today."

"We were celebrating when the doorbell rang," Ian added, wryly.

"Then I'm not sorry we interrupted." Jordan hugged her again. "Congratulations, darling." Then he reached around Lara and shook Ian's hand. "You, too, mate."

"Yes, congratulations," Regina added, with a sudden awkwardness. The dimensions had changed. She wasn't just among friends, she suddenly realized. She was with a family.

Regina didn't do families well.

As if sensing her discomfort, Jordan draped an arm around her shoulder. When she instinctively tried to step away, he pulled her tight to his side and kept her there. Too tired to fight, she leaned into him, surprised when this eased her anxiety.

"Lara," Jordan said. "Regina doesn't have any clothes besides the ones she's wearing. Someone torched her place tonight with her in it. I was hoping you might have some to spare."

"You've been busy," Lara commented, catching the look on Jordan's face. The hard line of his mouth, the set of his jaw, the slight softening around his eyes—told her that Jordan had gone into protective mode.

Interesting, considering the fight she'd interrupted when she came down the stairs.

But it wasn't only Jordan's reaction she noticed. The woman seemed to relax almost instantly once Jordan held her. Before that she'd seen the flash of panic, the wariness when she found out about Lara's pregnancy.

"It just so happens that I have some clothes," Lara said, keeping it light. "You lost everything?" She took the opportunity to study Regina, instantly liking the slight tilt of the chin, the proud set of her shoulders. "You're more Celeste's size then mine, but I'm sure I can find something."

"Celeste?" Regina asked, the wariness appearing almost instantly.

"My sister-in-law. Ian's brother's wife. If you can follow that," Lara joked, deliberately putting the younger woman at ease. "But don't worry, she won't mind."

Suddenly, Lara caught the scent of smoke. “Is that you two?”

Regina nodded. “We haven’t had a chance to really clean up—”

“You’re probably dying for a hot shower.” Lara tugged gently at Regina’s arm, separating her from Jordan. “You can use our guest shower if you want, Jordan.”

“I’ll pass. I can grab a shower back at the motel.”

“I don’t want to impose,” Regina insisted.

“You’re not,” Lara said, deciding the matter. “I’ll find some clothes for you, too, Jordan, if you want.”

“I have some, thanks.”

“Come with me. It’s been a while since I’ve had a chance to visit with another woman,” Lara whispered to Regina, lying without a hint of guilt. “You do mind, don’t you?”

Before Regina could reply, Lara stopped at the bottom step and glanced at her husband. “Why don’t you boys have some sandwiches made up and brought into the library?”

“Good idea. When you two are done, why don’t you meet us in there?” Ian said, studying the two women with an approving smile as they climbed the stairs.

“Stop ogling your wife.”

“I’m not, I’m ogling your girlfriend.”

“She’s not my girlfriend.”

“Too bad. She’s tough. A scrapper,” Ian said with admiration.

“Girlfriends end up being collateral damage in our line of business, remember?” Still, Jordan’s gaze followed Regina until she disappeared into the main bedroom upstairs.

"Can't argue there," Ian commented. "That's why I left."

"You left because you wanted to make whiskey. Just so happened, you fell in love with another operative. Just like your brother, Cain, did with Celeste and Roman did with your sister, Kate," Jordan pointed out. "They all still work for Labyrinth."

"None are field ops," Ian remarked. "You know as well as I do why Cain is the director of Labyrinth. He chose the desk job after Jon Mercer left, to protect Celeste and his boys."

"Celeste still profiles for Labyrinth. And Kate still works their technology division. And Roman is still contracted as one of their security specialists," Jordan insisted, then jabbed a thumb up at the stairs. "Regina owns a bookstore."

Ian raised an eyebrow. "So you're saying you're not tempted to sleep with her."

"Hell, yes I've been tempted. Have you looked at her, Ian? What heterosexual male wouldn't want her?" Jordan said, exasperated. "But I'm not going to. I promised Chris I'd protect her. No more, no less. The sooner I can figure out who tried to kill her, the quicker she can go back to her safe, ordinary life."

"You could always retire."

"And do what? I've been trained for one thing. I'm damned good at it, too."

Ian considered Jordan for a moment, not arguing.

Jordan was good at what he did. In fact, he was probably one of the best left in the field. "You were goading her on purpose. Why?"

Jordan shrugged. "I wanted to see if she would slip up with any lies while in a temper."

Ian snorted with derision. "You know as well as I do she's telling the truth."

"I knew pretty much before we even got here," Jordan admitted, wryly. "You're not the only one with instincts."

"So?" Ian prompted.

"So, it takes her less than ten seconds to get under my skin when she's in a temper," he admitted, aggravated.

What he didn't admit was that the angrier she got, the prettier she became. Her eyes sparkled, her face flushed pink and her mouth got downright sassy.

Just the thought of all that sass turning to passion shifted his baser instincts into overdrive. And frustrated the hell out of him.

"Most people call it foreplay."

Startled, Jordan stared at his friend.

Ian grinned, flashing a row of white teeth. "Only obvious when you're not caught up in it. Remember when Lara and I used to go at it?"

"Yes. You drove me crazy." A few years back, Lara and Ian had fought like cats and dogs up to the moment he chased her to France. Even then, it took a while for Ian to convince Lara he loved her. And at the time, she was seven months pregnant with Ian's baby.

Foreplay. Jordan glanced at the master bedroom one more time. Desire tugged deep in his gut.

Bloody hell.

"I like her," Ian remarked, his tone serious.

Jordan sighed. "Me, too. But I'm not happy about it."

Ian nodded. He'd known his friend too long to be surprised by the remark. Either way, the immediate future was going to get pretty difficult for Jordan. And Miss Regina Menlow.

"Then I guess we'd better save her," Ian suggested.

"I guess we'd better," Jordan agreed, then shot his friend a grim smile. "Before she tries saving herself."

Chapter Six

"I appreciate your meeting with me on such short notice, Archer." Jon Mercer studied his old friend over the rim of his glass.

"You're the President of the United States, Jon. I didn't realize I had the option of ignoring you and going home to bed."

Jon's laugh was low and easy—born from years of friendship and genuine respect for the man sitting across from him.

Archer Cordey wasn't one to pull punches. That's why he made an excellent Chief Justice in Jon's opinion. Although Jon couldn't take credit for appointing him during his presidential term, he appreciated the foresight of his predecessor.

The last few years had taken its toll on the seventy-five-year-old. A little less gray hair on top, a slower gait maybe, even a bit more slope to his shoulders. But his mind was keen, the gray eyes alert, his instinct still razor sharp.

"Besides, I know what this is about." Archer glanced

down at his glass of Scotch and sobered a bit. "Chris Beck was my friend, too, Jon."

"Word travels fast on Capitol Hill, doesn't it?" Jon settled back into his leather seat. "Tell me about Timothy Severs, Archer."

"I can't tell you much more than your dossier says on him."

"Fair enough. Give me your opinion, then."

Archer swallowed some of his whiskey. "He was an unstable son of a bitch."

"Intel says he was high. And greedy. Not unstable." Jon glanced around the Oval Office, taking in the navy blue carpet, the burgundy leather winged-back chairs. At a time like this, he almost preferred the decades where he risked his life, hip deep in jungle marsh, ferreting out the country's enemies.

Now, technology gave terrorists a whole new playing field. And at sixty-three, Jon sometimes felt just too damn old to step up to the plate.

As if reading his thoughts, Archer continued. "The bombing was an unforeseen attack from a very misguided young man. Nothing more. Nothing less. No one would have tagged him as a suicide bomber."

Jon studied the Resolute desk like so many had before him, feeling the burden each president dealt with when faced with a threat to their homeland security. "You've always told me, Archer, this office was a symbol of strength—the center point of integrity. If those foundations of belief were ever shaken, the aftershocks rock the nation."

Archer nodded. "I still believe that."

"Less than a month ago, a building no more than a few blocks away was nearly destroyed and this office was nearly brought to its knees by a government employee high on cocaine. I want to know why," Jon said.

"You know why. Your people stated publicly that Severs acted alone."

"Chris was an Ambassador to the United States. One that I could not protect. Right now, world leaders are watching, strategizing. Soon, the news will leak that Timothy Severs had unsavory connections."

"Do you know that for sure?" Archer asked, his eyes narrowing. "Because if you don't, I'm advising you—as your legal counsel now—hold to the original story. A mentally unstable young man—"

"Severs's bank accounts show that he got paid a small fortune to kill Christopher Beck. The fact that he spent a good chunk on cocaine and screwed up the detonation was stupid, not unstable."

Archer waved Jon's statement off. "Don't fool yourself. The boy was unstable. His father and I go way back, long before he was even born. There was something off about Timothy from the very beginning. Many were concerned, but it's hard to voice that concern when his father serves on the Supreme Court bench."

"David Severs is retiring soon. Claiming hardship."

"I'm not surprised. David is a decent man and now this will be his family's legacy. Do you blame him for stepping down?" Archer asked, sympathetic.

They both knew one wrongly placed comment had

destroyed many political careers. While the bombing only killed Chris Beck and Timothy Severs, the unanswered security questions had left many without jobs on Capitol Hill.

"No, I don't blame David. And I'll make sure he gets his full retirement and help out any other way that I can. But the fact remains that someone paid Severs to kill Chris."

"And?" Archer prompted.

"Timothy and your son, Scott, were friends," Jon commented. Scott Cordey had been West Point's golden boy. Star quarterback, class valedictorian.

"They were dorm mates. Big difference. They didn't have the same social circle. Hell, Timothy Severs had no social circle." Archer tapped the armrest, thinking. "Still, I'll ask some of Scott's friends about Timothy. Most stay in touch with me. I'll see if I can find out anything."

"I'd appreciate it, Archer. This one is more than a little personal for me."

"And me. Chris and I go back as far as you do." Archer finished his Scotch. "It's been a hell of a year, hasn't it?"

"Yes, it has," Jon answered, understanding the past months had been harder for his friend. "How are you holding up?"

Archer lifted a shoulder in a half-hearted shrug. "Some days are better than others. If I hadn't lost Eva to the cancer so soon after Scott, it would've been easier. But you play the cards you're dealt."

Archer raised the empty glass in a mock toast, before sliding it onto the desk. "Tell Ian this new batch of

MacAlister whiskey is pretty damn good. He made the right decision, taking over for his old man."

"I will." Jon paused for a moment. "You know, Shantelle was asking about you the other night," Jon said, a small smile tugged at his lips at the thought of his wife. "Why don't you come over for Christmas Eve dinner Sunday?"

"You're not going to Camp David for the holiday?"

"Not this year," Jon admitted, but didn't go into details. Some national issues he couldn't share. Not even with a close friend like Archer. "We'd both love to have you. Ian and Lara are coming over with the baby." Jon lifted the half-empty bottle of Scotch. "I'll have him bring you a brand new batch."

"I'd be tempted if you offered me a chance to hold the baby," Archer remarked, but not before Jon saw the flash of pain across the older man's features. "How is Clara doing? She must be what? Almost one now?"

"One and a half," Jon replied, unable to mask the pride over his only granddaughter. "All green eyes and fire-red curls like her mother. And energetic. She doesn't let anybody hold her until she collapses from exhaustion."

Archer laughed. "How are Lara and Ian holding up?"

"Frazzled. It's worth coming over just to watch," Jon admitted, grinning. "Damned if I don't enjoy that almost as much as the baby."

"You've convinced me." The judge chuckled, then settled back into the leather chair. He crossed one leg over the other. "I'd love to join you and Shantelle. I'll check my schedule and have my assistant confirm with yours."

The phone beeped on the desk. "Hold on a minute, Archer." Jon picked up the phone, knowing his assistant wouldn't have bothered him if it wasn't important. "What is it, Julia?"

"Sir, Ambassador Morris is here. He says it's important."

Julia Cutting had followed Jon from his previous post as the director of Labyrinth, to the White House. For the last few years, she ran his life. She went head-to-head with some of the toughest men and women on the Hill—most who'd dealt with world leaders—and all who had backed down to Julia at one time or another. Shantelle described her as the prettiest five-foot-eight, brown haired, brown-eyed tornado she'd ever seen.

Jon couldn't agree more. Half the men on Capitol Hill feared her while the other half were in love with her.

"If you would like, Mr. President, I can ask him to wait."

Jon smiled, imagining what Kyle Morris had to say just to get her to interrupt his meeting with Archer. "It's okay, Julia. Send him in."

He hung up and cleared his throat. "We're about to have company, old man."

The door opened suddenly. Julia came first, her hair coiffed, her navy suit sleek, trim and professional. She smiled at Jon and then stepped aside, allowing the two men through.

The first man, Kyle Morris, was tall, distinguished, with a bald head and goatee that Jon knew he stroked out of habit.

The second man, Calvin West, was taller, six-two according to his file, and more than a decade younger than Kyle's fifty years. Cal carried the political GQ-stamp of approval well—trimmed, shaven and groomed.

The Brits, Jon mused, always tended to have a pay scale better than the Americans.

"If I may interrupt, Mr. President," Julia asked, her concern genuine as she turned to Archer. "I can have your car brought around whenever you are ready, Your Honor."

"How about in ten minutes, Julia?" Archer suggested warmly.

She smiled in response, showing an attractive dimple just to the side of her mouth. "I'll have it waiting, sir."

Jon caught the slight double take from Calvin West and nearly smiled himself. He'll have to tell Shantelle that Julia had just added another admirer to the long list of many.

Unaware, Julia glanced at Jon. When he nodded, she closed the door behind her with a polite, yet firm snap.

"Mr. President, we have a situation that needs your attention." Kyle moved in tight, hurried strides to the desk. He tugged his tie twice, as if it were choking him. Another habit Jon noted Kyle hadn't broken in the four years he'd known him.

Calvin, on the other hand, wore the Dolce suit like a second skin. Fitted, relaxed. Having studied Cal's military file, Jon also knew the man wore jungle fatigues the same way.

"It can wait one minute, Kyle." Jon nodded toward

his older friend. "Archer, you know Ambassador Kyle Morris. Our British liaison."

"Only by reputation," the judge said with an easy smile. His politically correct smile, Jon noted. The one that didn't warm the steel-gray eyes.

Kyle shook Archer's hand. "Actually, sir, we met briefly last year at Lara and Ian MacAlister's wedding reception. At the time I was the British Counselor of Foreign Security. Attaché to Ambassador Beck."

"Then it's a pleasure to see you again, Mr. Morris." Archer's smile widened just enough for emphasis.

"And this is Calvin West," Jon continued. "The new Counselor of Foreign Security."

"In other words, you're MI6." Archer shook the younger man's hand, intercepting a glance from Kyle to Jon.

"At one point, yes, I was, sir," Cal admitted easily.

"That's all right. I won't hold it against you, West." Archer stood with difficulty, his legs already stiff from the few minutes in the chair. "Arthritis. Damn nuisance in the winter," he stated with a grim smile.

He grabbed his topcoat from the back of a nearby couch. "I believe it's time for me to go home, gentlemen. Obviously, you have business to take care of and I have a warm bed waiting for me."

"I think you have the better deal." Jon joined Archer on the other side of the desk. He placed his hand on the older man's shoulder and walked with him to the door. "I appreciated your input, Archer."

"I had very little to offer. But let me make a few calls,

Mr. President. I'll get back with you." He paused, swinging back to Kyle. "I suspect I'll be seeing more of you, Mr. Morris?"

"I look forward to it, Your Honor."

"And you, Mr. West?"

Calvin tilted his head forward briefly. "It would be a pleasure to see you again, sir."

Archer Cordey laughed outright, acknowledging the fact that Calvin used his own words against him, with the very same inflection. "This boy is subtle and smart, Jon. Watch out or he might have your job."

"He's British, Your Honor," Kyle pointed out, politely.

"I know." Archer winked at West and opened the door. "Merry Christmas, gentlemen."

"It's not everyday you meet a military legend," Kyle murmured as he watched the Chief Justice leave.

"A military legend?" Cal asked, curious.

"Archer Cordey was a platoon sergeant in Vietnam," Kyle explained. "During a routine sweep, his men were ambushed in the mountains outside of Khe Sanh. Fifteen U.S. soldiers against forty Viet Cong. The Yanks were pinned by automatic fire and rocket grenades. Their only real defense was a machine gun mounted on the back of a truck. But their gunner was dead, killed with the first shot from Charlie."

"Charlie?"

"Victor Charlie. Viet Cong," Jon answered, amused. "Rusty on your war history, Cal?"

"A little, sir," Cal admitted. "But with all due respect, Mr. President, Vietnam was your war history. Not ours."

"Not necessarily," Kyle continued, exchanging a look with the president. "During the attack, Archer Cordey jumped onto the truck and opened fire. And in doing so, he made himself the target. He took three bullets—two to the chest—but he held them off until the Americans worked their way around and killed the bastards remaining."

"Have a seat, gentlemen," Jon offered and waited while the two men settled into the winged-back chairs.

"Archer pretty much did the job himself. Hell, there were only a few to finish off for the rest of us in the platoon," Jon commented, then sat once again behind his desk. "And as for it not being your war, Cal, you're wrong. Chris Beck was our MI6 liaison. He survived the battle with a bullet in the shoulder. Of course, if you read the official report, Chris was never there. And the wound never existed."

Cal let out a soft whistle. "I had no idea."

Jon studied the younger agent. "How old are you, Cal? Mid-thirties, right?"

"Thirty-seven, Mr. President."

"It was before your time," Kyle explained. "You had no reason to know."

"A history lesson, then," Jon inserted, his features grim. "Bottom line is that Chris Beck and I owe Archer our lives."

The president leaned back, the steel of his eyes pinning the ambassador to his seat. "Down to business, Kyle. What's the problem?"

"You're not going to like it, Mr. President." Kyle

pulled two photographs from his suit pocket. "Our problem seems to be Jordan Beck. He just got placed on our most wanted list."

Chapter Seven

Lara studied the young woman sitting on her bed. She was pretty in a librarian sort of way, even in the drab sweater and boxy slacks. Lara had no problem picturing Regina with her hair pinned up, her lips pursed to hush some unsuspecting male student.

At least until those big, hazel puppy-dog eyes focused on that same student. Then that boy's hormones would never be the same.

"Do you wear glasses?" Lara asked, smiling warmly.

Regina glanced up, blinked. "Yes. When I read."

"Has Jordan ever seen you in glasses?"

"No." She frowned. "I lost them in the fire. Why?"

"Just curious." Lara decided she'd pay big bucks to be a fly on the wall when that moment happened. Jordan had a secret weakness for women in glasses.

Normally, Lara would've invited Regina out for lunch, maybe some casual shopping, then used the time to build a friendship that she instinctively knew was going to spark between them.

But time and circumstance didn't give Lara that luxury.

And if anyone needed a friend right now, it was Regina Menlow.

Lara sat next to Regina and placed her arm around her shoulder, taking it as a good omen when Regina didn't pull away.

"I know it's none of my business," Lara admitted, quietly. "But you really look like someone who needs a good ear, right now. And it so just happens I have two."

Regina shook her head. "I'm just tired."

"No better time to get things off your chest," Regina urged. "Can I ask you why Jordan would think you're his father's mistress?"

"Because Chris and I were close friends."

"For how long?"

"Two years."

Lara let out a slow, low whistle. "How did you meet?"

"First through phone calls. Business calls," Regina clarified. "Most of my business dealt in rare books. Chris was one of my best clients. He had a passion for collecting hard-to-find first editions."

"So you started out as business acquaintances."

"Yes," Regina replied. "Gradually it evolved into Internet discussions on various topics. Then one day he showed up at my shop."

"And the relationship was purely platonic." It wasn't a question, Lara could see the emotion in the younger woman's face. There was love there, but not the kind between a man and a woman, or even the kind of love between friends. "You cared for him a great deal."

"Yes. Chris was my best friend. My only friend," she corrected, deciding that if she were going to purge, she'd leave nothing back. "The thing that hurt the most is that I found out about his death on the news. He never told me he was the British Ambassador. I never went to his funeral."

"Don't be too harsh on Chris, Regina. Knowing him, he had good reasons."

"After the event, I kept telling myself he simply wanted an escape from everyday life on Capitol Hill."

"How did you meet up with Jordan, if it wasn't at the funeral?"

"Chris sent him to me. To protect me from the men who killed him," Regina replied, realizing she'd almost forgotten how cleansing it was to share thoughts and concerns. "I met him for the first time a few hours ago."

"Yet, I can see you trust him."

"Oh, yes. I trust him. Chris talked about Jordan all the time. Sometimes, it seems I've known Jordan all my life."

"Like a big brother," Lara commented, testing.

"No," Regina denied. "More like a..." Regina struggled with the word.

"Lover?" Lara suggested gently.

"Yes," Regina admitted. "Stupid, really."

"Not at all," Lara said, thinking of how at eighteen, she'd fallen in love with Ian. Ten years before he even realized it.

"But then he turned out to be so different in some ways." Regina shook her head. "And yet, exactly the same in others." Regina put her head in her hands. "I'm such an idiot."

No, Jordan's the idiot, Lara thought, as her heart ached for the woman beside her.

"What would you say if I told you Jordan wasn't showing you his best side right now?" Lara suggested, placing her hand over Regina's, then giving it a reassuring squeeze. "That the Jordan I know has risked his life time after time to save his friends' lives, and the lives of complete strangers. People he never knew or saw again?"

Regina found herself liking Lara. She recognized genuine kindness when she saw it. Being with Chris had taught her that.

Regina couldn't help comparing their lives, wondering if she and Lara would have been friends had they grown up in different circumstances.

"That's the Jordan Chris told me about," Regina said.

"What would you say if I told you that I've never seen Jordan hurting this much? And for some reason, I feel you're the only one who can help him through this mess."

Tears gathered in Regina's eyes. It had been a long time since she'd hurt this much herself. "I'd say that you're the first person I've talked to in a while who is telling me the truth."

"So what are you going to do about it?"

"Go to the library," Regina decided.

Lara chuckled. "Somehow I don't think you're going to find your answers in a book."

"You're probably right," Regina agreed. "But I actually meant your library. Jordan and Ian said they'd be waiting for us there, right?"

Lara laughed. "They can wait a little while longer."

"Don't discount the public library, either," Regina added. "I may end up there yet."

Lara draped her arm around Regina and hugged her. After a while, Regina moved away and saw the tears well in Lara's eyes. "I'm sorry, I didn't mean to make you cry."

"Don't worry. Pregnant women love to cry."

Regina nodded. "Crying actually releases endorphins that automatically raise a person's spirits."

"So you can't help but be happy after a good cry, is that it?"

"That's it," Regina laughed out loud at the silliness of it all. "The last time I laughed was with Chris."

"You miss Chris terribly, don't you?" Lara asked, sobering a little.

"Yes, more than I ever thought possible," Regina said. "But what's worse is that I think Jordan misses him more."

Lara reached over and grabbed them both a tissue. "You just proved my point. I think you're the one person Jordan needs right now. You both loved Chris the same way. Like a father. And only you understand how much Jordan's hurting right now. Even if he doesn't."

Startled, Regina stared at Lara. "I never thought of it that way. Thank you."

"No thanks necessary." Lara smiled and gave Regina another quick hug. "That's what friends are for."

"WHAT HAVE WE GOT?" Jordan asked, not liking the edgy feeling that seemed to catch him off guard. Regina had been upstairs for almost an hour.

"Don't worry, Regina couldn't be safer. Lara's a high-trained specialist. She can kick your butt any day."

It was an old argument. One Jordan figured Ian had brought up for a distraction. He was about to tell him so, when he heard feminine laughter through the door.

"I told—"

"If you want to live through the next two minutes, I wouldn't say a word."

Ian shrugged, but kept his mouth closed. After all, he could definitely empathize with what his friend was going through.

Regina's eyes were red and her hair was damp. The scent of shampoo drifted toward Jordan. Feminine, light.

She looked so much more relaxed in the chocolate-brown running suit, that he decided against commenting. Instead, he handed her a chicken salad sandwich. "Here, eat something."

He watched her take two bites before he was satisfied.

"Glad you two showed up. R.L. brought up quite a bit of names from our databanks. We're going to need a few more facts to narrow it down, Regina."

"Narrow it down from what?" Lara asked.

"About a hundred, give or take a few aliases. Illegal

arms dealing is big business these days," Ian said, before glancing at Regina. "Jordan said you memorized the journal." At her nod, he said, "All I need is a place, another name, an age. Anything."

"How's your headache?" Jordan turned to Regina, but she avoided looking at him and instead stared at the computer.

"Better. I can recite the page," Regina said quietly. She took a moment, closed her eyes and pictured the words. "They meet tonight. R.L. has promised the merchandise. Charlie is handling the exchange. Half now, half when the mission is complete. Of course, if he gets caught in the fallout...*sootbaa.*"

"Sootbaa," Jordan repeated. "That's Russian for the word 'fate.' But what's the fallout?"

Regina ran the words through her mind again, checked them against the other pages she had memorized. "He didn't reference that word or any other Russian words anywhere else in the journal."

"Fallout from the operation," Ian suggested.

"Or nuclear fallout," Jordan added. "We are talking about an arms dealer."

"It's a place to start," Lara murmured. She flanked Ian on the opposite side of Regina and pointed to the list on the screen. "Isolate the Russian nuclear experts."

"Right." Ian's fingers flew over the keyboard. "If we can at least narrow the names to a dozen, we can track their whereabouts. Might take a few days, a week max."

"We don't have a week," Jordan replied.

"Do you have a timeline?" Lara asked.

"No," Regina answered. "But there was definitely an underlining urgency to Chris's entries. Whatever is going to happen, will happen soon."

Ian leaned back with a grim smile. "Then I'm thinking that this must be your lucky day."

"I think you're right." Jordan leaned over the desk and studied the screen. "Looks like it might get a little nasty out there. Can I borrow your Hummer, Ian?"

Ian pulled out a pair of keys from the desk drawer, but held them away when Jordan reached for them. "Not so fast. The last time I loaned you my car, you blew it up."

"Technically Cain blew the car up. It was just my idea," Jordan corrected. "Besides, we saved the president, didn't we?"

"You wreck my Hummer, you replace it."

"All right," Jordan agreed. But when he reached again, Ian held them back once more.

"And," Ian added, twirling the key ring around his finger. "Lara and I get your estate for one week. Alone. Which means you babysit. Here."

Frowning, Jordan looked from Regina's stunned face to Lara's amused one.

"Fine." He grabbed the keys and pocketed them. "But I'm not going to wreck your car."

Chapter Eight

Fatigue had been riding Regina hard for the past two hours, but she didn't dare complain. Whatever Chris was involved in, wasn't long term. The urgency was there, hanging over her head like a guillotine.

She glanced at the dashboard clock. Just past two.

"You all seemed to take this whole situation with a good dose of humor," she commented.

"You learn to enjoy the people close to you while you can."

Jordan glanced her way before turning his eyes back onto the road. The snow had stopped, but the air still frosted windows, made the roads icy. "In our line of work, it might be the last chance you see them," he added.

"You said Lara is still active with Labyrinth. Doesn't Ian worry she might get hurt?"

"Sure, but he doesn't stop living his life because of a fear. If he did, he wouldn't be able to function," Jordan explained. "Two years ago, Lara had found out she was pregnant with Clara. At the time, she was finishing up a relatively harmless operation. Then, one of our oldest agents went rogue. He decided releasing a biochemical weapon on Las Vegas was the answer to his problems. Lara ended up getting shot in the stomach. It was a nightmare for Ian."

"Why doesn't Ian insist that Lara quit Labyrinth?" Regina asked, surprised. "They have a baby now."

"Lara isn't on active duty. She trains all our newest agents, so the chance of being in harm's way is very small. Smaller than being a cop these days. Or a firefighter."

"But it's there."

"Yes, but it's her career," Jordan said. "Lara is extremely good at what she does. Ian trusts in her abilities."

"Why didn't you ask them for more help?"

"The minute Ian said Lara was pregnant, I didn't consider it," Jordan said. "And right now, he's the only one I'd trust."

"How about you, Jordan?" Regina asked quietly. "How many close calls have you had?"

"Too many to count."

"Have you ever thought about getting out?"

"No. I'm very good at what I do, too," he answered, evenly.

Once Chris had told her about Jordan rescuing a sheik and his son from assassins. Although she would have died before admitting it, for weeks she pictured Jordan up on a horse, racing across the desert, his white cloak soaring behind him, a sword in his hand.

Not once did she ever picture him lying in the sand in agony, bleeding to death from a stomach wound.

"Who worries about you?" she asked. Chris had never mentioned a girlfriend or wife. But Chris also hadn't seen Jordan in two years.

"No one," Jordan said, a hint of a smile crinkling the sides of his eyes.

"So, why didn't you stay close with your father?" she asked. "I mean, if he was an agent, too, he understood the risks that you were taking."

"Most of the time when I was growing up, I never knew where he was at any given moment. His job took him all over the world for weeks, even months at a time. He made work his priority, not his family," Jordan answered. He shot her a sidelong glance. "If it helps, I've been told I'm the same way."

She had always wondered why Chris's memories were never of Jordan's childhood. Now she understood. "Did he have a choice?"

"We all have a choice, Regina. He made his long before I was even born."

"And after, when you became an operative?"

"Look, if you're trying to play psychologist—"

"I'm trying to understand." Before Jordan could respond, Regina added, "I loved your father. So it's hard for me to believe you didn't."

When Jordan raised an eyebrow, she didn't hide her annoyance. "Don't start on the whole mistress thing again, Jordan. Chris was my best friend." The words clogged her throat but she forced them out. "Actually, he was my only friend."

"Your only friend." His eyes flickered over her before returning to the road. "Looking for sympathy?"

"No sympathy required," she insisted, but the fact that he thought she'd stoop that low pricked at her pride. "I dealt mostly with rare books, so I didn't need any help. Most of my business was Internet-based. It was my choice to be antisocial."

"No regular customers off the street?"

"A few here and there. I deliberately didn't jump on the coffee shop bandwagon that most bookstores incorporated. Food and beverages attract too many people who like to linger over their purchases. Or worse, people who want to just hang out and work or study or something."

"I bet you cut down quite a bit on any steady flow of traffic."

"I was very good at discouraging loiterers."

"I bet," Jordan mused. "So you really don't like people."

"I like people," she insisted. But liking and socializing were two different animals. "I'm just not comfortable around them. Over time it just got easier for me to be alone, I guess."

"You seem fine with people now. Lara and Ian certainly enjoyed you."

"They are nice, aren't they? I enjoyed them, too." She studied the street before them. "Maybe your father helped me without realizing it."

"If you were that antisocial, what made my father different?"

"That's a good question," she replied, taking a moment to think about it. "Chris was the first person I found more interesting than any book I've read." She paused to smile. "And he was persistent. He wouldn't let me hide in my books."

"So, you hid from life in your books?"

She glanced out the window, watched the Christmas lights flash by in streaks of rainbow colors. "Something we have in common I guess."

"Lady, we have nothing in common."

"You hide from real life by being a government operative, don't you?"

"Trust me, being an operative does nothing but show you all aspects of life. Good and bad."

"I'm talking about your personal life. Other than a few close friends—that even *you* admit you rarely see—do you have a personal life?" When he said nothing, she added, "Like father, like son. You said it yourself."

"You've got a point," Jordan admitted. "A small one. He was better at diplomacy than spying. I've never been known as the diplomatic sort."

"But you could be. I think it's in you." Regina paused, debating. Deciding to go with her instincts, she pushed, "You regret not being on better terms with him when he died, don't you?"

"There's a lot of things I regret, sweetheart. Too many to start listing this late at night."

"You could always just give me the top ten."

"Nice try."

Silence settled between them.

"Jordan, I have to tell you something." When he

raised his eyebrow, she hesitated. "I don't like most people. But I like you."

His eyes snapped to hers. His jaw worked. "Well, don't."

Her sharp intake of breath broke through before she could stop it. But when he didn't take the words back, she blinked back the sting of tears and stared out the window. "Well, no worries there. It shouldn't be too hard to learn to hate you now. And I'm a fast study, remember?"

"Regina, I—" What was he going to say. He was sorry? Admit that he liked her, too? That he wanted her? That even if he started something, he would eventually be forced to walk away?

Suddenly, a car appeared in his side-view mirror. An unmarked black sedan with a suit driving. He let out a string of curses. "Do you have your seat belt on?"

"Yes, but what does that have to do with you—"

"Hold on to something." He snapped out the order.

She grabbed the front dashboard and he jerked the wheel, sending the car into a one-hundred-eighty-degree spin.

Shots rang out, pinging off the side panel of the driver's door. "Get down," Jordan yelled, pushing her head down to the seat.

"Who is it?" Regina kept her face against his thigh, but the fear was there, edging each syllable.

"Standard government-issued vehicle."

"The government's shooting at us?" Her head rose automatically before Jordan shoved it back down again.

"Did Ian turn you in?" she asked.

"Not bloody likely." But the doubt was there biting him at the base of his neck. Did Lara mention his visit to her father? Jordan instantly ruled the possibility out. She would have had to call Mercer before Jordan and Regina had even left her house.

"Then who?"

"Someone pretty high up on Capitol Hill from the looks of these guys."

He sped through a red light, jerked the wheel but didn't let up on the gas. "That car is no regular car. It's armor-plated and bulletproof."

"So even if we shot at them—"

"Wouldn't touch them," he bit out. "We're going to have to lose them the old-fashioned way."

"Are they far behind you?"

"No, they're right on my ass." More gunshots exploded through the dark, deserted street.

"If you tap your brakes for a long second, they'll hit theirs, too, in reflex. Then hit your gas. The trick is in the timing. Whoever is following us won't expect—"

"Don't tell me. Defensive driving book, right?"

"Human psychology," she said and actually sounded indignant. In the middle of a car chase. Jordan almost laughed out loud.

"The streets are slick from the ice and snow," Regina explained, her voice schoolteacher prim. "They might lose control. Then we can get away."

"Good idea." Jordan eased off the accelerator, watched the lights close in through his rearview mirror. "Or half of a good idea."

Jordan hit the brake, heard the screech of tires behind him. The sedan spun into a one-eighty, stopping when its back end hit a nearby light post.

"Hold on," Jordan ordered. He slammed the Hummer gear into Reverse and hit the accelerator.

The Hummer shot backward, its tail end headed for the driver's side of the sedan.

Regina cried out and grabbed the dash. The impact slammed her back, then forward again as metal ripped through metal.

"Stay here." Suddenly, Jordan was out of the car, gun in hand.

The two men in the car were pinned behind the Hummer. Their air bags inflated, the driver's window blown out from the impact.

"Who are you working for?" Jordan demanded his gun raised.

"You're dead, Beck," the driver said, his face more blood than skin.

Suddenly, the second man raised a Glock from behind the driver's shoulder. Jordan fired. The man flopped back, dead.

"I'll ask again," Jordan said, his voice low. "Who do you work for?"

"Go to hell." The driver reached for his partner's gun. Jordan fired. The bullet pierced the man's forehead before he even touched metal.

"You first."

Jordan didn't need to look up to see that Regina witnessed the killings and fully expected her to be hysterical by the time he reached his door.

Jordan slid into his seat, surprised to find her sitting quietly. He shut the door and threw the gear into Drive.

"Are you all right?" Jordan asked. She was pale, and her hands were shaking as she clasped them in her lap. But there was no sound.

"Yes," she answered, her voice strong but quiet.

When he pulled away, she looked back at the wreckage behind them in the street. The metallic scent of the blood followed Jordan back to the car. Regina's stomach rolled.

"Jordan," she said, swallowing the bile that burned the back of her throat.

"Yes?" His muscles tensed, waiting.

"I think you owe Ian a new Hummer."

THEY'D RETURNED TO the motel, but not immediately to the room. First, Jordan circled the motel until he was satisfied they weren't followed. Then, while Regina waited outside the doorway, he checked the room.

"Did those men tell you who they worked for?"

"No, they didn't. But I wasn't expecting them to. Those were government hitmen. Trained to do nothing but kill. They could've worked for any number of people, in any number of organizations. National Security. Central Intelligence," Jordan explained. He opened his bag and grabbed some clean clothes. "They must have waited for us outside Ian's. The question is, how did they find us?"

"Government hitmen," Regina repeated. "As in the United States?"

"Yes."

Stunned, Regina placed Lara's duffel bag at the end of the bed. Her new friend had filled it with enough slacks, sweaters, socks and pajamas to last a while. Regina planned on buying some underwear and shoes the next day.

"After I take a shower, I'd like to go over some more of my father's notes," Jordan said. "That tail tonight just upped the ante on us."

"It's almost three in the morning, Jordan. I'm half dead on my feet." She opened the case and rummaged for the nightshirt. Some of the clothes were a size or two bigger, but all things considered…

Jordan stepped closer and caught her chin with his thumb. "Just the highlights." He tilted her head up until his eyes caught hers. "No more than fifteen minutes," he promised.

She thought for a moment he was going to kiss her. His eyes drifted over her mouth. But then suddenly he was gone.

The bathroom door snapped shut and a few moments later the shower started.

Deciding it was better to change while he was in the bathroom, she took off her sweatshirt and immediately shivered in the chilled air. Finding the heating unit under the window, she flipped the switch.

Suddenly, something skittered across her foot. Regina

screamed and jumped away from a large cockroach that dashed under the nightstand.

Before another scream passed her lips, Jordan was there, his gun in his hand.

"What is it?"

"Cockroach!" Another darted across the floor and under the bed. This time Regina jumped on the bed and stood on her knees.

"A bug?" Jordan yelled, his wet hair plastered to his head. "You give me a heart attack over a bloody bug?"

"A filthy, *bloody* bug," Regina argued, amazed she found her voice.

"You don't even flinch when we're chased by some bad guys with guns. But a cockroach turns you into a screaming banshee?"

"Have you ever read about them? They're disgusting," she said, letting his temper prod hers. "And nocturnal. Which means they attack at night."

"I know what nocturnal means, damn it. And cockroaches don't attack."

He set his gun on the nightstand and took a quick glance behind it. "Nothing. You can calm your nerves now."

She glared at him. "Us mere mortals have weaknesses, Jordan. Mine just happens to be cockroaches. And I didn't ask you to come to my rescue." She glanced at the gun. "And as for overreacting…what were you going to do, shoot them?"

Angry, he stepped to the bed. "Call me crazy, but when you screamed I thought 'bad guys,' not cockroaches."

"Not my fault." She slapped a hand against his chest

to fend him off. "And stop crowding me. My reaction was instinctive. Not premeditated."

Hair—moist from the shower—tickled her palm, causing her fingers to curl into his chest.

Her eyes drifted down. Water had darkened the hair on his chest to a charred brown. Tiny beads of moisture, the size of small crystals, clung to his skin. While others broke free, running in a slow, lazy path down the V of his chest, over the tight abdomen, to the thin line of hair just past his navel.

This time when she shivered, it wasn't from the chill.

Regina shut her eyes, not ready to go farther.

"Regina." His breath shuttered beneath her palm.

Her eyes flew open. "Jordan, I—"

"Be quiet." His hands shook as he grabbed her by the shoulders and pulled her off the bed and into him.

He smelled of shaving cream, and soap. Spicy, masculine. She gave in to the urge to lean closer, to inhale deeper.

When the top of her breasts brushed against the moist hair of his chest, she nearly groaned.

"Regina," Jordan murmured her name like a curse. His eyes drilled hers, so clear, so sharp. If she let him, he would see into her soul.

She gripped the top of his shoulders, felt the hard muscles flex beneath her touch. "Jordan?" Desire slammed into her, shoving her off center, jumbling the thoughts in her head.

Cursing, he let go and she fell back onto the bed. "What you're asking for isn't going to happen, sweetheart."

It took a moment for his words to penetrate.

This time Regina closed her eyes tight, but couldn't stop her body from trembling. She'd spent her whole life alone, but never truly understood the feeling until that moment.

"Give me a few minutes to get dressed," Jordan said, his voice rough, but brisk. All business. "We can go over the notes and make another copy."

"I need a computer." That was twice he deliberately hurt her. Once in the car, once now.

"Not that I couldn't handwrite the whole book again, but it would take too much time." She faced him, her fists tight at her sides, her eyes on his face, not daring to look down again.

He reached inside the bathroom, grabbed a towel off the rack and wrapped it around his hips. "I have Ian's laptop. I put it in the car while you were changing. Will that work?"

"Yes," she said stiffly, showing no hint of the relief that rushed through her when he tied the towel in place.

Her eyes dipped down. She saw the scars then. One on his right shoulder, another slashed across his bicep. A third one, jagged over his left ribs.

Stabbings? Gunshot wounds?

Distressed, she licked her lips.

"Regina," Jordan said softly. "Look at me."

Her head jerked up, not realizing until that moment that she'd been staring at his chest again.

"Just remind yourself occasionally that you don't like me, sweetheart, and we'll both be better off," he answered, his voice hoarse. From anger or frustration, she couldn't be sure.

Before she could comment, Jordan turned on his heel and stepped into the bathroom.

Chapter Nine

Jordan leaned his forehead against the closed door, battling down the surge of hormones that heated his blood, sent his heart racing. The last thing he needed was complications. And Regina Menlow was becoming a huge complication.

In his mind, he saw her body, flushed pink with arousal. The small tips of her breasts clear through the white, gauzy cups of her bra.

He lashed down the desire that gripped his gut. But then her hazel eyes deepened as they drifted down his body. Each point they touched, each contour they followed set his flesh on fire.

Still, he managed to maintain.

But when the tip of her tongue slid between the row of white teeth, tasted her bottom lip—

Jordan nearly groaned out loud.

His last remark had been made out of pure desperation.

And not one guy on earth would have blamed him.

He heard Regina muttering from the bedroom. A reluctant smile tugged at the corners of his mouth when he heard the word jerk. She certainly had a way with words. Something he was learning to appreciate.

He dressed quickly in sweatpants and a T-shirt. No use pushing his control. One touch of her soft, silky skin against his, and he'd be in serious trouble.

When he stepped out of the bathroom, he expected to see her changed into pajamas. Instead, she was wearing a short night shirt with a big teddy bear Santa on the front. "Lara's idea." She shrugged. "It was going to be Celeste's Christmas present."

"That explains the fit." His eyes drifted down to where the hem of the shirt brushed the top portion of her thighs. The image of her high breasts, curved waist and slim legs wouldn't leave his mind.

"I think," Regina cleared her throat, "that I'll have a look at that computer."

"Good...idea," he mimicked her hesitation, letting her know the reason behind it didn't make him happy. "We need your notes as close to verbatim as possible."

"They will be. But you realize what I write down is hearsay now. It wouldn't hold up in court."

His eyebrow rose. "Another book?"

"Common sense," she said, then added grudgingly. "And yes, another book."

"Tell me something, can you recite every book you've ever read?"

"If I chose to, I could. Some I deliberately forget. I can read a book page to page in my mind if I've committed it to memory. I see both the words and the pages they're on."

Jordan pulled the computer from his case, placed it on the nightstand and opened the screen.

Regina sat down on the bed with her legs crisscrossed in front of the screen. Quickly she tucked her nightshirt around her thighs for modesty's sake.

A moment later, Jordan lay on his side behind her. The bed tilted, slamming her back into the curve of his rock-hard stomach.

"Do you mind?" She used her elbow against his stomach for leverage to sit up, taking satisfaction in hearing him grunt.

"I can see the screen better from here," Jordan explained. "You don't need to be nervous."

"You're not making me nervous."

When his hand slid intimately around her ribs, she jumped.

He dropped his hand. "The hell I'm not."

"*You* aren't doing anything. It's the situation making me nervous." She shifted closer to the nightstand. "Any person is bound to get a little nervous when they've never experienced this before."

"If you expect me to believe—" His face snapped to hers. "Are you telling me you've never had sex before?"

"You don't have to yell, Jordan. I'm right next to you."

This time it was he who jumped, putting a good foot or so distance between them on the bed. "You're twenty-eight years old. That's impossible."

She twisted around to see him. "Improbable in this day and age, but not impossible, I assure you," she responded primly, more than a little disgruntled. So what if she'd chosen not to get involved with anyone? It didn't make her a freak.

"Men aren't that stupid." His gaze swept over her, not leaving until pink flushed her neck and face. "And my father certainly wouldn't have been."

"I've told you before, your father and I had a platonic relationship."

A pithy remark shot from his lips.

Her eyes narrowed into twin slits of green granite. "Want me to prove it?"

"Bloody hell." In an instant, the blood drained from his head, pooled in his lap, making him hard. "I'm not going to give you a crash course in sex just to prove my father hasn't already slept with you."

"It wouldn't be a crash course. I've done my research."

Jordan couldn't believe she actually sounded insulted. "Don't you dare tell me you've read a book on the subject."

"Not one," she corrected. "I've read several."

"Well, I can tell you from experience, it's not the same." Jordan wanted to know how in hell he lost control of the conversation. For good measure he shoved a pillow in the middle of the bed.

"How much experience?"

"What?"

"I was just curious." Her head was down and she plucked at the spread. But he got a sneaking suspicion she was studying him from beneath her lashes. "If you have a lot of… I mean, if there's been quite a few women—"

"Too many to count."

"I understand." Hurt flashed across her features,

catching him off guard. Making him lean forward before he realized what he was doing.

"No, you don't. That's just the point. And I won't be the one enlightening you." But he wanted to. Enough that the thought left him shaking from anger and desire. He'd be her first. The thought of sinking into her, knowing no other man—"

He yanked a hand through his hair, drawing some sanity from the pain he inflicted. "A virgin."

"So you're admitting now that you're wrong. That Chris and I were only friends?"

Jordan went still. "You were proving a point?"

"Yes."

Frustration and desire boiled over into an icy rage. "Is that what this is all about?"

"Mostly." Regina was too busy being smug to notice the dangerous glint in Jordan's eye. "I haven't been with anyone. And you have to agree—"

The next thing Regina knew Jordan's body covered hers, pinning her to the bed beneath him.

"I have to agree what?" His tone slipped into a low, silky whisper.

"It's…it was a good argument." He was so close she could see silver flecks sharpen in the blue irises.

She could lose herself in his eyes. The clearest shade of blue, tranquil like a calm lake.

But when his temper stirred, the blue turned wicked, stormy. And tormentingly, just as enticing.

"Clever argument. Tricky clever." His mouth skimmed her cheek, nibbled on her top lip. "Baby, you're sweet."

"I am?" Suddenly, her throat went dry, her eyes fluttered shut. Regina shivered—not from the cold, but from the heat of his mouth.

"I've never been told…" She sighed when he left small bites along her collar bone until more delicious shivers rippled over her skin. "I've never been anything."

"Have you ever been kissed?" Jordan murmured, while his teeth grazed her throat.

"No." Her vision blurred and her head lolled back, allowing him more access, steeped in the havoc his mouth was causing. "I never dreamed…"

"Sweetheart, you have the sexiest mouth I've seen." With a groan, his lips touched the side of hers.

She sighed against his cheek as he nibbled his way across her bottom lip. "I didn't know kissing involved more than…"

She whimpered as his tongue slid over her upper lip. He took his time, tasting, enjoying the soft texture. "More than what, sweetheart?"

"More than what?" she whispered against his mouth, her hands tugging on his hair as she instinctively tried to deepen the kiss. Her breath, sweet as honey, caressed his jaw in a rush of warm, moist air.

"You said," he nudged her, his breath hot, his teeth sharp as he nipped her lobe—then soothed the spot with his tongue immediately after, "kissing involved more than what?"

Regina struggled to focus beyond wispy clouds that fuzzed her mind. "More than kissing."

A low masculine laugh rumbled against her ear,

doing delicious things. Things that made her tremble until she ached between her thighs.

"Regina." He shifted until she cradled him between her legs. Her body quivered against the hardness of his. Her feet moved restlessly against the back of his calves.

"Tell me what you want, sweetheart."

"You," she whispered, craving his mouth against her somewhere. Anywhere. Her hands curled behind his neck with impatience.

Then his mouth was on hers, hard, demanding. Incredible. The hot, heady masculine taste—the mixture of firm, sharp, soft textures.

Regina's lips parted, offering him whatever he wanted, taking what she needed. What she'd yearned for her whole life.

He didn't tease. He wasn't gentle. Having waited too much, played the game too long. Again and again he plundered. Again and again, she matched him stroke for stroke, need for need.

Instinctive and bold, Regina's response sent him careening toward the edge of control.

"More," he whispered. Ordered. Begged. "Give me more." His hand slipped down until he found the moist heat between her thighs. Felt her tremble beneath his palm.

"How?" Her eyes fluttered open, showing him the confusion and fear—and the trust he didn't deserve.

Reality slammed into him, knocking him back with one single punch. He staggered from the weight of it.

"Jordan?"

He jerked his hand away from her body, fisted it

above her head. When that didn't help, he buried his face in the scented curve of her shoulder, his breathing ragged as he fought for control.

"Jordan?" Regina whispered, confused. She rubbed against him in short restless movements.

"Don't." The command harsh from sheer desperation. He sucked in his breath. His body shuttered, his grip slipping on what little control he had left. He kissed her once more, hard, fast, but not deep.

Not again.

She was so vulnerable right now, so slight he could crush simply with words if he wasn't careful.

He brushed a strand away from her heated cheek. Tipped her chin until he could see her face.

"Listen to me, Regina." The trust was there again, open and honest.

His hand shook. Her vulnerability scared him to death.

"Look Regina, what we did was a—"

"Please don't say it was a mistake." Hurt edged her words, but it was the underlying loneliness that drew him. He resisted the urge to pull her close.

"Listen to me, sweetheart." It hadn't even occurred to him to think it was a mistake. Not until that second. Once again he found himself telling the truth. "I was going to say it was a close call. Another five minutes and—"

"I would have had you right where I wanted you?" she asked, her lips swollen and trembling from his kisses.

"Yes, I guess you would have," he agreed gently, ignoring the fact he was lying on her—his body hard, throbbing. Or that she cradled him between her thighs.

Slowly, Jordan stood. That alone almost killed him.

He saw the tears well up. "Don't cry," he warned, his voice strained, like a man stretched out on the rack. "I already feel lower than—" He bit off the obscenity. "If you only knew what a turn on—" He stopped again, his hands fisted. "How in bloody hell did you go this long without sex?"

"I told you I don't meet people…easily." She didn't want to listen to him berate her ineptness. With small jerky movements, she scooted to the edge of the bed until her knees bumped the nightstand. Only pride kept her from curling into the pain, weeping with the humiliation.

"You said it yourself in the car, Jordan. You don't like me. And if you weren't stuck with me, you'd be long gone."

He didn't deny it. He would've been long gone, but not for the reason she thought.

"And honestly, I've never reacted to any man," she continued, "like I have to you."

"Regina." He ground out her name, knowing his hold on the situation was slippery at best. "What we did. It's normal. I just don't want to hurt you because it won't lead to anything. Once we're done with this, I'm gone."

Her head snapped around. "So you're saying it wasn't me? It was you? That's why you stopped?"

"Yes," Jordan said slowly, feeling like he'd just walked into a minefield of some kind.

"So, you were being gallant," she reasoned, slowly. More to herself than him. "You didn't want to take advantage of the situation. Or me."

"I didn't want to complicate things," he explained, uncomfortable with the word "gallant."

"You know, Chris told me all these stories about you. Mostly about the missions you went on and the people you saved. I'd actually started thinking of you as some avenging angel or white knight or something."

He glanced at the bed. "Yes, well, I'm sorry to disappoint you."

"That's just it, you haven't disappointed me at all. You're kind. And sexy. And brave," she admitted, feeling the blush rise over her cheeks.

"Regina," Jordan warned, exasperated. "Do you always have to be so honest?"

"Somehow, I don't think you'd like me any other way."

"Sweetheart, if you think that, then you missed everything that happened on that bed just now," Jordan retorted. "I'd like you pretty much any damn way I could take you."

"That's not what I mean," she answered, letting out a long, shaky breath. "You've lived your whole life with lies and secrets, haven't you? First from your parents, then with the government."

"It's the nature of the business."

"I think it's become more than that. It's spilled over into your personal life, tainting it. It's became part of *your nature,* not just part of your business. But I don't believe it's who you really are deep down. You're nobler than that."

"Don't try to make me into something from one of those books, Regina. I'm no hero. I don't defend the innocent. Not anymore. I work strictly contract now. My talent goes to the highest bidder."

"You quit your job because you want to find your father's murderer," Regina insisted, her voice achingly loyal. "You might be killing, but it's for justice, not for money."

He shook his head, almost dazed. "Are you always so sure of people?"

"I'm sure of you."

"Don't be," Jordan said, then decided to change the subject. "Look, I know I promised only a few minutes on the computer, but if you've got the energy—"

"I couldn't sleep right now even if I tried. Let's just go and see what happens."

Jordan caught the double meaning, but decided to let it pass. He could still feel the soft imprint of her body against his, hear the small sexy sound she made when he nibbled her silky skin.

He rubbed the ache from his chest.

"Would you recite the journal to me as you type?" He grabbed the chair, flipped it around and sat on it backward, his arms resting across the top. A small barrier, but a barrier nonetheless.

"Yes."

He'd asked and not ordered. A small miracle.

"Jordan." Regina looked up and caught him watching her from the chair. For the first time in her life, she felt desirable, even sexy. Another miracle. She was on a roll.

"Yes?"

"That was a damn good first kiss, wasn't it?"

"Yes," he answered. A smile twitched at the corner of his mouth. "It sure was."

The smugness was back, but she couldn't help herself. She wanted to dance on the bed and scream to the world she was normal.

"Thought so." Then she did something she'd always wanted to do. She winked, slow and sexy.

"Regina," Jordan warned on a growl.

"Just testing," she said, smiling. "For later."

She turned back toward the computer, pretending she didn't here the obscenity he muttered under his breath.

"This day has definitely been life-changing." She pushed the button to boot up the computer. "And I think I owe everything to your father."

"Other than him making you a possible target, I don't see how he helped much at all."

"I didn't realize it until I was talking with Lara tonight. But somehow becoming friends with Chris must have made me more comfortable socially. It isn't totally natural for me yet, but it wasn't a struggle for me, either."

"What did you and Chris talk about?"

"History. Music. Philosophy. You," she said softly. "He was very proud of you."

"He said that?"

"Not in so many words. But it was always in his voice," she explained.

The computer beeped, stopping any comment Jordan might have made.

"It's ready."

"Let's go then," he said, more than ready to move on from the conversation.

"December twenty-fifth," Regina recited, the click of the keyboard catching the easy rhythm of her words. "Of my many regrets, none have haunted me more than my son's face. With each year that has passed—"

"Skip over anything personal about my mother or me," Jordan interrupted. "I'll read those entries later."

His tone was casual, but Regina wasn't fooled. She glanced back at him, knowing he wouldn't read them. But she decided, she'd already won something tonight from him, so she wouldn't press him now.

"All right, I'll fill the personal comments in after. And you can read them when you're ready."

Her fingers moved over the keys again. "December twenty-eighth. My first meeting with Alpha went as expected..."

"YOU'RE LATE, SOLOMON." Kyle Morris sank deeper into the hot tub. The heat seeped into his muscles, soothing most of them. He picked up the bottle of brandy and poured a good portion into a nearby glass.

"It couldn't be helped."

While the British residence served as his main living quarters, it was too close to Capitol Hill for Kyle to operate his other, more diverse ventures.

He'd been forced long ago to rent a flat on the more fashionable side of Washington, D.C.

"Tell me what happened." He tilted the brandy toward

the other man before taking a sip. The brandy was for those muscles the heated water wouldn't take care of.

"I got the book and torched her place. With her inside, of course." Solomon tossed the book on a nearby patio table. "I'm through cleaning up your messes, Kyle. I told you not to use Severs. He was too unstable."

"Severs was a necessary evil. And you missed killing the woman. Jordan Beck helped her escape." Kyle leaned back into the water and nodded toward the photos lying on the bar counter. "One of the witnesses took those with his cell phone. Then reported it to the police."

Solomon picked up the photographs. The first was of Beck and the woman. The second, a close up of Beck's car. "Got to love suspicious Americans."

"We have the license plate. But he's already killed the two men I put onto him. I need you to find him and the Menlow woman," Kyle ordered. "Find them, but don't do anything with them yet. His escaping actually might have done us a favor."

"How so?"

"Echo and I have agreed that having Beck involved might work to our advantage."

"Meaning?"

"We have three days until Christmas. The second package hasn't arrived here in the States yet."

"Isn't that your job to make sure it does?"

"Not anymore." Kyle grunted with satisfaction. "We still have plenty of time to set the explosive. I assured Echo that I would handle any problems that arise. But

I'm confident that Jordan Beck's involvement will work out perfectly."

"Like Christopher Beck? And Severs?"

"You can't always expect a mission to go without some hitches, Solomon. You of all people must be aware of that fact."

"Yes, I am aware of hitches." Solomon walked behind Kyle and pulled out his gun. "Echo talked to me as well."

Kyle took a sip of his brandy. "What about?"

Deliberately, Solomon checked the attached silencer, then pointed the gun at the back of Kyle's head. "He's decided now that we have Beck, we don't need you."

Chapter Ten

"Cain, I need a jet."

The office building looked like any other from the outside, except for the extra security staff. But once she entered the elevator, it all changed.

Green beams scanned them as they stepped off the elevator. For bugs and weapons, Jordan had said off-handedly.

Black and gray tiled corridors led them to a windowed office framed with steel beams.

"No." Cain MacAlister put down the file and leaned back in his desk chair. "Is there anything else?"

"Damn it, Cain—"

"And who are you?" Cain shifted his gaze from Jordan to Regina.

"Chris Beck's—"

"Regina," Jordan warned on a growl, not in the mood.

After an hour of work, they'd both decided to get some sleep. But Jordan hadn't figured in the fact that Regina had never slept with anyone, let alone a man.

The first hour she spent hugging the edge of the mattress to keep from rolling back into Jordan.

Finally, he pulled her to him and shifted her until she lay on her stomach in the crook of his arm and pushed her head down on his shoulder.

And for the next several hours she mumbled, sighed and shifted, until he was rock-hard and sleep-deprived.

She lifted a tired shoulder. "I was going to say that Chris was my friend."

"Cain MacAlister," Jordan introduced. "Regina Menlow."

"MacAlister?" Regina repeated, her frown turned on Cain. "Isn't Ian's—"

"He's my younger brother," Cain answered.

"Then Celeste is…"

"My wife."

"Small world," Regina remarked, eyeing the Director of Labyrinth. In her opinion, the two men looked nothing alike. Where Ian was mass and muscle, Cain was whip-lean with short inky black hair and smoky gray eyes.

"Not today it isn't." Cain studied her for a moment, his gaze taking her petite frame, the proud set to her spine before turning back to Jordan. "Okay, fill me in."

"I've got a lead on Chris's murder. An arms dealer named Rurik Losev. He's being held at a detention facility at Keflavik International.

"Losev mostly deals in upper-end weapons. Nuclear weapons. *Portable nuclear weapons.*"

"I know of Losev." Cain dug through some papers on his desk before snagging one. His eyes skimmed the sheet.

"They got him on falsifying his passport," Jordan said. "Not on arms dealing. He's being shipped to London for questioning about the subway bombing a few years ago. Seems he might have supplied the Severs."

"Might? Do you know for sure?" Cain dropped the paper back on his desk and placed his hands on his hips. "Or are you theorizing?"

"For sure," Jordan said, then caught Regina's frown.

Silently he cursed Regina and her honesty. And his own stupidity for feeling a twinge of guilt. "All right, not for sure, but it's my only lead and worth investigating."

"At least now I understand how Miss Menlow knows Ian," Cain acknowledged, wryly. "He accessed our files for you, didn't he?"

"Last night at his house," Jordan admitted. "Ian called me this morning and told me he couldn't get me a secured flight out to Iceland."

"No surprise there," Cain stated. "The president has the NSA security beefed up at all major airports for the holiday. All unauthorized flights are being held as security risks."

"Why?"

"The president hasn't told me," Cain answered, sharp enough for Jordan to realize Cain wasn't happy about that fact.

"It could have something to do with what you're telling me," Cain admitted, then thought for a moment. "All right. Let's assume there is a rogue nuke out there somewhere. Do you have any ideas where it might be?"

Jordan shook his head. "Any major city. Here or

overseas. We don't even know how many bombs we're dealing with yet. But I'm thinking Losev will have the answers."

"Maybe we need to find out." Cain hit the button on his phone. "Tamara, find Dr. D'Amato for me and tell her we're on our way down to her lab."

"Yes, sir."

"We don't have time for a discussion with Kate," Jordan argued. "If they extradite Losev, we may never get another chance."

"If they release him to London, we'll track him there."

"If I step foot in London, I'll never get to him," Jordan snapped back.

"I can always assign another operative."

"My father. My operation."

"And you need *my* help," Cain added. "I want to know what we're dealing with first. If I send you after Losev, you'd better know what you're walking into."

"IF LOSEV IS INVOLVED, then we're talking suitcase nukes." Kate MacAlister-D'Amato leaned against her desk. "Most likely two tons of power. That would wipe out a five-mile radius in any major metropolitan area. The radioactive fallout, depending on the weather, could travel fifty miles in any direction.

"The rumors have always floated around since the Cold War that the Russians had created a hundred or so suitcase bombs," Kate advised. "And over the years, have sold them at a high price to select terrorist groups."

The brother and sister definitely came from the same

gene pool, Regina mused. Handsome, aristocratic, with the classical lines of the Scots.

There were other similarities. The raven black hair—hers pulled back in a pony tail, his with threads of silver—the same smoky gray eyes. Cain in a charcoal-gray tailored suit; Kate in trim black, skirt and jacket. Both were efficient, understated and expensive.

"The Russians track all their plutonium and uranium. How could any, let alone a hundred, slip through their security?" Jordan asked.

"During the breakup of the Soviet Union, anything was possible. Several of Russia's foremost scientists testified that they were involved in or had seen some of these suitcases. Losev was one of those scientists. An astrophysicist."

"But I remember reading that the Russian government denied any knowledge of these nuclear bombs," Regina inserted.

"Very good," Kate remarked. "And it was a story that Moscow stuck to. After Losev testified about what he'd seen, Moscow sent him to Siberia for treason. After a few years, he was released and disappeared off the radar."

"Obviously, he decided to change his profession to arms dealing," Jordan said, studying the screen over Kate's shoulder. "More lucrative."

"If that's the case, he couldn't have picked a better career move," Kate acknowledged. "Dr. Rurik Losev got his Ph.D. from MIT."

"A genius with a chip on his shoulder," Jordan commented. "The best kind of person to be selling weapons of mass destruction."

"MIT? As in Massachusetts Institute of Technology?" Regina asked. "He went to college here in the States?"

"Most of the terrorists do. Some are even homegrown," Cain commented grimly. "Kate's input is nothing more than circumstantial evidence. You're going to need more proof, Jordan."

"My father's journal identified Losev as a possible link."

"The journal isn't enough proof to justify issuing a Learjet to a civilian. And right now, that's exactly what you are. A civilian. Officially, you lost any backing from Labyrinth with your resignation a month ago."

"And unofficially?"

"Unofficially, you're a civilian who's close to being arrested for any number of charges. NSA is just looking for an excuse." Cain shrugged. "Of course, they have to find you first."

"What did you do?" Regina asked.

"Resisted arrest," Jordan replied. "The National Security Agency holds an aversion to other government agencies interfering in their business. When they closed my father's case after no apparent investigation, I protested the decision rather emphatically."

"You broke an agent's jaw," Cain corrected, his mouth twitching with amusement.

"That particular agent made a derogatory comment regarding my birth right," Jordan indicated. "I decided he needed time to think before he shot off his mouth again."

"Which brings me to my other problem," Cain said, sobering. "Kyle approached the president late last night with your photograph outside Regina's bookstore. He implied that you were involved in your father's death."

"You're saying that Morris accused me of killing my own father."

"Yes."

"And why would I do this?"

"You tell me," Cain answered, irritated. "It wasn't a secret, you and Chris had a falling out. Only no one knows the reason."

"So I have a disagreement with my father and decide to blow him to pieces," Jordan stated sarcastically. "Did the president believe him?"

"He didn't at first."

"At first?" Regina asked the question. "What changed his mind?"

"Circumstances." Cain's mouth flattened into a grim line.

"Damn it, Cain. You know as well as I do if Kyle is accusing me of the British Embassy bombing, then he could be behind this. He's MI6 for Christ's sake, but that doesn't mean he isn't a traitor."

"Kyle Morris is dead," Kate inserted quietly.

"Dead?" Jordan glanced from Cain to Kate. "How?"

Cain folded his arms. "He was found shot in the back of the head and floating in his hot tub only hours after he implicated you in Chris's murder. There were no signs of forced entry. Whoever did it knew him."

"They left the gun lying on the floor," Kate added. "A gun with your DNA all over it, Jordan. Chris's gun."

"Dad had several different weapons."

"This was a nine-millimeter Sig Sauer. The one you received back with the rest of his effects after he died," Cain added. "The only reason you weren't arrested the minute you stepped foot in here is because there are some areas I still control."

"I left my father's things at my flat in London," Jordan explained. "Someone could have easily broken into my place and stolen his gun."

"Can you prove it?"

"I can," Regina protested, ignoring Jordan's sharp shake of his head. "He didn't kill anyone. He was with me last night."

"All night?" Kate asked, startled.

Jordan sighed. "She's not credible. We're lovers."

"Lovers," Cain snapped, glancing at Regina. The flushed cheeks confirmed his friend's statement. "Jordan, so help me God if we survive this, I'm going to kill you myself."

"Get in line," Regina murmured, angry at the lie. Obviously, Jordan didn't trust her as an eyewitness.

"All right, boys," Kate replied, using a stern tone. "Any ideas who might have killed Kyle? How about Calvin West? Do we know if he's dirty?"

"Hell, it could be anyone at this point. Even Scarface," Jordan remarked.

"Who the hell is Scarface?" Cain demanded.

"The bastard who torched Regina's bookstore." Jordan fisted his hands.

"He was after Chris's journal."

"The list of possible bad guys is getting longer," Kate commented. "What the hell is in this journal?"

"That's just it," Jordan explained. "Nothing really. Only vague details of possible meetings between people with nothing more than code names."

"The only thing we know for sure is that these people were associates of Chris's. So they could be holding high positions in any government," Regina replied. "We're missing something. There's nothing definitive. No evidence. Certainly nothing worth killing over. But Chris wouldn't have put so much importance on it for no reason."

"His enemies might not know what's in Chris's notes themselves and assume the worst," Jordan commented. "But whoever's behind this has enough pull to send two government hitmen after us last night."

"Information?" Cain asked, his eyes narrowing.

"None," Jordan replied.

"Dead?"

"Yes," Jordan said, knowing his friend took betrayal of any kind very personally. "I'll take care of it, Cain."

"Who else is on your list of suspects?" Kate asked.

"Too many to count. Hell, even the president is suspect right now," Jordan added.

Kate frowned. "How so?"

"He ordered the NSA on alert, didn't he?"

"He could've ordered the alert as a precaution after Kyle's murder," Cain stated.

"Jon Mercer isn't a traitor," Kate added defensively.

"Are you sure? The journal implicates my father as a terrorist," Jordan argued. "Jon and my father were the best of friends. Doesn't work in his favor, right now. Hell, I can't even rule out your father, Cain."

"Watch what you say."

"Quentin was friends with my father," Jordan stated quietly. "He has as many contacts across the globe as Mercer."

Kate straightened, instantly angry. "Quentin had nothing to do with this. My father wouldn't—"

"That's what I used to say."

"All right, you've made your point." Cain sighed and rubbed the back of his neck. "I'll get you the jet. But if this doesn't go well—"

"I'll be nuclear sludge if it doesn't go well. We all will."

"If you really believe that, Jordan, then you'd better follow me," Kate said and opened her office door. "I have a few gadgets that just might keep you alive."

Cain picked up the phone. "While you do that, I'll make the arrangements."

"Make some for me, too," Regina added. At Jordan's frown, she hitched her chin higher. "I go where you go, *lover*."

"WHAT WAS ALL THAT nonsense about you and me being lovers?" Regina asked. A few minutes before, they'd arrived at a private jet hangar and parked the Hummer.

"If you need to make it work in that little black and

white mind of yours, then consider the fact that we've slept together."

"It's not the same thing."

"Right now it's going to have to be."

"Watch it, your arrogance is showing."

"White knights are not arrogant," he countered, snidely. "They're confident."

Regina raised a delicate brow.

"Once Cain's delivery boy gets here, we can go."

"What's Cain sending?"

"Entry papers and a few other things." Jordan went through the bag of equipment that Kate had given them. He pulled out a cell phone, flipped it open. "This has a radiation sensor. While I'm questioning Losev, just keep it in your pocket as a precaution." He handed it to her. "If it swings toward the red zone, you'll know right away because the box will vibrate in your pocket."

"Does it work as a phone?" She tucked it into the pocket of her overcoat.

"Not well, no range. But it's good enough to fool anyone who is curious about it."

"Do you really think the plutonium will be there?" Regina snapped open the briefcase that Kate had given her. If she were going to pretend to be Jordan's secretary, she might as well start with Cain's delivery boy.

"No. But better safe than sorry. The Iceland authorities could've confiscated the explosive without knowing what they had." He reached into the back and pulled out a lighter and pocketed it. When he caught her raised eyebrow, he explained. "Blowtorch."

Regina watched him draw a pistol from the black bag and check the clip. Satisfied, he placed the new gun in his shoulder holster.

"What did Kate do with your gun?" Regina reached into the briefcase, pulled out a pair of glasses.

"I'll tell you later, right now we have to get going." Jordan glanced up as Regina slid the wire-framed glasses onto her nose.

He tightened his muscles, anticipating the punch of desire. And it hit—a heavyweight punch—low, below the belt.

"Where did you get those?"

"Kate gave them to me, along with this business suit and the overcoat. To add validity to my secretary story," Regina said, nudging the frames a little higher up on her nose. "They're even the right prescription."

Jordan reminded himself to breathe. "How would she know that?"

"I mentioned I wore glasses to Lara last night," Regina answered, puzzled. "Lara called Kate. My prescription isn't top secret. It wouldn't have taken much to find out what it was."

Jordan made a mental note to have a long discussion with Kate and Lara the next time he saw them.

"Take them off," he ordered, not wanting to deal with those big, moss-green eyes for three hours on the jet.

"Why?"

"You won't need them," he said, not caring if he sounded surly. Damn it, he was surly.

"They're glasses," she retorted, obviously annoyed at the order. "Get over it."

"You know something?" Jordan grabbed her coat, yanking her toward him. "You've got a smart mouth."

"Not my problem," she shot back. "Last night you said you liked my mouth."

Her words would've packed more punch if she hadn't looked at his mouth when she said them.

"Remind me why," he muttered, just before his lips covered hers.

He didn't go deep, but lord knew he wanted to. It wasn't the time or place. Still his mouth moved over hers hard and hot, demanding a response.

Groaning, she shifted closer, opened her mouth and sank her tongue deeper, kissing him with an uninhibited frenzy.

Desire exploded in him, rocking him back. Growling, he pulled her onto his lap, his mouth slanting over hers again and again, no longer satisfied with the stroking and teasing.

His slid his hand under her coat, cupped her breast. She moaned, her bottom moving restlessly against his groin.

Jordan shuddered, his control held in place by sheer willpower. He broke away, buried his face in the curve of her neck, forcing back his desire. "Damn it, Regina," he said, his breathing ragged.

Dazed, Regina sat back into her seat, her eyes wide, the irises deepening to the darker shades of a hazy rain forest.

"What the hell was that?" he asked, raking his fingers through his hair, annoyed that they shook in protest.

"Unexpected," she whispered, pushing a strand of hair away from her heated face.

Suddenly, a flashlight blipped in the distance, signaling that the jet was geared up.

"Let's go." Quickly, he zipped the bag, then hit the handle of the car and stepped out. The cold air hit Jordan in the face, but it didn't chill his heated body, the heaviness in his loins.

Unexpected was an understatement.

"Ready," Regina said, coming up beside him.

Suddenly, headlights shot across the tarmac, and skimmed over the couple. The car pulled up in front of the nose of the Learjet and parked, blocking their path.

Calvin West stepped from his car. "Where are you going, Beck?"

Jordan swore. A moment later, his pistol appeared in his hand. He pointed it at Cal's chest. "Go find someone else to annoy, West."

"You won't shoot me." But the man still stopped ten feet away, Regina noticed. "I'm an official of the British government."

"Now you're just giving me a reason to pull the trigger, aren't you?" Jordan raised the barrel slightly.

Ignoring him, the other man tilted his head toward Regina. "Hello, Miss Menlow. I'm Calvin West, Minister of British Foreign Security."

"Hello," Regina replied, slowly, more than a little confused.

Jordan snorted. "I expected you to bring some backup. You MI6 chaps like to work in packs."

"Times have changed. You would know that if you hadn't defected to Labyrinth. Couldn't stand having to walk in your father's footsteps, could you?" Cal taunted. "Same old Jordan."

"Chose not to, big difference." Jordan relaxed his stance, but the pistol remained in position. "But you're not here to talk history, are you?"

"No. I'm here to talk plutonium."

Chapter Eleven

"I'm sure you are," Jordan responded, his voice deadly low. "And if I find out you're involved in my father's death, you won't find a crevice small enough to hide in."

"I didn't kill your father, you idiot. I worked for your father. Kyle was dirty, not me."

"And I should believe you, why?"

Calvin folded his arms. "An autopsy found heavy traces of high-quality cocaine in what body parts we could locate of Tim Severs."

"If you don't tell me something I don't know already, I'll shoot you just for the hell of it."

"At President Mercer's request, Archer Cordey asked some of his son Scott's friends about Timothy Severs's illegal activities. Friends that knew both Scott Cordey and Timothy. It seems the boys went to college together."

"And?"

"Archer discovered the name of Severs's drug supplier. A supplier the DEA had in custody," he advised. Calvin reached for his pocket.

"I'd be very careful right now," Jordan warned.

Slowly, with two fingers, Cal pulled a photograph out of his coat pocket. "This is the man we believe picked up the drugs from the supplier for Severs."

Regina peered around Jordan to see the photograph. "Scarface."

"His name is Solomon Kashin. Ex-KGB, full-time mercenary. An expert in demolition. Among other things."

"So you're saying he would have knowledge on how to detonate a nuclear weapon?" Jordan questioned.

"Possible. Although nuclear is far different from any other explosive he would have used in the military."

"So we have one player," Regina commented.

"Possibly. We just don't know who's hired him," Cal answered. "I'm hoping your trip will find out for us."

With the same two fingers, he pulled out a manila envelope from inside his jacket. "Here's the paperwork you need to land in Keflavik. It's also all the information I have on Kyle. And what we have on Russia's suitcase bombs."

"You're the delivery boy?"

Cal nodded. "We'd suspected Kyle Morris was dirty. Last year, Chris volunteered to take the case. But over the last six months or so, things changed."

"Changed how?"

"Chris became more secretive about his investigation. Didn't file any reports. Didn't keep me informed. I need you to find out why."

"You think he was a traitor."

"I liked Chris. More than that, I respected him, which is hard to do in this business." Cal handed Regina the file. "Number Ten isn't happy. He believes Chris crossed the line."

"Number Ten being the prime minister," Regina commented logically. England's prime minister lived at Number Ten Downing Street in London.

Cal nodded. "And now with Kyle's murder, you've been listed as a traitor. I need you to prove both counts wrong."

"Don't worry, I will," Jordan managed, understanding, but still not trusting. Still, he shoved his pistol back into his shoulder holster. "But not for MI6."

"Fair enough. As long as the results are the same. You've got tanks of extra gas on that bird. Should be plenty to get you to Iceland. Refuel there."

With a short salute, he turned away, only to turn back again. "By the way, I want my jet back undamaged."

"*Your* jet?"

"Who do you think Cain called? He couldn't pull one on his own without Mercer finding out. And unlike him, I don't have to tell your president everything."

"Now why would MacAlister trust you?" Jordan asked.

"We worked a few missions together a few years back. Guess I impressed him. Good thing, too," Cal commented. "Or you'd be out of luck right now."

The British agent glanced at Regina, his lips twitching with humor. "Jordan's an idiot, but I still consider him a friend. Sometimes his temper gets the best of him, but don't hold it against him."

"I won't," Regina promised, smiling. In that moment, she decided she liked Cal.

"If you get tired of his fits, though, look me up." The MI6 agent gave her a slow, sexy wink.

"The hell she will."

Cal ignored Jordan. "I might not have royal blood, but I'm certainly better looking." With that, he gave a short wave and was off.

Jordan waited until Cal reached his sports car, then called out. "So what was the cost, West?"

Cal swung back. "For what?"

"To have that cocaine supplier turn over on Solomon Kashin?"

"A 'get out of jail free' pass," admitted Calvin, jerking open the car door. "So make sure you nail this bastard, Jordan. Because I let go one of the DEA's most wanted and now I owe them a huge favor. And you know how much I hate that idea." Calvin climbed into the BMW and drove off.

When the tail lights grew smaller, Regina turned to Jordan. "Would you have really shot him?"

"Yes." Once again he cupped her elbow as they walked to the jet.

She glanced up at his profile, studying the granite-like features. "I believe you would have."

"Right up to the part where I found out he'd made a deal with the DEA, anyway," he admitted reluctantly.

"And then?"

"Let's just say it will be worth keeping him alive, so I can watch him pay back that favor."

Regina smiled, sensing somehow that Jordan and Calvin had been carved from the same stone. "What did Cal mean, when he said his blood wasn't royal?"

"He meant mine was."

Regina stopped, her mouth dropped open. Jordan laughed and kissed her quick and hard. "Relax, sweetheart. I'm twenty-ninth in line for the crown."

"That's not so bad, I guess," she replied, more bemused over the quick kiss than the lineage. For the first time, he had kissed her simply out of affection.

"Now that my father's dead I'll inherit his title."

"Which is?"

"Earl. I'm the Ninth Earl of Beck." Uncomfortable with the subject, he changed it as they approached the steps. "Regina, if you've read any books about piloting private jets, I don't want to hear about it. Got it?"

"I've read them," she teased, instinctively knowing he needed to keep the moment light. "But I've also read about the human brain. Doesn't mean I can walk into an operating room and perform brain surgery. You're safe from my flying skills." She took the manila envelope from Jordan. "Besides, I have some files to commit to memory."

KEFLAVIK INTERNATIONAL LAY on the coast of Iceland. Covered in snow, the main terminal and outlying buildings appeared not more than white mounds against the night sky.

They had no idea what awaited them, but certainly Regina wasn't expecting a full contingent of security when they stepped off the jet. Jordan stiffened beside her.

A man in his mid-forties stepped toward them, dressed in a navy blue military uniform. "Jordan Beck?"

When Jordan nodded, the man smiled a smile that didn't quite reach the brown eyes. "I am Chief Inspector Dagur Jonsson."

Regina noticed the four uniformed men moving toward them. Dressed in navy blue military with navy blue fatigues, they formed a wall of Kevlar vests behind their leader.

The Viking Squad. Jordan had warned her on the trip in about the Iceland special operations unit.

Dagur was shorter than Jordan by a few inches, but broader in the shoulder and bigger in the head, she thought with amusement.

Dagur shook Jordan's hand with a firm, friendly grasp. "Have we met before?"

"No," Jordan replied, the lie slipping easily over his tongue. The inspector's name hadn't been listed in the file. "My first time here." He faked a shiver. "And hopefully my last. No offense."

"None taken," Dagur answered, his gaze steady. "And this is?"

Regina stepped forward and at the last moment, remembered to adopt a British accent. "I'm Regina Menlow. Mr. Beck's secretary."

"A pleasure, Miss Menlow." He indicated a nearby black snow vehicle. "I received a call from Calvin West. Your timing could not have been better since Rurik Losev is scheduled to be extradited to London tomorrow over a subway bombing."

Jordan knew the man was fishing. "I wouldn't know about that, Inspector."

"I've allowed your visit with Rurik Losev simply because the information you might be able to get from him can help us with some of the gun running problems we have been experiencing here. That and your Mr. West can be quite formidable when he wants," Dagur admitted.

"Yes, he can," Jordan muttered as they climbed into a nearby SUV. The squad all grabbed jeeps and flanked the threesome in the SUV. "Lead the way, Inspector. I'd like to get this over."

DAGUR DROVE TO A compound nearly a mile beyond the airfield. From the outside, it appeared to be a set of warehouses surrounded by fence and barbed wire.

"Follow me." Dagur led them past several modified snowmobiles to a nearby building.

Jordan grabbed Regina's elbow and pulled her close. "Dagur and I have had a run-in before. An international drug bust gone wrong. I just happened to be undercover on the wrong side of the law when it happened. Someone warned the cartel and at the last minute it became an all out battle for survival. I gave our friend here a broken nose and managed to escape. The good guys lost that one. If he remembers me, the situation is going to get nasty fast," Jordan murmured into Regina's ear. "Stay alert."

"Okay."

Dagur paused in the office and indicated a metal detector arch. "For security purposes." He pointed to the wall beyond. "On the other side there is a camera. We just ask you to look into the camera and count three. We keep photo records of all our visitors."

"No problem."

Regina followed Jordan through the procedures, then whispered, "Do they have your photo on file?"

"Probably not."

"Rurik Losev is waiting in one of our interrogation rooms," Dagur advised. "If you would both follow me."

"We agreed this conversation would be a private one between myself and Dr. Losev. He has to trust there will be no repercussions from the information he provides."

"Yes, by all means. I assured your people that we would not eavesdrop as long as you provide information to us in a written report within the next twenty-four hours," Dagur assured him. "Losev is not our priority. It's his contacts we want."

"That's why I brought my secretary."

Regina handed Jordan a recorder, in front of Dagur, like Jordan had instructed her to do on the jet.

"Miss Menlow will transcribe the conversation on our flight back and fax it to you once we land back in Washington."

Jordan pushed a button on his watch. One that Kate's people designed to disrupt the microphone frequencies, leaving only static.

Dagur could not complain about the reception, if he wasn't supposed to be listening.

Losev was a frail man, no taller than five-and-a-half feet. Bruises on the older man's face told Jordan that he had not been treated well during his stay.

"Hello, Doctor. I'm Jordan Beck."

"Thank you for the kindness." Losev smiled. "It has been a while since I've been called Doctor."

"I have some questions to ask you Dr. Losev." Jordan indicated the chair on the opposite side of the table. "Do you mind?"

"Not at all. One of us should be comfortable," Losev joked. He raised his wrists, displaying chains and cuffs.

Jordan sat and placed the recorder on the table between them. He pushed the button. "We have it on good authority that you have been black-marketing illegal weapons. Is that true?"

Losev glanced at the door. "No. It is not true."

"They cannot hear you. I promise."

When the older man said nothing, Jordan reached over and turned off the recorder. "Look, I don't have time to go through the usual persuasive questions until I hit on a bargain for the information I want. So why don't you tell me what you want in exchange for the details of your transactions."

Losev studied him for a long moment. Then nodded. "All right, Mr. Beck. I will give you what you want, if you can guarantee my staying here."

"Here in Iceland?"

Losev sighed. "Yes. I wish to stay here."

"But your trial—"

"Can be postponed, can it not?"

In that moment, Jordan saw fear in the older man's eyes. More fear than a few bruises on his face would have caused.

"It's a deal. You have my word that I'll contact the right people and delay your trial. For how long?"

"Six months."

"Six—" Jordan bit the rest down on his back teeth. "All right. Six months. Agreed?"

"Agreed."

"Now, I want to know about your nuclear arms business."

Losev's features flickered in surprise. "You have guessed much."

"No guessing involved," Jordan commented. "I have information regarding your connection with suitcase bombs."

"What you say is true," Losev stated. "A few months ago I struck a bargain to sell two Soviet suitcase bombs that I...acquired...to a certain individual with one hundred million dollars."

"Two?"

"Yes, fifty million apiece," Losev stated and smiled. "Other than that, I cannot help you."

"You're saying he had no contact with anyone? You sold them blindly?"

"For one hundred million dollars, you don't ask questions, Mr. Beck."

Jordan leaned back in his chair and studied Losev. "You don't strike me as a stupid man, Doctor. Surely you'd want to know something about the buyer. Not everyone has that much cash lying around, now, do they?"

"You're very astute for being so young." Losev nodded in approval. "I admit I was curious. The deal had been struck through the proper channels, so I had no reason not to trust the buyer."

"But you did see him."

"Yes, simply because I was curious," he admitted. "I stayed hidden, of course, at the drop-off location."

Losev leaned forward; his mouth curved into a small grin. "You see, up to that point, all my dealings were done with absolute anonymity. The technical age makes it very easy these days.

"However, marketing two nuclear weapons was the biggest deal I had ever arranged. A deal that took less than a week from start to finish," Losev explained, frowning. "Who has access to that much money so quickly, I asked myself. Such a person, I would like to see."

"And what *did* you see?"

"A man about six foot tall, muscular. Fairly ordinary face. Walked like a soldier. You know, light-footed but still rigid enough to show training. I saw many of his kind during my career in Moscow. He was a middleman, nothing more." Losev sat back and waved his hand in disgust, the chink of the chains punctuating his gesture. "My bones froze out on the canal for no reason."

"Froze? You mean this happened recently?"

"Yes," Losev said, frowning. "Less than a month ago. Right before I came to Iceland, in fact."

Jordan swore. And right before his father's murder. His father must have known.

"This middleman, did he have any distinguishing marks?"

"He had one. A curved scar that creased his left cheek. Hideous actually."

Jordan showed no reaction. "No name?"

"No. His e-mail address was Charlieone," Losev informed him. "But I doubt if it still exists."

"Anything else?"

"An observation," Losev added. "This man, Charlie-one, does not care about human lives."

Jordan stared at Losev, understanding. "That's why you want to stay here, isn't it? You know these bombs are set to go off and you want to stay well away from their effects."

"I know nothing for sure," Losev replied with caution. "But my family has already moved here from Moscow. To be close to me."

"Give me a hypothesis, Doctor."

"If what I suspect is true, the world will be thrown into chaos within the next few weeks. No one will care about an overaged arms dealer."

"Why Iceland?"

"Why not?" he retorted. "I prefer the snow over the heat. And who will detonate a nuclear bomb here? It would serve no purpose. But the United States? Germany? England? Even Asia. Imagine what a nuclear explosion would do to the global market."

"You believe that is the reason? Someone is out to destroy the world's economy?"

"What other reason would there be? Unless, you wanted to start another world war. Or commit genocide."

Chapter Twelve

"Solomon Kashin is Charlie," Jordan murmured as he and Regina stepped into the open air. "Losev said his contact had a scar on his face."

"You're sure?"

A guard stood less than twenty feet in front of them. Jordan kept his back to him.

"I'm as sure as I am about anything right now," Jordan murmured, handing her the recorder and giving the impression to anyone observing that they were discussing business. "Did the sensors get a read on anything?"

The three guards assigned to escort them hadn't followed them out yet. Still, Regina stepped closer to Jordan, then pulled the black box halfway out of her pocket.

"Nothing." Regina shook her head. "I even asked to go to the bathroom and made sure I wandered a bit before being directed back to you. And still nothing."

She shoved the meter back into her pocket. "I'm really glad to be out of there."

"Don't relax yet," he said, and grabbed her arm. "We're not safe until we're back in the air—"

Sirens exploded around them, rocking the icy tarmac beneath their feet.

"We've been made. Come on!"

The soldier stepped toward them. Not hesitating, Jordan smashed a fist in his face, knocking the man out cold.

He grabbed her arm and pulled Regina to the nearest snowmobile. "Get on." He took her briefcase and threw it to the ground.

Regina jumped onto the seat. Snow and heat fogged her glasses. She took them off and shoved them into her pocket. "What about the jet? They'll have guards waiting at the airport."

"We'll worry about that when we get there. If we get there."

Regina barely had time to wrap her arms around his waist before the snowmobile surged forward.

A staccato of gunfire burst from behind them. "Keep down." Fear caught him in the gut. If he didn't do something the Viking squad would end up putting a bullet in Regina's back.

As if reading his thoughts, she shouted, "Don't worry about me. Just get us out of here."

Jordan deliberately steered the vehicle off the path. "Keep your head down behind me. We're out in the open. There are no trees for cover."

Regina knew she slowed them down because there were two. Another round of bullets spattered snow in front of them.

Suddenly, a snowmobile swung in beside them. Regina screamed a warning.

Jordan kicked out his leg, hitting the driver's arm. The soldier jerked the steering wheel and sent the machine into a deadly tumble.

Snow sprayed her face, choked off her oxygen. Regina buried her face between Jordan's shoulder blades.

Without warning, two more snowmobiles approached, flanking Regina and Jordan. The man on the right waved his weapon, yelled at them to halt.

"Hold on," Jordan yelled to Regina, as both men raised their machine guns. Jordan hit the ground with his foot, and swung the snowmobile into a one-eighty. Snow kicked up, blinding Dagur's men.

The two machine guns exploded, missing Jordan in the crossfire. The men lost control. One snowmobile exploded and crashed into the other.

Jordan stopped the machine. He glanced at the burning wreckage and the two drivers, dead in the snow. "Bullets hit the gas tanks."

A sharp, searing pain tore through Regina's shoulder. Stifling a gasp, she tightened her grip on Jordan.

"Are you okay?"

"Yes." Regina placed her face against his back, telling herself she didn't lie. She was okay for right now.

But the throb in her shoulder told her she wouldn't be okay for long.

JORDAN PARKED THE SNOWMOBILE in a ravine at the edge of the airstrip. From their spot, he counted six men, all with Uzis, standing guard by the jet.

Jordan reached under his coat and ripped out a long piece of its lining. "I want you over there." He nodded up the ravine and to the left about thirty feet. "Keep your head down."

Regina watched him take the gas cap off of the tank and shove part of the fabric in until the fuel soaked the rag. "Go, Regina. Now."

Startled, she hurried to the spot, making sure her head stayed below the top of the ridge. White-hot knives jabbed at her shoulder. A thin veil of sweat broke out over her skin by the time she reached the crest.

Suddenly, Jordan was behind her. "Come on," he whispered. "We've got about thirty seconds to reach that utility shed."

He grabbed her wrist and nodded toward the field shed at the end of the runway. "If they see us, we're dead."

They darted across the field, keeping their heads low. Once, Regina stumbled, but Jordan's gripped tightened and she recovered her footing.

When they reached the shed, she leaned against the wall, grateful for the moment of respite.

Suddenly, an explosion set the night sky on fire.

The soldiers yelled, their guns raised as they ran toward the burning snowmobile.

"Now!"

Jordan tugged on her bad arm, making Regina bite back a cry of pain. She ran beside him until they got to the jet. Jordan shoved her against one side. "Stay here."

He crept behind the guard and hit him over the head

with the butt of his pistol. Soundlessly, the man slid to the ground.

Jordan pulled the blocks from beneath the wheels.

"Let's go." He opened the passenger door and lowered the stair. Regina hesitated, her knees buckled.

"What's the matter?" He pulled her to him, catching her when she stumbled. "Come on."

He noticed it then, the smear of blood against the jet's white panel. The crimson patch vivid in the runway flood lights. "You've been shot?"

"Yes." Regina hugged her arm to her chest. "And I don't think I'm okay anymore."

Jordan shoved aside her coat and saw the blood. "Can you hold on a little longer?"

"Yes."

Once they climbed into the cockpit, he maneuvered her into the co-pilot seat and snapped the safety belt around her. He tugged the buckle, satisfied, then slid into his own.

Gunfire burst from the fields, spattering the side of the jet. "Hold on," Jordan ordered, flipping switches until the engines roared to life.

Strong gusts shoved the wings of the jet back and forth as it started down the runway. "This isn't going to be smooth."

Regina watched him handle the airplane's wheel with firm, capable hands. Outside, snow and ice slapped at the windshield but she felt no fear.

A single snowmobile pursued them but stopped when it fell a hundred yards behind.

Regina stared out the window. Another plane was taking off at the same time. "Jordan! Look out!"

Jordan shoved the nose of the jet down, barely missing the mail plane as it skimmed over the top of them.

"That was close," Regina murmured. Resting her head against the back of the seat, she gave in to the black void of unconsciousness.

DAGUR PULLED THE KEYS from his pocket and reached across the table. Losev held up his hands as the other man unlocked the cuffs.

"So did they get away?" Losev asked and rubbed his wrists.

"Yes," Dagur answered. "Although Beck almost killed himself by hitting our mail plane."

"Was our package on board his jet?"

"Yes." Dagur tossed the cuffs and keys on the table.

"I'll pick it up, once they land in Washington D.C.," Solomon said as he walked into the room. "We lost a few men. He was damn clever. Before two of them could intentionally ditch their machines, Jordan managed to get them to kill each other."

"I can't afford to lose anymore men," Dagur noted before turning back to Losev. "Beck scrambled the microphone. Did he believe your story?"

"Yes." Losev stood and rolled his neck. "Notify Echo that Beck is on his way back to the States with the woman and that we can go ahead as planned." He rubbed his cheek until the makeup came off and left his face with no more bruises. "Is the bomb in place in London?"

"Yes," Solomon answered. "And is set to go off at the expected time."

"Excellent. Using Beck was a good idea, I think," Losev acknowledged. "Be ready within the hour, Solomon. You and I are flying to the United States. We shouldn't face any delays now."

"If Beck gets through security," Solomon inserted.

"He won't have to go through customs. Trust me." Dagur grunted.

"I still have concerns." Losev stood. "Beck located me quite easily, wouldn't you say?"

"I would have been concerned if he hadn't," Dagur countered. "The woman obviously read the journal. Without it, they wouldn't have found you so soon. We have the journal. And one of Labyrinth's finest is our courier. It has all worked out for the best." Dagur slapped Losev on the shoulder. "Do not worry, comrade."

"You are right. I'm being an old woman, I think." Losev grinned. "Good work, gentlemen. Now we just have to see if Jordan Beck takes my bait. Once he gets back, he should come after you, Solomon. Just make sure he finds you *after* your pickup."

"And if he finds me before?" Solomon asked, stroking the mark on his cheek.

"Then kill him."

"REGINA! WAKE UP!"

Her eyes fluttered open.

"I need you conscious, sweetheart." Jordan's hands were still on the steering. "Can you check your wound?"

She glanced down at her coat and slowly slipped it off. Her body felt lethargic, too heavy to even breathe. Her head lolled back against the seat.

"Regina!"

She turned her head toward Jordan.

"I need you to stay with me."

"I will." Slowly, she shifted forward, until she sat straight in the seat. Blood soaked her sleeve, warm and sticky against her skin. Bile rose to the back of her throat.

Forcing the nausea back, she grabbed the sweater and tried to take it off over her head. The sleeve material caught on her wound. Pain, white-hot, skewered her shoulder.

"It's stuck, Jordan," she whispered, sweat broke out on her forehead.

"Okay, this is what I want you to do." Jordan unclipped his belt. "Switch seats with me and steer the plane."

"You're kidding, right?"

"No. There are controls on your side, but I can't get to your right arm. And I have to stop that bleeding. I'll put the controls on autopilot, but you still need to keep your hands on the wheel just in case," he explained. "While you're controlling the plane I can patch your wound."

Jordan tossed her coat into the back and out of the way. "Don't tell me you haven't read anything on piloting?"

"I told you that earlier."

"I thought you were—"

"Don't you say it."

"Kidding."

Temper flushed her face, distracting her. By the time she realized what he'd done, she was sitting in the pilot seat.

Smart man.

"Is this anything like flying a Harrier? I've read about Harriers."

Jordan's eyebrow rose.

"I'm joking, Jordan." She sighed. "You really don't have a sense of humor, do you?"

"Apparently not," he answered dryly. "The auto pilot will handle most of the job. But I need you to keep an eye on that dial." He pointed to an illuminated circle on the control panel. "It's the artificial horizon. If the indicator moves, tell me."

"I will."

He leaned in until they were nose to nose. "You lost your glasses."

"They're in my coat pocket."

He gave her a quick kiss. Warm. Tender. "Hold on while I grab the first aid kit." If she hadn't already loved him, she would have then.

"I'll be right back," he whispered.

"I'll be right here," she whispered back, mimicking him.

"Cheeky." He spoke the word softly, like an endearment.

Regina's heart fluttered in her chest.

She leaned back and stared out the front windshield. Thank goodness, the night remained cloudless. Stars patterned the black sky.

Regina heard Jordan stepping next to the seat. "Do you realize the day after tomorrow is Christmas?"

When she'd been small she would stare out her window on Christmas Eve and make a special wish. It wasn't the right day, but in her heart it was the right moment. She closed her eyes and wished.

"No, I didn't." Jordan snapped open the red kit and started digging through the contents. "But Christmas hasn't gotten any attention from me in a long while."

"Why?" She turned her head toward him.

"I'm always in the middle of one operation or another. The life of a secret spy," he joked. He unwrapped a pair of sterile surgical scissors. "I'm going to cut away your sleeve, all right?"

"Yes."

"By the way, I distinctly remember asking you if you were okay back there," Jordan rebuked. "You sure picked a hell of a time to lie to me."

"I didn't lie. At the time I was okay."

Jordan snorted, telling her exactly what he thought of her splitting hairs.

"If you had asked me if I'd been shot, I would've told you the truth," she added defensively. More for herself, she realized with guilt. "You wouldn't have been able to do anything anyway. We were being chased."

A sharp sting on her arm caused her to jerk. "Sorry, the material is sticking a bit to your wound." He pulled the remaining material free and tossed it to the floor. "Good thing you weren't wearing angora, or this would've been a nightmare."

"How about we save the nightmare opinion until this is over, okay?"

"Yes, ma'am."

He grabbed a flashlight disc from his bag. He stuck it to the ceiling above her arm and turned it on. "I've got to clean around the wound so I can see what I'm dealing with."

"You sound like you've done this before." Regina remembered the scars on his chest and arm.

"Too many times to count." He opened a packet of antibiotic wipes. "Relax and breathe. This is going to sting."

More than sting. A thousand pins jabbed at open nerves. Tears pricked her eyes but she maintained her grip on the steering.

"It's okay to cry," he said softly while he concentrated on her arm. "No one here but me."

"If I cry, I won't be able to see the dial." But lord knew she wanted to. Instead she did what he said and tried to breathe through the pain.

"Good girl," Jordan said, with admiration. Within moments he was tossing aside the cloth. "Okay, I've got good news, bad news and really bad news. Which do you want first?"

"The good news."

He laughed at that, expecting her to take the bad news first. "I bet you open all your presents before Christmas, too."

"I don't know if I would. I haven't had a present from anyone since I was four," she said without thinking.

It wasn't until he let out a long hiss that she realized what she'd said.

She turned her head, saw the hard line of his face. "It's okay, Jordan."

"The hell it is." He grabbed a pair of surgical gloves.

"What's the good news?"

"It's a four inch gash across the backside of your arm. And there's no bullet."

"The bad news?"

He snapped the first glove over his hand, then reached for the second. "The wound is deep so butterfly bandages aren't going to help. I'm going to have to suture it shut. But before I can do that, I need to remove some bits of fiber left from your sweater."

"And the really bad news?"

His gaze caught hers, the blue of his eyes strong, concerned. "I don't have anything to numb it with, love," he answered softly. "This is going to hurt."

A wide smile spread across her face. Regina could see from Jordan's frown she confused him. But she couldn't help herself.

After all, she'd just gotten her wish.

He had called her his love.

Chapter Thirteen

"Ready?" He held up a fine-pointed forceps that appeared no different from a set of big tweezers.

"Let's do it."

"I'm going to have to move the skin a little, open it up so I can get to the sweater fibers," he explained. "It will be better if you try not to think about what I'm doing."

"I'll give it my best shot," she said, even as she bit her lip.

"Why don't you tell me something? A story?" Jordan leaned over her arm. "Tell me why you haven't gotten a present since you were a child."

"I don't remember any earlier ones before my parents died," Regina said.

"Your file said that they died in an airplane crash," he said, studying her arm.

"Yes, I think that's when I first turned to books, actually," she agreed. "My father used to say, knowledge is power. And somehow reading gave me back some control of my life."

Regina gasped. The first probe sent a white-hot rod of pain through muscle and bone.

"What did your father do?" Jordan wiped a small thread on a nearby cloth.

"He…he was a professor of ancient civilizations," Regina answered, trying to focus on her story. "They died in a plane crash while on a lecture tour. A second honeymoon when I was four. At the time I was staying with my Aunt Aida. My father's sister."

"And after they died," Jordan prompted.

Another jab, this time through her shoulder. Her stomach lurched, bile slapped the back of her throat. Regina closed her eyes, forced herself to breathe.

"How's the horizon looking?"

Her eyes flew open. "We're fine," she said, checking the lines.

"You didn't answer my other question," Jordan said lightly as he continued. "What happened after your parents died?"

"Nothing really, I just continued to live with my aunt."

"How about your Christmases with her?"

"I only remember one," Regina managed to say through another probe. Her skin was on fire, flaying the muscle and bone beneath to no more than open nerves.

"How old were you?" he said softly, his hands never stopping.

"Eight." Regina tightened her jaw and tried to lose herself in the memory. "The holiday gave my aunt a chance to show off her money with a big party every Christmas Eve."

"Sounds wealthy," Jordan commented and wiped the forceps once again on the cloth.

"Aida's hobby was marrying wealthy men. She's on her fifth right now and is currently residing abroad," Regina explained, arching back against the seat when another poke hit a nerve. "Where, I don't know. We don't exactly keep in touch."

"Nice way to make a living." With gentle fingers, Jordan shifted her arm farther into the light.

"Yes," she agreed after a moment. "I was never invited to the holiday parties, of course. The first few years I was too young, so I didn't mind so much. I hung out with one of the maids or, more often, by myself."

"Reading?"

"Yes, reading." She would've laughed if it hadn't sounded so pathetic to her ears. "On my eighth birthday I asked if I could go to that year's party." Regina paused, amazed how a memory could still make her cringe. "She told a friend later that day in her sitting room while they were having tea. They were laughing at my expense. She called me a freak.

"I confronted her right then, with her friend."

"What happened?" Jordan asked "Did she apologize?"

"No." Regina shook her head. The burning intensified in her arm, but the bone-jarring pain had ceased.

"Actually, she seemed relieved. She didn't feel it necessary to hide her feelings from me anymore. If I were old enough to ask, then I was old enough to understand. I guess I never realized I was different until then."

"You're not so different, Regina," Jordan stated. "But I can see why you don't lie."

"Actually, I try not to lie because of what I said earlier. I'm not good at it. I might be able to memorize books, but I can't keep all the lies straight in my head."

"But the truth can hurt," Jordan commented, then leaned back, wiped the forceps one more time. "Done."

"Good. Worst over," she teased.

"Half over," he said, with a heartbreaking, handsome smile.

"You're gorgeous, Jordan."

He laughed. "Thank you. You're pretty gorgeous yourself."

She knew he was just teasing, but she couldn't help the sudden leap in her pulse, the tingle along her nerves.

"Are you going to be one of those patients who fall in love with their doctors?" he joked, catching the look in her eye.

"I might," she said lightly. "So you'd better be careful."

He didn't say anything. There was nothing really to say.

"No worries, Jordan," she assured him. "You're safe."

"It's your safety I'm worried about. And look what happened." He took off the gloves with a snap, breaking the tension. "The bleeding has slowed down. I have to clean the forceps and thread the needle, so you have a small reprieve."

"Thank you."

He opened the alcohol wipes. "So what happened after the run-in with your aunt?" He wiped down the forceps.

"Within weeks, she sent me away to school. I spent

all my holidays at the school with the staff. She paid extra for me, so I could. I actually preferred it. It's hard to be where you're not wanted."

He held up the needle with newly gloved hands, cut the thread and slipped it through the eye.

"Ready?" she asked.

At his nod, she looked straight ahead.

The needle pierced the skin, going deep. Regina bit back a gasp. Tears pricked her eyes.

"I'm sorry, love," Jordan whispered, "but I have to get most of the layer or it won't heal properly."

Regina refused to cry. "I'll let you in on a secret," she said, her voice hoarse from the strain of holding back the tears. "This is only the second time I've ever been hurt."

"The second?"

Another fiery pinch. Regina bit her lips.

"Yep." She struggled to stay casual. "That tells you how boring I was growing up."

"What was the first?"

"The bump on my head yesterday."

Something clutched at Jordan's chest. He took a deep breath. "And I had just decided you were an accident just waiting to happen."

He wiped away some blood and pushed the needle through the first side. A whimper caught deep in her throat.

"Am I going to have a scar?" she whispered, her voice cracking only slightly as he placed the next suture.

Lord, he was proud of her.

"You sound like you want one." Up through the other

side. He saw the muscles of her neck tighten. He'd known many others who'd be throwing up right now from the pain. Or crying like babies.

But Regina held firm. "That's my girl. We're halfway there."

"If I'm going through all this I'd better get a damn good scar out of it." She stopped when he inserted the needle once more. A small whimper escaped from her lips. "All the kids at school had them."

"You're going to have a beauty." He glanced at the white-knuckle grip she held on the steering, saw the paleness of her skin.

He put another stitch through, heard another whimper, this time deeper.

"Almost done, sweetheart," he coaxed. Sweat beaded on his forehead. He dried it with his sleeve.

"When I was about twelve, I can remember being envious of one of the girls who'd run down a hill too fast and broken her leg."

"You wanted a broken leg?" He was talking fast now, filling the void with something other than the pain.

"I did. But I was such a coward, I couldn't bring myself—" Her voice broke on a sob.

"You're not a coward," he whispered, stitching another small section of jagged meat.

"Oh yes I am," she whispered the words. "It hurts, Jordan."

A single tear rolled down her cheek. It was almost his undoing. "Almost done, love. I promise."

Knowing she was close to losing control, he took the

needle through quickly two more times. Sobs burst inside her chest, but she didn't let them free.

"Hang in there, baby," Jordan cajoled, forcing himself to go through one more time before tying the knot and cutting the thread.

A moment later he scooped her into his arms, putting his faith in the auto pilot, needing her there as much as she needed to be there. He didn't know who was shaking more, her or him but he no longer cared.

"Shh..." he soothed, his voice no more than dry brittle leaves. He tightened his grip as she wept silently against the crook of his neck.

"No more. I promise," he murmured, rocking her back and forth. "No more ever."

TO REGINA'S SURPRISE, they didn't return to the Carlton-esque. Instead, Jordan booked a suite at an upscale hotel.

Regina would have enjoyed the effort more if the tension between them hadn't grown so thick.

He had rocked her until she no longer wept. Exhausted, she fell asleep only to awaken when the jet touched down a few hours later.

"Stay here." He pulled out his gun, then stepped through the doorway. It was second nature to him, she realized and wondered how many times he'd done the same over the years.

When he reappeared, his gun had been holstered once again under his coat. "It's clear."

After he grabbed the luggage, Regina followed him through the door.

The suite was a rainbow of tans, browns and golden hues. Elegantly simple in its design. Impeccable in its crisp, clean lines.

They were on the fifteenth floor. Far enough to get a glimpse of the D.C. skyline from the terrace.

"How's your arm?" Jordan asked from behind her, making her jump.

"Sore, but tolerable." She'd taken some aspirin as soon as they'd gotten off the jet. It took the edge off the pain.

He help her remove her jacket, then laid it across the top of the bar. She had no other, so both of them had been forced to deal with the heavy, tinny scent of dried blood on the way home.

"Jordan," Regina began. "I don't know what happened on the jet."

"You were shot," he said, deliberately cutting her off. "No more, no less."

"I mean, between you and me," she clarified, her temper simmering. "I don't know what happened between us. I fell asleep next to you, and woke up next to a stranger."

"Nothing has changed. I think we both just need a couple hours of sleep," he stated, the lie slipping easily over his tongue.

She took a deep breath. "I know I fell apart on you. I'm sure Lara or Celeste or even Kate would have handled the situation much better. My only excuse was that it was my first time being shot. I'll promise to do better next time."

Her words hit him, ripping a layer of skin off with

each syllable. "You handled it fine," Jordan answered sharply. "None of them would have done any better. And I'll make sure there isn't another time."

At least that was the truth. She'd come close to dying only hours before. He wasn't willing to risk Regina's life. And he couldn't change his. The closer they became, the more her life would be threatened.

I see." Regina let out a quiet breath. "And how are you going to manage that?"

"It's what I do," Jordan said, his tone brisk.

"Why haven't you said more than two words to me since we left the airport?"

"There's been nothing to say." Jordan wouldn't risk her life because of his choices. If that meant pushing her away, then so be it. Fighting the urge to touch her, he walked behind the bar, using it as a barrier. He grabbed a bottle of water from the refrigerator beneath. "Are you hungry? Do you want something from room service?" He took a long pull from the bottle.

"No. I don't want anything except for you to be honest with me, damn it," she screamed. "Just once."

"If you don't want anything to eat, you should probably clean up," Jordan responded flatly. "The bathroom is all yours. If you decide to take a shower, watch your stitches. Don't get them wet."

She saw the tense set of his shoulders, the tightly clenched jaw. For whatever reason, he was freezing her out.

Frustration knotted with anger until there was no beginning or end. "You're trying to hurt me deliberately, Jordan. I don't know why, but I do know I won't let you."

"Go take your shower, Regina."

"You told me once that everyone has a choice," Regina said quietly. "You didn't have to do this. All you had to do was be honest with me."

"Go take your shower, damn it!"

Shaking, Regina walked into the room. She went to sit on the bed, but noticed the white comforter. All cotton and lace.

Instead of sitting, she walked into the bathroom and turned on the shower.

With heavy limbs, she stripped off her clothes. Too late, she realized she'd left her toiletries in the living room with her bag.

She slipped on the white hotel robe and belted it with a tug. Softly, she padded from the bedroom.

THE ROOM WAS DARK, the silence deafening.

Only the moonlight shone, turning the shadows into decipherable patterns.

Jordan stood by the terrace doors, one forearm high against the thick, paned glass and stared unseeingly at the city lights that flickered beyond the terrace wall.

He'd almost lost her.

And in doing so, realized he loved her.

The image of her pale skin, her bloodless lips as she fought through the pain and fear. She'd suffered with each probe, each jab he inflicted on her tender flesh.

The pain was hers. But the blame was his.

For hours, a battle raged in him.

A war against passion and love—until the injustice screamed in his blood.

At her. At himself. At the world just beyond the patio's glass door.

It was a battle of body and soul.

And he was losing both to her.

Suddenly a soft tapping of bare feet sounded behind him.

"I thought you were in the shower," he rasped quietly. "I heard the water running."

"I am," she said, and took a quiet step forward.

"Stay there!" he snapped out the order but didn't turn toward her.

She froze. "I—I forgot my bag."

"On the couch." He nodded once with a quick jerk of his head. Still, he continued staring through the windows, his back rigid, his shoulders set.

"Jordan. What I said earlier—"

"Go take your shower, Regina," he snarled.

"I could really hate you, right now," she whispered.

Her words stung like a sharp slap to his face.

Better hate than dead.

He swung his head around. "That's the idea, sweetheart."

Jordan knew he'd made a mistake the moment he turned.

The muted light from the terrace cast a spotlight of soft, pearly hues and captured her features in a shimmering haze. Guilt prodded him, desire slammed into him, both a warning to turn away.

But he was beyond redemption. Beyond reason. Submersed in the torment of his roiling emotions.

She stood there with her huge eyes of misty heather-green and soft waves of brown hair framing her face. A robe—two sizes too big—overwhelmed her small form, leaving only bare toes peeking out from under the hem.

Jordan tightened his fists, willed her to leave him in peace.

"Get away from me." He growled the words, with no more than a tenuous leash on his control.

"And if I don't?" She threw the words down between them.

"Then I'll have you. Under me. Over me. Riding me." His voice lowered into a hot, smoky tone—cinder rough—that touched off a fire in her eyes. "Each time you quake, each time you quiver, I'll feel it. Because I'll be inside you, buried deep."

She trembled, he saw it just before she took a step forward.

"Stop!" It was a battle cry born from desperation, sharpened by need. "With me there is only tonight, Regina. There is no love. No happy ending. If you can't accept that, go back to the bedroom and lock the door." Desire reared back, a snarling beast biting and clawing through flesh and bones. "And you'd better do it soon, sweetheart, while you still have a choice."

"Well, then..." She stepped forward again—a small, tentative step—her hands already tugging her belt free.

"If I get to choose…" She shrugged the robe off her shoulders, caught it just above her breasts.

A hiss escaped from between his teeth.

"Say it, Regina." But he was already closing the distance, the words only a formality once the robe parted over her shoulders.

Jordan shoved the blades of guilt back, ignoring the slices it took from his soul. Understanding when it was over, they'd both bleed.

"It's simple." Another delicate shrug and the robed slid down her arms. Just for a second the terry cloth caught on the curve of her hips, keeping her secrets hidden, until with a sweet sigh of cloth against skin, it dropped, pooling at her feet.

"I choose you."

Chapter Fourteen

Jordan thrust his hand into her hair, letting his fingers get tangled in the soft waves. His mouth slanted over hers, greedy, carnal.

Regina wound her arms around his neck, arching against him until his own desire unleashed hers. She'd never known making love could be breathless, hot, frantic and tender at the same time.

Suddenly Jordan broke away, but only far enough to tilt his forehead against hers. "Regina, love. We got to slow down."

"Why?" She tried to tug his head to her mouth. When he resisted, she hitched up her legs and wrapped them around his waist.

Jordan groaned. "Honey, you're not making this easy."

Frustrated, she pulled at his sweater, lifting it up over his head and then throwing it to the floor. "That was easy enough." She leaned into him, sighing with pleasure when her breasts rubbed against his chest.

"Regina," Jordan murmured against her mouth. "Do you trust me?"

"Yes," she whispered. She nibbled his lip like he'd shown her before, felt the burst of power when he shuddered against her.

"Undo my pants, sweetheart." He held her away from him, just enough for her to reach down and unsnap his jeans. Within seconds both pants and briefs were shed and left on the floor.

His arousal pushed at her, heavy and hot, promising something that left her squirming to get closer. How could she ever have existed without this, without him?

His hands slid under each round cheek, and for a moment let his fingers stray to the sweet spot between. The muscles quivered at the base of her spine. "Oh my," she whispered, then nipped at his jaw, enjoying the whiskers rasping against her tongue.

Jordan growled, a rumbling deep in his throat as he fought for control. "Honey, we need to slow down or I'm going to hurt you."

In spite of his words, his mouth covered hers. This time thrusting with hard, deep strokes, setting a rhythm that left them both frantic.

"More," he groaned against her lips. Her mouth opened wide beneath his, allowing full access to the secrets within.

With long, quick strides, he carried her to the far side of the room and he pressed her against the patio door.

"Jordan." She gasped his name. The icy glass touched her heated skin. She arched up toward him, leaving only her shoulders against the door.

"Slow and easy, love," Jordan murmured. "With the city's Christmas lights behind you."

Her breasts rose to meet him. They were round and small, the rosy pink nipples hard little nubs. He lifted her higher, caught one between his teeth, sucking it against the roof of his mouth until she whimpered with pleasure.

Her thighs squeezed his hips until her stomach quivered. With one hand he soothed, sliding it down to the moist triangle of curls between her legs.

"So tight," Jordan rasped through gritted teeth. Sweat broke out on his forehead. His finger found her heat, moved it in her, back and forth, getting her used to the rhythm.

A heat built up inside her, making her legs shake. Her low moans deepened into a low humming at the back of her throat. She squirmed against the glass, her palms moist as they pressed against the smooth surface for leverage.

"Look at me, love." Blood pounded in his ears, thundered through his veins. The need to take her stormed through him. A tempest of raging desire.

Her eyes opened, the lids heavy, the moss-green now deep pools churning with need.

The base of his spine tightened, urging him to drive into her, sink himself deep.

He kissed the spot between her breasts, breathing in her fragrance mixed with the headier scent of her arousal.

Her hand fisted in his hair. "Jordan, please," she rasped the demand. "Now."

His hands gripped her under each thigh, pushing her flush against the chill of the glass. Her skin, a pale gossamer against the blur of holiday colors, emphasized the soft curve of her belly, the softer flare of her hips.

"Spread your legs, love. Wide." Jordan groaned when she opened herself up to him, all pink and wet.

A thin sheen of sweat broke out over his skin, as he fought the urge to slam into her until he was buried to the hilt.

Instead, he covered her mouth with his, making them both burn, until she whimpered.

Regina quivered, her body open and vulnerable. Slowly, he lifted her. She saw the hard set of his features, the muscles that tightened and flexed across his chest and shoulders, corded his neck.

The first nudge brought an intense ache, then throbbing between Regina's thighs. She tightened her legs around his hips, wanting him closer, needing him inside her.

"Easy, love." Sweat darkened his hair, his eyes smoldered with a vivid blue fire.

Another nudge this time with a blunt pressure that stretched her and left her gasping. The ache intensified between her thighs, burning for relief. A relief she knew only he could provide.

"Now, Jordan!" Suddenly she locked her hips tight, squeezing him, telling her with quivering muscles she was done with his teasing.

With a growl, he slid through the barrier and to the moist heat beyond.

There was a pinch of pain, then a rush of pleasure so sharp she cried out.

She arched up to accept him, taking him deep, deep inside her. Just as he'd promised.

When she would have leaned forward, he shifted

away, keeping her balanced flat against the glass until the only connection was at their hips.

Slowly he moved within her, rocking her, controlling the tempo until she shivered and quaked. Her eyes hazed with passion, her skin flushed with desire. The lights of the city bursting behind her.

Soon his thrusts moved from gentle to hard, then from hard to urgent in the space of a heart beat.

Her body clenched then tightened around him. Her head moved side to side as her whimpers turned into long, ragged moans.

With a cry, her climax hit, erupting into a volcano of liquid heat, sweeping him along, taking him to a place he'd never been. A place he never wanted to be until that moment.

She took him home.

Chapter Fifteen

The jet hangar stood empty, insulated against the bluster of winter outside.

The man called Echo took his gun and placed it in his pocket, no longer worried about being discovered. He flipped the fuse box switches, leaving the room pitch black.

With gloved hands he slipped on his pair of infrared goggles, casting the area in a green glow.

The jet's stairs had been left down. One less thing to worry about. He noticed the bullets in the side panel. Some more that had come dangerously close to the right engine.

Fools, he thought. Any closer and their collateral would have ended up in the Atlantic.

He climbed the stairs, ducking his head before he stepped into the cabin. A quick glance out the window showed he was still alone.

He bypassed the lounge chairs and reached for the floor latch. Two sharp tugs opened the trapdoor.

Underneath laid the black suitcase. The man smiled. Solomon hadn't arrived yet.

For the first time in the last two years, the man called Echo didn't seem so alone.

Soon, there'd be many souls to keep him company.

"ARE YOU EVER GOING to tell me what drove your father and you apart?" She snuggled in close under the bed covers, catching the fresh scents of soap and sweet moisture from the shower they'd just shared.

"I'd rather have you recite some of those sex books you bragged about yesterday."

She let her fingers stray across the crisp, springy hair of his chest, rub a hard nipple until he caught her fingers between his hand and the hard muscles of his chest.

"Later," she said, almost giving in immediately, simply because he flashed her a gorgeous, disgruntled look. "I'd really like to hear about your father."

"Sweetheart, didn't any of those books tell you that this type of conversation right after sex isn't good for a relationship?" Jordan said, then kissed her forehead to soften the jest.

"But this isn't a relationship," she pointed out gently.

He paused, not liking how her words unsettled him. "For tonight it is."

"Chris was my friend, Jordan. I'm just trying to understand."

"All right, but I don't know how. Since it's still hard for me to understand." He shifted her slightly, careful not to bump her arm. She settled her head against his shoulder.

"You already know my father was MI6. He'd joined in the mid-sixties and spent much of his time over in Vietnam," Jordan said, decided she more than anybody was entitled to know. "Even as a British Ambassador, he still remained in close communication with the MI6 organization."

Jordan let out a long sigh. "Throughout my life, he wasn't there for me or my mother. Instead, he was in some foreign country fighting the bad guys."

"And the holidays? Your birthday?"

"I can't remember the last time we spent a Christmas together. Or any holiday for that matter.

"Christmas is what I remember most." Jordan absently tightened his arm around her, drawing her closer against his heart. "Probably because it was hardest on my mother. Brave during the day, heart-broken and sobbing during the night."

"That must have been hard to understand as a child," Regina whispered.

"I made excuses for him. Told myself he was a hero and heroes made sacrifices."

"Then what happened?"

"I grew up and followed in his footsteps. I think he was proud, but sad at the same time. Maybe he wanted me to be a doctor, I don't know." Jordan shrugged. "There was never any heart-to-heart talks between the two of us."

"And the resentment just grew?"

"No," Jordan replied. "Quite a few years ago, our paths crossed when my father had uncovered a British double agent.

"I was relatively new to MI6 at the time, so not recognizable by most of the other agents. I was ordered to meet with my father at a hotel in London for a briefing." Jordan's tone took on a bitter edge. "Damned if I wasn't excited."

"What happened?"

"I showed up a few hours early. Eager to save the world. Father and son reunited."

Jordan stared at the ceiling, lost in the memory. "When he answered the door, I could have knocked him over with a feather." Jordan's lips curled with derision. "I remember laughing at the shock on his face." He turned farther into Regina, grabbed a lock of her hair, still damp, and rubbed the strands between his fingers. "Did I mention the double agent was a woman?"

"No." The hurt, the betrayal caught her in the chest. "You don't have to tell me the rest, Jordan."

He kept on as if he hadn't heard her. "A beautiful woman actually. Long, russet hair with legs that stretched to her armpits, I imagine," he said, his voice filled with contempt. "I know because she stepped out of his bedroom wearing nothing but a short, silk robe.

"Young, too. No more than half my father's age." Jordan paused. "You see, she heard the knock on the door and thought I was room service with her breakfast."

"They were sleeping together," she said dully.

"Yes."

"Jordan, I don't—"

"The thing is, in this business it happens. You use sex as a tool or a weapon, depending on the situation. Or just simply a way to release energy or emotion."

Pain sliced through her heart, understanding she was another in a long list of many.

"In this situation, I couldn't separate my father from the agent. Or stop thinking about the years my mother wasted being married to him."

"And your father?"

"He pretended I was an attaché assigned to him and dismissed me with some trivial errand. Later on, we nailed the woman for treason and went our separate ways."

He paused for a long moment. "That was the day I stopped making excuses for him."

"And you never told your mother?'

"No," Jordan acknowledged. "Oh, I thought about it, but what purpose would it serve? She was already suffering. Finally, a few years before he became Ambassador, she divorced him."

"You make him sound so cold-blooded. The Chris I knew was extremely sentimental," Regina said quietly. Taking a chance she recited one of his last entries. *"December fifteenth, Another Christmas is here. As I write this, 'O Christmas Tree' has come on the radio. Apropos, considering the path I have chosen to take. I loved my son more than any father. I never told him. Another regret."*

Regina laid her hand over Jordan's heart, feeling the steady beat beneath her palm. "Maybe he changed his mind about going through with the killing because he loved you."

"Maybe," Jordan agreed, for her sake more than his own. He shifted her until she lay on top of him, using her warmth to fight the chill that suddenly seeped into his bones.

"Now why don't you tell me about one of your books?"

"All right." Sensing his need for lightness, Regina slid up over him, smiling when he hissed his pleasure. She wondered if she'd ever get used to the fact she could draw such a reaction from him. Make him want her.

"I read once that one should communicate exactly what they want from their partner during sex," she murmured against his neck. "Do you know what I want you to do?"

"No."

She nuzzled his jaw, enjoying the rasp of whiskers against her cheek. "I want you to—" She whispered a few particularly descriptive words against his ear.

When Jordan groaned, she laughed low and easy. No, she'd never get used to her newfound power.

"If you like those words, Jordan. I have more. Lots more."

LUXURY, RURIK LOSEV NOTED, came at a high price. And that price was five million lives.

One he was more than willing to pay.

"It's gone." Solomon Kashin walked into the high-rise apartment. Thirty floors above Constitution Avenue, the two-bedroom penthouse provided a panoramic view of Capitol Hill.

Losev preferred the more stoic, traditional view of Moscow, but that couldn't be helped. One must travel where business is best.

"What do you mean?" Losev asked. "It was in West's Learjet. If the authorities had discovered the explosive, Echo would have contacted me."

"I looked under the flooring and it was gone, I tell you. Beck must have discovered it somehow."

Rurik had known Solomon for almost two decades. The one man Rurik himself had brought into the group of five. "Check with any intelligence channels you still have contacts with. Find out if your theory is correct. We need both of the suitcases in place for our plan to work."

"And Echo?"

"I'll contact him," Losev answered, his mind already racing ahead. "Where is Beck?"

"I don't know." Solomon went to the bar, poured himself a shot of vodka and slammed it back.

"Then I suggest you find him after you finish there," Rurik bit out. "If the suitcase is missing, chances are he'll know why."

"And when I find him?" Ignoring the comment, Solomon poured himself another shot, then tossed it back without pause. Only the white knuckle grip on the bottle showed the depth of his rage.

"Make sure he tells you where he's hidden the bomb before you kill him."

"And the Menlow woman?"

"Use her to persuade him. I have a feeling it would be very difficult for Mr. Beck if he had to watch her suffer while he withheld information."

THE SUN BROKE OVER the horizon, laying fingers of hazy gold across the bed.

From the bedroom doorway, he watched her sleep tangled among the comforter and sheet.

For the most of the night, Jordan had lain in the bed watching the expressions fade and sharpen across Regina's features. He'd never seen anyone so animated when they slept, or so restless.

Three times, she had kicked off her covers, only to shiver in the chill of the room.

Jordan finally pulled her on top of him while his fingers caressed her back in long, soothing strokes. Within minutes, Regina settled into a deep sleep, the mumbling giving way to a deep sigh of contentment.

He'd crossed the line just as his father had. Oh, Jordan wasn't married but he knew better than to care. No woman could survive what he did for a living. Hadn't he watched his mother suffer?

Waiting at night for someone who might never come home. Wondering what he was doing the whole time he was gone. Him not being able to tell her.

Frustrated, he turned back to the living room.

He could offer Regina no better than a life full of secrets and without trust.

He grabbed her coat from the chair, angry when he saw the blood again. Disgusted, he reached into the pocket and pulled out the cell phone.

Out of habit, he checked the gage. Then swore.

The red zone registered earlier in the evening.

He flipped on the lamp, made sure the readings were correct, then noted the time.

They had been on the plane.

Quickly, he returned to the bedroom. He pulled on his jeans and slipped his sweater over his head, then went to the bed.

"Regina," he whispered. Giving in to the urge, he moved his mouth over hers for a few moments. Knowing for the last time he'd enjoy the soft, sleepy texture of her lips beneath his.

Her eyes slowly opened, heavy from sleep, then her arms curled around his neck when he started to pull away.

"Hi," she said, tentative.

Jordan groaned, his body tightened. His hand slid over her hips, more for him than her, enjoying her flex and stretch beneath his palm like a well-fed kitten. "Time to get up, love. We've got to get going." The words were brisk, more from desire than anger.

"Where?" She blinked.

Jordan pulled away. He reached into his pocket, took out his cell phone and punched in the nine-digit number. "We've got a nuke to pick up."

THE HANGAR WASN'T secured. Logically, it had been long enough for the explosive to be taken off the plane, but Jordan was hoping for a lead.

"Follow me," Jordan ordered Regina. He held the flashlight toward the jet.

They climbed into the plane and immediately saw the space open in the floor.

"Let me guess, the suitcase was in there?" Regina asked.

Jordan passed the sensor over the area, watched it spike. There was no doubt the plutonium had been stored under the flooring.

"Bloody hell." He shoved the box back into his pocket.

Suddenly, a pistol prodded his back. "My sentiments exactly."

Regina gasped, drawing the man's attention.

A light flashed in his eyes. "Regina." Calvin West swore.

His gun dropped to his side. "What the hell are you two doing here—"

Jordan tackled Calvin, sending them both crashing out of the jet and onto the cement floor.

Cal hit the floor with a thud, stunning him. The pistol clattered off to the side. Jordan's fist connected with Cal's chin, and he grunted in satisfaction. "You're a bastard, West." He gripped the other man's collar and drew him up until they were face to face. "Where is it?"

Calvin threw an elbow into Jordan's gut, had the satisfaction of hearing him suck wind. For moments the two wrestled. Finally, Jordan pinned Calvin to the ground with a forearm to his windpipe. He snagged his gun from its holster and shoved the barrel under the British agent's chin.

"Jordan!"

"Stay out of it, Regina," Jordan ordered, his eyes not leaving Cal's face. "Tell me where it is or I blow your head off, West."

"I would, if you would get the hell off me and tell me what you're rambling about."

Jordan stepped back, took the radiation detector out of his pocket and threw it down at Cal. "This is what I'm talking about. Where are the explosives that you had Dagur stash in your jet?"

Calvin caught the gadget and glanced at the dial. "You mean you brought a nuke into the country and didn't even know it?"

"I might not have, but you sure in hell did."

"Look, mate." Cal struggled to his feet. "I'm going to tell you this one more time and honestly, I don't care if you bloody believe me or not. But I am not behind this. If someone put a nuke on that plane from Iceland, then it was meant for someone else here. Someone who knew you had papers to bypass inspections."

"So you just decided to visit your jet in the middle of the night?" Jordan sneered and grabbed Cal's collar.

Suddenly the ceiling lights flooded the hangar. "He came because I called him after I got off the phone with you." Cain walked in. "Let him go, Jordan."

"You called him?" Jordan released his grip, then stepped away from Calvin but didn't lower the gun.

Calvin rubbed his jaw, licked the blood from his lip. "Cain told me about the damage to my jet." Cal pointed to the bullet holes on the side panel and wing. "The last time I loan you anything, by the way."

Jordan lowered the gun. "If the bomb wasn't delivered to you, who else knew about my flight plan?"

"Iceland," Calvin answered.

"Dagur Jonsson," Jordan acknowledged. "I assumed Dagur remembered me from a drug bust I was involved in a few years back. He chased us out of Iceland with some gun-touting guerillas." Jordan swore. "It must have been a setup."

"If that's the case, Dagur was taking a chance you wouldn't discover the bomb," Cain commented wryly.

"Not much of a chance," Jordan admitted. "We were being chased. I was preoccupied with getting Regina out alive, not inspecting the jet when we boarded again."

"And after?"

"A bullet creased Regina's arm, so we had to take care of that. The last thing on my mind was the possibility of them planting a nuke in the cabin," Jordan explained. "I didn't discover the reading on the radiation detector until after we got back to our hotel room."

Cain glanced at Regina. "Are you okay?"

"Yes," she answered, surprised at the concern in the Director's eyes.

"The question is, who picked up the package? And where is the other?" Jordan shoved his gun back in its holster.

"There are two?" Cain asked the question.

"If Losev was telling me the truth, there are," Jordan responded. "And I think the first one is in London. I just don't know where in London."

"Are you positive?"

"Losev made a deal with me. He gives me the information, I arrange for him to stay in Iceland. The last place he wanted to be was in London. It's the place I'd start."

"A place to start?" Calvin said. "Europe's a bloody big place. That nuke can be anywhere."

"Which is why we can't tell anyone yet. If this gets out people will go into a blind panic."

"One of us needs to go to London." Jordan slanted a look at Calvin.

"Me?" Calvin asked. "So in the space of two minutes, you decide to trust me and then suggest I go chasing after your nuke?"

"Look at it this way, Cal." Jordan managed to take a little bit back in the Brit's discomfort. "Someone has to save the Queen. So it might as well be you. Besides, you've been jealous over my title for years. This might just get you that knighthood you've been after."

Chapter Sixteen

The wind had settled, taking the bite out of the air. The sun was just peeking over the horizon, turning the snow into shimmering gold.

"You were pretty hard on Cal," Regina said.

"He deserved it."

They rounded the corner of the hangar to where the Hummer was parked.

Suddenly, three men stepped out from nowhere, pistols pointed directly at Jordan.

Fear ripped through Regina. One of the men moved forward, his cheeks pink from the cold. All except the white crescent scar on his cheek.

One of the other men, a tall man with a protruding forehead and spiked blond hair, pushed Jordan face first into the wall. Deliberately, the man pulled the pistol from Jordan's shoulder holster and the knife from his pocket.

"Let's go," Solomon said, using his gun to point to a nearby black SUV. "Joseph, you drive."

Joseph was easily six-three, a good couple inches

over his boss. His hair, cropped military short, was black. Two bushy eyebrows lay over sharp, brown eyes which sat deep under a wide forehead.

"Put the woman in the front with me," Solomon ordered. Joseph grabbed Regina's arm and shoved her into the front seat.

Quickly, she looked around for a weapon but saw nothing.

Then, Solomon punched Jordan in the stomach.

Jordan grunted, doubling over in pain. "That is just a warning. I will do the same to the woman every time I don't like your answer. She is small, right? How long do you think she will last without a broken rib or internal injuries? I say, possible five or six times."

Jordan nodded, still catching his breath. The blonde shoved him into the car and climbed in next to him.

Joseph turned the key in the ignition. The dashboard lit up with the roar of the engine, the lights reminding her of the jet's control panel.

Solomon slid in beside Regina, grabbed her chin and pinched it between his fingers until she faced him. "Miss Menlow, if you try something I will put a bullet in that beautiful little head of yours, understand?"

"Yes." She jerked away and in doing so bumped her knees against the dash. She cried out in pain.

Solomon just looked at her, placing the gun next to her neck. "Do not move again."

She nodded.

They pulled onto the main street.

"Where are we going? To see your boss?"

"Actually, you are going to tell us where to go, Beck," Solomon said, twisting sideways in his seat to face the man behind him. "You have something I want."

"If you're looking for the journal, you torched it with everything else in the bookstore."

"Don't play games with me," Solomon snapped. "I want the case."

"The case? I have no idea—" Jordan let out a low whistle. "You lost a nuke?" His laugh was harsh. "Your partners are really going to be upset with you then, because I don't have it."

"Dagur and Losev made sure it was put on your jet," Solomon replied, his eyes skirting over Regina's. "That's one, Beck."

"They must have forgotten to tell me." His anger gained momentum, but schooled his features. His stomach was on fire. No way in hell Regina would survive a punch like that. "Looks like one of your partners pulled a fast one on you."

Jordan couldn't see Regina's face, but he understood the fear would be etched in her features. "What are you planning on doing, Solomon? Ransoming off the nukes?"

"Why not?" Solomon answered. "Even with one, we can make billions, but with two?"

"Why now?" Jordan pushed. "Rurik has been sitting on these for a while."

"You need more than the product, Beck. You need the salesman," Solomon answered. "It just took a while to find the right person with the right contacts. Dagur is our salesman."

"And Kyle Morris? Was he the boss? The one who planned the whole operation?"

"Morris?" Solomon laughed. "He was no more than the delivery boy. Being a British Ambassador comes in handy when transporting illegal weapons of mass destruction."

"Well, one of them screwed you over. Because you don't know where your suitcase is," Jordan taunted. "Maybe they placed it already, set the timer to go at a different time. Plan on taking you out with the rest of us."

"Boss, the tree," Joseph commented.

"Shut up, Joseph," Solomon snapped.

"You lie." He pointed the pistol at Jordan. "That's two."

Fear snaked up Jordan's spine. "All right, I might know where to find the suitcase," Jordan admitted, buying time. "But its not somewhere we can get to by car. Not fast anyway."

"Tell me."

"We had a sensor on board the jet. It triggered almost immediately after we took off." Jordan raised his hands. "It's in the left pocket of my jacket."

"Get it, Yurich," Solomon ordered the blonde. Solomon turned a little more toward Jordan and pointed his pistol at him. "For her sake I hope you're right."

Yurich patted the pocket, then reached in and grabbed the box. He handed it to Solomon.

Solomon scanned the reading. "Okay, now we're getting closer to the truth."

Regina saw the truck ahead of them stop at the red light, saw Joseph tap the brake.

Judging the distance between their vehicles, Regina fought back a surge of panic. Now or never.

Without warning, she threw herself toward Joseph and slammed her foot down on the accelerator.

The SUV shot forward. Metal tore through metal, screeching as their SUV plowed into the back of the truck.

The impact slammed Regina into the dash. Dazed, she looked around, forcing her vision to focus through the pain and confusion.

Solomon and Joseph lolled against their seats. Neither man moved fast. But only Solomon was shaking his head, struggling with awareness.

"Regina!"

"His gun, Jordan." Solomon's lay on the floor by the big man's feet, too far out of her reach.

"Never mind, damn it."

Jordan grabbed her and pulled her over the seat and into his lap. "We're getting you out of here. Now!"

He shoved open his passenger door. "Let's go!"

Solomon groaned.

"Now." Yurich lay dead in the backseat, blood covering his face and chest.

"Solomon's gun went off when we crashed, killed the bastard," Jordan said and kicked open his passenger door. "Come on."

Jordon tugged her out behind. Solomon yelled and grabbed at Regina, catching her coat. With a cry, she slipped out of it.

Jordan gripped her wrist, pulling her down the street.

"Where are we going?"

"Crowds." Jordan spied a skating rink down the block. "Over there. Come on. He won't follow us in. Too many witnesses."

Bullets pinged over the top of Jordan's head, some hitting a lamppost, others the brick building beyond. People screamed and scattered.

"Go!" Jordan grabbed Regina and pushed her across the street.

Cars honked and brakes squealed as tires slid. Metal crunched against metal.

Solomon stumbled after them, his face dripping with blood, his pistol raised.

The outdoor ice rink was packed with an early evening crowd. Many were adults with their children enjoying their Christmas school break.

Jordan tugged Regina through rows of table and chairs toward the ice. "Damn it. Solomon is out of his mind."

They made it to the rink benches where people were changing their shoes for skates.

At the edge, two children skated in front of them. Jordan swore and skidded to a stop but the momentum took them both down on the ice.

Without warning, Regina was grabbed from behind and dragged up by her hair. She screamed and struggled.

"Hold it, Beck!" Solomon ordered. He shoved his gun barrel against her temple.

"You're going to kill her in front of all these witnesses, Solomon?"

"You mean all these people who will be dead by tomorrow?"

Jordan froze, his breath coming in deep gasps. "I told you I don't have your nuke."

"Then you don't have a girlfriend, either." Solomon pulled the trigger and heard the hollow click as the gun jammed. Regina slammed her elbow into Solomon's groin. He grunted, loosening his grip as he doubled over in pain.

She dropped and scrambled away.

"Run, Regina!" Then Jordan was on him, his features a mask of fury.

Both men flew into nearby benches, scattering skaters.

Solomon pinned Jordan under his big body, his hands locked around Jordan's neck.

Oxygen caught in his chest, left with no escape from his lungs. Solomon slammed Jordan's head against the ice and cement. Razor sharp stars exploded inside his skull, bile backed up in his throat.

Jordan caught the glint of metal out of the corner of his eye. He reached toward it, his fingers clawing at the snow.

"Look at it this way, Beck. It is better to die now. Otherwise you would have to choose between your loved ones here or across the ocean."

Jordan felt it then, the cold steel blade of a nearby skate. With one last heave, he grabbed the skate and slashed the blade across Solomon's neck. Blood gushed. The big man leaned back, releasing Jordan. His hands frantically tried to stem the blood pumping from the exposed artery.

Jordan dropped the skate as Solomon slumped over, dead.

"You son of a bitch!"

Jordan looked up into Joseph's pistol. Blood smeared the man's forehead, dripped in crimson lines down his nose and chin.

Suddenly, Jordan heard a scream, saw Joseph stiffen and turn, a skate embedded in his back.

Joseph raised his gun and in that moment, Jordan knew he wouldn't be fast enough to save Regina.

Jordan yelled a warning even as a gunshot exploded.

Joseph staggered, the pistol fell from his hand as he dropped to his knees. The big man looked at his chest, then fell forward.

Cain walked up, gun in hand and nudged the dead man with his foot.

"Regina." Jordan staggered to his feet and then she was in his arms. "Are you okay?"

When she nodded, he grabbed her and kissed her hard. The scent of blood, tinny and sour, hung between them, but neither seemed to notice.

"Hey, I thought I saved the day," Cain remarked, stepping up to the couple. "I should be the one who gets the girl."

Regina leaned over and gave Cain a kiss on the cheek. "Thank you," she said softly.

"You're welcome," he said just as softly.

Jordan pulled her back to his side, sure he wouldn't let her go for a long while.

"How did you know?"

"I saw Ian's Hummer and their car pull away. When I didn't see you, I assumed the worst. I was on your tail, until you rammed that truck. The damn traffic jam you caused slowed me down. Had to follow on foot." Cain's smile was grim. "Looks like Regina had it under control though."

Jordan looked down, now that the fear was gone, the rage came. "I thought I told you to run?"

"You did—"

"Then why the hell didn't you run?" he roared.

"Because, I just couldn't," Regina answered. "Solomon had you pinned. Then when Joseph appeared I had to help you somehow."

"He could've killed you!"

"Stop yelling!" she said. "But he didn't kill me," Regina pointed out.

"You'll be lucky if I don't."

"She saved your life," Cain inserted quietly, the understanding in his gray eyes. "But you were lucky. If the air bags had gone off, you wouldn't have gotten away." Cain had been in Jordan's shoes too many times not to be empathetic.

"It wasn't luck, I clicked the indicator off on the dashboard with my knee," Regina corrected, crossing her arms.

"Smart woman," Cain said, impressed. "Want to work for me?"

"Maybe."

"No," Jordan snapped. "Once we're done with this, you're done with it all."

"We're not done yet. We're still missing the nuke." Cain glanced down at the dead men. "Did you get anything?"

"Yes."

Jordan looked at Cain. "I hope Calvin's jet makes record time."

"I gave him a Harrier. He'll be there within a few hours."

"Good call. Because I'm betting Solomon left presents for us under a couple of trees. And Christmas is going to come early."

Chapter Seventeen

"Here is the damn journal." Losev tossed the book onto the desk. "Solomon is dead!"

Echo glanced down, flipped open the cover. "This is a fake. The handwriting's different." Echo shoved the book away. "It doesn't matter now. We have both explosives set."

"We don't have the second," Rurik bit out. "The suitcase was missing from the jet when Solomon got there. He went after Beck."

"And Beck killed him?"

"Yes."

Echo sighed. "You should have notified me before you sent Solomon after Beck. I have the suitcase, not him."

"You? That wasn't our plan," Losev argued. "What have you done with it?"

"That's none of your concern, Beta. The plan has changed."

"What do you mean?" Losev frowned, never liking his code name. It was too American. "We agreed twenty five billion, or we'd trigger the nukes."

"The nukes will go. This was never about the money. It was about payback. I spent my life being patriotic, putting my country's needs before mine and the first time I asked for my country's help? They betrayed me." Echo leaned back in his chair, his gaze bland, almost dead. "You're just as guilty, Beta. You helped them by selling our ammunition and explosives to the terrorists. Our enemies."

"What has that—"

"No, there was never any profit for you."

Losev suddenly understood. He reached into his pocket, but was too late. The silencer whispered across the desk. Losev looked down. The words of disbelief formed, but he couldn't get them past the heaviness blooming in his chest.

Losev fell over the desk, gasping.

"Now you can join Solomon." Echo opened the desk drawer and shoved the weapon inside. "Think of it this way, Beta. You were dead, anyway. We all are."

Realization cemented in his eyes as Losev's head dropped to the desk, lifeless.

THE DULL SCRATCH OF PEN against paper ceased. Echo closed the book, placed it in the middle of his desk, then dropped the pen back in his drawer. He studied the pictures on the corner. A memoriam placed in a semicircle of frames. His son. His wife.

Both gone now.

Faith. Family. Country.

Wasn't that the creed of most? A creed he'd forgotten in the ambitions of his job?

A creed his country forgot when they forced him to abandon his son for national security?

He glanced out the window. Christmas Eve had settled in. The snow had picked up. Fat flakes fell, dusting the capital. Echo grabbed the book and went to the wall. He moved the portrait of Valley Forge to the side and reached for the safe behind.

The evening seemed unusually quiet, especially for Christmas Eve. But the silence suited his mood.

He placed the book inside the safe, shut the door. After, he slid the painting back into place.

The metallic scent of blood permeated the stale air. Echo opened the closet and stepped over the dead man on the floor.

He pulled a white suitcase from the top shelf. His wife's suitcase from the seventies. She never could throw anything away, he mused.

He set the case on his desk, opened the lid. After checking the cylinder, he set the detonator to two hours.

Calmly he shut the lid, then pulled his nine-millimeter Glock from a nearby drawer.

A necessary precaution.

He pushed the intercom button on his desk and waited for his secretary to answer. "Rebecca, something unexpected has come up. Please have my car brought around to the front." He shrugged on his jacket, shoved the gun into the pocket and grabbed the suitcase. "And cancel my evening plans. Send a bouquet of flowers along with my apologies. It's Christmas Eve and I think I want to be alone." He clicked off the intercom button. One glance back at his office, he shut off the light and closed the door.

"IT'S NOT HERE." The president's tree shimmered with hues of gold in the dusk of the evening. Jordan sank to his knees in the snow. He'd been right about the clues.

The reference to "O Christmas Tree" from the journal. Joseph's comment in the car.

He found a hollowed out part of the trunk at the base of the tree. But there was no plutonium.

"A decoy?" Regina asked, dropping beside him.

"No." Jordan shook his head. "Solomon was telling the truth. Joseph's reaction proved that. We've got a maverick nuke loose."

"This is a nightmare." She shoved her hair back from her forehead and glanced around. "Talk about a needle in a haystack."

Suddenly, Jordan's cell phone vibrated in his pocket. He snagged it and flipped it open. "Yeah?"

"We found it," Cal's voice came over the line, tired but satisfied. "They'd hollowed out the bottom of the Trafalgar tree."

"Is the nuclear specialist team there?"

"Yes, they're defusing it right now," Calvin responded. "Have you located the second one yet?"

"No." Jordan heard Cal swear on the other end. "We found the hollowed trunk in the president's tree but nothing. At least we're on the right track."

"The timer shows a little less than two hours, Jordan. You're running out of time."

"We've got Black Hawks flying over every major city," Jordan said. "Kate has them armed with radiation sensors but we can't evacuate until we know which one or we'll cause an uncontrollable panic."

"If I were to guess," Cal said, "both bombs were set to detonate at the same time."

A flurry of chatter interrupted Cal. "I've got to go, Jordan," he said abruptly. "I'll let you know when we're in the clear."

"Just make sure you succeed. My mother lives just outside of London," Jordan said, his voice low. "I'm kind of fond of her."

"My mom does, too, mate," Cal said and hung up the phone.

"They found it?"

He nodded. "They have over one hour to defuse it. But we're running out of time."

"We can't cover all the major cities. Assuming it's been left in a city. Assuming it's been left in this country."

Jordan swore. "There has to be something we missed."

So many people were going to die. She might not have family, but she certainly understood loss.

Loss? Without warning, she grabbed Jordan's arm and squeezed. "You just told Cal to keep your mother safe. I thought your mother was dead?"

"No, she's very much alive. The only reason why I haven't called her is because she'd refuse to leave her estate, nuclear bomb or not."

"But in the journal, your father grieved over her death," Regina insisted.

"I don't remember reading anything about my mom, Regina."

"You didn't. It was toward the end. Remember, I said he wrote the last half dozen pages about you and your mom. You didn't want to read it so I didn't put it in the computer."

"I remember."

"Chris wrote that your mother died of cancer over a year ago." Regina thought for a moment. "He hardly mentioned her to me, other than the fact that they divorced years ago. I always wondered why, until I read his journal. I just assumed it was too painful for him to talk about."

"Cancer?" Jordan stopped, then swore. He grabbed Regina by the shoulders. "It wasn't his journal. My father sent you someone else's journal." He grabbed his phone and punched the number. "Cain, listen to me. Who lost their wife to cancer a year ago? Someone who knew Chris." Jordan's eyes pierced Regina's. "Chief Justice Archer Cordey. And what about his son?" Jordan nodded. "Dead two years now."

Regina sat back in disbelief.

"I think I know where the second bomb is," Jordan continued. "Get Kate's unit to his wife's cemetery. Make sure Kate has an open frequency in case I find it before she does. If there's another nuclear bomb expert somewhere available, get them out to Arlington. Stat. That's where we'll be. And in the mean time, find out where in bloody hell his son's grave is and call me back. We've only got one shot at this."

Jordan hung up. “Cain said Scott Cordey was military, special operations. Two years ago, he was captured and executed by terrorists. But only after the American government refused to pay a ransom demand.” He looked at Regina. “It wasn’t the plans outlined in the journal that Archer Cordey wanted back. It was the personal entries.”

“There was never supposed to be any ransom,” Regina realized. “Millions are going to die because of a grieving father?”

“Bloody hell.” Jordan grabbed her elbow and pulled her to her feet. “If I’d read the personal entries, I would have known it wasn’t my father and we could have stopped this thing days ago.”

Chapter Eighteen

Rows of Arlington gravestones boasted their military precision. Like white dominoes, they lined the hills, allowing only an occasional snow-covered tree to disrupt their unbending ranks.

They found Archer Cordey sitting on one of these stones.

When they approached, he pointed his pistol at them. "Don't tell me you've come unarmed, Beck?"

"Yes, sir. It wouldn't do me any good to kill you now, would it? I need to know where that bomb is."

Archer looked at Regina. "Did you bring my journal, Miss Menlow?"

"No, sir. It was destroyed in the fire," Regina replied, trying to understand how a man like him could kill so many.

He nodded. "I started wondering if you would ever put all the pieces together. If you hadn't figured it out, Jordan, I think it would have disappointed me. I always believed you were the image of your father. And he was a smart man. He almost stopped me."

"I will stop you."

"How, son? It's too late. Do you really think I would leave the bomb here with me? Do you think I'm going to tell you where it is?"

"What I think is that murdering hundreds of thousands more children won't bring Scott back," Jordan reasoned.

"Or your father, for that matter," Archer agreed, jabbing a little. "Chris wasn't supposed to die, you know. I wanted him to suffer. So the plan was to frame you for Kyle's murder. After he'd brought the suitcases into the countries, of course. Then eventually kill you, making your death appear to be a suicide."

"I thought you and my father were friends."

"So did I at one time." Archer lifted a tired shoulder. "It was on Chris's recommendation that Jon Mercer did nothing to save Scott."

"Scott understood the risks, Archer. We all do."

"I would say, wait until you're a father, Jordan, then you'd understand. But you'll never be one now."

"You know, I've always disagreed with that statement, sir. In fact, I've always thought it quite arrogant. You don't have to be a parent to understand that kind of love—or grief, when that loved one is taken away," Jordan replied, pushing. "You can be a son…" he glanced at Regina "…or daughter, for that matter and understand. Maybe you don't comprehend that type of bond as a child. Still, children shouldn't be expected to, should they? They should just be allowed to thrive in that unconditional love.

"But as adults—not just as parents—we recognize it, whether we choose to take it to heart or not."

"Possibly," Archer considered after a moment, his keen gray eyes studying Jordan. "I think Scott would have liked you." He glanced up at the sky, saw the snow swirl down. "He died Christmas Eve, two years ago. Then my Eva, not even six months after."

"Eva died of cancer," Regina inserted, her voice hoarse with emotion.

"She died of a broken heart. Cancer just made her misery end quicker," the judge corrected softly.

"The two of them, Jon and Chris, sat me down in the Oval Office. Gave me a speech. Scott gave his life for his country," Archer said flatly. "Then they stood by me, shoulder to shoulder, and watched them lower my boy into the ground beneath us."

Archer snorted. "The president presented me with the flag. As if that made it all better."

"I'm sure the president meant no disrespect," Regina added quickly.

"I'm sure he didn't, either, Miss Menlow," Archer agreed. "But it doesn't make everything better."

Archer smiled at her. "Chris liked you, you know. He wanted you to marry his Jordan here. Matchmaking, smug bastard, no more than a few months after Scott died."

Jordan automatically took a protective step toward Regina. "Leave her out of this."

But the judge didn't hear him. "The day of Eva's funeral, I burned Scott's flag. And you can be damn sure, I meant it to be disrespectful."

He looked at Jordan, but his eyes were lost in the past. "I saved your father's life and he repaid me by letting my boy die. I wanted Chris to see you in the ground, dead. Suffer a bit."

He waved the gun. "Do you realize you wouldn't have existed, if I hadn't saved your father's life in Vietnam?"

"I don't know my father's reasons, sir. But I know my father. He would have never let Scott die, if it were possible to save him," Jordan argued. "How did my father figure out your plan?"

"I left my journal out when I got drunk on Eva's death anniversary. Chris came around to check on me. He did that occasionally and knowing how hard—" Archer's voice broke. He cleared his throat. "Chris read enough of it to suspect my plans but I had deliberately kept it vague so it wouldn't be more than circumstantial. He stole the book a while later. But in the end it was too late. I'd already made the deal with Losev and secured one of the suitcases."

"Archer, please tell us where the bomb is," Regina implored. "I read your journal, if he is everything you said he was in your entries, Scott wouldn't have wanted this."

"How could you know what he wanted?"

Regina closed her eyes and recited the last entry. *"In the end, you were a better man than I ever hoped to be, son. And that is your legacy to me. An old fool."*

"Very good, Miss Menlow. Did you memorize the whole thing?"

"Yes."

"So Chris wasn't so stupid after all," Archer mused. "Neither was Jon Mercer. Although Jon did me a favor when he asked for my help. It gave me a chance to lead you to Solomon. I figured it was a win-win situation for me. One of you would end up killing the other."

Regina took a step toward Archer. "You don't think Scott would want you to kill millions of innocent people. Certainly, Eva wouldn't want you to."

"No, they wouldn't and that's a cross I will bear. But then again, they weren't betrayed. I was. And now I'm tired."

"Archer—"

"Looks like snow." The judge jabbed his thumb at the sky and for the first time, Jordan saw the glint of insanity.

"Fallout snow." With that he put the pistol to his head. "See you on the other side of hell, Beck."

"No!" Jordan reached for the older man, but knew instantly, he was too late.

The explosion ricocheted off the wind. The blood from Archer Cordey's head puddled beneath him, turning the snow above Scott's grave crimson.

Jordan pulled out his phone and dialed. "Ian, did you find it at his wife's grave?"

"That's a negative. Not yet."

"Keep searching."

Regina pulled the radiation sensor from her pocket. "Please let it be here."

Suddenly the sensor spiked. "Here." She dropped to her knees and started digging through a mound behind the gravestone with her hands. Jordan was beside her and pulling out the suitcase.

He hit the dial on his phone. "Kate. All right, we found it. I'm going to give you to Regina. I need both hands."

Regina grabbed the phone and put it on speaker. "Can you hear me, Jordan?"

"Yes."

"How big is the suitcase?" Kate asked.

"Two feet by one foot. About ten inches deep."

"Check for a trip wire on the suitcase latch. Carefully, Jordan."

"Okay, give me a minute."

"That's about all you got," Regina whispered.

Jordan flashed the light over the suitcase, then slowly ran his fingers over the edges. Satisfied after a few moments, he hit the mechanism on the latch and opened the lid.

"We've got twelve minutes."

Dagur stepped up to the tombstone, his pistol raised. "Time's up."

Jordan swore but both his hands were on the suitcase.

"You really almost screwed this whole operation up, Beck." Dagur glanced at the dead body. "But I guess on the other hand, you did me a favor."

"How?"

"By eliminating my partners," Dagur said. He patted Jordan down, grabbed his gun from its holster. "I had decided quite a while back that I wasn't a good sharer."

"So it was the money."

Dagur shrugged and without looking tossed Jordan's gun several feet away. "And revenge. Scott and I had a business relationship. And I did owe you one for messing up one of my biggest deals."

"Drugs."

"Of course. You don't still think Scott was busted for spying?" he mocked. "He was busted for drug smuggling. A deal gone bad."

"You were partners." Jordan slowly eased back, shifting his weight for a better position. "All those years ago, you were the one who blew the drug exchange."

"I couldn't have let you arrest all my suppliers now, could I?"

"And Timothy Severs? You gave him the cocaine."

"Severs was a little puppy constantly following Scott around. Scott thought it was funny when he got Tim hooked. He kept him supplied. Made him pay for it, though," Dagur laughed. "In exchange, we would get information that we needed now and again from the inside.

"Actually, Severs warned me about your drug bust," Dagur commented. "When Scott got caught, Jon Mercer and Chris found out. It was one of our biggest shipments, so Scott decided to ride along. Bad luck that some terrorists intercepted them en route. The terrorists might have killed him immediately, except Scott told them of his father's connections."

"Hoping Archer would save his life," Jordan inserted.

"Somehow, Chris found out about Scott's capture first. Maybe through his MI6 channels," Dagur reasoned. "Chris decided not to tell Archer that his son was a drug runner."

"And Jon Mercer?"

"My guess would be that he knew. Your father would have needed help keeping the drug bust from going public. Both understood, ransom or not, Scott would die anyway. They chose to let their friend's son die with a good name. And some medals."

Jordan glanced at the timer. Under eight minutes. "So you you're doing this for Scott, too."

Dagur's laugh echoed in the night air. "No, I didn't like him that much." Dagur motioned Jordan to move back with his pistol. "His father knew that I was Scott's partner. Scott let it slip a while ago. But covered, saying I was his intelligence partner."

Dagur reached down toward the wires, keeping his gun on the couple. "Archer called me, hinted toward revenge. So I put on my best sympathetic face and met with him for dinner. It took a while but I earned his trust and eventually he shared his plan with me."

"Jordan, what's happening?" Kate screamed from the phone. "We don't have time."

The interruption startled Dagur, jerking him up. He eyed the phone. "Give it to me."

Jordan dove at Dagur, knocking the gun from his hand. Both men hit the tombstone but only one grunted in pain. Which one, Regina couldn't be sure.

Both men were well matched in strength and training. Both landing kicks and punches, drawing blood and ragged breath. Neither conceding their position.

Suddenly Dagur roared and rammed Jordan, taking him down.

Jordan scrambled for an advantage underneath Dagur, realizing the clock was ticking.

Suddenly, a shot rang out in the night air and Dagur

stared into Jordan's face for a brief moment before going limp, his dark eyes wide open.

Jordan shoved the dead man off him.

Regina stood with the gun in her hand, her arm shaking as she pointed it to the ground. "We didn't have time."

Gently, Jordan took the pistol and hugged her to him. He'd forced her to kill for him. Another scar she'd carry for the rest of her life.

"No, we didn't have time," he agreed quietly.

"Jordan. I love you."

He kissed her forehead, unable to say the words she wanted to hear. "Come on. Let's get this done." It was the hardest thing he ever did, letting her go. "We need to find the phone."

A moment later, Jordan found it smashed against the gravestone. He patted down Dagur, but found no phone in the dead man's pockets.

"Regina, you read about the bomb in Calvin's files, right?" Jordan asked, the blue of his eyes sharp, concerned.

"Yes."

"Tell me you memorized the file."

"Yes," she said, taking a shaky breath.

"Walk me through it then, sweetheart." Carefully, Jordan flipped the lock, then lifted the lid.

In her mind, she pictured the page she needed. "There are two cylinders set parallel, one on either side of a ten-by-three-inch box. The timer is to the left and what looks like a battery is to the right." Regina paused, studying the parts. "There are also two other small black cylinders with wires connected to the longer, middle box."

"Neutron generators?" Jordan asked.

"Yes," she said after a moment, her mind racing across the pages.

Jordan counted the wires leading from the battery to the timer. "Okay, we have three. Red, green and yellow. Two of them will probably trip the bomb."

Fear slithered around Regina's spine.

"Which one won't detonate, sweetheart?" Jordan asked the question as he knelt next to Regina.

"I don't know." She shook her head. "The file wasn't specific about the colors. And there is a third wire that wasn't mentioned."

Jordan studied the counter as it dropped to one minute. "Hell, we're going to have to take a guess, aren't we?"

Regina glanced at Dagur then froze. "No, we're not." She reached down and pulled the red wire.

The counter stopped at thirty seconds.

"How in the hell did you know to do that?"

"It was the wire Dagur was reaching for when Kate startled him."

"Not bad, Menlow." He hugged her. "Not bad at all."

Chapter Nineteen

Yellow tape looped the area, draping the charred remains of the bookstore like sagging decorations. Its lettering boxed and black. Its warning clear.

Keep out.

Regina stepped past the tape, ignoring its warning. Her thoughts were only on the work ahead of her.

Nothing was left. No furniture, no books. The small bits that weren't burned were melted, waterlogged or smoke-damaged.

"Merry Christmas, Regina," she whispered softly. The sun just rose over the skyline, bringing with it the sweet scent of a new day. Christmas day. She hugged her arms tight around her coat, fighting off the chill that had seeped into her bones.

Well, what better day is there for embracing a new life, a new beginning?

"Only a few hours back among civilians, and you're already breaking the law."

The words were easy, almost too relaxed, too friendly.

Slowly, Regina turned, more saddened than surprised. "Hello, Jordan."

He glanced around the blackened, hollowed-out structure. "The fire was thorough," he commented, while his face remained set, unreadable.

"It's just things, right?" She glanced at her home again. The ache from that was much easier to deal with at the moment than the ache from seeing Jordan again. "The fire marshal said I was lucky to be alive."

Jordan's eyes drifted over the charred wreckage of the apartment still lying in the middle of the floor. "We both were."

"Why are you here, Jordan?"

"Where else would I be on Christmas morning but home?"

"Home?" she repeated, confused. "This isn't anyone's home. Not anymore."

"They found another journal in Archer Cordey's wall safe," Jordan said, changing the subject, confusing Regina more. "It was a lead-lined safe. Custom-made to protect the journal from the explosion."

"A legacy of death," Regina commented. "So what he told us at the cemetery was true."

She wore a white, goose-down jacket over a black sweater and jeans. Suddenly, he missed seeing her in his own leather one.

"Yes, it was true," Jordan acknowledged. "You know about Dagur. It seems Archer had known Losev on and off during the Cold War. Losev brought Solomon into the plan. According to Cordey's new entries, Losev had done business with Solomon over the years."

"Why did they kill Kyle Morris then?"

"On the delivery to London, Kyle got skittish after the plutonium came close to being discovered. One of the baggage handlers dropped the case."

"So Solomon, Losev and Dagur were only in it for the money."

"Yes," Jordan replied. "Wouldn't have surprised me if those three had made plans to kill Cordey once the money came in. They just underestimated the old man."

"One thing I don't understand, Jordan," Regina commented. "Why didn't Archer wait until the bomb exploded? Why did he shoot himself?"

"My guess is that by dying in the blast, he would've died with his enemies. In his day, it was better to die alone, by your own hand."

"I hope he's found peace." Regina shivered, but this time it wasn't from the cold.

"How about you, Regina? Have you found peace?"

"No," she admitted. Knowing it would take a long time to find peace without him. "But I'm working on it. I'm going to rebuild my bookstore. Maybe add a coffee shop with magazines and other items. Mugs, stationery. After meeting Clara, I'd really like to expand with a children's section. One that might include some educational toys."

They stepped out of the building and into the sun.

"When did you meet Clara?"

"Last night," she replied, not willing to add more.

He didn't push. "Don't tell me, you're actually

going to be seeking out customers? Trying to make them comfortable, maybe enjoying hanging around your establishment?"

"It feels right," Regina replied with a slight smile. "Timing is everything, I guess."

"Speaking of timing," Jordan quipped, catching her elbow to help guide her back over the tape. "Yours was pretty lousy yesterday."

"Isn't that a matter of opinion?" she asked.

Within moments after they stopped the timer, the cemetery had been overrun with helicopters, rescue vehicles, bomb squads. Jordan took charge, directing those he could, dismissing those who weren't needed.

Not wanting to face saying goodbye to Jordan, Regina caught a ride back to Lara and Ian's with one of the ambulances that wasn't needed.

"I was trying to make it easier on both of us." Regina let out a quiet breath, watched it plume in the cold air. "You go back to your world. I go back to mine. Isn't that what you said?"

"Yes, but that was before my whole world shifted off balance." Jordan stopped, looking up the street. He noticed the Santa was back, ringing his bell next to a new coin bucket.

Things do tend to come full circle in life, he realized.

"Honest and up-front. That's how we're going to play this, right?" His eyes found hers. He caught the flash of hope in her eyes and on its heels the heartache, and to a lesser degree, suspicion. The first filled his heart, the second made it hurt. The third made him smile.

"Honest. Right." He let out a long sigh, shoved his hands in his pockets. "You know, Regina, when I first received my father's letter I was prepared to hate you before I even saw you."

"Because you thought I was Chris's mistress, I know."

"No, that's not the reason. Although I did think you slept with him at first," Jordan admitted when she frowned. "I couldn't help it, considering my history with him. Although I think it made me even angrier for a while when I realized you hadn't."

"Jordan, you're not making sense—"

"Hear me out." He cut her off, knowing he'd never get through this if he stopped. "My whole life, my father never asked anything of me. Nothing. He never needed me for anything," Jordan admitted, finding the words came easier as he went along. "Then after he died, for the first time ever, he asked me a favor."

"What favor?"

"He asked me to protect you from harm," Jordan explained gently. "I resented the hell out of that."

"Then why did you do it? At the time you didn't know about the book."

"Because I'm gallant." He winked.

She lifted a delicate brow.

"Honestly, at first, I didn't know why I accepted," he confessed. "I told myself it was out of curiosity. Who could my father care about so much?"

"The obvious answer for you was a mistress." Regina folded her arms.

Jordan shifted, suddenly feeling warm in spite of the

chill in the air. "And it was an easy concept for me to accept. For a while anyway."

"And when you realized I wasn't?"

"That wasn't so easy to accept," he replied, shoving his finger through his hair. "Because it left me with only one other answer. He loved you as a daughter."

"Sibling rivalry at its extreme?" she inserted, the confusion only deepening.

"Something like that," Jordan agreed, even though he knew she was half jesting.

"But he loved you, too," Regina insisted. "I told you that time and again, Jordan."

"You told me, but he never showed me," Jordan responded, softening his words with a tender smile. "And at the time I didn't like you. So why believe you?"

"Well, I think you're wrong about the favor. I think all these years, he'd been asking you to do something else, but you didn't realize it."

"And that is?"

"To love him. In spite of the kind of father he turned out to be," Regina said quietly. "I think that might be why he carried your Santa letter around with him. It was the last piece of proof he had that you loved him."

"Maybe," Jordan replied. The fact that he even considered her point made Regina do a double take.

"Where are you staying, Regina?"

"With Ian and Lara," she replied hesitantly. "They said I can move in with them until I find a place of my own."

"The hell you are," he snapped.

"They're my friends, too, now. You're just going to have to deal with it."

Jordan sighed. "That's not what I meant. I'm glad they're your friends, sweetheart."

He snagged her hand in his, surprising her. When she tugged, he tightened his hold.

"What I meant is, if you're going to stay with anyone, it's going to be me."

"I don't even like you, Jordan. Why would I want to stay with you?"

"You love me," he said. "You told me yourself."

"I don't have to like you to love you. Besides, the first one will help me get over the second," Regina commented. Although it would take a lifetime of concentrating, she added silently. "I've done it before."

"The hell you will." Jordan yanked her up against his chest. "I'm not some bloody stomachache you can get rid of."

Tears flooded her eyes, fell on her cheeks. He kissed them away. "I love you, Regina. And you're going to love me back. Got me?"

"I don't—" She choked on the lump in her throat. "It hurts too much. And I told you before, I'm a coward."

"You're anything but." Jordan smiled, hugging her. "A coward doesn't think clearly while being chased by bad guys with machine guns. A coward doesn't stab a man in the back with an ice skate. A coward doesn't shoot a bad guy when that guy is threatening someone she loves." He shifted higher, until her mouth hovered beneath his. "A coward doesn't walk away from love, just because her lover's been stupid," he said softly.

"I can't—" Her voice broke on a sob. "Don't you see? Dagur, Joseph, those government hitmen—they all tried to kill you. Everyday, someone tries to kill you."

"Regina—"

"No!" she yelled and shoved him away. "I can't live everyday knowing you might die, then keep it light when you come home to dinner. I can't laugh about a Hummer that blows up, or the fact that my lover can unarm a nuclear bomb."

"Actually, you unarmed the bomb—"

"Stop it!" she screamed, her fists balling at her side.

When he took a step toward her, she stumbled back. "Don't touch me, Jordan. I don't want you to touch me again."

Instead, she hugged herself. "Life is precious. If I haven't learned anything being alone all these years, I've learned that," she said dully. "It amazes me that as much as you face death everyday, you still take life for granted."

She shook her head when he tried to reach for her. The tears stung her cheeks, frozen there by the chill and the wind.

She wiped them away with the heel of her hand. "I think, I'd rather live a long time, and live it alone. Than live my life lightly."

"I might have taken life lightly. Who knows? You get caught up in it. But I don't take what I found with you lightly," he added. "I quit black ops, Regina."

"That's not funny," she bit out, miserable. Why couldn't he just leave her alone?

"I'm telling you the truth, love." He walked slowly toward her, taking advantage of her stunned expression. "But my new job will still require some traveling."

"Traveling?"

Giving into one need, he pulled her into his arms and nearly groaned when she came willingly, even if somewhat stiffly. "You like to travel, right?"

"I…I don't know." Stunned, Regina could only shake her head, bumping his chin. "I've only been to Iceland. And I wouldn't recommend another trip back."

He smothered a laugh in the crook of her neck, inhaled the soft feminine scent. "How about England, then?"

"Jordan. You're not speaking sense to me." But her body trembled against his, telling him she wanted to believe, to understand.

"This morning I found out that my father discussed the possibility of having me join the Diplomatic Service with the prime minister."

"You're kidding?"

"Actually, they had more than one discussion about the possibility," Jordan acknowledged. "Now that I'm no longer a traitor and somewhat of a hero, the prime minister wants me to fly out tomorrow and discuss my options."

"Tomorrow?"

"Why not? It would give you a chance to meet my mother."

"I've never met a mother before," Regina said solemnly.

Jordan laughed. "Well, mine is going to be very pleased to meet you."

Regina flushed pink.

He kissed her mouth. "Well?"

"I love you, Jordan."

"It's about time you admitted it," Jordan said, content. "You know, I wonder if this is what my father meant all along."

"You mean, what Archer Cordey said about his matchmaking?"

Jordan nodded, kissing the top of her head. "Jon Mercer gave me Chris's military file."

"He did? I thought that type of information is classified."

"It is," Jordan stated. "But I think Jon considered it a thank you for finding the suitcase."

"He's paying for my new store, too."

"Really?" It was Jordan's turn to be surprised. "Good."

"Can I read the file?"

"Yes," Jordan said, then kissed her temple, thinking. "You know, I'm sorry that the journal turned out to be Archer's. I would have liked having the chance to understand Chris better. Not the agent, but my father."

"I think I can help you with that."

"What do you mean?" This time it was Jordan who pulled away, but only far enough to see her face. "Are you saying he actually wrote a book and you didn't tell me?"

"You didn't want to know anything personal about the other journal, why should I mention anything else to you?"

"All right," Jordan conceded, after a moment. "So did he keep a journal?"

"No, but I did."

"Where?"

"In my mind," she said slowly. "It takes very little effort for me to commit words I see on paper to memory. Conversations are much harder, because they flow much faster. But if I really concentrate I can picture the words in the conversation and then memorize those words. I don't do it often because it's extremely difficult. But it can be done."

"What are you trying to tell me, Regina?"

"I pretty much remember every conversation I had with your father, verbatim." She spread out her hands. "There's enough probably to fill two journals, maybe more. In fact, I had already decided to write them all out and leave them with Ian to pass on to you."

"I don't know what to say."

"It might be a little late, but I'd like to give it to you as a Christmas gift. I'll even recite the words to you as I write them down."

Jordan just looked at her for a moment. The sun cut a shimmer across his eyes, made it look suspiciously like tears before he blinked.

Softly she patted his arm.

Damned if she wasn't comforting him, he thought.

And then realized, he wanted to be comforted.

"You recite and I'll write them down," he suggested, but only after he was sure the emotion had cleared from his voice. "We'll start tonight."

"I'd like that."

"But it still leaves me with one problem."

"What?"

He lifted her chin and gently kissed her mouth. "What could I possibly get you that would come close to that kind of gift?"

"Oh, I've already got my present," Regina said softly, the love in her eyes leaving him no doubt about her gift.

They started walking down the street, their arms wrapped around each other's waist. "Tell me, did you memorize anything I said to you?" Jordan remarked.

"Some. Only the highlights," she said, laughing. "I much preferred your father's stories about you."

"What do you mean by highlights?"

"I love you, Jordan. And you're bloody well going to love me back. Got me?" she said, taking on his accent once again.

"And you did, didn't you?" He laughed, hugging her.

"I did what?" she asked innocently, batting her eyes.

"You got me," Jordan whispered, his mouth hovering over hers.

"Yes," she murmured. "Just in time for Christmas."

* * * * *

THE MAN FROM NOWHERE

BY

RACHEL LEE

First published in Great Britain 2010
Harlequin Mills & Boon Limited,
Eton House, 18-24 Paradise Road, Richmond, Surrey TW9 1SR

ISBN: 978 0 263 88280 3

46-1210

Harlequin Mills & Boon policy is to use papers that are natural, renewable and recyclable products and made from wood grown in sustainable forests. The logging and manufacturing processes conform to the legal environmental regulations of the country of origin.

Printed and bound in Spain
by Litografia Rosés S.A., Barcelona

Rachel Lee was hooked on writing by the age of twelve, and practiced her craft as she moved from place to place all over the United States. This *New York Times* bestselling author now resides in Florida and has the joy of writing full-time. Her bestselling Conard County series (see www.conardcounty.com) has won the hearts of readers worldwide, and it's no wonder, given her own approach to life and love. As she says, "Life is the biggest romantic adventure of all—and if you're open and aware, the most marvelous things are just waiting to be discovered."

For Kristin T who daily makes lemonade out of some of life's sourest lemons. I admire you!

Chapter 1

Patricia Devlin, Trish to her friends, felt edgy, edgy enough to come to the sheriff's office. A pretty woman of about thirty, with auburn hair and moss-green eyes, she drew a lot of male attention and spurned all of it. She had and kept her secrets. Only children and fools did otherwise.

Gage Dalton welcomed her warmly in his back office at the Conard County Sheriff's Department. With his burn-scarred face and tortured past, he'd once earned the nickname in the county of "Hell's Own Archangel." Nobody thought of him that way anymore. Today he was the "new sheriff," a moniker that would probably take years to erase after he'd replaced the town's long-time and well-beloved sheriff, who'd retired a few years ago. But it was "Hell's Own Archangel" Trish was here to see. The man Gage had once been, maybe, would understand.

"Hey, Trish," he said when he saw her at his office door. He smiled and waved her in. "What can we do for you this morning?"

Trish, dressed in the local uniform of jeans, cowboy boots and a light jacket over her shirt, returned his smile and slid into the creaky old wood chair. She wasn't at all sure she was doing the right thing. "Well, I'm not sure you *can* do anything, Gage. I'm probably just being paranoid."

He leaned forward a bit to rest his arms on the desk. "I never ignore paranoia." His tone was encouraging.

"Yeah, but I don't like to give in to it."

"Apparently, something is bothering you enough to come here, so just tell me. We'll figure out how to handle it."

She hesitated, biting her lower lip. "I don't want to get anyone into trouble."

"I doubt you'll get anyone into trouble who doesn't deserve it. What's going on?"

His logic made her smile again, uncomfortable as she was. Once more she hesitated, reconsidering, but then reminded herself this was the whole reason she'd come here: to get information so she could put this matter out of her mind. She had enough on her plate already without worrying about some stranger who was acting a little…odd.

"Well, there's this guy who comes and sits in the park

across from my house every night at one in the morning. At first I just thought he was resting there, but..." Again a moment of hesitation. It sounded so stupid when she said it out loud, but she forced the words out, anyway. "He sits in the same bench every night, Gage, and it's like he's staring straight at my house. He just sits there and stares. Not at my windows or anything specific that I can tell. Just at the house. Then about twenty minutes later, he gets up and walks away."

Gage frowned slightly.

"I know, I know," Trish said quickly. "Public park and all that. And he limps so badly, he's probably just resting. And if he was any threat, why tip his hand by doing it every night?"

Gage held up a hand. "Hold on. Every night?"

"Since I first noticed him. I mean, honestly, I thought it was nothing, but when it kept happening night after night...well, finally I started checking to see if he's there. He is, every night." She sighed and looked down at her hands, feeling even more awkward now that she'd framed her concern out loud. "It's probably nothing. I'm making too much of it."

Gage shook his head. "You're not. You have every reason to feel uneasy. And you're not the only one who has noticed this guy, although I hadn't heard before that he's going to the park."

Trish's curiosity rose. "What does he do?"

"He's staying at the motel. Walks into town every night at the same time, gets a drink at Mahoney's and leaves. It's enough to get a few people speculating, but not enough to get anyone wound up. But this park thing… You're sure he's looking at your house?"

"It could be coincidence. The bench is right across the street. But it's like…" She spread her hands, trying to find the right words. "He never looks around. Never looks away. Just right at my house. Now maybe I'm overreacting from all the stress at work lately. I haven't been sleeping very well, which is why I'm looking out my window at that hour. But if he'd just turn to look in another direction I wouldn't even be worrying about it." Which might not be exactly true, but she'd be worrying a whole lot less.

Gage nodded. "Okay, I'm going to check him out. We'll run a wants and warrants on him, a background check, find out what's going on. Trust me, if there's anything squirrely, we'll uncover it. Should I call you at work?"

"Try my cell." She reached into her pocket and pulled out a small wallet, withdrawing a business card. She passed it to him. "I'm taking a few days of vacation time to try to relax."

Gage smiled. "I could use a few of those myself. Emma wants to take a cruise, but I have trouble imagining being confined to a boat for a week."

Trish laughed. "I hear they come into a port every other day. You'd survive."

He winked. "What Emma wants, Emma gets."

She knew full well Emma would get her cruise, because Gage would lay the world at her feet if he could, and not because she'd give him a hard time. She laughed, anyway, knowing that's what he wanted to see.

After she left the office, she stood on the sun-drenched street, feeling the kiss of autumn, that amazingly wonderful sensation of crisp air and warm sun that always made her glad to be alive.

Even if she was worried to death about work.

With a supreme effort of will, she forced her job from her mind. She'd taken these few days to get away from that, and she refused to spend her vacation time worrying about her work problems.

The problem, however, was that in taking her vacation on impulse like this, she'd made no plans about how to spend her time, hadn't made arrangements with her friends to take off at the same time so they could go backpacking or drive into a bigger town for some shows and shopping.

A planner by nature, she laughed at herself now for not having thought this through, then decided she'd practice winging it. Her friends often teased that she wasn't happy unless her life was laid out two weeks ahead in her datebook. The criticism might be a little on the extreme side, but there was more than a kernel of truth to it.

So, here she stood, and decided there was no time like now to try making up her day as she went, first with a trip to the bookstore down the street. It would be a perfect day, she decided, to curl up with a novel in her backyard. A little chilly, but that's what she had the clay fireplace out back for. She could light it, drink hot chocolate and coffee, and enjoy the luxury of uninterrupted reading until the sun sank too low.

Feeling her spirits lift, she hurried down the street to the bookstore, a tiny, musty and wonderful place full of new and used books that covered the entire spectrum. A fictional world was just what she needed right now. Vampires, maybe, or ghosts and ghoulies. Something so far away from everyday that she could truly escape.

Bea's Books seemed to be open all the time, but maybe that was because Bea lived above her store and loved books more than anything in the world. She could sit in a cozy corner of her shop with a mug of coffee and delve into new arrivals by the hour, distracted only when she had a customer. On weekends the place was usually full, but on weekdays it was a place where you could sit and read, and Bea never pressed you to buy the book first.

But today Trish was on a mission, and the weather was too beautiful to want to spend it inside. She chatted for a few minutes with Bea, who directed her to a stack of recent acquisitions that hadn't yet been shelved. In ten minutes Trish found three books that appealed to her and paid for them.

Outside she inhaled a deep breath of the fresh air and began her walk home, books tucked under her arm. It was such a perfect day, she thought. Exactly the kind of day she had returned to Conard County for, that and being able to walk almost everywhere she needed to go. Not until she'd moved away to go to college and then to take a job with a big accounting firm had she realized how much growing up here had taught her to yearn for the outdoors and open space.

People she passed on the street, even those she

didn't know except by sight, all nodded and smiled. Many said hello. The breeze ruffled the leaves, making them whisper of approaching winter even as they brightened with autumn color. Not colors like she had seen in the northeastern part of the country, but still colors.

The breeze seemed to push gently at her back, hurrying her along the sidewalk toward her house. Gradually a spring came into her step, and she started smiling about nothing at all. It just felt good to be alive.

That mood lasted until she neared her house and saw the park bench where the stranger sat every night. Immediately the nervous feeling returned, much as she had tried to minimize it, both in her own mind and when she had spoken to the sheriff. Deep inside somewhere, she didn't really believe the stranger's presence was an accident.

Even though he wasn't there now and probably wouldn't be back until late that night, her sense of pleasure in the day evaporated. Maybe she shouldn't sit outside, just in case. Maybe she should stay inside until Gage told her there was no threat at all.

Maybe she was nuts, but she ought to take just a few reasonable precautions. After all, she'd been growing increasingly uneasy even before the stranger's appearance. And sometimes, she had learned, it paid to listen to your intuition.

In the end, she decided not to sit out back in her own yard, but rather to wait inside for news. Opening a window in the living room to allow fresh air to enter was the only compromise she would make.

* * *

Gage paid her a personal call that evening just after dusk. "Sorry it took so long to get back to you, but we had to do an intensive search."

She invited him in and offered him coffee. "What do you mean?"

"I'd love coffee. Then we'll talk."

Nodding, she went to get that mug of coffee for him and refreshed her own mug. When he'd stepped through the door, she'd felt the cold clinging to him, a reminder that days were growing short, and as they shortened the winter chill approached, especially at night.

She joined Gage on the couch and wrapped her hands around her mug, looking at him. "So it's nothing?"

"I can't say for sure at this point. I couldn't find out anything at all about him. No criminal record, period. No outstanding traffic warrants. No driver's license record at all, in fact. No real estate holdings here in Wyoming, and he wasn't born here. He pays cash in advance at the La-Z-Rest. Came to town about a month ago and didn't use a credit card. Now before you get nervous, none of that means anything bad. Lots of ordinary citizens come up blank on a background check."

Relief started to creep through her, then she had a thought. "Nothing? You couldn't find anything? I mean, you're cops. You should have been able to search in ways I couldn't."

"You'd think." He hesitated, sipped his coffee, then set the mug on a coaster on the end table. "But there are limits on where and how I can search without a warrant or a subpoena, and I don't have probable cause for either. I'm sure he has bank records, but I wouldn't know where to look for them. There's a half dozen people with similar names in the credit agencies, but none of them near his age."

"So he's using a phony name?"

He shook his head. "Look, there *are* people who live off the grid, as they say. People who don't own anything and haven't done anything that would pop up on a background check. Some just don't like using credit. Some want to be anonymous."

"I can't imagine a good reason for that."

"That's the thing. Like I said, not everyone who chooses to live that way is necessarily a bad guy. You see the problem?"

She hesitated, aware that her nerves had begun to coil again. "I don't like this."

He sighed, rubbed his hands together as if to warm them, then reached for his mug again. "How nervous are you, Trish? How far do you want me to go with this? Because there are limits to what I can legally do."

She couldn't find a reasoned answer, which surprised her. Generally speaking, she was a reasonable person.

"What's got you so nervous? Apart from the fact that this guy sits in the park every night for a little while?"

She lifted her brows. "What do you mean?"

"I've known you long enough to know that you don't shake easily. Yeah, the guy sitting out there every night might get your attention, and you'd watch him, but you wouldn't worry about him."

"Maybe I wouldn't." She hesitated, then finally said, "I've got a little thing going on at work. I think I found that some product is missing, but I'm not a hundred percent sure. So I notified the CFO about it, but I haven't gotten an answer yet. And I'm wondering if I messed up."

"Messed up how?"

"Well," she admitted with a wry smile, "I'm the chief accountant. If it turns out I did my numbers wrong, I'm likely to be the *ex*-chief accountant."

"Ahh." He took a deep drink of his coffee, then shook his head. "Relax, Trish. Nobody gets fired for one mistake."

"Yeah, maybe." And he was probably right. She should just stop worrying, check her office e-mail before she turned in for the night in case the CFO replied, and then put it out of her mind.

But part of what made her such a good accountant was her accuracy, and sitting around wondering if she'd made a mistake, no matter how many times she had re-checked her numbers, made her feel utterly unsettled.

And that, she decided, was the only reason she'd even gotten paranoid about the guy sitting in the park. She was just in a paranoid mood to begin with. "Sorry I put you to so much trouble, Gage."

He shook his head. "No trouble at all, Trish. Tell you what I can do."

"Yes?"

"I can do a stop and identify. Ask for his ID. Maybe we can get a little more info on the guy. But that's all I can do unless he does something he shouldn't."

She nodded. "Thanks. Thanks, Gage. I'd appreciate it. But I guess I should just forget about it. It's probably all perfectly innocent."

"That's what I'm supposed to be telling *you*. And most of the time it is. But since I can't say so for absolute certain, I'll try to get a little more information."

She thanked him again. He finished his coffee and headed for the door. "We'll keep an eye out, Trish. We won't just ignore it."

She was certain of that.

Put it from your mind, girl. Let it go.

But not until she checked her e-mail.

Powering up her laptop in her tiny home office, she checked her work e-mail account. And there, answering her uneasiness, was finally a response from the company's CFO, the man who had trained her at the corporate headquarters in Dallas:

Trish, thanks for alerting me to this. Sorry my reply was so slow in coming, but your memo somehow got routed to the bottom of the stack on my desk. Apparently my secretary didn't see the urgency.

I'm having an independent auditor come look it over. Of course, I hope you just mismatched some things, but if not, we'll find out. Either way, you've done your job exactly as you're supposed to. I tried to call this morning and they told me you're on vacation. Enjoy the time. And thanks again for the great job you do. Hank.

There it was. Done. No need to remain on tenterhooks any longer. No suggestion that if she'd screwed up she was in trouble. The head office in Texas had basically said she'd done exactly what she should.

She put the message in her private file on her home computer, then logged off.

Nothing to worry about. Nothing at all.

Except the stranger who sat out in front of her house every night.

Chapter 2

He was out there again. This time she started watching early and saw his painful approach as he limped down the sidewalk and finally dropped onto the park bench with evident relief.

She had twitched the curtain aside just the tiniest bit so that she didn't have to hold it as she peered out, because she didn't want him to know she was spying on him.

And now, watching him, seeing the way he stared at her house as if nothing else on the street existed, made her feel like a creep herself. Was she losing her marbles or something? Her house was locked. She had a shotgun upstairs, a hand-me-down from her father, which she could load with birdshot in no time at all. If the guy tried anything, he wouldn't be able to get away with it. With birdshot she wouldn't even need a good aim to plaster him painfully enough that she could escape.

So what was wrong with her? Why couldn't she just ignore it? What if it had been someone local, someone she knew by sight, doing the same thing? She wouldn't be at all worried.

But he wasn't local, and that made her nervous.

Okay, she told herself, *try being rational.* The guy obviously had suffered some kind of injury, which made him less than threatening to begin with. Maybe the injury had also affected his neck and he was having trouble turning his head.

Possible, yeah. That stare might be nothing but a stiff neck.

Maybe she just needed to cool it and stop acting and thinking like someone on the edge.

Of course she did, but the realization didn't help. At some level something was niggling at her and wouldn't give up.

She saw a deputy's cruiser pull up near the bench. The man didn't move, so apparently he wasn't disturbed by the approach of the police. Then Gage climbed out after training his spotlight on the man, who made no attempt to shield his face from the light.

Man, she thought, Gage was working a long day. And all because of her. But his concern warmed her. He wasn't treating her nervousness as if he thought she was simply a ditzy spinster with too much time on her hands.

She watched as Gage walked over to the bench. Apparently he said something, because the man pulled out his wallet from his hip pocket and passed something to Gage. Gage took it, spoke for a minute, then returned to his patrol car.

No doubt running the guy's ID. Finally Trish allowed relief to trump over nerves. Gage would sort it out, and the stranger was on notice that he had been seen. Good.

The man had turned on the bench so that he was looking directly at the sheriff's car and away from her. So maybe he *did* find it difficult to turn his head.

All right, she should just go to bed and forget it. Gage would let her know if anything should concern her.

Except that she remained rooted. A sign, she decided, of having had too much time on her hands. She wasn't the type to stand at her window and watch the goings-on outside, unlike some of her nosier neighbors.

After a few minutes Gage climbed out of his vehicle again, approached the man and handed him something—probably his ID or driver's license. They chatted for a moment and then Gage got back in the car and drove off.

Okay, so there was no immediate evidence that the guy was a threat. She glanced over at the digital clock on her DVD player and realized there were only minutes before the guy moved on again, assuming he followed his usual, almost compulsive, schedule.

Driven by some impulse, maybe the need to put the matter to rest *now,* she hurried into her kitchen, poured two mugs of the coffee she'd made a couple of hours ago, still hot and rich-smelling. Then she slipped on her jacket and went out the front door with the two mugs.

As she approached him, the man on the bench appeared startled in a way he hadn't when Gage had stopped to speak with him. She guessed he hadn't expected a homeowner to come out at this hour.

Reaching him, she could finally make out his features. Nicely chiseled, although not Hollywood handsome. She couldn't tell the color of his eyes and could see only that his hair was dark, short, but unkempt. The rest of him, seated as he was, remained mostly a mystery within a heavy jacket, jeans and work boots.

"Coffee?" she asked.

"I was just leaving." Nice baritone, smooth enough to indicate a nonsmoker and probably a good singer.

"Well, you can drink fast," she said, thrusting a mug at him. "It'll be cold in a minute or two, anyway."

He couldn't refuse the mug without being rude. Which was exactly why she'd done it. She took the other end of the bench and sipped her own coffee. Yeah, it was already cooling down.

Then she looked straight at him. "Why do you sit out here every night?"

"Because there's a bench." Yet the reply hinted at a question, almost as if he was wondering if she was looking for a particular response. If she was, she didn't know herself what it was.

"You limp pretty badly," she said bluntly.

"Accident."

"Will it heal?"

"Eventually." He made *eventually* sound like a very long time, not something that might happen in the next couple of months.

"I'm sorry."

He shook his head slightly. "Things happen. I was the lucky one."

He spoke that like a mantra, as if it was something he told himself again and again, yet didn't quite believe. Some part of whatever had happened, she guessed, was never going to feel lucky, but she didn't feel she could press it.

She offered her hand. "Trish Devlin."

He hesitated, and finally shook it. "Grant," he said. Not a full name.

Trish let it pass, thinking that Gage probably had all the rest of it now, anyway, and maybe a lot more. She watched him take a gulp of coffee and realized he was about to make a quick getaway.

Despite running to the sheriff with her paranoia, Trish had never been a wimp. She wasn't going to let the stranger off that easily.

"You've been making me nervous," she said. "Sitting out here every night staring at my house."

He seemed to grow still, as much inwardly as outwardly. Then he said, "I guess that's why the sheriff stopped."

"Could be."

She thought she saw the faint flash of a small smile. "Could be," he agreed. "I didn't mean to make you nervous."

"Well, you did. You keep staring at my house."

He shrugged. "It's right in front of me." He gulped more coffee.

"So it is," she agreed, then waited, trying to let silence do what her questions couldn't: make him talk.

"Sorry," he said. "I'm just resting, for obvious reasons."

He was a lousy liar, she decided, because she didn't believe that, even if it did fit. But if he was a lousy liar, that was a good thing. It meant he wasn't practiced at deceit.

"Okay," she said finally. "Don't let me keep you."

But he didn't move. Instead, he said something she wondered if she'd heard right. "Everything's wrong tonight."

"What?"

Again that little shake of his head. Then, "Look, I'm really sorry. I don't sleep well at night, never have. So I'm walking. Waiting, I guess."

She seized on one word. "Waiting?"

He drank more coffee, this time sipping, as if to put off his moment of departure, quite different from when she'd first approached. "Do you know anybody who doesn't have a rucksack full of emotional baggage?"

"That's some question!"

"But an honest one."

So she gave him an honest answer. "I guess not. More for some than others."

"Well, mine's pretty full. So I guess you could say I'm waiting for some resolution."

"Don't you usually have to work at that, not just wait?"

"I am. Believe me, I am."

In spite of herself, Trish was growing more intrigued. But then he sighed and passed her back the empty mug.

"Go inside before you get chilled," he said. "Thanks for the coffee."

"What are you going to do?"

"I'm going to walk back to the motel. Maybe pop into the truck stop for a wee-hours breakfast."

The truck stop was indeed the only twenty-four-hour business for miles.

He rose, and even in the darkness she could see him grimace. "Nice talking to you, Ms. Devlin." He started to limp away. But after three steps, he paused and looked back. "If you want to join me at the truck stop, I should be there in about thirty minutes."

She hesitated. "I could give you a ride." The instant the words escaped she wanted to snatch them back. Was she nuts? Completely nuts? She knew nothing about this man.

"Sometimes," he said, "walking is the only way." Then he resumed his painful departure.

Trish watched him until he vanished into the shadows. Only then did she realize she was growing cold.

Damn! Meet him at the truck stop? Give him a ride? Had some evil spirit taken over her brain?

Shaking her head at her own behavior, she went back inside.

Forget about it and go to bed. Wise advice to herself. Except she couldn't forget about it and didn't seem to want to get ready for bed despite the late hour. She grabbed the new novel she'd started earlier and tried to read it. But all she could think about was meeting the stranger at the truck stop and maybe learning more about him. Actually seeing his face in the light. Getting his measure.

It would be safe at the truck stop, a busy place at any hour. Safer than what she had just done by accosting him on the darkened street.

A minute later she was grabbing her keys and heading out the door.

The truck stop restaurant was indeed brightly lit, and in addition to the staff held about a dozen drivers, all eating some version of early breakfast or late dinner, every occupied table boasting a generous carafe of coffee. Some of the drivers seemed to know each other. Others greeted each other, table to table, strangers in a common place and time.

Grant sat alone at a table backed up to the wall. He already had coffee, and she noted that an extra mug was at the seat facing him. Whether for her or for someone else she didn't know.

She ignored the interested looks she received from the truckers as she eased her way between tables to Grant's.

"Hi," she said. In the light he proved to be good-looking, if a bit wan. Silvery threads of gray sparkled in his dark hair. His eyes were dark, that brown so deep it would sometimes appear black. He returned her greeting with a faint smile and motioned her into the seat facing his.

"I got you a cup," he said.

"You knew I'd come?"

"Anyone who'd come out onto a dark street to beard a stranger who frightened her must have more curiosity than a dozen cats."

In spite of herself, she smiled back and took the chair. "It gets me into trouble sometimes."

"I imagine so. On the other hand, you probably don't run through life with a load of nagging questions."

"Not often."

He reached for the carafe and filled her beige mug. The table already held a saucer full of little half-and-half containers. She reached for one, opened it and poured the contents into her coffee. At this hour of the night, even her beloved beverage could give her heartburn. The half-and-half would help.

"I haven't ordered yet," he said. "Take a look at the menu. I'm buying."

"I can buy for myself."

"I'm sure you can. But since I caused all this uproar for you, this seems like the least I can do. And believe me, I can afford it."

So she reached for the menu and began scanning a list that exceeded Maude's City Diner in variety, but probably not in saturated fats. Here she could even find artificial eggs and vegetarian omelets. It gave her a glimpse of the new generation of truck drivers.

But what the heck. She settled finally on their "fluffy" pancakes.

The waitress came and took their orders, his a full-size breakfast with all the trimmings. He certainly wasn't worrying about his weight *or* his cholesterol.

With the menus tucked back into the wire holder behind the salt, pepper and ketchup, they stared at one another over coffee mugs. Trish found herself strangely reluctant to grill him, even though she'd started their conversation back on the bench by doing precisely that.

Finally he spoke. "So what can I tell you that will ease your mind?"

"What do you *want* to tell me?"

"That I mean you no harm. A statement that is absolutely meaningless without anything to back it up."

She couldn't argue with that. "Seems like one of those lines in a bad sci-fi movie that always winds up being the prelude to something terrible."

"Hey, I like those old science fiction movies. The older and more awful, the better."

"The ones with nuclear bombs that are both the cause *and* the solution to whatever is ravaging the world?"

He chuckled. "Yeah, those. Science as the be-all and end-all."

"I take it you don't believe that."

He hesitated. "Not anymore," he said finally.

She eyed him directly. "What changed your mind?"

"Let's just say I have reason to believe that science is less of an answer and more of a question. It should be a search, not a conclusion."

"Interesting way of putting it."

The waitress interrupted, serving their breakfasts with a smile that seemed almost obscene at this hour of the night. Either the woman was a native night owl, or the need for tips made her pretend to be one.

After a bite of pancake, which did indeed prove to be very fluffy, she posed a question. "What brings you to Conard City? Sure, the state highway runs through, but it's not the kind of place where people usually stop and stay without a reason."

"I've been on the road for a long time. Guess I finally realized you can't outrun yourself. Seemed as good a place as any to wait for the rest to catch up."

The answer sounded pat. Too pat. She looked down at her mug, then picked up the spoon to stir her coffee pointlessly. "Really," she finally responded.

"Really," he said. "Sounds like a bad novel, right?"

She met his gaze again. "No, not exactly. Just...stock."

He nodded slowly. "There's a difference between citing a cliché and meaning it."

"Well, yes."

"And clichés become clichéd because they're often true. Otherwise people wouldn't use them so much."

In spite of all her suspicions, she felt more intrigued that ever, and sensed the beginnings of an actual liking for this guy. She didn't want that.

He shrugged finally. "It's true. I ran from myself. From an unhappy time in my life. And like all people who run, I found all the troubles and grief just came along with me. Some memories can't be erased. They stick like burrs on your cuffs."

"Yes, they do. Would you want to erase your memory?"

"There've been times I've actually thought that would be a good thing. But other times...well, frankly, Ms. Devlin, you can't give up the bad without giving up the good." He looked out the window, but there was clearly nothing to be seen beyond the reflections of the interior of the restaurant. Darkness turned the windows into mirrors.

"I had to put my favorite dog to sleep a couple of years ago," he said slowly. "Best dog I ever had. She taught me a lot about being a better person."

"How so?"

He looked at her again, and there was no mistaking the heaviness in his sad, dark eyes. "I could be lazy. I could be impatient. I sometimes made her wait for the smallest of her needs. Sometimes I yelled at her for no better reason than that she was asking for a simple thing like a walk, or water. Because she was interrupting something I thought was more important at that moment. But she never held it against me. She'd go away and wait quietly, and the minute I gave her the attention she had asked for, she was hopping with joy and gratitude."

Trish nodded. "It's been a long time since I had a dog, but I remember it."

"Endless love. Endless forgiveness. Endless patience. Anyway, she was a lesson, and she began to get through to me about all the truly important things in being a decent human. Simple things, every one of them, but so difficult to do. Unless you're a dog."

"They do seem to do it naturally."

"I have a friend who tags her e-mails with 'WWDD: What would dogs do?'" He smiled faintly. "A little over the top, maybe, and probably offensive to some, but to some extent my dog became my touchstone, so I understand what my friend is trying to get at. Anyway, I finally had to put the dog down. I'd waited too long because I needed to hang on, but finally I realized I was hurting her to put off my own guilt at the decision I knew I had to make."

"It's an awful decision to have to make."

"It is. I guess part of me hoped I'd wake up one morning and find she'd passed peacefully in her sleep, so I wouldn't have to make a choice at all. Life doesn't always allow us to do that."

"No, it doesn't." She paused, then took another bite of pancake, waiting for whatever else he might volunteer.

"Thing was, much as I grieved for Molly, I learned another lesson from her—it hurts, but you have to remember the good times, not the very end, which was so hard."

Despite her determination not to respond emotionally to this guy or his story, Trish felt her throat tighten. She put down her fork.

He seemed to recognize her reaction, because he said quickly, "Sorry, I'm not trying to tug your heartstrings. It's just…you'd think having learned that with the dog, I'd be better at handling stuff. But I'm not. When the rest happened, well, I didn't want to be around anything that reminded me of it. So here I am, on a quest for some kind of peace. Very sixties California except it's nothing like that. I got here and saw my journey coming to an end. So I'm going to hang around until it's over. And then I'm going home."

She nodded. His story made sense to her, although she would have liked to know more about what had put him on the road. However, she felt it would be prying too much to just come right out and ask. As she knew herself, some things were painful to talk about, even with friends, and impossible with total strangers. And hadn't she herself come running home to Conard County because of a past she didn't want to face every single day?

People did things like that, rational or irrational.

He resumed eating. She followed suit, absorbing what he had told her, weighing it in her mind and deciding that on the face of it, she didn't need to be paranoid. People had seen them together, Gage had stopped to check him out. If he meant her any harm, he was certainly on notice now that he'd be the prime suspect.

"Are you a scientist?" she asked, at once trying to learn more about him and direct the conversation to less explosive territory.

"In a way. I work in computers. Software and system design. At least I did."

"Will you go back to that?"

He put his fork down and for an instant he looked almost eager. "You know, sometimes I think about it. I was getting into some really interesting research."

"I didn't think computer people did research."

Again that half smile. "Not all of us sit in cubicles and write code. Some of us are, or were, busy looking toward the future."

"In what ways?"

"Well, we're approaching the possibility of quantum computers. Do you know anything about quantum physics?"

"I had a physics course both in high school and

college. I wouldn't say I'm well versed, but I have a nodding acquaintance."

"When it comes to the quantum world, nobody really understands it, anyway. All we can do is make predictions based on large numbers. Sort of like playing the odds."

"Oh, that makes me feel secure."

His smile widened. "We're both here talking, and the restaurant hasn't vanished. So the large numbers work just fine for most purposes."

"But in quantum computers, what happens?"

"That's the problem we're trying to sort through. Things get dicier, of course, at such a small scale. But then studies actually proved the so-called observer effect—have you heard of that?"

"Something about the act of observing affects the measurements?"

"At the quantum scale, yes. But it goes way beyond that. I won't bore you with details, but a number of experiments show that conscious intent can affect the basic randomness we expect at the quantum level. One extended study of them at Princeton, in fact. The effect wasn't huge. Just a nudge this way or that, tiny but statistically relevant. That throws a big monkey wrench into quantum computing."

"Wow. And you were working on that?"

"Doing some research, yes. You can't move into nanotechnologies unless you can guarantee reasonable accuracy. If a process relies on quantum randomness, you have to correct for influences that actually *reduce* that randomness."

At that she felt herself smile. "Now I'm in over my head. I just know how much I depend on my computer to be accurate."

"Exactly. So there's a lot of work to be done. But it's unleashed some fascinating questions."

"And that's why you said science should be about questions, not answers."

"Well, partly." His face shadowed a bit, but he continued. "We need solutions, but solutions aren't necessarily *answers,* if you get my drift. And some people don't even want to ask the questions." He fell silent, then dipped a corner of toast in his egg, and popped it into his mouth. He appeared to have gone elsewhere in his mind, whether to his former research or some darker place she couldn't know.

But one thing seemed to be clearer for her: there was no reason to believe this man intended her any harm whatsoever. Once again she began to feel embarrassed by the mix of emotions that had led her to go to Gage.

Even though the sheriff hadn't thought she was out of line for being nervous about this guy sitting across from her house every night in the wee hours, she herself felt as if she had made a mountain out of a molehill.

"I'm sorry," she blurted. "I overreacted by getting the sheriff involved."

It took him a moment to drag himself out of the well of thought he'd fallen into. "I understand perfectly. The world being what it is, you'd be strange if you hadn't gotten nervous about me sitting across from your house every night. It's not like I'm someone you know from around town." Then he shook his head very slightly and smiled faintly. "Not that anyone can be sure of anyone just because they know them by sight."

"You've lived in a big city?" His answer would seem to suggest that.

"Yeah. So I understand. I may be out there a few more nights, because it's a convenient place to rest."

She noticed he didn't ask if that would continue to bother her. Apparently he felt he'd answered her questions sufficiently. And just like that, she felt nervous again, because the bottom line was that she hadn't learned a damn thing about him really. The death of his dog? A personal tragedy? References to computer research? Conveniently lacking any verifiable details?

All of a sudden she didn't feel silly anymore. In fact, she wondered if she'd just been treated to a good sales job.

She pushed back her plate and stood. "I feel stalked," she said flatly. Then she grabbed her purse, threw bills on the table and walked out.

No one followed her to her car. When she glanced back as she was about to climb in, she saw Grant still sitting at his table, staring into space.

Yes, she felt stalked. That was exactly the word, the one she hadn't actually put her finger on until just now.

And there were a lot of good reasons for her to feel paranoid about that.

Chapter 3

Trish's computer hummed quietly as she searched the Net for information. Outside, another bright, cool day was beginning to degrade into cloudiness that might bring rain or even snow. She didn't know or really care. She was too busy trying to verify what Grant had told her last night about the research he'd been doing, then trying to find out if it led her to him.

Either she didn't know the best search question to ask or the subject wasn't one of the most popular. Either way, several hours passed during which she scanned articles that hinted at the matters Grant had spoken of last night without success.

He appeared to be right about one thing: from what

she was seeing, not many scientists wanted to ask whether conscious intent could affect the quantum field.

She did, however, gradually realize that some terms were appearing repeatedly without explanation, as if they were understood. And she realized there was a certain evasiveness when they came up. Either that or they were used within such strictly defined limits that she couldn't get the meaning.

Finally she changed her search criteria from quantum physics and linked *conscious* with *Princeton.* Up popped a Web site link for the Princeton Engineering Anomalies Research Lab.

She might not have studied physics in depth, but as an accounting major with a minor in economics, she had studied a lot of statistics, and as she delved deeper she discovered that the things Grant had discussed in loose generalities were actually being investigated with mind-blowing results. While the ultimate conclusion was that conscious intent had such a small effect on random number generators that it could be ignored, the fact remained: the statistics showed the effect to be way, way beyond chance.

Good Lord! she thought. What a door to open: human thought could affect the functioning of a machine…or the rate of radioactive decay. In small ways, yes, but even those small ways were a window to a whole different view of the universe. And it further elucidated what Grant had meant about some scientists being afraid to ask the questions. Of course they were afraid to ask. None of them would want to be labeled fringe lunatics.

She sat back in her chair, stretched and thought about what she had just learned. Grant, whoever he was, hadn't been spouting some kind of extremism last night, but a valid scientific viewpoint, however much mainstream science might try to skirt it. That much at least hadn't been a sales job.

However, there was no way to search for him, not with only one name, first or last she didn't know. No matter how many ways she tried it, the word *grant* came up more often for grant applications and awards than anything else. How convenient.

She sighed, then spoke aloud to the empty room. "Get over this obsession," she told herself. "Just get over it. Load the damn shotgun if you're that worried, and then forget about it."

Not a normally obsessive person, her behavior, her contradictory responses, had begun to seriously trouble her. The man limped around town in the middle of the night, sat on a public park bench for a whole twenty minutes, had spent time last night trying to reassure her in some way, and there was nothing left to do except regain her own sense of proportion and rationality.

Sitting here at the computer working the "Grant problem" as if she had nothing better to do with her time was out of character.

Wasn't it?

She sighed again and rubbed her eyes. "What is going on?" she asked the room. The room, of course, didn't answer.

But some little voice in her head finally did.

It's not about this guy, it's about another guy. A guy who lied to you.

Was she really in some subconscious way trying to make Grant a stand-in for Jackson?

Oh, yeah. Now you've got it.

At once she leaned forward and pressed the button to hibernate her computer. Then she shoved back from her desk, realizing only as she stood that she had grown stiff from not moving for so long.

"Idiot," she said to herself.

In the kitchen she made a fresh pot of coffee and a turkey sandwich.

Yeah, she was an idiot, she decided, but only because, however indirectly, she had opened that damn Pandora's box again, the box named Jackson Harris.

That box containing a torrid fairy tale, an all-consuming eight-month romance that had ended in the heart-stopping, earth-shaking discovery that he was a married man. That he had lied to her all along, claiming he was divorced. An instant of discovery and shock that had seemed to kill everything inside her in one icy blow.

Until the pain started. To this day she couldn't say what hurt worse: losing love, being used or being betrayed so callously. It had certainly hurt to leave her job in Boston because she couldn't face the constant reminders.

But at least she had managed to find her way home. Maybe she had thought it would all get better here. Instead, just as Grant had remarked last night, she'd brought her baggage with her. *You can't run from yourself.* Probably one of the oldest clichés in the world. And so, so true, as Grant had pointed out.

She sat at her kitchen table and bit into her sandwich, thinking about the tangled mess of her mind. A mind that she always preferred to believe was relatively neat and orderly…yet as of this moment seemed anything but.

What was the psychological term? Transference? No, more like projection? Whatever, it disturbed her to think that she might be reacting to Grant in a way dictated by her experience with Jackson. After all, what had Grant done except sit on a park bench in the middle of the night? So maybe her suspicions resided less with his actions and the timing of them than they did with the horrendous betrayal she had suffered at Jackson's hands. Maybe she felt uneasy and threatened for no other reason.

Probably a good time to have a heart-to-heart with one of her girlfriends, but a glance at the clock told her that they were all still involved in the middle of their workdays. Not the time for a conversation like this.

She took another bite of her sandwich just as her cell rang. With a muffled groan as she tried to chew and swallow fast, she pulled the phone from her pocket as the ring tone played the same bars of "Carmina Burana" for the second time.

"Hello?"

"Hi, Trish, it's Gage."

"Oh, hi, Gage. Thanks for calling. I'm sitting here concluding yet again that I'm overreacting to that guy."

"Conclude away. I did the 'stop and identify' I promised you I would last night."

"I saw you. You're going to think I'm nuts."

A quiet laugh escaped him. "Not a chance. Why?"

"Because after you left I went out and talked to him. And then I met him at the truck stop and we talked longer."

"Well, I'll give you credit for guts and curiosity, but I'm not going to tell you that was a wise thing to do with a total stranger."

"Well, since I'm getting concerned about the state of my own mind right now, I have to agree. I bounced from he's not really a threat to feeling stalked, and now I'm on my way back again."

At that Gage really laughed. "It's hard to reach a conclusion in the absence of facts. But I have some facts for you. Interested?"

"In anything that might help me get my balance back. When I have to stand back and look at my own mental workings, something's not right."

She could hear the smile in his response. "Smart people do that all the time. It's the idiots who never self-examine. Anyway, I *do* have some info for you."

"I'm listening."

"I couldn't find anything on him yesterday because he used a fake name on the motel register."

"Not good."

"Not a crime. When I stopped last night and talked to him, I got his driver's license. No wants, no warrants, great credit rating and he owns property in California."

"That's a long way away. Anything else?"

"Actually, yeah. But nothing that raises a red flag."

Gage fell silent a moment. "Did he give you his full name?"

"No, just Grant."

"Well, until the guy does something wrong, I don't feel I have the right to share any more. Sorry, but there are limits. Just ask him his full name. Then you can find out what's in the public record just as I did. But I don't have the right, legally or ethically, to go beyond what I just told you."

She almost sighed, but knew he was right. How much would she want Gage to invade her own privacy just because she made someone feel uneasy?

"Thanks, Gage. I appreciate your help."

"You're more than welcome. If he does anything else to concern you, let me know immediately, okay?"

"Sure thing."

She closed her phone, slipped it back into her pocket and felt an urge to laugh at herself. Oh, it was so shocking! Yep, really shocking. Some guy sits on a public park bench, legal even at one in the morning, and nobody could do anything about it.

For some reason, her grandmother's voice floated into her mind, the woman's plainspoken way of telling someone to think about what they were doing: *Are you tetched in the head?* Always delivered in a kind voice, but always in its own way like a jerk back to a calmer state of mind.

"Are you tetched in the head, girl?" she asked out loud.

Yeah, maybe she was. And maybe tonight she'd go out and ask Grant for his full name. Or maybe not. Just because Jackson was a lying scoundrel didn't mean every other man on the planet was.

She finished her sandwich in a calmer frame of mind. Then she grabbed a heavy flannel shirt and her book and went out back. Ten minutes later she had a small fire burning, and she curled up on a chaise with her coffee to read.

Clouds might be moving in, but that didn't mean winter had arrived.

Yet.

The deepening night chill, which had begun its arrival with rain in the late afternoon, bit at Grant's exposed skin as he limped his designated path from the motel to Mahoney's, where he spent fifteen minutes sipping an excellent rye, and then again as he limped his way toward the park to sit in front of Trish Devlin's house. He shoved his hands deeper into his pockets, but the night managed to bite even through his jeans, and his hood couldn't cover his cheeks. If he was here much longer he might have to upgrade his clothing.

But he had no choice yet. His path was ordained, by what he couldn't really say. All he knew was that he'd ignored something like this before and had lived to regret it. He wished he hadn't lived.

So he followed the plan, according to what he knew, even though it was entirely possible he couldn't make any difference at all to the outcome. How would he know? Science didn't like these questions and had never tried to answer them. Theology even tried to steer away from this place.

But here he was in the midst of it. After nearly a year of thumbing rides around the country, trying to deal with his demons, he'd become aware of a different demon. And somehow he'd known he'd arrive in the right place at the right time.

The minute that last rig had pulled into the truck stop here, somewhere deep inside, he'd known: *this is it*. Certainty as strong as a compulsion had led him to check into the motel, then hunt for the bar he was sure he'd seen before. The clock he recognized over the bar. The time that had been nagging at him. The subsequent walk to a park and a bench that were somehow familiar.

Sometimes he wondered if his experience was something like that of serial killers who talked about a compulsion, an inner pressure to hunt a victim whom they somehow recognized even if they had never met.

Sometimes he wondered if he'd gone off the deep end. Sometimes he wondered if he himself was the demon he was hunting.

But he was here, guided by God knew what to this out-of-the-way place, and fear of failing yet again made him follow this set path night after night. The only reassurance he had that he wasn't the demon was his own distaste for making Trish Devlin nervous.

He wished there was another way.

But there wasn't. He just knew he had to be on that bench at that time. Period. And he couldn't explain it to another soul without getting himself committed.

Smothering a sigh, ignoring the grinding pain in his hip and the stabbing pain in his thigh and the incessant ache in his back, which probably came from limping around so much, he plowed through the night, feeling as if he were walking through an iceberg rather than air. At times it was almost as if something pushed back at him, told him to turn around. But the compulsion overrode everything else, and because he hadn't trusted that compulsion before, to his great grief and horror, he had to trust it now.

Time, he reminded himself, was an artifact of the large-number world he existed in. At the quantum level, past and future became one in a timeless present. So his experience was possible.

Possible.

Just possible.

A lot of rational people would tell him he was nuts. There'd been a time he would have agreed. But not since the…accident.

Except now he lived in a world where he knew there were no "accidents," only probabilities, and there was one probability he had come here to prevent.

It was possible he had already prevented it just by coming here and making this walk every night. But the compulsion remained, so he remained, too.

He lowered himself to the bench again with a gasp of both pain and relief. Maybe when this compulsion let go, maybe when he dealt with whatever he'd come to deal with here, he'd be able to allow himself the gift of the hip replacement the docs had wanted to give him. A hip replacement he'd denied himself out of guilt.

He almost smiled then, realizing that he might actually be doing penance for something that had arisen from the morass of quantum probabilities, probabilities over which he could exercise only minimal control by making decisions. He had made a rational decision that time.

This time he was making an irrational one in order to atone.

And he was evidently scaring the woman who lived in that house. He felt bad about that, but maybe his whole purpose in doing this was to scare her. Because if he was right, she *needed* to be scared.

The last thing he expected to see was Trish Devlin come out of her house and march toward him. After their meeting at the truck stop, he expected her to avoid him like the plague. Instead, here she was, striding purposefully toward him, her snorkel hood up on her parka, her hands in her pockets.

When she reached him, she stood over him. The snorkel hood, even though it wasn't fully zipped, managed to shadow her face completely.

"Who *are* you?" she demanded.

"A very cold guy who is sorry he keeps disturbing you."

"I'm finding that hard to believe. The sheriff says you appear to be okay."

"Then you shouldn't worry about me."

"Well, I can't stop wondering about you. I go from being annoyed to being frightened to being just plain curious. Either way, I can't sleep until you leave. So why don't you just come into my house and tell me what the hell is going on?"

"Why should anything be going on?" He genuinely wanted to hear her answer to that.

"Because after what I told you about feeling stalked, a gentleman would have chosen a different bench tonight."

"Reasonable," he said. "But not possible."

"Why the hell not?"

His answer was simple, and as true as he could give her. "Because I can't."

"That's not true. You can walk any direction you want, sit on any one of another dozen benches."

"Theoretically."

She made a disgusted sound. "Why do I feel as if I'm caught up in a conversation with an evasive Zen monk?"

"I should be so lucky."

"Then just give me your full name."

"Why?"

"So I can do a Google search on you. So maybe then I'll be able to sleep."

"I don't want you to sleep at this time of night."

She swore then, a phrase he suspected was totally uncharacteristic. It didn't seem to pass her lips easily. "Do you always talk in riddles?"

"Enigmas, actually. I can't explain." He hesitated, but sensed there was no danger in the revelation. And feelings were about all he had left to guide him in this unknown territory. "But I *will* give you my full name. The search engines should take you on an interesting journey."

"I hope so."

"My full name is Grant Frederick Wolfe." He spelled the last name for her. "You'll probably find me most often as Grant F. Wolfe, or even G. F. Wolfe, which is the name I used on most of my papers."

"Thank you," she said stiffly, then turned to walk back to her house.

This should be interesting, he thought as he watched her disappear inside. Because he had a pretty good idea what the search engines would bring up.

He glanced at his watch. Ten more minutes, then he could go back to the motel's warmth.

Maybe, at some point, the universe would reveal to him why he'd been chosen for this particular hell.

Because *he* sure didn't have any idea why.

Chapter 4

The morning was chilly enough to cause Trish's breath to fog. The rain yesterday had cleared the air so well that the trees seemed even more colorful, the sky even bluer and the sun even brighter. They were in the height of autumn, with a brief burst of Indian summer in the forecast for tomorrow. She looked forward to those few warmer days.

But this morning she had a mission. By nine-thirty, she was hammering on the door of Grant's room at the motel. A few minutes passed, then the door opened and he looked out at her with sleep-puffed eyes.

"Come in," he said. "Except you'll have to excuse my state of dress. I haven't even brushed my teeth yet."

She stepped into the warmth and glanced around the

room. It showed its age, of course, but Grant was evidently a neat person. His few possessions appeared to be stowed away.

On the other hand, Grant himself was something else. Maybe he slept in the buff, but he'd pulled on nothing but a pair of jeans to answer the door, and he hadn't even bothered to snap them.

Trish's thoughts raced down an alley she didn't want to enter, but it proved impossible for her to ignore the fact that he had a broad, smoothly muscled chest, arms that said he could lift more than a laptop. And then there was that faint sprinkling of dark hair below his navel that acted like an arrow, pointing directly to the open snap of his jeans.

The man was beefcake, for crying out loud. He could have posed for one of those calendars.

But then he turned swiftly away, grabbing a sweatshirt on the foot of the bed, and she saw his back. Her awareness of his musculature vanished as she saw the patchwork of scars. They looked like surgical scars, but she could only imagine the injuries they represented.

Almost as if the strength had been sucked from her, she sank into the one chair beside the window.

Sweatshirt on, he dropped onto the end of the bed, facing her. "So," he said. "Can I buy you a coffee or breakfast? I could use a cinnamon roll myself."

"I want to talk."

He nodded. "I figured that out. You wouldn't be here otherwise. But wouldn't it be better to talk somewhere public?"

"For you or for me?"

"For both of us, maybe."

Thinking about what she had learned during her Internet search, she could understand that answer. "Okay," she said. "I'll meet you across the way."

"Actually, I was thinking about the diner. Mahoney told me the food is fantastic."

"It is if you're not worried about the state of your arteries."

At that he smiled faintly. "I'm not. Are you?"

"All right, I'll drive you there. My car's right out front."

Outside she stopped to pull in a lungful of cold fresh air. How could she have forgotten how attractive a man could be or how good one could smell?

Shaking her head, she climbed into her car, switched on the ignition and turned up the heat. Grant Wolfe now posed a new kind of problem, one she felt less able to deal with than a stalker. She absolutely could not afford to feel attracted to him.

Five minutes later he emerged from his room, dressed for the weather now and quite a bit less distracting. He climbed into the passenger seat of her little four-wheel Suburu and smiled. "Thanks for the ride," he said. "I honestly don't feel like walking this morning."

She managed a smile in return. "Too cold," she said. "In another few weeks I won't even notice it, but this change was too sudden and too big. I'm freezing."

"I come from near L.A. Nice climate. Moderate, most of the time."

"That's what I hear. But I think I'd miss the seasons."

"I hear that all the time from people when they move to my area. The funny thing is, after a year or so they don't seem inclined to move away."

She gave a little laugh and nodded. "From what I've heard, it can be pretty seductive."

"It can be."

"I don't know if I could handle the earthquakes."

He cocked his head. "That's another thing I hear a lot about. But if you really give it some thought, you realize that no place is totally safe from Mother Nature's wrath."

She nodded slowly as she pulled into a diagonal parking place in front of Maude's. "You're probably right about that."

At this hour of the morning on a weekday, Maude's diner was empty of all but a couple of knots of retirees and a couple of tables occupied by somewhat younger women—probably ranch wives who'd come to town to do the weekly shopping. Glances came their direction from everyone, but conversations barely stopped. Just enough noise and activity to make quiet conversation possible.

After the chill outside, Trish chose a table by the window where a bright sunbeam made its way inside. It was getting close to that time of year when, because it was too cold to stay long outside, she'd stand at a window just to feel the sun on her face.

Grant limped behind her and lowered himself gingerly into the chair.

"You really hurt," she remarked.

"It's worst when I first get up. Once I move around a bit, it eases."

The inevitable cups of coffee arrived, slammed down by Maude herself, who regarded Grant with evident suspicion. "Know what you want?" she asked in her graceless way.

"Cinnamon roll, please," Grant said.

"They're big," Maude warned. "'Course, you look like you could use some fattening up." Then she turned to Trish. "Don't see much of you around here. Watching that tiny waistline?"

Trish almost blushed. "Actually," she said carefully, "I just like to cook at home."

Maude sniffed. "Well, you're here now, so what'll it be?"

"I already had breakfast, so the coffee will be fine."

"Rude not to eat when you're with somebody who's trying to enjoy his breakfast. I'll get you a roll, too. I figure that one—" she pointed at Grant "—will probably want whatever you don't."

As Maude stomped away, Grant cocked a brow at Trish. "You get a roll, too, even if you don't want one?"

Trish grinned. "She's an institution in this town. Maude's way or don't set foot in here."

"I get that sense."

An awkward silence fell. Understandable, Trish thought. She didn't really know how to address what she'd learned about him, or where it was safe to start, or even how to frame an appropriate apology. She felt as if anything she said might break eggshells.

And, of course, Grant wouldn't want to talk about some of it at all.

But at last the huge, hot, fresh cinnamon rolls occupied plates in front of them, along with butter for those who needed additional calories, and their coffee cups had been topped off. Impossible to avoid talking any longer.

It was Grant, however, who broke the silence. "I doubt," he said, "that you found out anything about me that I don't already know. I imagine you have questions."

"Not questions, really," she said, trying not to squirm. "More like a feeling I owe you an apology."

"You don't owe me one at all. I scared you."

"I leaped to conclusions."

"Maybe not such bad ones. Especially given that I'm a total stranger."

She cocked an eyebrow at him and caught again that haunted, hunted look, but this time she knew where it came from. "I'm sorry about your family."

He nodded, his lips compressing.

"But we don't have to talk about that," she said hastily. "That's not what I wanted to talk about, anyway. I read the newspaper stories. It was awful. I can't imagine surviving a plane crash that took your wife and daughter."

Again he nodded, his face twisting a bit. "Some things you just have to live with."

Words deserted her, leaving her with no other option than to return his nod and look down at the roll she now wanted even less than when Maude had slapped it down in front of her.

After a minute or so Grant sighed. He picked up his fork, cut off a bite-size piece and popped the sweetness into his mouth. He chewed, swallowed, then said, "There are still good things in life. And this must be one of the best cinnamon rolls I've ever eaten."

"Maude is without compare in the kitchen."

"So it would seem." Back to inconsequentials. She was happy to keep the conversation on safe ground. "You wrote a lot of papers."

He almost smiled. "I think I was a little manic. I loved my work, and sharing the things I learned was one of the best parts. Working the ideas through in my head enough to actually express them cogently in papers."

"Well, I couldn't understand a thing you said, but I was impressed by the number of your publications."

"A natural outflow of my work. You probably also noticed some of them weren't exactly greeted as mainstream."

"I gather you were pushing frontiers. Maybe some of the rest of the world just needs to catch up."

"That's a kind way of putting it."

"It's the best I can do." She gave a self-deprecating smile. "I'm an accountant, after all. In my world anomalies usually result from mistakes."

"I like numbers. They don't lie."

That gave her a little start, harking back as it seemed to her recent discovery at work. When numbers didn't add up, something was definitely wrong. It might be her mistake, or it might be that there were real problems with the plant's inventory, but either way, numbers didn't lie. "You're right about that," she said. "At least not if you've got the right ones."

"That's often the question, isn't it?" He took another bite of his roll.

Trish pushed hers toward him. "I can't possibly eat. If you don't want it when you're done with that one, take it with you. Maude will object only if we leave it behind."

"I can do that," he agreed. "So what did you conclude from your research?"

He wasn't going to let her off the hook. She'd insisted on checking him out, and now, whether she liked it or not, he wanted to know what she thought. This man could not be easily diverted.

"Such as?"

"Just give me an overview. I haven't done a Google search of my own name in a long time. I'm a little curious, actually."

She decided to stick with facts as much as possible and leave her impressions out of it, if he'd let her. "Well, you own a huge interest in a company called Causal Designs, a computer systems engineering and research firm."

"I still own it?" He frowned faintly. "I told my attorney to sell my interest to my partners."

"Apparently, they didn't listen. If they did, it wasn't noted anywhere. I may not be able to read your papers, but I can sure read financials. You still hold the controlling interest. What your partners and your attorney *did* do was try to find you. For all I know, they're still looking. Apparently, you made the news when you disappeared ten months ago."

"I went on the run," he said quietly. "I told you that."

"I know." She felt a painful twinge of sympathy. "But you asked what I'd found. I'm telling you."

He sighed, put his fork down. "Go on. Maybe at some point I'll connect with this in a way that doesn't make me either sad or mad."

She paused, feeling compassion flower, and tried to find some item she'd picked up that wouldn't disturb him. "You're quite the philanthropist."

He waved a dismissing hand. "I don't like it when that gets publicized. Besides, giving something back is required of everyone."

"I wish everyone agreed."

"People do what they can."

"Some of us, anyway. And you must be a pretty likable guy."

"What makes you say that?"

"Because you have partners and friends who want you back. People who have been searching for you, who are worried about you. That probably impressed me most of all."

Again he fell silent, taking a trip through his thoughts that she couldn't follow. "I guess I should give them a call, let them know I'm still breathing."

"They'd appreciate that."

Another long silence, then, "I don't know if I'm ready for that."

She didn't need him to explain. She could well imagine

that touching base with his friends would lead him right back to the places and associations he'd said he was running from. "Would you like me to call for you?"

That clearly surprised him. "Why should you do that?"

"Because if someone I cared about had been missing for nearly a year, I'd love to get a call from anyone who could confirm he's still alive."

"Let me think about it." He started to pull at another piece of his roll with his fork. "The thing is, if you call them, they'll find out where I am."

A prickle of suspicion was quickly washed away in the memory of this man's tragic story. "Would that be so bad?"

"It wouldn't surprise me if Jerry or Dex came racing to my rescue."

"And that's bad why?"

"Because," he said, looking her straight in the eye, "I'm the only one who can rescue me from this nightmare. They'd just come out here and cloud the issues."

"Which issues?"

"All of them."

He spoke so emphatically that she pulled back a little.

"Sorry," he said quickly. "I didn't mean to bark, but I can promise I don't bite."

She relaxed again and now reached to pull her plate back toward herself. She needed to put something in her mouth if for no other reason than that it would keep her from talking. Maude's cinnamon rolls were at least the most delicious gags in the world. The first bite almost melted on her tongue, a delicious contrast of spicy cinnamon and brown sugar. Almost in spite of herself, she closed her eyes so nothing else could interfere with the moment of pure enjoyment.

Maude had apparently decided it was late enough in the morning to add some music to the mix of diners and diner sounds, because Willie Nelson began to sing out of the recently installed speakers.

She opened her eyes again and found Grant had cocked his head as he listened with a smile. "You like Willie Nelson?" she asked.

"Oh, yeah. Doesn't everyone? I used to listen to him a lot when I was working."

"Funny, I'd have thought you'd go for some other kind of music."

"Why? Because I'm a computer nerd? I like classical, jazz when it's not too complex, blues, some country, good gospel…oh, all kinds of music, really, as long as it doesn't sound like a broken cement mixer."

She laughed. "That's a matter of taste, I guess."

"Also a matter of synesthesia."

"Syne—what?"

"Synesthesia. Something else for you to look up on Google. Some people hear sounds and see colors. That's me. I can't listen to Bach, for example, because the colors I see get too jarring and change too quickly."

"That's amazing!"

"Studies are beginning to show that a lot of us have various forms of synesthesia. Seeing sounds as color, seeing numbers as colors and number lines as shapes, even occasionally tasting words as if eating something. For some these connections are strong enough to interfere with ordinary life in unpleasant ways. For most of us it's more of a background thing. And then there are a lot of people who have forms so mild they're hardly aware of it."

"That's fascinating. I *will* check it out. But doesn't that interfere with you working?"

"Not at all. At least as long as I pick the right music. I can't work when I'm listening to Bach because too much of my brain gets involved in racing to keep up with the colors. It can leave me feeling exhausted and edgy. In fact, I could say the same about going to a big party. Too many colors from all the voices and background music. But other stuff is just soothing. And I don't work well in total silence. It's as if part of my brain needs to be occupied with other things in a way that frees me to think."

"I can understand that. I need music when I'm working, too. It's as if it locks down distractions."

"I've thought about that sometimes. It seems to me as if the brain insists on multitasking, so people get their best focus going when they induce controlled multitasking by listening to music, or maybe running a TV in the background. Whatever it takes."

It struck her then that this man was opening up entire new worlds of thought to her. He definitely came at life with a different perspective. And she liked it.

Danger! screamed a little voice in her head. She had to watch that. This man might be widowed, but to her way of thinking he was still a married man, the worst kind of married man, because there was no way you could divorce a dead wife you still loved.

Ugly thought, maybe, but she'd been burned before, badly. Sometimes compassion had to give way to self-defense.

"So," she said, clearing her throat, "can you give me an example of what you mean by seeing colors when you hear music?"

"Sure. Ravel's 'Bolero.' I always see a kind of kaleidoscope of reds and blacks in various shades. I'd call it a visually coherent piece of music."

She nodded, trying to imagine it. "Another one?"

He cocked his head, then named the music coming over the speakers right now. "'On the Road Again.' It's mostly in shades of yellow and browns with a background thread of…hmm…greens. You know, when I concentrate on it, it gets harder to define because the colors are shifting. This song certainly has more colors in it than 'Bolero.'"

"But not enough to bother you."

"No."

"Wow. You really have a different way of looking at the world."

One corner of his mouth lifted. "I've heard that before."

"But wouldn't you have to in order to perform research?"

"I suppose I could use that excuse. I am what I am. But enough about me. Who are you, Trish Devlin?"

The question surprised her, even though it was a fair one. And it caused her to think. How *did* she think of herself? What did she see of herself reflected in others, like her friends?

"That's a hard question to answer," she said finally. "I don't think of myself in those terms."

"Then how do you think of yourself?"

"I'm a CPA. I have a pretty good job and I'm chief accountant at the semiconductor plant here. I own—well, the bank owns—my own home, that cute little house you've been staring at. I have friends, some I've known my entire life. I lived in Boston for a few years where I worked for a large accounting firm, and then spent about six months in Dallas at corporate headquarters where they trained me for my current position." She gave a little shrug. "It's been a pretty ordinary life so far." With one glaring exception, which was probably pretty ordinary, too, no matter how painful.

"You sound job-oriented."

"I guess mostly I am. Is there something wrong with that?"

"I'd be the last person to suggest any such thing. Until…last year, I was pretty job-oriented, too. Any hobbies?"

"I'm a pretty avid reader, I love hiking and I actually look forward to winter because I love to cross-country ski."

"If it snows before I go home, maybe I'll give cross-country a try."

"Wouldn't that be painful?"

"Probably. There's very little that isn't right now. If I let it stop me, I'd be in a padded cell."

She nodded, not quite sure how to respond. The usual phrases that sprang to mind didn't seem very useful. And somehow she suspected that he didn't want to hear

I'm sorry. So she switched tack again. "You seem pretty certain you'll be going home soon."

He closed his eyes a moment. "Yeah. I think that's in the near future. I can't run forever. Not that it's done me much good."

Another reason to push down her awakening interest. He'd be leaving. A sigh almost escaped her, because she was a normal woman, despite her past stupidity, and she would have liked to once again be in love. To know those wonderful, heady moments, the indescribable elation and joy. Nothing else in life could ever compare.

In fact, she was getting to the point where she would have liked to have a fling, something emotionally unthreatening, something to give her days the promise of excitement and pleasure around the next corner.

Heck, she thought in a moment of uncharacteristic sourness, she was becoming utterly drab. Boring.

"Penny?" he said.

She understood the reference immediately. "More like a quarter these days. But sorry, I'll just keep these thoughts to myself."

He leaned back a little, his dark eyes reflecting something kind. "I know that sort of thing all too well. How about we blow this joint and take a little walk in the cold? I need to move before I get too stiff."

"Won't the cold make it worse?"

"Not as much as the sitting."

He insisted on paying the bill and she didn't argue. Now that she knew who he was, it would be ungracious. Surely her mother had raised her better than that.

They put their carryout boxes in her car and began to head up the street toward the courthouse square. Like many old county seats, the town had been built around the square, the old brick building with its pillars and dome fronted by a couple of acres of park with paths and benches and the requisite metal statue. An old-timer with a gun. Settler? Civil War vet? No one seemed to know for sure, and no one really cared.

She pointed at it. “See that statue? It’s been painted many times over the years by the graduating senior class. Vandalism? Of course. But fun? Oh, yeah. The sheriff seldom makes a serious attempt to find the pranksters and cleaning the statue had become a standard part of the town’s budget. We wonder every spring which color it’s going to be. I even hear there are bets riding on it.”

He chuckled. “I like that. Most places would probably get upset about it.”

They crossed the street, then stepped onto the sidewalk that ran around the edge of the entire square.

“When this place was a frontier town,” she remarked, “the park was used for grazing.”

“Like the Commons in Boston.”

She smiled at him. “The same, only smaller. But we were a much smaller town back then. You could number the families in the dozens at most.”

He limped along beside her, but didn’t seem to want her to slow her pace any. “Go on. Nobody’s bothered to share the history with me in any of the places I’ve been.”

“Maybe not everyone cares or knows. Anyway, the founders were people who had come west on the

Oregon Trail, then stopped shortly after they got to Fort Laramie. Apparently, they saw something attractive in all the grasslands."

"Seems to have worked so far."

"So far. Good times and bad times. We even had a brief gold-mining rush up there in the mountains. The ruins of their little town and their mines are still up there, but dangerous to visit. The mines collapse sometimes, and the buildings themselves are on the verge of coming down, too."

"But people go, anyway."

"How did you know?"

He actually laughed, a very nice sound. "Something about human nature, I guess."

"Well, I've gone up there myself. I guess most folks around here have at one time or another. It's like a different world. The park service has roped off the areas they know to be dangerous, and there are lots of warning signs."

"Just more temptation."

"Apparently. Anyway, historically speaking, the lodes ran out fast. Placer mining lasted longer, and from time to time someone will camp up there to pan in the creek. Occasionally someone finds a bit of gold, but there's never enough to make it more than a fun vacation."

"I think we've pretty much found all the worthwhile gold deposits."

"That would be my guess." They reached the square and began to walk around it, first passing the sheriff's office in its corner storefront across from the square.

"Are your founding families still around?"

"Gage Dalton's wife is descended from one, the original Conard family. I think others left over the years. Life here was never easy, and for people who came here in the first place looking for greener pastures, well…it would be my guess some thought another place might be greener."

"I'd agree with your guess. Imagine the kind of people willing to pack up their lives and move into the unknown, with all its dangers, to try to find something better."

"I think that attitude still infects a lot of us."

"Maybe it's genetic. Who knows." He paused, looking up at the courthouse, then to the businesses that framed the square on the other side of the street. "There's something almost New England about this place."

"I don't think that was an accident."

"I don't think so, either. But you've got your share of ugly sprawl around the edges."

"Oh, yeah. And more since the semiconductor plant came to town. We've actually grown a little bit, which I guess is good considering we were shrinking for a long time. Kids tend to stay now, and we'll probably get a junior college in the next couple of years."

He resumed his limping walk around the square. "You were fortunate to get the plant. Most of that work is going overseas these days."

"Not *this* kind of work."

He paused again and looked down at her. "I see. *That* kind of work. On stuff that can't be legally exported."

"Basically."

"I'll be honest with you. I'm of two minds on that."

"Why?"

"Well, I'm a researcher. I've had papers pulled prepublication on national security grounds. And I got annoyed because knowledge grows faster when you can share it. When you box it off by itself and limit it to only a handful of minds, you can hold back progress."

"I guess I can see that. So what's your other mind on this?"

He half smiled. "It keeps jobs here. And God knows, I've seen enough people hurt by companies that are looking for cheaper labor in other parts of the world."

She nodded. "That's absolutely true."

"So," he said, resuming the walk, "I can see both sides of the issue. And I guess if preventing technology from being exported without a license keeps jobs here, then I have to approve of it. I didn't move *my* company to Dubai, after all. Everything I needed was right here, and I was willing to pay fairly for it."

"How many employees do you have?"

"Three hundred the last time I counted. Cozy, actually."

"Is everyone in research?"

"Naw. We had projects in other areas, nuts and bolts stuff. The place where the rubber meets the road." He glanced at her almost impishly. "Just because I was living in an ivory tower most of the time didn't mean that's all we did."

If she wasn't careful, she was *really* going to like this guy. And considering the strength of the physical attraction she had felt earlier, that was no good. Not if he was leaving soon.

Almost as if he read her abrupt change in mood, he started limping faster, back toward her car. “Can I cadge a ride back to the motel?” he asked. “I need to rest this hip.”

“Sure. Want me to bring the car over here?”

“I can make it.”

Or maybe, she thought after she dropped him off, he’d sensed the same growing attraction she had.

And maybe he was running from it just as fast as she was.

Chapter 5

He was going to have to tell her.

Grant lay on the bed in his motel room and stared at the ceiling, waiting for the grinding and throbbing pain in his hip to ease up a bit. He took nothing for pain anymore except over-the-counter stuff, which gave him minimal relief, but didn't cloud his mind the way a prescription medicine would have. Nor did they raise the specter of addiction.

Although sometimes he wondered why he even cared about that. Life, until just lately, had become something to be endured, not something to be enjoyed. He hadn't cared whether he lived or died.

But something was changing. He could feel it inside. Good or bad, he didn't know, but on some level he'd always known the time would come when he would move on emotionally. He just didn't know if he was ready to yet.

Besides, there was a far more important issue: Trish Devlin.

God, how was he going to tell her? She probably already thought he was crazy, with his talk about synesthesia. Until recently, even science had thought synesthetes were merely nut jobs. Why had he even brought that up?

But he knew why. He needed her to know him, so she wouldn't just totally dismiss him when he told her what was happening. Because he was going to have to tell her. And in order to get her to understand, he was going to have to revisit the tragedy that had put him on the road in the first place.

He closed his eyes against the sting of tears that invariably still welled up when he thought of his family. The day-long crying jags were gone, as were the mindless rages, but tears still came.

He swore and tried to roll onto his side without unleashing another dagger of pain. He succeeded, and with a sigh of relief opened his eyes again. The lone tear that had managed to escape dripped onto his pillow.

Nothing interesting to look at, not even the framed Western-themed prints that posed as art on the walls. This was where his journey had brought him: a fleabag motel on the outskirts of a town that seemed to live on the edge of world. Certainly on the edge of any reality he had ever really known.

He liked the place. Despite being a stranger in a strange town, despite being questioned by a cop in a way he had never before been questioned. Despite being on some foggy kind of mission that he couldn't quite bring into focus beyond a few visual images and an overriding compulsion.

He even liked Maude's manner. At Maude's, he had concluded, you got what you got and, damn, it tasted good. None of the expense of nouvelle cuisine or soy milk for people who couldn't just give something up, but demanded a substitute. God help your arteries. If you cared about them, anyway, and he'd quit caring about that, along with a whole bunch of other things.

So his lawyer hadn't sold his business to his partners. Well, actually, his partners had probably refused to buy his share. Don was a good lawyer and would have done exactly as instructed, regardless of whether he believed it to be temporary insanity.

Maybe it had been. After talking with Trish today, he'd started to feel the itch again, a desire to return to his unfinished research. To the equations that painted pictures in his mind of a reality that maybe only someone like Picasso could begin to grasp.

But now Trish had stopped being afraid of him. Which would have been good, except Trish Devlin still needed to be afraid. She very much needed to be afraid.

But how could he tell her? How could he get anyone to believe the truth of why he had come here?

He believed it only because of experience. Only

because the last time he hadn't believed, he'd paid the dearest price imaginable.

So he had to figure out how to tell her. How to persuade her. Because if he failed, it could cost her everything.

Slowly, he began to turn things around in his mind, examining what he thought he knew from every angle, seeking the key that would get through to her.

And then he noticed something he'd never noticed before.

Popping up from the bed, he pulled on heavy clothing and set out on yet another mission.

After dropping Grant at the motel, Trish had taken a drive through the country, soaking up the beauty of the day from the warmth of her car. Then she made a short stop at the grocery to find something she felt like cooking for her dinner. After that she did a little research on synesthesia, decided Grant was far from nuts and took another walk, a short one because despite the promise of warmer temperatures the next day, today seemed to be growing ever colder.

Just as another bank of clouds began to move in, darkening the afternoon, she answered her front door to find Grant standing there with a squirming ball of fur in his arms. "You need a dog," he said without ado.

"I do?" She stared blankly.

"You do." He held the animal out to her. It appeared to her untutored eyes to be a mutt with golden fur. "Shouldn't you have asked me first?"

"Probably, but then I'd have to explain."

"You're going to have to explain, anyway."

A rueful smiled curved his mouth. "Why did I figure that would be your reaction?"

"Maybe because you don't dump this kind of responsibility on someone without clearing it first."

"Point taken." His smile vanished. "Trust me, you need a dog. This guy was abandoned at the vet's by someone who couldn't pay a bill. He's in perfect health, he's had all his shots, doesn't have worms, and I even paid for day care for him in advance so you don't have to worry about what he might get up to while you're at work."

How was it that he was making her feel ungracious by not taking the dog?

Just as irritation began to replace shock, those big brown eyes turned toward her, and she received the full impact of floppy ears and an imploring gaze.

"You are so unfair," she said, whether to Grant or the dog she didn't know. She reached out, took the dog in her arms and instantly fell in love. Which was every dog's stock-in-trade, of course. Instant love. When he licked her cheek tentatively, the deal was sealed.

"He's adorable," she admitted.

"Small, but not too small, if you know what I mean. The vet says he's not much of a barker unless something makes him uneasy. Good watchdog."

Watchdog. Why should he think she needed a watchdog? The back of her scalp began to prickle uneasily. She looked from the dog to Grant. "I think we need to have another talk. Come on in."

He hesitated. "About what?"

"About why you think I need a watchdog."

"Poor choice of word, maybe."

"Somehow you don't strike me as the type who chooses his words poorly."

As she watched him, he seemed to go away to some distant place again. Finally, he spoke. "Look, it's hard to explain. I bought stuff for the little guy, so let me just get it."

She looked past his shoulders and saw that he seemed to have arrived in one of the few cars available for rental in town. "Uh, no," she said. "He can survive with a bowl of water for a little while, and I can provide that. You're not going to escape so easily."

He sighed, seemed to check some inner barometer, then nodded and stepped inside, closing the door behind him. She led the way to her kitchen, where she filled a soup bowl with water for the dog. He seemed grateful for it and lapped happily at it.

"How old is he, and what's his name?"

"Vet says he's about a year old. Housebroken, although you might have to remind him the rules haven't changed just because his house has. As for his name…I didn't ask because I figured you'd want to name him."

"How thoughtful." She couldn't quite keep the tiniest edge of sarcasm out of her voice. But she waved Grant to a seat at the table and poured coffee for them both.

He thanked her as she took a seat across from him.

"So let's get back to this watchdog thing," she said, refusing to skirt the issue. "Why did you say that?"

"It's...just a feeling I have."

"Must be a pretty strong feeling."

Again a moment of hesitation, then, "Yeah, it is. *Very* strong."

"Enough to make you dump a dog on me."

He returned her stare squarely. "Most definitely."

"And I'm supposed to believe your feeling?"

"You don't have to believe it. I'm the only one who has to believe it. Although it might help if you'd at least try it on for size."

She had been leaning forward on her elbows, but now she leaned back and straightened a bit. "Grant, do you have even the foggiest idea how weird you sound sometimes?"

"Oh, believe me, I do. I sound weird to myself, even after what I've experienced."

The dog, still nameless, had begun to sniff around her ankles, learning something about her. The inevitable resulted: she reached down to gently scratch some very soft fur around some very soft ears. "Maybe you need to stop being so enigmatic and start telling me straight out what you think is going on here."

"I'd like to. And I will, once I figure out how."

"What is so hard about it?"

"You won't believe me."

They sat there, staring at one another. Trish honestly didn't know what to say. Worse, even in the face of frustration and annoyance, she was feeling that inexorable tug toward him. That unmistakable yearning that wanted to pool between her thighs. How was it possible to feel desire and impatience at the same time? Both a longing to take him into her bed and throw him out?

But that's what she was feeling, and her breath caught as she saw a spark flare in his eyes, as if he felt it, too. And then she saw the same shock she had felt, the awareness that this was not something he wanted to feel.

"I'll go get the dog stuff," he said abruptly. With a grimace, he pushed out of his chair and limped back to the front door.

"What the hell?" Trish said to the empty room. If she hadn't known better, she might have thought the universe was laughing at her discomfiture.

For the first time in a long time, the atmosphere seemed pregnant with possibilities.

"God, no." She put her forehead in her hand and closed her eyes.

She wasn't going to fall for some nut job who was just passing through. Maybe he hadn't always been a nut job, but whatever else he was, he was *leaving soon.*

A few minutes later he returned to the kitchen carrying a couple of large plastic bags in one hand, and a huge bag of dog food over his shoulder. She looked up and blinked at the size of the dog food bag.

"What did you give me? A Saint Bernard?"

"No, but the dry stuff lasts and I didn't think it would be nice to leave you with a dog and no way to care for it. And you have thirty days to take him back to the vet if it doesn't work out."

She looked at the dog, maybe just a little larger than a cocker spaniel, which started sniffing around the bag of food as Grant put it down. "As if anyone can return a dog after thirty days."

"Well, then, tomorrow if you can't stand it. I'll even do the dirty work."

Afraid of feeling the attraction again, she nevertheless looked up at him. And there it was, a sudden pang in parts she'd been pretending no longer existed. Maybe, said some imp in her mind, it wouldn't hurt just to have one roll in the hay.

Even if she wasn't normally the type to do that.

Grant sank into his chair again, opening the plastic bags. "Dishes," he said, showing her the contents of one—two large stainless-steel bowls. "Toys, collar and leash," he said, opening the other and emptying its contents.

He picked up a plush toy covered in fake lamb's wool and squeezed it. It squeaked, which caused the dog, for the very first time, to let out a bark of excitement. Grant tossed the toy and the dog skittered across the linoleum at high speed, crashing into the refrigerator just before it snatched up the toy. The pressure of its jaws made the toy squeak again.

Now it was time for the kill. The animal began to shake the toy back and forth. Trish didn't want to admit how adorable the dog was. But he was, anyway.

"Tennis balls," Grant continued, pulling out a pack of four. "The vet says he loves balls. Rubber chew toy, rope tug and some treats. Vet says no more than one pig ear every couple of days, but rawhide is fine."

Finally she said the necessary words. "Thank you. I mean it."

At that he smiled, a heart-melting smile. "I'm glad," he said simply.

The dog seized the toy again, making it squeak, then darted off to another room.

Grant cocked his head. "I think he's already at home."

Somehow those words tugged painfully at her heartstrings. Without a conscious decision, she rose and walked around the table to place her hand on his shoulder.

Grant looked up, and then, as easily as if he did it all the time, slid his arms around her waist and pressed his face to her midriff.

"God," he said shakily.

Tangled in a morass of emotions she couldn't label, Trish stroked his hair with her other hand. One thing she knew for sure: she'd been missing this kind of human touch.

Apparently, so had he, for he pulled her a little closer and turned his head so that his cheek rested against her. He didn't say anything, didn't try anything. Just held on to her as if they were both adrift in a stormy sea.

The problem was, he seemed to be the only one who knew the dimensions of the sea.

Forcing herself to ignore impulses as old as nature, she eased away. It almost hurt physically to do so. He dropped his arms and looked up at her.

For a while, they simply stared at one another. She was fighting an internal struggle between wisdom and need. Whatever he was thinking, it seemed to darken his gaze even more and make him look a little bit lost. As if he needed rescuing.

And he probably did, but she wasn't in the rescuing business, she reminded herself. She'd fallen for that hook, line and sinker in Boston, and had ever after sworn off any man who appeared to need rescuing.

But the ever nosy observer in her head reminded her, Jackson had claimed he needed rescuing. This guy hadn't asked for it in even the smallest way. Quite the contrary, he kept intimating that *she* needed rescuing or protecting.

"You *have* to tell me," she said. "You *have* to. How else can I ever trust you?"

"I know." He sighed and ran his fingers through his short hair. "I've been trying since you dropped me at the motel to figure out a way. I guess all I can do is spit it out and let you make your own judgments, good or bad. But in the meantime, can I move to a softer chair?"

"Sure. I'll bring more coffee into the living room. Sit wherever you're most comfortable."

She joined him only a minute later. He'd settled at one end of the couch, his lame leg stretched out before him and propped on the small hassock.

"Thanks," he said as he accepted the mug. Nearby the dog was pulling at the squeak toy, holding it between his paws and tugging with his teeth, evidently determined to get at the source of the noise.

Trish took the easy chair, which placed her close to Grant, but with an end table between them. "So start," she said.

"I'm not sure exactly where to begin, so I may ramble."

"Ramble away."

"Okay." He took a deep breath. "I've always been afraid of flying. I don't know why. I mean, logically it's about the safest way to travel, and I had to do it all the time. You'd have thought that uneasiness would wear off." He looked at her.

"Sometimes people feel that way because of control issues," she offered. "They feel safer in a car, even though they're not, because they're at the wheel."

"Maybe. Someone suggested that to me, so I took up playing with a flight simulator. Learning how to fly a plane in the safest place possible—my own desk chair."

"Did it help?"

"I thought so. A little. I was just getting to the point of deciding that maybe I needed to take a few flying lessons. Try to push myself over that hump. I mean, I know I didn't have a true phobia, because I could still get on a flight, but at the back of my mind I feared that if I gave in to it at all, it *might* become a full-blown phobia."

This guy, she thought, had a lot of grit and determination. Most people she knew with phobias preferred not to even think about them, let alone face them head-on. "Back in Boston I had a coworker with such severe claustrophobia she refused to take the elevator. So every day she went up and down nine flights of stairs."

"Good for her health," he remarked with a small smile.

"That's what she said when anyone suggested she might want to get treatment. It made a good excuse, but when you consider her claustrophobia wasn't limited to elevators, it didn't make sense. She couldn't stand to be in windowless rooms, for example. She couldn't fly anywhere if she had to get on one of those small puddle-jumpers. You know the flights I mean. Thirty passengers max. She felt like the plane was closing in on her and might crush her."

He nodded. "That's tough. And lots of people seem to have that fear."

"Along with the fear of flying," she reminded him.

Again that small smile. "Right back to the point."

"Sorry. That's the way I am."

"I like it." Again he hesitated. Another deep breath.

"So, anyway, I thought I was getting past my fear of flying a bit when I started to have these…visions, for lack of a better word. I would suddenly see myself at the controls of a plane that was nose-diving straight for earth."

"That must have been awful."

"It got worse yet. At first it was just glimpses. Weird, because I'd never been in the cockpit of a 767, let alone at the controls. I brushed it off, figuring my fear was just trying to get the upper hand. I even told myself I was going to get some lessons in a flight trainer so I could put that to rest."

She nodded encouragingly, but realized her heart had begun to thud. Somehow she knew there was horror coming.

"Anyway, I had to fly to New York to give a talk at a conference. I decided to take my family because Laura loved the city and Penny, our daughter, had never been there. She was only seven. Big family vacation is what I thought, maybe even a stopover in D.C. to introduce Penny to some of our history."

"That would have been lovely."

"Yeah, it would have. We never got to do it." He clenched his teeth and his hands tightened into fists. "From the time I made the reservations, those visions became more insistent. More frequent. I kept telling myself it was just ramping up because of the trip."

"A reasonable assumption," she said quietly. *Here it comes.* She didn't know if she could bear to listen.

"Anyway," he went on, "the night before the trip I had this vivid dream. I was at the controls of the plane again, but this time as we augered into the ground I could hear my wife and daughter screaming."

"My God!" Her heart was hammering now, and she could see sweat bead his brow even though the room was a little on the chilly side.

"Yeah," he said almost bitterly. "I woke up from that nightmare and spent the next hours before boarding telling myself it was only a nightmare, it couldn't possibly be anything else, and besides, I'd been warned that when you fight something like a phobia, one of the stages is when the phobia pushes back hard. At least that was the thinking. Besides, how could it mean anything when I saw myself in the pilot's seat?"

She nodded, knowing what he was going to say, knowing there was nothing she could offer to change any of it, any part of it.

"I was afraid to give in to a fear," he said harshly. "I was going to master it. Yeah, I really did a good job. You read the stories about what happened. It wasn't till I woke in the hospital three days later that I realized my dream, my *vision,* had been true. I'd just seen it from the *pilot's* perspective."

"Oh, God," she whispered, knowing now what he'd meant about guilt. Her chest tightened until she wondered if she could draw another breath. Aching for him, she closed her eyes and kept her silence. The horror was beyond imagining, yet what she *could* imagine hurt beyond words. How in the world did someone deal with something like that?

"I had some back surgery," he went on, his voice low, tight. "Some physical therapy, even some psychological therapy. But nothing, absolutely *nothing* could prepare me for going home to an empty house when it was my fault."

"It wasn't your fault!" The words, useless in the extreme, burst out of her.

"It will be *this* time," he ground out.

Her hammering heart seemed to stop. Shock washed over her in a cold wave. Finally she managed to stammer, "Wh-what do you m-mean?"

But he chose not to answer her directly. At least not right away. "You know I went on the road. I've been hitchhiking all over the country. Moving. Always moving, as if I could get away from my own head. And of course, I couldn't. I'll never get away from my own head."

All of a sudden she realized her fingers ached. Looking down she saw that she had dug them into the arms of her chair. With effort, she loosened her grip. She didn't want to hear this. She *didn't.* But as if she was caught in a waking nightmare, she couldn't tell him to stop.

"I wasn't just running from grief and guilt," he said after a moment. "I was running from what those visions and dreams might mean."

"How so?" But did she really want to know?

"I've spent a year wondering how it could be possible to see the future. And if it *is* possible, can we change it? Was that crash a fixed future event regardless of what I might have done? Or could I have changed something?"

He heart resumed a heavy beating, not a pleasant feeling. Some part of her wanted to stop this conversation *now,* while another part argued that she had to get her answers, like it or not. Apart from finding Grant sexually attractive, he had another characteristic that made her extremely uncomfortable: he could raise more conflicting feelings in her than rooting for both teams in a football game. She hated feeling conflicted, and she wasn't sure she liked the way he was changing her view of the world. There was something to be said for the familiar, after all, but he was leading her to the edge of things she wasn't sure she could, or wanted, to deal with.

Conflicted or not, however, she was pretty sure she was going to take this journey one way or another.

"Theoretically," he said slowly, "these are fascinating questions. When they become personal, though, they get a whole lot tougher to deal with."

"I'm feeling pretty much the same thing right now."

He looked at her, his eyes reflecting an old pain. "In theory, quantum physics says precognition is possible.

But in theory time can move backward. How often do we see that?"

"Not very."

"So as a rule, you go with the way the world works. Time doesn't move backward. Okay. But there is some experimental evidence that we can foresee probabilities in the future. Most of those experiments suggest we could look ahead three seconds max. Not enough to really count in any big way. But then you come up against something like my visions and nightmares."

"Yeah," she said softly, trying to turn it around in her mind. "Yeah. Hard to explain, hard to believe, hard to even imagine *why*."

"Until it happens to you. Then you believe, but everything else gets harder."

Again she felt a pang for him. He must hurt in ways she couldn't even begin to grasp, in ways no amount of reassurance could ease. "But you couldn't possibly have known that nightmare was anything except a nightmare."

"True. Doesn't help much, but true." He looked at her. "But you see, it had an effect. An abiding effect. So about six weeks ago when I started to have more visions, I knew better than to ignore them. I paid attention. I waited, because somehow I knew that if I was envisioning this stuff, I was going to wind up exactly where the vision showed. Just the way I wound up on that plane."

She drew a sharp breath, and fear began an icy crawl along her spine. "What? How…?" The only thing she knew right then was that she wasn't going to like what he was about to say.

"I got to the truck stop here, and I knew. I just knew. This was the place. And when I found the bar, just as I'd seen it in my vision, I became convinced. So I started walking and I found that park bench right across the street. Just the way I had seen it."

She wanted to yell at him to shut up, to stop, that he was scaring her and he must be insane. But all the protests died before they reached her lips as the cold fingers of fear tightened her throat.

"Someone," he said, "is going to try to kill you."

Chapter 6

"Are you out of your mind?" She leaped up from her chair and glared at him. "Is this some twisted kind of joke?"

His face tightened, but he said nothing. Merely shook his head, very slowly.

"You come here from nowhere, worm your way into my life, and now you expect me to believe you've had a vision that someone is going to kill me?" She had raised her voice, but she didn't care. She was tumbling, tumbling fast into an alternate universe of shock, disbelief and the darkness of fear. Only, she had no way to know what exactly she should fear.

"*Try* to kill you," he said evenly, quietly.

"What difference does it make? Are you threatening me?"

"God, no!"

She could see him coil as if to stand, but he didn't. Maybe he hurt too much. Maybe he thought it would appear intimidating. As if she cared.

He spread his hands beseechingly. "I don't care if you ever talk to me again. I don't care if you throw me out. All I want is for you to be on the alert. And all I'm going to do is sit on that damn park bench every *damn* night until I'm sure you're safe."

Then he did push up off the sofa, using his arms for leverage. A small gasp escaped him as he straightened, but he didn't hesitate. He took two steps away from her, giving her space, before saying, "Call me crazy, call me names. But I ignored these visions once, and I owe it to my wife and daughter not to do it again. If you have a gun, load it and keep it close."

Then he limped toward the door.

She stood frozen, angry and stunned. Wanting to grab him and make him take it all back. And afraid, so very afraid, that he might not be crazy at all.

The front door closed behind him.

"Lock it!" she heard him yell from outside. Then, moments later, the car he had arrived in sped off.

She locked the front door. She ran through the house and locked every window, checked every door, all the while telling herself that Grant had been pushed over the edge by the loss of his family, that he couldn't possibly mean what he was saying, and even if he did he couldn't possibly *know* anything about the future....

And then she collapsed on a chair in her office, wrapped her arms around herself, and began to rock back and forth, unable to believe, unable to *dis*believe him.

Eventually something nudged her leg gently. She looked down and saw the nameless dog. He gave an uncertain wag of his tail, looking up at her hopefully. Helpless to do anything else, she scooped him up into her arms and held him close for comfort. Apparently, he liked that enough to lick her face with a soft tongue. Just a couple of tentative licks, as if testing the relationship.

Trying to let go of her knotted emotions, she buried her face against his soft, furry neck and rocked gently in her chair.

She should call Gage about this. But then she knew she couldn't. For the same reason that Grant had had so much difficulty telling her, for the same reason he hadn't merely come into town and headed straight to the sheriff's office with his story.

Who would believe his vision? And if you didn't believe him, there was only one other conclusion to reach: he was insane.

And if you reached that conclusion...

She sighed and eased her hold on the dog. He used the opportunity to give her another tiny lick, then burrowed himself in close against her shoulder.

"I need to name you," she said, hardly aware of the words escaping her, not even really thinking about them.

She had read plenty about Grant Wolfe on the Web.

Plenty. All of it showed him to be a responsible citizen, a brilliant man, someone who had suffered a tragedy beyond imagining. Did she want to be responsible for adding to his problems by passing along a story that might get him into trouble?

Even as horrified and angry as she felt by his prediction, if you could call it that, she wished the man no ill.

Gently she put the dog down. "Tad," she said, though she had no idea where the name had come from. "You're Tad."

He wagged his tail as if he liked it.

Then she went to do the only thing she could: she got her dad's shotgun.

Bonehead! That was probably the nicest name Grant applied to himself in the next hour. After dropping the car off at the rental place—a garage, really, where they had a handful of cars to rent—he limped back to the motel and dropped onto the bed like a six-foot slab of stone.

What had he been thinking?

But of course, that really wasn't the question. Unsure of his own ability to successfully intervene in the vision that plagued him, he'd made the really *boneheaded* decision to tell Trish so that she'd be on guard. That's what he had been thinking.

Had he even for one deluded moment believed she would accept that news as if he'd just remarked that it was a nice day? Of course not.

In fact, right now he wouldn't be surprised if the sheriff showed up again, this time to tell him to get out of town. That would make things easy; he'd be driven off and wouldn't—couldn't—drive himself nuts with this feeling of responsibility. Hah! Sure. You bet.

But part of him had hoped Trish wouldn't totally sunder the tentative relationship they'd begun, because he really felt it would be best if they could work together somehow.

Or maybe, if he was honest with himself, he was actually enjoying making a human connection for the first time in a long time.

But if that was so, what the hell was he thinking, racing headlong into the one thing he could have told her that would cause her to never want to see him again?

Had he become self-destructive?

Possible. Entirely possible. He had thought he'd moved past the days early on when he had sometimes contemplated suicide as an antidote to the grief that had been tearing him apart. But maybe he'd just moved to a different phase.

The sheriff didn't knock, of course. Even if Trish had called him, Grant doubted that anyone had the authority to throw someone out of town. That was for Gary Cooper and John Wayne, for movies, not for reality.

Instead, he lay there waiting for night to come, waiting for his mission to resume. Turning his memory of his visions around in his mind as he sought any possible new clue.

The visions were scattershot. First he had seen someone in a darkened house with a silenced gun, stalking a woman who had turned out to be Trish, reaching her room, then raising the gun, pointing it toward the bed in the shadows….

Nothing.

Then he'd seen a man sitting at what had turned out to be Mahoney's bar. He'd gotten a clear vision of the clock over the bar showing the time—twelve-fifty—as the man got up and walked out into the night.

Then the park bench.

Then the outside of Trish's house. The sight of a hand cutting a wire. He assumed a phone line, but he didn't know for certain.

And he'd gotten the clearest vision of Trish. He'd known her before he clapped eyes on her.

Gradually, over the past month or so, a picture had emerged, enough that he had been able to piece together a sense of what he needed to do. Knew the instant he reached the truck stop across the highway that *this* was where he needed to do it.

So every night he walked into Mahoney's bar and waited until the hour at which the gunman was supposed to leave. Waited to see if some stranger arrived, then left on time.

But he was the only one who arrived and left at that time. So far.

Then he limped down the street to the park and Trish's house, and he waited. Waited because someplace deep inside he knew the killer wouldn't approach from the front. Knew that his presence on the bench wouldn't prevent what might happen.

He knew, somehow, that every night he was following the killer's intended path until the point where he reached the house. Right before that, except for the vision of the gunman in her bedroom, everything splintered.

Maybe because everything wasn't fixed in cement. That was the only hope he could cling to. That something he might do, that something Trish might do, could keep that man from shooting her in bed.

That between them, one or both of them would do the critical thing to shift the probabilities just enough to save her life.

He had to believe that. Even before he had met Trish, he had had to believe that.

Because he couldn't stand the thought of living in a world where the future was fixed. Couldn't even begin to believe in such a place.

But now, there was something he couldn't stand even more: the possibility that Trish might die.

With a groan, he rolled onto his side and pounded the mattress just once with his fist. The theories that had fascinated him for so long had become more than theories. They had become a living hell he couldn't seem to escape.

That night Grant was on the park bench again, and just like every other night, he left after about twenty minutes. Only then did Trish go to bed.

The next morning she ran errands and tried to stay out of the house, taking the dog on a long walk in the countryside and finally returning home in the late afternoon, tired and somehow more frazzled than she'd been earlier.

The smell of gun oil hit her nose the instant she

entered the kitchen, and carried her back to the days when she and her father had often used the shotgun on critters in the field behind the house. They hadn't really wanted to kill anything, just scare them away.

"Trish," he'd said to her on more than one occasion, "birdshot is really all you need. And I wouldn't load anything more powerful into this gun unless I decided to go hunting big game. It's enough to scare the birds, and inside the house it's the safest load for self-defense. Inside of twenty feet, it'll hit as hard as buckshot. Do we have anyplace in the house big enough to need more than that?"

She still didn't have any place in the house to need more than that. What's more, she didn't want to be shooting anything that might go out her window and into a neighbor's with deadly force.

The birdshot she loaded into the gun had been purchased recently. Her dad had always told her to keep fresh ammunition, so she regularly bought a new small box and donated her old stuff to the local gun club.

The trip back to childhood made her close her eyes. Her mom had died when she was ten, bled out on the kitchen floor from an ovarian cyst while no one was at home, and then she'd lost her dad to a heart attack just after she graduated from college. The last time she had seen him alive, he'd been beaming from ear to ear at her graduation dinner. Then she had flown to Boston to join her new firm, only to come home a month later for a funeral.

But her dad was still with her, especially as she held his old shotgun. She could still see his work-hardened and gnarled hands holding it, showing her how to treat it with respect and caution.

How he would say, "I know plenty of folks who say guns don't kill, people do. To some extent they're right. But guns can also kill in the hands of people who don't know how to handle them. So you're going to learn how to handle this, Trish. You never know when you might need it."

So out they would go to some isolated place on their small ranch and shoot away for an hour or two. It had been fun, actually. Lots of fun. Maybe because it was time with her dad when they weren't busy with chores. Maybe because target shooting was just a fun pastime.

And in the weeks immediately following her mother's death, target shooting had even felt therapeutic.

Birdshot is just as good as buckshot within twenty feet. She checked the load yet again, five rounds, and closed the chamber. Then she flicked on the safety.

And wondered briefly if she was nuts to even be doing this.

No, she decided, this was not nuts. No more nuts than making sure she always had fresh ammo on hand, as her dad had taught her. This was just caution, plain and simple. It didn't mean she believed Grant was right, it didn't mean she believed someone would actually try to kill her. It merely meant that if something bad *did* happen, she'd be ready.

That was most definitely *not* nuts.

Sighing, she looked down at Tad, who was lying patiently on her feet on the linoleum. He seemed to be a singularly content young dog. She probably ought to take him for another long walk, but after Grant's announcement yesterday, she was absurdly skittish about going outside, even if Grant did seem to think the threat would come in the middle of the night.

Like most people, she couldn't imagine why anyone would want to kill her. But the thing was, the world was littered with innocent victims who'd never done a thing to deserve such an attack. There didn't have to be a reason. If you let yourself really think about it, that was the scariest thing of all.

So people didn't think about it, herself included. Until today.

She thought once again about calling Gage, but she could just imagine how he'd react if she told him about Grant's vision. Hell, he would probably be even more annoyed and disbelieving than she was herself. No, that wasn't the route to take. Not unless something more happened.

She took Tad out back to do his business, then returned inside, where she discovered she no longer felt entirely comfortable. Grant had done that to her. The safety of home no longer seemed inviolable.

That alone should have been enough to make her furious with him. Instead, now that the first shock had passed, she was feeling sorry for him. If he'd really had those visions before he lost his family, then she could understand why he was so obsessed now. Guilt. Atonement. Maybe a type of sad mental disconnect, an attempt to recreate an awful event in order to ease his guilt.

Sighing, she put the shotgun on the table, then rested her forehead in her hand, as she often did at work when faced with numbers that weren't working right.

Time to examine her own beliefs about things, she decided. Time to think about where Grant Wolfe fit into her worldview. Time to figure out what disturbed her more: what he had said yesterday or that he might somehow be right.

Did she believe in ESP? Telepathy? Yeah, at some level she did. Like many people, she'd experienced those moments of knowing something she shouldn't have, like who was about to call just before the phone rang, or thinking about someone she hadn't thought about in a while for a day or two before a letter arrived, or an e-mail. As if she knew they were thinking of her, too.

At times, with Jackson, it had been often enough and significant enough to really catch her attention. With her dad sometimes, too, although she had always put that down to knowing him so well.

But precognition? Knowing the future before it happened? That stuck in her craw. She didn't like anything about that.

But Grant's story about his visions and his dream before the plane crash—that was something she couldn't dismiss easily. He hadn't made that up. He believed it. In fact, he'd believed it all along, not just now, because she had read in one of the news articles that he'd said, "I knew something was going to happen. I just knew."

That was something a lot of people said.

She sat up a little straighter. A lot of people said that. How many times had she heard a friend say just that. Or herself? How many times had it been laughed off?

I knew I was going to spill that.

I had a weird feeling at that intersection yesterday, and look what happened to me!

Honestly, when she thought about it, people frequently intimated that they knew something was going to happen before it happened. Big or small, explicable or laughed off, they said things all the time that indicated they had somehow known *something.*

Well, what if it wasn't coincidence? *What if sometimes people really do know?*

She'd been feeling uneasy for days before Grant had shown up on that park bench. In fact, that very uneasiness had been the only reason she'd looked out and seen him, the only reason she kept looking for him, the only reason she'd been having trouble sleeping.

Then she had transferred all that uneasiness to Grant, an obvious target.

"Hold on," she said aloud. Tad lifted his head quizzically. "Not you," she said.

He put his head back down, but didn't stop watching her.

"Back up," she said to the empty kitchen. "Go back to the beginning. Think it through."

Rising, she grabbed her wall phone and dialed. Not the sheriff, but the motel. She wanted to talk to Grant, and she wanted to talk to him *now.*

* * *

He was waiting for her outside the motel. The warm front had clouded the sky completely, though it had brought not even a spatter of rain yet. He wore his jacket, unzipped now as the temperature rose, and climbed into her car with her without a greeting.

"I thought," he said, "that you'd have liked it better if I left town."

"I thought so, too, yesterday. But that wasn't a reasoned response."

At that he looked at her. "Do people in real life actually talk that way? I thought only psychologists did."

"I'm a fairly logical person. Not always, but often enough to catch myself eventually."

"Where are we going?"

"My place."

"I'm not sure...." But he trailed off.

"My place," she said firmly. "I don't want to be somewhere with constant interruptions, and I want to eat. Besides, thanks to *someone* I have a dog to worry about."

He gave a bark of laughter. "I seem to be at the core of all your problems."

"I'm not so sure about that anymore. So we're going to talk."

Tad had behaved himself during her brief absence. Indeed, he had chosen to settle into a corner of the living room on a soft patch of rug, sandwiched between a bookcase and some floor pillows she had stacked nearby. A little nest.

"Are you hungry?" she asked Grant.

"More than I should be. I have a fast metabolism."

"Then let's sit in the kitchen while I start dinner. I'm roasting a chicken and steaming broccoli. Do you like your potatoes mashed or baked?"

"Either way. I like potatoes just about every way they come."

He paused on the threshold as he saw the shotgun on the kitchen table. "You didn't exactly ignore me."

"No, I didn't. The safety is on." But she moved the gun, anyway, standing it in a corner, wedged against a cabinet.

"Can I help with dinner?" he asked.

"Just sit. I'll pour us both some coffee, then get started."

He followed her direction, pulling out the chair he had sat in before. Tad decided to join them, and leaned into Grant's leg. Grant obliged with some scratches around the ears.

Grant remained silent, evidently giving her space to marshal her thoughts. She washed the chicken while the oven preheated, then patted it dry. She rubbed it with olive oil and seasonings, taking her time about it, then put it in the roasting pan and popped it into the oven. When she had set the timer and washed her hands, she joined him at the table at last.

"I usually hang out in here until it's time to turn the temperature down," she explained, "but if that chair is uncomfortable for you, let's go into the other room."

He shook his head. "I'll be okay for a while."

"Let me know when you need to move."

He nodded, watching her, slowly scratching the dog behind the ears.

Trish wrapped her hands around her mug and hesitated. "I don't know how to piece this together for you, exactly. You know how the brain works—it hops all around making intuitive connections, then you try to explain it to someone and it's mush."

He nodded. "I'm all too familiar with that. So just go ahead and pick a place. We'll get it together."

"Well, I was sitting here this afternoon, kind of taking a journey down memory lane." She reached out and touched the shotgun, running her fingers lightly over the stock. "This gun was my dad's. We used to use it for scaring birds out of the fields and for target practice. So smelling the gun oil, holding it, took me back. And it made me think about the fact that I had actually cleaned and loaded it—because of what you told me."

He nodded encouragingly, saying nothing.

"So I decided to think about what's been going on, and that's when I realized that for all you unnerved me with what you said yesterday, I had been uneasy even before I saw you."

"Really? Over what?"

"Let me get to that in a minute. I was trying to think about these so-called paranormal things. I guess I already accept telepathy to some extent. I think a majority of people have experienced it one time or another, if not more frequently, and then dismissed it. But precognition…that bothers me."

"Me, too," he agreed. "I can't tell you how much."

She met his gaze. "I think we're probably pretty

close together on that. I mean, who wants to think the future is fixed?"

"I certainly don't. But there's other ways of looking at it."

She drew a deep breath, then said, "I just want to know one thing before I go on."

"I'll tell you if I can."

"How do you know it's *me?* Because you found my house? Or something else?"

"I saw you before I ever met you. I saw you getting ready for bed just before…" He closed his eyes.

Her heart thudded. So *she* had been part of his vision, too.

"You were in your bedroom. You climbed into bed. Then he shows up."

"God." The word came out thinly. With effort, she gathered herself. "Okay. Let's leave that alone for a minute. I can't stand to think about it just yet. But I realized something this afternoon, something important."

"Which is?"

"How often we say or hear others say, *I knew that was going to happen.*"

He sat up a little straighter, dog forgotten, dark eyes growing intent.

Trish hesitated, seeking words, slowly finding them. "We always brush that reaction off. Or almost always, anyway. We say that we must have noticed something subconsciously that warned us. It must have been a coincidence. Lots of reasons to dismiss it."

"Yes, there are."

"But the thing is, *we all say it.* And even if only just a very small percentage of the time there was no clue other than the internal sensing that something was about to happen, that's...that's mind-blowing."

He nodded. "I told you there is experimental evidence that at a rate well beyond statistical chance people are looking two or three seconds ahead."

"Right. Well, like I said, even if only a *very small* percentage of the time, that's what's really happening, then it must be possible sometimes to look even further ahead."

"It's possible," he agreed. "Scientifically possible, whether or not most scientists want to put their heads on the block by saying so."

"Someday, when I'm feeling really brave and really intelligent, I'll ask you about that stuff." She gave him a weak smile. "But right now I'm focused on only one thing."

"Understandable. Go ahead."

"So what I'm talking about here is not necessarily your premonition. It may be mine."

"Yours?" He leaned forward intently.

"Mine. Like I said, I was uneasy before I ever clapped eyes on you. And in retrospect, I was clearly far more uneasy than I should have been. Uneasy enough to get seriously worried about you sitting out there every night, something that I am absolutely convinced wouldn't have bothered me at all up until just recently."

"I'm not sure about that," he said wryly. "I mean, a

total stranger sitting across from your house every night at one in the morning? A lot of people would get uneasy."

"I went past uneasy. I went to the sheriff, feeling like a paranoid idiot for doing so. You did nothing threatening. If I hadn't already been so nervous, I would have thought you were just sitting there to rest your leg. I am, frankly, not usually the kind of person to get in a twitter over nothing."

He nodded. "Okay, we'll take that as a given. I don't know you well enough to say otherwise."

"So I thought back and realized that what I had done was transfer my job anxiety to you."

"And why were you anxious about your job?"

"That's the thing." She looked away, weighing it yet again. "I found some discrepancies between the number of microchips we had manufactured and shipped, and the number we had in inventory. Basically, we're missing chips. So I notified the CFO in Dallas and sent him my numbers. Ordinarily I'd have just put it from my mind then. I'd done my job, I'd reported a discrepancy, and someone would explain it. A batch got destroyed and not reported, a shipment was damaged, my numbers were wrong. Any way you look at it rationally, it was probably no big deal."

"Maybe not."

"What was not rational was the way I started to get nervous. On edge. I started worrying that I'd made a mistake that would get me fired. Which, in all honesty, was a ridiculous overreaction. Even if I *had* made a mistake, all that would happen would be a warning. At the very worst. A warning."

He nodded. "People don't usually get fired over a mistake like that."

"Unless it's on a tax return, anyway." She smiled mirthlessly.

"Well, that's one place it might cause a serious problem," he agreed. "But on inventory? Not likely."

"Exactly. But I couldn't shake the feeling that something terrible was going to happen, and by the time the CFO responded—quite nicely, actually—I'd focused all my anxiety on *you.*"

He nodded. "I see what you're saying."

"But I was sitting here this afternoon, thinking it over, and it struck me, what if all that anxiety I was feeling after I made that report to the CFO had some kind of basis? What if I sensed that it had set something bad in motion, something bad for *me?*"

"Damn." He whispered the word and his gaze grew distant as he thought. She waited, almost on the edge of her seat. The delicious odor of roasting chicken had begun to waft from the oven, and she heard a faint spattering and sizzle. Homey sounds, so far away from what they were discussing.

He finally spoke. "Did the CFO contact you again?"

"I don't know. I'm on vacation, so once his first e-mail put the matter to rest, I stopped checking my work e-mail. I haven't wanted to know, I guess."

He nodded, but now he seemed tense, too. "Do you happen to remember what kind of chips were missing?"

She shook her head. "I don't know one chip from another."

"Is there some way we can find out? Because I *do* know chips."

"Sure." She glanced at the oven timer. "Let me just wait until I turn the chicken down. Five minutes. What are you thinking?"

"I'm not really sure yet. Just show me what you've got so I can noodle it around."

As soon as she turned the chicken down and reset the timer, they went into her small office with one of the kitchen chairs. She insisted that he take her softer task chair while she herself sat on the hard seat of the kitchen chair. Her computer came up quickly from hibernation, but just as she was about to open her e-mail to see if she had anything additional from the CFO, Grant stopped her.

"Are you wireless?"

She twisted to see him better. "No, the company hooks us in by dedicated lines."

"Okay, good. So nobody can see what you're doing."

"Not unless they're watching me on the server."

He nodded. "Go ahead."

She opened her office e-mail, and her heart skipped when she saw another e-mail from Hank. "The CFO wrote me again."

"Check it out."

Did she really want to? But did she have any choice? Telling herself it was probably just a note about when she could expect the auditor, she clicked on it.

* * *

Hey, Trish. The auditor wants to know if you've brought anyone else in on this, or if he needs to wait until you've finished your vacation. Hope you're having fun. Hank.

"Well, that's nothing," she said, but even as she was about to close the e-mail he touched her hand.

"Let me read that again, Trish." He leaned forward, scanning the mail. Then he shook his head. "I don't like that."

"Why not?"

"Because the damn auditor could have contacted you about this directly. Because I doubt he can get an audit going this fast, anyway. I ran a company, remember? I just don't like it. But let me see what chips are missing. Do you have to access that on company files?"

She shook her head. "Actually, no. I sometimes download files here so I can work on them, and that's one of them. But they don't have any technical details, just coded numbers."

"Of course not. Just get me whatever you have about the chip number or description. Write it down. Then let me at your computer and let me use your phone."

"That I can do." She noted that he leaned back so she wouldn't have to worry about him viewing one of the company's internal files. She opened the e-mail she had sent to the CFO to begin with, and quickly on a scrap of paper scribbled down everything she had about the missing chips, including their production number.

She then closed her e-mail account at work and handed Grant the paper. "I'm sure the chip number is a code."

"Most likely. But I have sources."

She left him at her computer and went back to the kitchen to finish dinner preparations. On the face of it Hank's e-mail seemed totally benign, but on another level she knew Grant might be right. If the auditor had a question, he would have her contact information. Someone at Hank's level wouldn't deal with that kind of piddling stuff, would he?

Nope. The answer came to her clearly. So what was going on?

Diced potatoes were boiling on the stove and she was preparing broccoli for the microwave when Grant returned. He limped into the kitchen, dragging the chair with him, then sat at the table.

She faced him. "Well?"

"I've got an old friend looking into the chip involved. He can do it without drawing attention your way." He smiled faintly. "He was glad to hear from me."

She turned back to the broccoli, adding a little butter. "I'm sure he was. I'm sorry if your cover is blown."

At that he chuckled. "It wasn't really cover, and it actually made me feel good to phone Dex and hear his voice again." He paused for a long moment. "Trish. They want me back."

"That must feel wonderful!"

He looked as if he couldn't decide whether to smile or cry, and then simply nodded. "Better than I expected."

She sprinkled a tiny bit of mustard powder onto the

broccoli, then tucked it into the microwave to be turned on just before the chicken was done. A check of the potatoes told her they were boiling at just the right rate. With nothing left to do, she rejoined him at the table.

"So," she asked, "do you think you'll go back?"

"I don't know." He sighed. "I'm starting to feel an urge to get back to work, but I don't know if I can go back to the same place, if you know what I mean. Too many memories, I guess. But the nice thing about my work is that I can do it anywhere. I'll have to think about it. But when Dex asked, 'When are you coming back, G….', I… Trish, I didn't realize how alone I'd felt."

She nodded. "I can understand that. Before I came here, I had a good job in Boston that I had to leave for the same reason. Well, not exactly the same reason, because what happened to me was minor compared to what happened to you. But I couldn't stand all the reminders. And I ended up in Dallas without any friends or family. It's like we don't know who's there until they're not."

His brow elevated. "Can I ask what happened?"

This was something she'd been reluctant to share even with her girlfriends, a subject she had tried to leave behind her in Boston. But maybe the only way to exorcise a demon was to face it head-on. "It was practically a country-Western song."

At that he smiled. "Most of life is a country-Western song."

"I'm beginning to think so." She bit her lower lip, then

said, "I had an affair with a married man. I didn't know he was married, in fact, he told me he was divorced. It's not something I would have done knowingly."

He nodded encouragingly.

"What killed me was discovering that he'd lied to me. If he could lie to me about that, how many other things had he lied about? I felt betrayed and dirty. Used and humiliated."

"I'm sorry," he said gently.

Remembering, she closed her eyes. Anger tried to surface again, but she didn't allow it. "I guess I still feel those things," she said quietly. "All of them. And sometimes they're still strong."

She opened her eyes and peeked at him, daring to see his reaction. All she found was kind understanding, no judgment.

"I'm sorry," he said again. "Sometimes people can do unforgivable things."

"Yeah. And I keep telling myself that his wife must feel a million times worse."

"That doesn't negate what he did to *you,*" Grant said.

"No, but of the two of us, I think she got the worse deal. Getting out was easy for me."

"Did she leave him?"

Trish shrugged one shoulder. "I think she did for a while. I heard something about them going to counseling after a bit. And that's when I decided I needed a new job. People may be well-intentioned, but I didn't want to keep hearing the gossip."

"Are you sure it was well-intentioned?"

"What difference does it make? Oh, I imagine some folks thought I must have known he was still married, but my friends defended me. They, at least, knew better. Still, it's awful to know you're the subject of conversations at the water cooler."

"How did it get out, anyway?"

"His wife. She wanted me fired."

"Ouch." He winced. "I think I'd have fired *him,* not you."

"Nobody got fired, but I sure had an uncomfortable interview with the partners." She could still squirm, remembering. "I guess that's the reason a lot of businesses have a rule about not dating coworkers."

"That rule isn't worth the paper it might be written on. People meet at work, they feel attraction, some even get married. Yeah, a bad relationship can cause disruption, but only if the people involved aren't mature enough to keep it out of the workplace. That's all I ever asked of my employees—don't bring it to work."

He shook his head. "In a case like yours, I probably would have fired the guy. For using you the way he did, and for his wife bringing it into the workplace by trying to have *you* fired. I would have considered him more trouble than I wanted, both then and down the road." He gave her a slight smile. "I don't need unscrupulous guys like that working for me."

She felt herself smiling back almost shyly. "The partners seemed more intent on finding out if I was inclined to be a home-wrecker."

"Then they were idiots. The home-wrecker was *him,*

not you. *He* was the one who was supposed to be off the market."

"You really mean that."

"Of course I do." He waved a hand. "I just don't subscribe to this notion that men shouldn't have to exercise self-control, and that women are always at fault when some guy can't keep his pants zipped."

A small giggle escaped her, whether from his irritation or his description, she wasn't sure.

He cocked a brow at her. "You think I'm funny?"

"Not exactly. It's just the way you said it."

"I'm only saying what's true. There's a tendency in society to accept that men are ruled by rampaging sex hormones and it's up to the woman to keep her head. Nuh-uh. I don't buy it. We may tend to think sexually more often, but that doesn't mean we're slaves to our drives. And if we *are* slaves to our drives, maybe we ought to pack it up and go home and let women rule the world, because after all, women are supposed to have enough self-control for *all* of us."

Now she was giggling more loudly, and the twinkle in his dark eyes said that was exactly what he had wanted.

"So you'd have fired him," she said, still chuckling.

"I'd have booted him so fast his head would have been spinning."

"I would have liked to have seen that."

"I bet you would."

Her chuckle faded, and she sighed. "He had kids. I'm glad he didn't lose his job for their sakes."

"*He* should be the one worrying about his kids, not you. But I guess you have a generous heart."

"I hope so." She smiled. "I like you, Dr. Grant Wolfe."

He shook his head. "I prefer just 'Grant.' 'Doctor' sounds like I should have a rubber glove and a stethoscope. And I'm glad you like me."

Just like that, the air became pregnant. Their eyes locked, and Trish stopped breathing. Every cell in her body seemed to be reaching for him. Madness. Sheer madness. Wonderful madness. Everything else vanished in a longing so intense it took her totally by surprise.

Then the oven timer dinged. *Saved by the bell.*

"Oh!" she said, startled. "I haven't even started the broccoli. And the potatoes…"

She jumped up to get to work, feeling as if she had just peered over a steep cliff and had almost fallen.

No, she told herself as she started the broccoli and began to make mashed potatoes. No. She didn't know him, really, and anyway, he was the worst possible kind of married man.

Married to a ghost.

Chapter 7

They talked randomly through dinner, and afterward he insisted on doing the dishes. She sat at the table, chatting with him while he loaded the dishwasher and scrubbed the roasting pan. They carefully avoided discussing any matter of seriousness, avoided allusions to the events that had brought them together.

In short, they took a break.

But then he said he had to go back to the motel.

"Why?" she asked. "Why can't you just stay here until it's time to go sit on the bench?"

"Because I feel a compulsion to follow the path. It's like I have to do it." He sighed and ran his fingers through his hair. "I'm sorry, Trish, but I really have to do this. Maybe I'm nuts, or maybe there's a reason. I don't know. I just know what I *have* to do."

She nodded, and realized she was trying to hang on to something that was only going to go away eventually regardless. She had to let him go because she couldn't afford to let him stay.

He took a few moments to check his messages on her computer, but all he heard from Dex was, "Still looking. Will take a bit longer."

"Maybe by tomorrow," Grant said after he showed her the message.

"It might not be related," she reminded him…or maybe she was reminding herself. Everything had gone off-kilter, first with Grant's arrival and now with her own doubts about the anxiety that had been plaguing her.

She wasn't being herself at all. Not at all. Best to take Grant back to the motel and try to find her footing again.

So she did exactly that. But for some reason it didn't help at all.

At midnight Grant was on the bench again, watching her house, exactly as he had every previous night. The compulsion hadn't weakened at all, which he interpreted to mean that the threat still remained, despite warning her.

He kept hoping for another vision or a dream. Something, anything that would tell him Trish was out of danger.

But somehow he felt the web drawing tighter around him, as if he were being sucked into the vortex of whatever he had foreseen.

The night was cooling rapidly, and he zipped his coat

as quietly as possible. Haunted by memories of the premonitions that might have saved his family, he could no more have budged from that bench than he could have stepped out in front of a racing train. For some reason he had to be here. Somehow he had to atone, if only by giving witness to his belief that such premonitions could happen, could be real. And if there was a damn thing he could do to save Trish from that shadowy figure with the silenced gun, he would do it. At any cost.

Abruptly the compulsion let go. He glanced at his watch and saw that twenty minutes had passed. It always let go at the same time, which to him indicated that whatever he had been brought here for, it would be over in about twenty minutes.

And then what? A woman saved? Or would he be too late, helpless in the face of a predestined future?

He could absolutely *not* bear that possibility.

He closed his eyes for a few moments, remaining on the bench. Quantum probabilities argued against a fixed future. Instead, they argued for something even more complicated: a future that contained *all* probabilities. In which case, you had to steer your course, make your decisions, do everything you knew how to bring about a particular outcome.

Somehow, some way, a murderer had become a high probability in Trish's life. Somehow he had been dragged into the whirlpool of that probability. But he had to believe it was *just* a probability, not a certainty. He had to.

Sighing, he opened his eyes and levered himself up from the bench. The instant he did so, Trish's porch light came on and she stepped out. He waited, but felt nothing wrong, so he started to cross the street.

"At least come in for a hot drink," she called as he neared.

He couldn't for the life of him find anything wrong with that idea. The compulsion was gone, the night-mare darkness that hovered around the edges of his mind had withdrawn. Somehow he knew tonight was not the night.

"Thanks," he said as he reached her steps. A painful climb with his hip stiffening, but he made it. Just four steps.

And then they were back in her kitchen and she was offering him hot chocolate.

"It's the instant kind," she said almost apologetically.

"That would be great. It's the only kind I've ever had."

"Remind me someday to make it for you from scratch. But it's too late at night now. I don't want to fuss with much except heating water."

"That's plenty of fuss. Am I turning you into a night owl?"

She shook her head as she put the kettle on. "Anxiety is doing that. Otherwise I would never have seen you on that bench."

All of a sudden he asked, "Did you reply to that e-mail from your CFO?"

"Hank? No, not yet."

"Good. Don't. Use vacation as your cover. Leave him wondering."

She sat facing him, waiting for the kettle. "What brought that on?"

"I don't know. I guess it must have been niggling at me somehow." He spread his hands. "I can't really explain any of this, Trish. I wish I could."

"I know." She took a paper napkin from the wicker basket she always kept on the table and began folding it with origami skills nearly forgotten, but learned with great enthusiasm as a child. She doubted she would make anything other than a mess, but it kept her hands busy.

And she needed to keep her hands busy, because her fingers kept wanting, as if they had their own mind, to touch Grant. To stroke his hair. To feel his skin. To trace the muscles and scars until they had discovered every inch of him.

She forced her wandering mind back to matters at hand. The kettle began to whistle, so she rose and quickly poured water into the mugs that already held the mix, then topped them with a little bit of cream to make the cocoa richer.

With habit so old she didn't even think about it, she stuck a teaspoon in each mug and carried them back to the table.

Grant sat stirring his cocoa with his head slightly down. "This stinks."

"Any part in particular, or all of it?"

He looked up, weariness etched all over his face. "Any part of it. All of it. Take your pick. My visions are vague. The compulsion to be out in front of your house every night is overwhelming. But none of it tells me *enough.*"

"So now you want high-definition precognition?"

He appeared startled, and then a short laugh escaped

him. "Yeah. In full living color, with a beginning, a middle and end."

"The end," she said quietly, "has not been written."

The words seemed to hang on the air, thickening it and chilling it until she felt something icy snake along her spine.

Their eyes met, and for an instant, just an instant, electricity seemed to zap between them, like static on dry air. Then it was gone, giving way to darker things.

He pressed his lips together, appearing to try to gather himself in some way. Trish needed a moment, as well. The change in mood had been so sudden, up then down in an eye blink.

"Do you think," he asked finally, "that your sheriff would listen to me?"

"I'm sure he'd listen. I don't know whether he'd believe you. Or me. I mean, this is weird. I'm not sure I'd talk to my best friend about this."

"I hear you."

"But Gage…well, Gage might not believe it, but he wouldn't ignore it. He'd probably park someone right outside my house."

"Then we should call him."

She started to agree, but then something else struck her, maybe the most chilling thought of all. "No," she said.

"No? Look, Trish, I'm not sure I'll be able to do enough to help you. If you think your sheriff will listen to me, then we *have* to tell him. Even one sleepy deputy might be enough to tip the scales."

"No," she said again.

It was his turn to grow impatient. "Are you out of your mind? You need all the protection you can get."

"I'm not out of my mind," she said quietly. "But think about this, Grant. If somebody really wants to kill me, if I'm not just some kind of random target, putting a deputy out there will only change the place and time. Right now you're pretty sure about where, when and how. What happens if we change things in a way that makes your vision invalid? Can you be sure I won't just be attacked in the parking lot at work? Or when I go out in the morning to walk the dog?"

"God, I don't like this. Don't be crazy, Trish. If you need a round-the-clock guard, then we'll get you one."

"But how will I know? How will *you* know? Don't you see? Unless we let this play out, we'll never know when it's over. We'll never know that I'm safe. I don't want to spend the rest of my life looking over my shoulder."

He drew a long breath. "Okay. I understand. But that doesn't mean I'm going to give up trying to find a way to better protect you."

"I have a dog and I have a shotgun," she reminded him. "And be honest, Grant, why are you so determined to be out there on that bench every night instead of in here or in your motel room? I asked you to stay after dinner, but you wouldn't even consider it. Because you *know.* You absolutely know that if you don't follow the exact pattern, you'll change what happens, and you're worried that we wouldn't be prepared then. Admit it."

He clearly didn't want to admit it, but she also saw that he couldn't argue about it.

"Nothing is fixed," he said slowly.

"No. It's not. I can't believe it is. But what you've seen…well, that's what we need to prepare for. If we do something that makes it impossible for that guy to do what you've seen the way you've seen it, how can we even guess where he might come from, instead?"

"I really, *really* don't like this."

"Neither do I," she admitted as a little shiver of apprehension ran through her. "But how else can I handle this? If I leave town for a week or a month or forever, how can I be sure this guy isn't hunting for me? At this point I'm convinced enough that *something* is wrong that I'm willing to take the chance on you, rather than maybe becoming a target when I'm not ready for it."

He stood up, paced her small kitchen with mug in hand. He took a couple of sips before setting it on the table. "I don't know," he said. "But honest to God, I don't feel like I know anything anymore."

"How so?" she asked, following him with her eyes, hating the way he winced a little bit with nearly every step.

"I used to be high on knowledge," he admitted. "I chased it like the gold at the end of the rainbow. I worked in a world of uncertainties that fascinated me as if I was playing with magic. Theories, equations, thought experiments. I was your ultimate geek, more plugged into a computer than the day-to-day world."

"But you ran a successful business," she reminded him.

"It was a means to an end. But yeah, I learned how to do that because I had to, in order to chase my pot of gold. But for heaven's sake, Trish, my *dog* had to teach me how to be a decent person. My *dog* taught me how to be a passably good husband and father."

"I'm sure that you had some of the basics already."

At that he paused a moment, then resumed his pacing. "Yeah, maybe," he said finally. "I had good friends. The kind of people who still give a damn, even though I walked out on them ten months ago and never did a thing to reassure them I was still alive. People who kept searching for me when they could have just bought me out of my business and gotten wealthier without me."

"So you had some contact with the real world."

"I always had contact with the real world. The problem was that I was focused on the reality we don't see, the world too small for most of us to even notice. The world nobody really understands and probably never will."

He drew a long shaky breath.

"Grant—" she started, aching for him.

He cut her off. "I loved my wife and daughter. I loved them. But I didn't love them enough. I should have given them more time, should have put my work aside more often. But I'd get hot on the track of some idea and I might not come home for days. I'd lock myself in my lab, catching catnaps when I had to, living on coffee and junk food. Laura always said she understood, but in retrospect...maybe she was just being nice. I couldn't have been easy to live with."

"Did she complain? Ever?"

"No."

"Then," Trish said gently, "maybe that's the thing you should focus on."

He looked at her from haunted eyes. "It's too late now. Isn't this the point where I should say, I hope I've learned something?"

She nodded slowly. "Maybe. If it's true. If it helps."

"God knows, I've had plenty of time to think about my shortcomings."

"Yeah," she said quietly. "I know all about that. Funny how we get so fixated on what we messed up that we seldom think about what we might have done right."

"Well, I messed up the ultimate and it cost my family their lives."

"As if you were supposed to know."

He froze, brows lifted.

"People get those little twitches all the time."

"Twitches?"

"Flashes of things. Visions. I dunno. If I believed everything that popped into my head in vivid detail, I'd never go out my front door."

"Meaning?"

"Meaning there's no way you could have known you were having precognition. Let me give you an example."

He came back to the table and sat facing her.

"A couple of years ago in Boston, I came to an intersection I drove through every day. I stopped at the stop sign and then this weird thing happened."

He nodded, listening.

"I all of a sudden had an absolutely vivid impression of my car being struck on the passenger side and spun around. I could literally *feel* the impact and the spin. It shook me enough that I double-checked to make sure the intersection was clear and there was no oncoming traffic. The feeling followed me home. I dismissed it as a moment of imagination and drove through that intersection the next day and every single following day without anything happening."

She waited, but he didn't comment.

"So," she said after a few moments, "given what you told me about possibilities and all that stuff, I guess I should conclude that I sensed a probability, one that never happened, and it may not have happened only because I became aware of the possibility of having an accident and took extra care."

"That's entirely possible," he agreed.

"Or I could say it was just a weird brain backfire. Regardless of what it was, I didn't presume it was a vision of something that was absolutely going to happen. I had no reason to think so. Nor did you have any reason to think your visions of a plane crash were anything but anxiety about flying. It's not like you'd spent your life foreseeing the future."

"I know that, intellectually. It's at the gut level I'm having a problem."

"I understand," she said gently. She wished that she could hug him fiercely and erase his awful burden of guilt. But only time could do that, she reminded herself. He'd have to find his own personal resolution, just as she was having to.

A minute or so later he unleashed a long sigh. "I still think there must be a way to let your friend Gage in on this."

She drummed her fingers on the table a moment, thinking, trying to ease back from some of the raw feelings he'd exposed and made her feel. This was a time to *think,* not get emotional.

"Tell me exactly what you've seen," she said. "Everything you think you know."

"I told you it's splintered. Glimpses. And I can't tell what I'm seeing from *my* perspective and what I might be seeing from *his.* Like the plane crash thing. I don't know why I kept seeing it from the pilot's perspective. If I'd seen it from my own, I might have grasped it."

She put her chin in her hand. "Maybe all that simulator training just made you interpret whatever information you got from that viewpoint. Does it really matter why you saw it that way?"

"Not really. At least in terms of what's going on now."

"Let's work on now. I think you're probably going to spend the rest of your life trying to figure out this conundrum."

"Maybe so. I doubt I'll find any hard and fast answers, though."

"You never know."

He smiled again. "The carrot is always out there." Then he took a deep drink of cocoa and put his mug back down. "Okay, what do I know about this current situation?"

"I'm all ears."

"I know the guy is going to leave Mahoney's at ten to one in the morning. I see the clock, I see him briefly from the back as he gets up and leaves. So I go there every night looking for him."

She nodded.

"Then I get this feeling of walking. And it's not me walking because there's no limp or pain. So in that part I'm seeing it from his viewpoint. And that's why I walk every night, following what I'm fairly certain is his path toward your house."

"You're hoping you'll run into him."

"Well, I'm hoping I'll catch sight of him at least and then I can do something to stop him when I'm sure I have the right guy."

Chin still in hand, she narrowed her eyes in thought, wondering how she had managed to divorce herself enough from this situation that she was able to think about it like a number problem to solve. She ought to be quaking, maybe crying, calling the cops…

No cops, she reminded herself. At a minimum, if all this played out, this man had to get into her house in order for him to be arrested. Until he crossed her threshold uninvited, he would have committed no crime. And unless they could get him arrested, they'd never find out important details, such as who, what and why.

Without warning, her detachment snapped and she realized she was shaking. "Oh, man…" The words came out of her almost like a whimper.

Grant rounded the table as if he didn't have a bad hip, and so fast the sound had barely finished escaping her. He pulled her up into his arms and held her snugly against his chest. Strong, warm. He felt like safety.

"I can't believe this," she whispered. "I can't believe this."

"Of course you can't."

"What's wrong with me?"

"Nothing that I can see."

She tipped her face up, still shaking. "One minute I'm so calm, and then it hits me like a freight train…"

"I know," he murmured. "I know. I've been doing that for a year now." He lifted one hand and stroked her hair gently. "I've been doing it, too."

"I can't believe I'm sitting here talking about this like it's a puzzle to be solved, or something in a game."

"It's no game," he said grimly. "*Now* will you let me call the sheriff? All I care about is that someone is watching over you."

But one thought kept rising to her mind, scary though it was. "Grant, I've got to be the bait. I've got to. Because if we don't catch this guy I'll never be safe. You know I'm right."

"Assuming I'm not totally crazy and didn't just dream this up out of some kind of guilt."

She shook her head. "We've been over that. The sense that something awful is lurking just ahead of me in time started before you showed up. And it's not going away."

He stroked her hair once more, then tightened his hold on her, just enough to make her feel surrounded by strength.

"We can't keep tossing this ball back and forth between us," he said. "We'll both go nuts. In the morning I'm going to call your sheriff if you won't."

"But it might do more harm than good, Grant!"

He shook his head and touched her cheek with his fingertips. "Don't you see what we're doing? We're running this round and round without finding any really good options. You're talking about being bait, I'm wondering if I'll be able to help at all if this guy shows up, hoping against hope I can figure out what to do, and hoping against hope I'm not just going to be a silent witness."

"Oh, God." She pressed her face to his chest, trying to grapple with stark imaginings, horrific possibilities and the way they jangled against the world she had always believed in.

"You know I'm right," he said quietly. "We need a more objective head. Some other input. Otherwise we're going to stay on this hamster wheel for God knows how long."

"You didn't want to tell *me,*" she said, lifting her head. "But now you want to tell the sheriff?"

"You've reinforced my feelings. I've reinforced yours. We'll go to him together. And maybe Dex will come up with something that will pinpoint a reason for all this. I hope so, because it would be nice to go to your sheriff with *something* tangible."

"The chips," she said, her voice cracking. "The damn chips. I wish I'd never looked at those numbers."

"And maybe it's a damn good thing you did. Do you even know why some of those chips can't be outsourced? Why they're classified?"

"Not my area."

"Well, I can assure you it's not because they could be used in a home computer."

She sighed again and closed her eyes. "God, this just keeps getting scarier."

Before she could open her eyes to gauge his response, she felt something touch her lips. A light touch, and for a second she thought it was his finger. Her heart and breathing seemed to stop, as if she wanted time to hold still.

Then she knew: he was kissing her. Lightly, almost questioningly, as if he wasn't sure about what he was doing. As if he wasn't sure how she would respond.

If her brain had engaged, she surely would have stepped back. But brain cells stopped operating in a huge rush of naked desire. She needed this. More than anything she needed to be held and kissed and cuddled and…

Aching, she leaned into his kiss, parting her lips just a little, inviting more because nothing else in the world mattered right now except that she celebrate being alive in even this small, primordial way.

A kiss, a touch…a reminder of all that was good, all that *could* be good. Feelings she had sworn off years ago when she convinced herself they didn't matter anymore.

But they mattered. They definitely mattered, and now they swamped her with an ache that filled her every cell.

"I'm sorry," he whispered against her lips. "I'm sorry. I can't…"

His apology hit her like a douche of cold water. At once she reared back, pulling out of his arms, turning away.

Of course he was sorry. He was still a man locked in grief. And she was a fool to have forgotten that for even a second.

Still aching, still yearning, feeling a bubble of anger rise and burst because her entire body was screaming for something she hadn't even really wanted until he kissed her and then pulled away, she kept her back to him.

"I'm sorry," he said again. "I shouldn't have."

"Don't say that," she said tautly. "Please don't say that."

"I just meant..." But he trailed off, evidently guessing that explanations wouldn't be a good thing right now.

Finally, he asked, "Can I use your computer? Maybe Dex has already found something."

"He doesn't sleep, either?"

"Not when he's curious."

She turned slowly, seeking stability. "You guys must really be fun."

"Oh, yeah, like a basket full of kittens."

She couldn't quite look at him. "Go ahead, you know how to turn it on."

She was grateful when he walked out toward her den, grateful to have a few minutes to scold herself and get past the absolutely huge frustration she felt.

She didn't even bother to run over for the umpteenth time all her reasons for avoiding men, particularly men who were still attached to someone, living or dead. She didn't bother to remind herself that this guy would take to the road any day now.

She didn't remind herself of one damn thing because she knew it all.

So she settled for a silent *You idiot!* and reclaimed her seat, sipping cocoa now gone lukewarm. At least it was chocolate. Wasn't that supposed to create the same feeling as being in love, without all the hassles? Maybe she should drink four or five mugs of the stuff and get herself a bar of dark chocolate in the morning. Purely out of self-defense, of course.

"Trish?"

She heard Grant call from the office-den, so she picked up her mug and went reluctantly to join him. "Yes?"

His back was to her, the only illumination the screen of her laptop. Was this how he worked? In the dark?

"Dex found it. Those missing chips of yours?"

"Yeah?"

"They are definitely not for export. Dex says approval has to come from the Department of Defense, because they're used in weapons applications."

"Oh. My. God." Her hand started to shake and she had to set her mug down on top of a cluttered bookcase so she didn't spill it. A cold wind ran through her body and she wrapped her arms around herself. "Oh, my God," she said again. "Is he sure?"

"Dex is not one to say something he doesn't absolutely believe to be fact."

"How could he know? All I have are code numbers." Her voice cracked as she spoke, as she tried to absorb the enormous implications. Her knees began to feel rubbery and she leaned back against the doorjamb.

"Let's just say Dex knows his way around computers enough to get a look at things most people couldn't see without a ten-digit pass code and a retinal scan. He's being cautious here, and I'm sure as heck not going to ask him for details this way. Even with a dedicated line, anyone could be tracking your computer traffic."

Another chill ran through her. "Can I see his message?"

"Sure." He rose and let her take the chair.

Trish sat. Cautious was an understatement she realized as she stared at the screen.

Dod only wepapp.

"That's not cautious," she said, "that's downright cryptic! How can you be sure?"

"Because I know Dex. Because we always used to misspell things to confuse anyone who might stumble on something we wanted private. So look at it again. *Dod* is Department of Defense. Given what I asked him earlier, the rest falls in place. *Only* means the chips can only be sold to the Department of Defense. *Wepapp*… well, just say it out loud. It means this chip has weapons applications."

She might only be a bean counter, as some people might like to call those in her profession, and she didn't know a thing about what was actually going on with technology at the plant, she could put two and two together to make a nice round four. Classified projects, chips that couldn't be sold without an export permit…

Oh, it made an awful kind of sense. She could only begin to imagine the kind of money some people might pay to get their hands on chips that had weapons applications, because you'd have to be talking about *smart weapons.*

The chill that had washed through her minutes ago came through again. She turned her head jerkily to look at Grant. "If this is true..." She paused. "Do you need to do anything else?"

"At the computer? No. Dex doesn't need to get in any deeper, and I don't want to create a buzz of traffic on your computer that might draw attention. Log me out and shut down."

With her hands shaking, she couldn't seem to do that fast enough. Finally she was able to push away from the desk and stand.

"I'm in shock," she announced for no particular reason except that she felt extraordinarily weak and everything looked odd, as if her office had suddenly become a different world.

Grant took her arm as if to steady her, and guided her to the living room where she dropped ungracefully onto the sofa. What had she stumbled into? The thoughts buzzing through her brain like angry bees didn't want to settle anywhere.

He went and got their cocoa and passed her mug to her. She held on to it like a lifeline as he took the armchair facing her.

"That settles it," he said.

"Settles what?" She was still trying to absorb the magnitude of what she had discovered.

"We're talking to the sheriff in the morning. If someone is selling those chips illicitly, it would be ample cause to murder you for having discovered it."

She nodded slowly, accepting the truth. Then she whispered, "What if Hank is part of it?"

"I don't know. I mean, his response to you may have

been just because he knows *exactly* what those missing chips are and he's worried about it. Maybe hoping he can somehow find them without having to call in the feds."

"Maybe." Her lips felt dry, almost cracked. Her heart was beating hard, though not fast. And she was feeling far colder than the room temperature should have allowed. "Maybe *I* should call the feds."

"And say what? That there are some missing chips, you're not completely positive they're missing, you don't know what they are...? Because I can't drag Dex into this. They'd want to know how he found out, and how he found out is something no one is supposed to be able to do."

She forced herself to expel a long breath and reach for calm. A sip of cocoa, getting colder by the minute, seemed to help.

"Okay," she said. "Assuming Dex is right, there's a good reason for someone to want to shut me up." She couldn't bring herself to say *kill me.* "If Dex is right, I have no way to prove it to anyone without getting him into trouble, and I'd really prefer not to do that. I don't want to get anyone into that kind of trouble."

Grant leaned forward. "If it seems like the only way, I'll drag Dex into it."

She shook her head. "There has to be another way. You're talking a federal crime, even if you're not saying it. Even I can figure that out. So no, we don't mention Dex to anyone. What we need is another way to prove what's going on."

"We need to catch the guy who's coming after you. He'd be the link in the chain."

She nodded slowly. "Okay, I give in. We talk to Gage in the morning. Privately. This is too big to keep to ourselves." And now scarier than ever.

"Good. If he listens at all, we might be able to figure out something better to protect you than me sitting on a park bench."

"This is so surreal!" The complaint burst out of her, but even as it did she felt silly for making it. She'd been through surreal before. They happened, those moments or times when something changed everything in a fundamental way. Like Jackson. Complaining about it did no good. "Sorry," she said.

"Don't be sorry." He put his mug aside and came to kneel in front of her. "Trish, I hope to God I just had some kind of nervous breakdown, that these images that have been driving me like a whip are just fantasy. But I don't dare take the chance."

She looked into his eyes and felt again the forbidden ache. Loneliness welled up in her. All the friends she had couldn't help now. The only person who was with her in this scary time was a near stranger, and that didn't ease her need *not* to be alone. She needed to be grounded by people she knew and trusted, people who could give her emotional support. But the thing was, she didn't want to risk pulling anyone else into this.

"I should go back to the motel," he said slowly.

"No. Please. I don't want to be alone with this."

"But if that guy is already in town and watching..."

"Then he already knows you're here." Shaking her

head, trying to batter down a welter of emotions, she sought doorways, exits, escape. But until whatever this was played out, she was trapped.

Truly *trapped.*

Chapter 8

Trish dozed on the couch, Grant on the recliner. Neither slept well, and often Trish would open her eyes to see Grant looking at her. As if she was a puzzle. As if he was trying to figure out something.

Maybe he was as confused by all of this as she was.

Morning dawned hazy, hinting at the summery day to come in the waning weeks of autumn. Grant joined Trish in the kitchen and proved he was adept at slicing grapefruit and cooking eggs. They didn't have much to say. Trish was dreading the meeting with Gage. She suspected Grant felt the same, but at least he looked determined.

At eight o'clock, the sun still far in the east, Trish called the sheriff. Gage took her call promptly.

"I'm sorry to bother you," she said, "but I may have a serious problem."

"What's going on?"

"Grant Wolfe and I need to talk to you. Privately."

There was no hesitation. "Are you at your place? Both of you?"

"Yes."

"I'll be there in ten."

She hung up and looked at Grant. "You're sure about this?"

He closed his eyes a moment. "It doesn't feel wrong. And that's all I've got to go on, really."

Gage arrived in his personal vehicle, dressed in jeans and a black leather jacket. He often eschewed the uniform, but with his scarred face, everyone in the county recognized him on sight, so what did it matter? Gage was a totally unforgettable man.

He joined them in the living room, crossed his legs loosely, ankle on thigh. "So what's going on?"

Trish hesitated. "This is one of those things you're going to have a whole lot of trouble believing. And the two of us need some…"

"Objective thinking," Grant said when Trish trailed off. "We've been discussing this for a couple of days, and I don't want us to get into a folie à deux. If we're not already there."

"I'm listening." He gave Trish an encouraging smile. "And trust me, I've probably heard weirder things than you can dish up."

"I'm not so sure about that," Trish said. "Maybe I

should start at my beginning and let Grant take over with his part."

Grant nodded agreement. "Sounds like the best approach."

"Okay," Trish said. "I told you I was edgy because some numbers hadn't matched at work, and that was probably why I was overreacting to Grant being on the park bench every night."

"I remember," Gage said. "Seems you got past that, since you're both here."

"Well, not exactly. But let me tell you some details. I was uneasy because I'd discovered an inventory discrepancy. Microchips unaccounted for. I don't know how much you know about what we do at the plant, but a lot of it is on government contracts."

"I've heard," Gage said. "Security clearances and all that. I've been part of more than one background check when the FBI has come to ask questions for someone's security clearance. So missing microchips could be a big deal, not just a monetary matter."

Trish felt a wave of gratitude toward this man for understanding so quickly. "That's part of the reason I was uneasy. Not just because I might have made a mistake, but because it could cause the company a real hassle regardless of whether I was right or wrong. That's why I mentioned I might get fired. Not likely, if we sort it out ourselves, and it turns out to just be a miscount on someone's part, including my own. But even if it's a miscount and the feds hear about it, we could have problems."

"I get it. So you had cause for anxiety. Then Grant shows up. Yeah, I'd be watching him, too, if I were you, and getting paranoid."

"The thing is, I didn't know if those chips were classified. We make unclassified ones, too, and everything is coded. So I might have discovered that some run-of-the-mill chips were missing. I mean, it was really all up in the air, and the main thing—I *thought,* anyway—was that I was worried about my job. I wasn't looking past that. Until Grant."

Gage trained his gaze on Grant. "So how do you fit?"

"This is the part where you're going to want to toss me out of town," Grant said, obviously trying to make the words sound light. He didn't quite achieve the effect.

Leaning forward, he told Gage his whole story, start to finish, his voice breaking a bit when he spoke of the plane crash, the death of his family and the visions that had preceded it. The sympathy on Gage's face was unmistakable.

"But it doesn't end there," Grant continued after a moment of silence. "I started having new visions a few weeks ago. And they brought me here. The compulsion has been overwhelming to be outside this house every night at the same time."

"Why?" Gage asked quietly.

"Because someone is going to try to kill Trish. I see it. Over and over I see someone standing in her bedroom in the dark with a silenced pistol."

"Damn," Gage said expressively.

Hurrying, in case Gage might dismiss it all, Trish

jumped in. "What's more, even though at first I thought Grant was just, well, a nut, I began to realize that I'd been having feelings that something bad was going to happen. That something was lurking right around the corner. Think about it, Gage. How many times do people say 'I knew that was going to happen.'"

"You don't have to convince me," Gage said flatly. "I've had experiences that make me think we don't *begin* to understand these so-called paranormal things. Okay, so you both have an idea that someone might try to kill Trish. Give me something solid."

Grant hesitated. Trish finally spoke. "We managed to find out that the missing chips are classified. They're for weapons systems, and they can't be sold to anyone but the Department of Defense."

"I won't ask how you figured that out, considering Trish just said everything is coded."

"Thanks," Grant said. "Thanks for that."

"Well, if those chips are really missing, and someone knows you found out, that's ample cause for murder. Either to protect the thief or to protect the company."

"My thinking exactly," Grant said.

"But the thing is," Trish interjected, "it struck me the only way we can find out is to let this guy come after me just the way Grant sees it. Otherwise, if this is really happening, I could be targeted somewhere else."

Silence greeted her words. Even Gage looked as if he had swallowed something awful.

"Bait," he finally said.

"Exactly." Her voice was subdued. "It scares me,

Gage. Grant can tell you I was actually shaking last night. I want to run, I want to hide. But how can I ever have a life again if this doesn't get resolved somehow?"

"So what you're saying is to let Grant's vision play out. But what if it doesn't?"

"I can't even think about that now." A small shudder passed through her. "Since we found out what the missing chips are, I'm more terrified than ever. I don't want to spend the rest of my life looking over my shoulder."

One corner of Gage's mouth tightened as he thought. "I could call the feds, let the chips fall—no pun intended—and go into witness protection. Except I know the costs of that. You not only lose your whole life, but you still can't be sure no one will find you. It doesn't happen often, but it happens." He paused. "And frankly, I don't know why you should pay such a heavy price when you've done nothing wrong."

"There's a heavier price," Grant said.

"True."

But Trish shook her head. "Would I like to run? Hell, yes. I think I've already said that. But…give up everything and still have to look over my shoulder for years at least? I don't want to do that. Something in me says I should take this risk, terrified or not. But to do that, we have another problem—we can't do anything that will materially change what Grant has foreseen. That's why I *didn't* want to come to you. If you put a guard on me and this killer finds out, the whole game changes."

"I already figured that out," Gage said.

Tad chose that moment to wander in and hop up

beside Trish on the couch, laying his head in her lap. She stroked his silky ears and waited. Her chest felt tight, her heart heavy, as if this moment was freighted with an entire future of terrible possibilities. And maybe it was, given Grant's vision.

"Okay," Gage said after a few minutes of thought. "We have to make sure we don't shift anything out of alignment, for lack of a better word." He looked at Grant. "Do you think we might have already?"

"I don't get that feeling. But I'm running on feelings here, and we all know how easily I could be wrong."

"For the sake of being able to do anything at all," Gage replied, "we're going with your feelings. I need to figure out how to set up some kind of protection for Trish that won't scare this guy off. And I need you, *both* of you, to keep me clued in to anything you see *or* feel that might indicate something is changing. I'll be honest with you—I don't know how much stock I put in these visions, but I know I'm not willing to just dismiss them. Trish is right. Every one of us has said or felt that we knew something was going to happen before it did. In law enforcement we get used to that and call it a hunch. And I've never been a man to dismiss hunches out of hand."

Trish felt something inside her begin to uncoil. "Thanks, Gage."

"I'll let you know what I come up with. I won't let it drag on, though. It seems to me we need to act fast."

At the door, though, he paused and faced Grant. "I've been through the same hell you have," he said. "Let me tell you one thing I finally learned."

"Which is?"

"That guilt doesn't fix a thing or change a thing. All it does is rip you apart and make you useless. You're not God. Let Her do Her job and you do yours."

Trish dropped off Grant back at the motel, and he went in to shower and change. Both of them figured the killer in his vision wouldn't know that Grant was any kind of threat, let alone that anyone was aware of him, so it wouldn't hurt for the two of them to be seen together, as long as Grant stayed away during the hours that he deemed dangerous.

After his shower, still a little damp despite toweling himself, Grant flopped naked on the bed, determined to catch up on some sleep.

But sleep proved elusive. Gage's words had stuck in his head, and where before that kind of advice had struck him intellectually, somehow this time it had hit emotionally.

You're not God.

Sage words, and something in his reaction told him they were words he needed to hear. Laura wouldn't have wanted this for him, he knew. He'd known that all along, but grief was an unreasoning taskmaster, one that yielded not one wit to sense or logic.

Yet grief wasn't the same as guilt. Guilt. It was the guilt he needed to let go of, the guilt that whipped him endlessly, especially because, sadly enough, he was beginning to let go of grief.

If he gave himself half a chance, he'd probably turn

that natural healing into guilt, too. It wasn't that he didn't miss Laura and his daughter each and every day. But the ache for their loss, the emptiness in their wake... that was becoming a familiar, quiet companion. A hole that would always be there. Maybe you never stopped grieving, maybe you just got used to it. Maybe time eased the ache a bit simply because it had to. Life went on, even when it seemed like a mortal insult.

But guilt...that was a whole different thing. That remained fresh, vivid and clawing. Like grief, it didn't yield to logic, but it also didn't yield to time.

You're not God.

He sighed and rubbed his eyes, wishing sleep would carry him away from this constant, nagging, *endless* misery for just a little while. But sleep remained stubbornly elusive, leaving him mired in his own company.

Because that's what it was beginning to feel like in his head: a mire. Quicksand that wouldn't let go.

But maybe it was a quagmire of his own making. Lately he wondered if he clung to guilt and grief for fear that he might discover there was nothing else left inside him. That the tragedy of his loss had transformed him into a mere husk, capable of feeling nothing but pain.

It wasn't your fault.

Almost as if she stood by the bed, he heard Laura speak. The mere memory of her voice was enough to make his throat tighten.

It wasn't your fault.

That's exactly what she would say. She'd give him hell for beating himself up about something he hadn't properly understood. She'd stand there wagging her finger and tell him that he had another responsibility now, and lying around feeling guilty would only keep him from taking advantage of the lesson he had learned, the lesson that had caused a series of visions to bring him to this out-of-the-way little town and hunt down a total stranger.

She'd tell him: *The only failures in life are the ones you don't learn from.*

He could even hear her saying it, as she had so many times before to him, to herself, to others she knew.

Laura had believed life was a school, that everyone was bound to screw up at times, and the only proper response was to dust yourself off and not repeat your mistakes.

She was right about that. And by this point in time, a year later, she'd be getting pretty annoyed with him for beating himself up. And she'd be cheering him on for having learned his lesson and trying to help Trish.

Trish. Feelings for her were beginning to edge their way into his heart. He didn't know if he was ready for that. But there they were, stealthy invaders he had tried not to notice. She was a lovely woman, and like any normal man he had noticed how attractive she was.

And like any man who'd been without a mate for so long, he felt the sexual pull like a huge undertow. All that held him back was the fear that he might hurt her, because he hadn't resolved his own issues yet.

But damn, he wanted to make love to her. He wanted to feel her silky skin against his, feel her body rise to meet him, hear her moans and whimpers. He wanted to take a journey with her to that one place in life where you touched the stars. Just the thought made his body ache with need.

But that wasn't enough. It wouldn't be fair to her.

And he was scared to death of the things that *would* make it fair to her.

He didn't know if he could ever allow himself to be that vulnerable again. The price might be enormous.

He ought to know; he'd paid it once already.

"Howdy!"

Startled, Trish looked up from the mail she was pulling from her porch mailbox and saw a woman walking her way from the house next door. A stranger, not one of the house's residents. Yet the woman, about her age with cinnamon-colored hair, wearing jeans and a denim jacket, carried a leaf rake as if she'd just been working in the yard.

Trish's heart skipped a beat. Who said an assassin had to be a man? But it was still late afternoon, there were other people driving by, kids were starting to fill the park. Wrong time, wrong place.

"Hi," Trish answered uncertainly.

The still-smiling woman, rake in hand, climbed the steps of Trish's porch. "I hate this raking," she said cheerfully.

"Not my favorite thing, either." Trish had to battle an urge to dash into the house and lock the door. But it was already too late. The woman reached her, staying a step back, and with her free hand lifted her jacket.

Trish gasped with relief when she saw the badge on the woman's belt.

"Lori Morgan," the woman said, keeping her voice low. "Try to act like you know me."

"I wish I did."

Lori laughed as if Trish had said something funny, then lowered her voice again. "Invite me in for coffee so we can talk."

Wrong time of day, Trish reminded herself. Besides, that badge looked all too real. "Hey, take a break," she said in a normal conversational voice. "Come on in for some coffee."

"Don't mind if I do." Lori propped the rake against the house and followed Trish inside.

Once the door closed behind them, Trish faced the woman uncertainly. "*Would* you like some coffee?"

"Am I a cop?"

At that Trish smiled. "That joke is worn to death."

"In all its ten thousand variations," Lori agreed as she followed Trish to the kitchen. "Oh, I like this," she commented as she took a seat. "You've made this room so homey."

"Thanks. I feel the heart of any home is the kitchen."

"You're right about that." At that moment Lori was distracted by the arrival of Tad. He bounced into the kitchen, carrying his tennis ball, only to drop it when he saw Lori. The serious sniffing began around Lori's ankles and shins. "Cute dog," she said.

"If he bothers you…"

Lori interrupted her with a wave of her hand. "He

doesn't bother me. My house is run by a Saint Bernard and a malamute, and two cats fill in as kings."

Trish had to laugh. "That's a priceless image."

"Well, I'm away so much they consider me a mere appendage to their lives."

Coffee poured, they sat facing each other at the table.

"Okay," Lori said. "Gage asked me to come over and fill you in."

"Oh. I thought he'd call or drop by."

Lori shook her head. "He wants this totally under wraps. Seems to feel it might cause you some trouble if he's seen around here too much."

Trish nodded slowly. "I suppose it could. I don't know."

The other woman shrugged. "Gage knows what he's doing. So here's the deal. My partner and I have come to town to visit the Callahans next door. Not really, but that's the cover. Believe it or not, I'm actually related to Moira."

"Really?"

"Second cousins thrice removed or some such Conard County thing. We were close as kids, moved apart, but we've met a few times at family reunions and stuff, so Moira was glad to have me visit, along with my partner, who is passing as my boyfriend."

"Okay."

"We're actually cops in Laramie. And we're here, as I understand it, because somebody might want to kill you."

"That seems to be a distinct possibility."

Lori nodded, her expression serious. "I was told we're to avoid doing anything that might scare the guy off for all those reasons that cops both hate and love."

Trish nodded reluctantly, queasiness filling her. "I'm bait. I have to be or I might never be safe."

"Yeah, that's pretty much what Gage said, and I can tell you he's no more thrilled about this than we are. I suggested doubling for you in the house and hiding you somewhere else."

"No!" Trish was surprised at the vehemence of her own response. Scared as she was, she also felt the danger. "If we make any changes… We can't do that. Trust me. I'm already worried that we might do something that'll mess this up." She shook her head. "Just call it a major hunch."

Lori sighed. "That's pretty much what Gage said. Regardless, we're going to be watching over you as best we can, given the restrictions of needing to catch this guy in the act."

"At least in the act of entering my house."

"Yep. And if that's the only way we can make you safe, that's what we're going to do. Anyway, Gage called us in because nobody in town knows we're cops, and apparently he doesn't want that hitting the rumor mill."

"That could create a problem, all right."

"So I just want you to know, my partner and I will be right next door watching. And I think Gage is looking for a couple of other people he can insert without generating comment. Regardless, you'll have two of us watching every minute."

"Thank you." Trish felt a sting in her eyes. "I can't tell you how much that means."

"You don't have to tell me," Lori said. She leaned

forward so she could pat Trish's hand gently. "Gage said he has reason to believe that the dangerous time will be between midnight and two, but we'll take turns watching round the clock, anyway. And with the dog, we'll be alerted by any serious barking."

Trish glanced down to find Tad chewing on his tennis ball. "He's only barked once before."

"Wow. How long have you had him?"

"Just a few days."

"Maybe he's just settling in, then. Some dogs don't bother to bark much. Others…well, you wish they'd shut up."

Trish managed a smile. "It's great just knowing you're there."

"Thanks. Anyway, I'll just finish this coffee and get back to raking leaves. They don't rake themselves, and it's a good excuse to be outside…in the sunshine."

But Trish knew Lori didn't want to be outside for the sunshine, however cheerfully she might say it. At least four people now believed someone was trying to kill her.

Five, including herself.

Chapter 9

Grant should have felt more relaxed when he awoke. Gage Dalton seemed like a good guy, and more than that, a good cop. Trish had called earlier, interrupting a dream he'd thought important at the time and now could not remember, to say Gage had brought in a couple of Laramie cops undercover to watch her. That was good news.

And at least now Dex knew Grant was alive. Grant wasn't yet ready to deal with how that felt. Hearing Dex say, "So when are you coming back, G?" as if Grant hadn't left without as much as a goodbye. As if he hadn't tried to sell out of the company. As if he hadn't left his best friends to wonder if he'd been swallowed by the earth itself, or worse.

No questions. No recriminations. Just, "So when are you coming back, G?"

He looked at the faint print in the wallpaper, a trellised pattern so subtle he had to lean close to be sure it was even there, and wondered how much of life was exactly like that: patterns engraved in our existence that we don't even notice. We look right past them, he thought, willfully blind both to risk and opportunity, to trap and treasure.

Oh sure, he knew he liked Dex and the other guys. They had started with an idea—no, a *dream*—and they'd turned it into reality together. You didn't do something like that and not form bonds. But they were the guys at work, after all. Yeah, you talked about lives and wives and kids and ups and downs, but they were just the guys at work.

Until you abandoned them, wallowing in grief and self-pity and guilt. Walked away from the dream you'd built up into reality together as if it was so much litter on the sidewalk, already just another tattered shred of history. You went off chasing a cockamamie vision that you couldn't tell a soul for fear of ending up in a psych ward, but you couldn't ignore it for fear of worse. Then you met your vision, up close and in real life, and that just scared you all the more because *things like that did not happen.* But they did.

And did you call home for a reality check? Call home to apologize? Hell no. You called home to ask a friend to commit a federal crime for you. And he did it without a moment's hesitation. And he said, "So when are you coming back, G?" as if you'd done nothing more than take an afternoon off for a round of golf.

If a God existed and really gave a damn, was really fair, all of the other good stuff that people with faith said they believed, there was a special place in heaven for people like Dex. And rather than kick himself for what he'd done, or wondering why Dex was the kind of man he was, Grant decided to do the one thing that made even the slightest sense in a moment of reflection in a hotel room in a faraway town he'd stumbled to in a bizarre vision. He picked up the phone.

It was silent for a moment, and then Grant heard the voice of the front-desk clerk. "Can I get you something, Mr. Wolfe?"

So she had learned his real name somehow. Everything he'd heard about small tight-knit communities appeared to be true. But of course it was. His throat tightened briefly as he thought of the close-knit community he'd left behind. Dex and Jerry and all the others. "Yes. I need to make a long-distance call. I guess you need my credit card for that?"

"We usually would," the woman said. "But since it's you, just make the call. Hold on and I'll give you an outside line."

"Um, thanks, but—"

"Mr. Wolfe," she said, "I don't know much. But when Gage Dalton says 'good people,' I know what that means. You just go right on being 'good people' and make that call. Okay?"

Grant swallowed. "Okay, sure. Thank you."

"And Mr. Wolfe?"

"Yes?"

"Don't waste much time on apologies. Good friends don't need it and the rest won't listen. And somehow I bet you're calling the kind of friend who won't need it."

My God, he thought, as he waited for the dial tone, did this whole town read minds? Or had someone at the sheriff's office gossiped? Most likely the latter, he decided.

Moments later he had a dial tone and punched in the numbers from memory. "Dexter Flagler's office," the woman said. What was her name? Karen.

"Um, Karen…this is Grant. Grant Wol—"

"Oh, sure, Mr. Wolfe. I'll put you right through."

He had to let himself smile.

"Hey, buddy!" Dex had once thought he'd be a football coach, and he certainly had the voice for it. "What's up?"

"Nothing, really," Grant said, only now truly realizing how badly he missed Dex. He had one of those moments that had happened too often since the plane crash, a surging flood of memory. This had been a good part of his past, but still, did everything have to be painful?

He cleared his throat and spoke again. "I just woke up and realized that I didn't explain anything when I called you yesterday. Not why I left or anything. Just asked you for a favor. A big favor, as it turned out. It was selfish of me and—"

"One more word like that and I'm hanging up," Dex said. "You know me better than that, or you wouldn't have called and just asked for that favor. And I did it. So you not only know me, but you're right. So no explanations and no apologies, okay? We're all just happy to hear you're okay. Or the rest of them are."

"Oh?" Grant asked.

"I didn't tell them anything. Just that you called and you're okay. I couldn't tell them the rest. And I'm not sure how much I can say on this line. Get me?"

"Yeah," Grant said. "I get you. I don't like what I'm getting, though."

"You shouldn't, buddy," Dex said. "That stuff you asked about is serious, big-time, 'up your rectum from a thousand miles away' kind of stuff. That far and that accurate. Still getting me?"

"I am. And I'm liking it less and less."

"Then you're hearing what I'm saying. Keep your head down, buddy. Whatever you're doing, whyever you're doing it, keep your head down. We want you back, but not for a funeral. Okay?"

"You got it," Grant said. "Head down, no funeral. I think I can still fathom simple instructions."

"I keep it too damn simple cuz you're too damn smart," Dex said. "As always."

Grant managed a laugh. "Yes, sir, coach."

The tension in Dex's voice lapsed for an instant, and he actually chuckled. "*Now* I know you're getting me."

"You're the best, Dex. I want to say that much. And I want to say thank-you. That's what I really called to say. Just…thank you."

"You'd do it for me," Dex said. "For any of us here.

We always knew that. So do what you need to do and get your ass back here, where your friends can babysit you. And if you've met some friends there, and it sounds like you have, bring them back with you. Always need more friendly folk in this city."

"We'll see," Grant said, feeling his chest tighten again with emotion. "I gotta go, Dex. Thanks again."

The tension returned. "Head down, buddy. Way, way down. That's the no bovine manure, straight-up scoop."

"I get it, Dex. I get it."

"Get it, and don't forget it."

Always the coach, Grant thought as he hung up the phone. And always the friend. More's the point, if Dex's instincts were right—and they were rarely wrong—Trish was in a lot more danger than Grant had imagined. If those chips were the reason someone wanted Trish dead, that someone wouldn't be sending any amateurs. He'd find pros.

"She needs the Secret Service," Grant said to the trellised wallpaper. "And I'm just a half-crippled geek."

You're not God, Gage Dalton had said. But what was the rest? *Let Her do Her job, and you do yours.* Well, he wasn't sure what his job was. But he was damn sure going to try.

It was still early afternoon when Grant returned. Trish saw him on the porch and immediately opened the door, greeting him effusively and reaching for his hand to draw him inside.

Grant looked startled, but she didn't explain until she closed the door behind him.

"That was for the benefit of my guardians."

"Oh, the cops."

"Exactly. So they don't have to come over to check you out."

"Oh." He looked a little downcast, but then an impish smile, utterly unexpected, appeared. "I wouldn't have minded at all if you'd meant it."

Her cheeks colored faintly. "You seem to have… changed."

"I had a good talk with Dex. I—" He broke off. After a moment he found his voice again. "I realized that in running from the bad things, I ran from the good, too. I need to start reestablishing my connections with the good things."

"I'm happy for you." And she was. In spite of feeling a strong pang in her heart, because that meant he would be leaving as soon as this business was over. But hadn't she known that all along?

Still, the pang persisted as they went to sit in the living room so he could be comfortable. Sitting on the couch side by side should have made her feel close to him, but the gulf was still there, larger than the twelve inches between them would have indicated.

"I'm glad you talked to Dex again." And she meant it. It was only a small, selfish part of her that didn't, and she pushed that part back.

"Me, too." A long breath escaped him, as if he were releasing something. "It's amazing. He acted like I never went away. And just like that, it felt like I never had. He wouldn't even let me apologize."

"They say you can judge a man by his enemies, but if you ask me, you can judge him better by his friends. You seem to have some very good ones."

"The best," he agreed. "God, I don't want to choke up again."

"Why not? You're allowed to."

He glanced at her. "Haven't you heard? It's not manly."

"Where you've been, I think it would be less manly if you pretended to feel nothing."

"I haven't been able to pretend that for a long time."

"So don't start."

He turned sideways and reached for her hand. When she didn't object, he closed his fingers around hers and squeezed gently. "There's more to talk about than whether I'm very lucky in my friends."

"I don't know that I'd call it luck, but go on."

"Dex said something that scared the bejesus out of me."

She tensed. "Do I want to know?"

"I think you have to."

She pressed her lips together, knowing that thoughts she'd been avoiding since Lori had left were about to be stirred up. "Give it to me."

"These chips are for smart weapons."

"I kind of figured that out. Nobody would want any other kind."

"Well, we're talking about orders of magnitude here. I won't quote Dex exactly because you might not like his language, but let me put it this way. You're familiar with the size of a bull's-eye on a target?"

"Of course." Her fingers gripped his as tension returned in one massive slam.

"Well, imagine being able to hit one from a thousand miles away."

"Oh, my God!" She clapped her other hand to her mouth as if she could hold something in. Her heart turned over and her stomach sank like a stone.

"Exactly. This is a huge breach. And frankly, Trish, if this killer doesn't turn up soon, we're going to have to go to the FBI with this. We can't allow stuff like that to get into the wrong hands."

"Of course we can't. Oh, God! I had no idea we were doing something so critical!"

"Of course not. Everyone would want a low profile on this, and there's no reason anyone at the plant should have to know exactly what these chips do. It's not their part of the job."

"But…" She looked at him, panicky. "I need to let someone know right now."

He shook his head. "Trish, you already let the CFO know. It's in his hands."

"But what if…what if…" She couldn't even bring herself to say it.

"Could anyone else know what you found?"

"In theory, of course they could. I mean, I didn't ballyhoo it, but people knew I was looking into things and getting a little disturbed. If someone at the plant had done something wrong, and he knew I was sniffing around it...how smart do you have to be?"

"Not that smart," he said grimly. "Okay, here's what you do. Call Gage now. Or I will. Have him contact the feds. I'm sure there's a way he can keep them from bumbling into the middle of this in a way that will scare off our only possible link to the bad guys. They should have as much interest as anyone in making sure they don't blow this."

She felt gutted, hollowed out, and looked at him even as she felt terror pinch her eyes. "You know what this means?"

"What?"

"If those chips weren't just miscounted, they're going to send a pro after me. A thing like this...it's too important to screw up."

His mouth tightened, but he didn't say anything. He didn't have to, apparently. Instead, he gave her hand a quick squeeze, then pulled away. "I'll be right back. I'll find a way to let Gage know how serious this is without getting any of us in trouble."

She nodded, watching him walk out of the room to use one of her phones, feeling as if her last lifeline had just deserted her.

And suddenly she saw dominoes starting to fall in a long chain. Because she wasn't the only one who knew. She'd told Hank. So Hank would be under suspicion unless he'd already reported it. Assuming he knew what those chips were for, and at his level in the company he probably had some idea.

Regardless, he had been informed, so if someone wanted to kill her because she'd discovered a discrepancy, they'd have to kill him, too.

And of course, the FBI would want to know how she'd found out the importance of the chip. And that would drag Grant and Dex into the middle of the maelstrom of a federal investigation that might get them all jailed.

Telling herself she was protected because she hadn't realized the significance of the missing product was nothing but a thin wall against the questions that were going to be asked now. Questions she couldn't answer without getting other people into trouble.

God, it just got worse and worse!

"Trish?" Grant returned and sat beside her. "Gage already called the feds."

She was shocked. Hadn't he said…or maybe he hadn't. The whirlwind in her head was making it difficult to sort out what had happened, what they thought might happen, who knew what when…

"It's okay," Grant said, taking her hand. "It's okay. He told them that you'd mentioned an inventory discrepancy at the plant involving microchips, and that you'd reported it up the company ladder. He said you just mentioned your concern to him."

"And?"

"And he said they were all over it like white on rice. He also told them to stay away from you for now because there'd been a threat made on your life and he didn't want them in the way. They're going to start their investigation at the top."

She smiled thinly. "There goes my job."

"Maybe. But what's more important?"

"Not my job, of course. Obviously not my job. God, if I'd had any idea what those chips were for, I'd have reported it to the feds myself at the same time I notified Hank. I wish I had."

He took her hand again and squeezed it. "You couldn't know. You followed the only procedure you could."

"Maybe." The grip of his hand comforted her, but only a little bit. Things seemed to be getting murky beyond her ability to sort through them. But one thought did make it through. "Oh, my God!"

"What?" He leaned toward her, intent.

"Hank is in trouble, too. Because whoever wants this silenced will have to go after everyone who knows."

He nodded. "And?"

"And it just struck me. Hank is the *only* person I told exactly which microchips were missing."

Grant's expression grew grim indeed. "That might clarify things, actually."

"How so?" she asked.

"If he knew what chips they were, he should have reported it. If he didn't report it, well…once the feds contact him, we're playing against a short fuse."

She nodded, her heart pounding, stomach souring, mind spinning. "I can't…I can't…" She couldn't take in air, as if her ribs refused to let her lungs expand.

"Easy," Grant murmured. "Easy…"

Then he pulled her onto his lap, cradling her head

with one hand, his other arm wrapped tight around her. "Easy…."

One of her hands curled into a claw and gripped his shirt as she hung on for dear life. Every time she gasped for air, her throat locked up. The world spun like a crazed merry-go-round and blackness seeped in from the edges. Then there was nothing.

Impossibly, when she came to, she was lying on her bed. Grant lay with her, holding her close, murmuring soothing words, his hand rubbing her back. How he had carried her upstairs she couldn't imagine.

When her eyes fluttered open, reluctantly, they were face-to-face.

"Thank God," he said. "I almost called EMS, but once you passed out your breathing steadied."

"How long was I out?"

"A couple of minutes. Probably a much needed vacation from reality."

He was trying to make light of it, but reality wouldn't back off even that much.

"I've never done that before."

"You've never been in this situation before." His hand slipped up her back to stroke her hair briefly, then slid down again to resume its light, soothing rub. "And I have to admit, this situation takes the cake."

She closed her eyes again, allowing herself to enjoy a few moments of comfort in his nearness. She was entitled to that, surely. Last meal for the condemned woman, or whatever.

The moment of black humor told her she was getting past the shock and beginning to function again. She *had* to function if she was to survive this mess.

"Okay," she said after a minute or two. "I've got to start thinking. Planning. Getting ready. Because if you're right about everything speeding up from the instant Hank gets that call, time just became critical. I need to print out everything I have for you to give to Gage. Just in case…in case…"

Her chest tightened again, and she struggled to calm herself.

"You don't have to do anything right now. If there's one thing that keeps coming to me, it's that nothing has changed. That guy is going to come in the middle of the night. Tonight, tomorrow night, whatever. It's still afternoon. Whatever's going to happen, it's not going to happen right now. Right now you need to unwind so you can be on top of things when it matters."

She nodded, unable to speak, curling a bit closer to him because he seemed like a bulwark, warm, comforting and strong. When she reached out a hand to try to draw him closer, he obliged with little urging. She needed to feel him, all of him, along her entire length. She needed to remember something good about life, because right now her options seemed awfully limited.

She couldn't pinpoint the exact moment when things began to change. Maybe there wasn't an exact moment. The atmosphere shifted, her awareness shifted, her breathing quickened a bit. The cells in her body began to send a new kind of message, an intense, in-the-moment message, like sparks zinging along nerve endings.

"Trish..." he whispered, and just as the horrible thought sprang to her mind that he was about to put her off, he whispered her name again and she knew beyond any shadow of a doubt that he felt the same tug, the same yearning, the same ache.

"Grant..."

As if speaking each other's names was all that was needed, the last barriers slipped away.

In an instant they pressed together, tangling, his leg between hers, denim against denim, his thigh against her pulsing center.

A tide of weakness ripped through her. Everything else fled except a driving need as old as time. Their mouths met hungrily. Hands traveled everywhere like desperate seekers needing answers just out of reach. Through her clothes, he traced her curves, every one he could reach, stroking, teasing, promising, evoking, until she could no longer stand the inhibiting layers.

As if he read her mind, he reached up beneath her shirt. With one short twist he released the clasp of her bra and found her breast, covering it with warmth and igniting a fury of flame. A moan escaped her and she began to rock helplessly against his thigh, needing more and more.

Something like a groan escaped him, and for one awful minute he seemed to pull away. But then her shirt and bra were yanked off with a hunger that fed hers even more.

When his mouth left hers it was only to fasten on her breast, sucking her nipple deeply into his mouth, so hot and wet. A noise escaped her and her whole body arched in offering.

He continued to suck, each pull of his mouth sending sparks and then waves of desire to her core until she began to ache so fiercely she was lost completely in the sensation.

But oh, he was not done, not nearly. He seemed determined to drive her to the edge of madness. He certainly seemed determined not to let her have one single coherent thought. She never really knew when or how the rest of her clothes disappeared, leaving her as vulnerable as a newborn babe. Nor did she care.

He was there, still fully clothed himself, guiding her up the stairway to the stars with his mouth and hands. His fingers trespassed between her legs as his mouth continued to tease and torment her breasts. Those wicked, knowing fingers that knew exactly how to touch to lift her even higher without giving her a chance to crest.

He turned her into a writhing, demanding woman with no thought of anything beyond him and this moment, and reaching her ultimate destination.

A finger slipped inside her even as his thumb continued to tease the almost painful knot of nerves he had excited to full flower. A cry escaped her and she clamped her legs around his hand, rocking desperately, needing, all need, nothing but need…

And then he was atop her, his weight bearing her down, his jean-clad hips pressing into the tenderest of flesh between her legs.

Erotic, so erotic, to bare herself and feel him still

clothed, to feel denim, not flesh when she was utterly and completely open.

Another soft cry arose from her lips, and he answered with another thrust of his hips, knowing just how hard to rub against such a tender place. His mouth seized hers again, his tongue thrusting in and out in time with his hip movements, his chest raised just enough that with each movement his shirt brushed against her swollen, aching nipples.

Lost. Oh, she was lost with only one goal in mind, arching up against him, denied that last little bit that would carry her over the top.

She needed more, just that little bit more, and desperately she began to pull at his clothes.

"Trish." He spoke hoarsely.

Oh, no… She opened her eyes just a slit, her body still determined to find culmination, but aware that something was not right. *Please, don't stop*. She didn't know if she said it or only thought it. She couldn't tell where she ended and the rest of the world began. It was all one big bundle of need.

"Trish, I don't have a condom. Leave my clothes…" It was almost a groan.

She got it then. He was going to satisfy her just like this, even if it meant denying himself because he was going to protect her in this, just as he had been protecting her for days.

"Drawer," she gasped. She indicated the bedside table with a quick movement of her eyes.

He moved, twisting, baring part of her to air that

suddenly seemed chilly, and she wanted to cry out in protest at even that minor separation.

He reared up then, tearing off his own shirt while she pulled at the snap and zipper of his jeans. She didn't even get them all the way off before he was tearing at a condom packet with his teeth. She grabbed it from him because this was one pleasure she was not going to be denied, no matter how much she ached and hated this intrusion.

His staff was hard, hot, eager, and she rolled the latex onto him with deliberately teasing strokes, because she wanted him to feel some of the torment he was causing her. Such delicious torment. Such exquisite torment.

He groaned and remained on his knees for a few moments, his eyes closed, his teeth gritted as she ran her fingers over him and reached beneath to that hot, sweaty place, knowing that she was making him as helpless as he had made her and loving every bit of this momentary power.

But then he grabbed her hands and pulled them away, holding her by the wrists near her head. When she tried to tug free, he wouldn't let go.

She opened her eyes a bit wider and saw the most devilish grin on his face, even as his own eyes seemed to be heavy with passion.

Then it happened. She was opened wide, wet and ready and throbbing, and he found her opening as if the two of them were puzzle pieces meant to be matched. With one long, hard thrust he entered her.

Hot. Hard. Everything connecting in just the right way, exactly what her body had been crying out for.

He came to her again and again, and the climb resumed, each thrust a step on the ultimate stairway. Higher she climbed, the ache building and building until…

Until.

She had never felt so open, so hungry, so helplessly enthralled.

Then, in an instant, the expanding bud of desire blossomed into a brilliant rose that shot its petals everywhere, multicolored, bright and oh, so full of beauty.

But just as she started to drift down with the petals of desire fulfilled, he moved again, and before she knew it, she was shooting upward like a rocket, aching even more than before…and finally exploding like fireworks into a place and a peace she had never before known.

Moments later, she felt him follow her.

Chapter 10

"You used to cook a lot," Trish said, watching Grant chop a leek into slices so thin she could see through them.

They had napped for an hour after making love, the first time in days she'd felt truly relaxed. Both awoke hungry and wanting to move out of the bedroom. She had offered to make an evening breakfast—eggs and bacon—but he had declined.

"I'm going to treat you to an old specialty of the Wolfe household," he had said. "Oven-fried chicken with maple-vinegar glaze."

Her stomach had rolled at first, but now as she smelled the scents blending, she grew surprisingly hungry. He had butterflied the chicken with poultry shears, even tucking the ends of the drumsticks into slits cut in the breast skin, seasoned it with salt and pepper, and browned it in a thin layer of olive oil before putting it in the oven. Now he was chopping leeks, if so clumsy a term as *chopping* could apply. *Shaving* was nearer the mark.

"I cooked some. Laura did most of it. For me it was only a hobby." He finished the leek and flipped the root end over his shoulder, landing it not only in the sink but in the side with the garbage disposal, before dabbing his fingertips on the towel over his shoulder. "Something to do when I couldn't think anymore. Just trust my hands and eyes and nose. A way to turn off the hamster wheel."

"As if," Trish said, watching him with admiration approaching envy. It did not escape her that he had just spoken comfortably of his wife for the first time. "First, I'm betting your brain never turns off, period. And second, nobody handles a nine-inch razor blade like that unless they've had a *lot* of practice."

He shrugged and smiled. "Let me have some modesty, okay?"

"Cordon bleu?" she asked, playfully rubbing her shoulder against his arm. "Paris?"

He shook his head. "Not quite. But my boss had."

"Your boss?"

"Stanford's an expensive school," he said. "Even if you're on scholarship. And Palo Alto is an expensive place to live. So I thought—I have to eat, why not get a job where that's included?"

"You worked at a restaurant?"

He nodded. "Started as a dish boy and the head chef

noticed I really cared about the food. He made me a sous chef and there you go. I didn't make a lot of money, but at least I didn't have to buy dinners."

Trish smiled. "That's…charming. I mean, it's one of those 'who'da thunk it' things."

"Few people's lives are straight lines," he said.

"That's true." She laughed, remembering her own early life. "I was going to do weather. Meteorology."

"Really?"

She smiled. "Yup. I had it all figured out. I was going to get a PhD and be on TV for a few years and then do research on hurricanes, when I could squeeze it in around being insanely rich and happily married."

He laughed, a huge belly laugh like she'd never heard from him before. It was, she realized, a laugh she'd like to hear a lot more often.

"Okay," he said, finally taking a breath. "So when did that train derail?"

"Probably right about where you would have gotten interested," she said. "Quantum physics. Turns out that meteorologists have to know that stuff. And I couldn't get it. Period."

"It's not intuitive," he conceded, splashing white wine vinegar into the sautéing leeks.

"Not intuitive?" she asked. "Try incomprehensible for ordinary human beings!"

"There's a saying among physicists," he said. "Anyone who claims to understand quantum theory… hasn't studied it enough."

"*Now* you tell me!" Trish said. "If my professor had

just said that, I might've stuck around. Instead, because I was good at math, I went into accounting. Of course it's not as interesting as being on TV, researching hurricanes and being insanely rich and happily married."

"Been interesting enough lately, though, hasn't it?"

And there it was. Trish remembered the old Chinese curse: *May you live in interesting times.*

"Yeah," she said. "I guess it has. Speaking of, I need to print out my files. If Hank is involved, he may decide to scrub the server. I want hard copies, just in case."

"Good idea," he said. "I'll be a few more minutes here. You have time before dinner. And print two copies, okay? I'll take one with me when I leave."

"Leave?" she asked. "Can't you…?"

Grant shook his head. "No, I can't. I've never seen it from here. I wouldn't know what to look for. I have to follow the vision, and that starts at Mahoney's." He paused and looked at her. "You were the one who said we can't change anything that might affect what I've seen."

She remembered only too well. The thing was, she didn't want to let Grant go. Not even for a few hours. But fear was riding her shoulder again. "Yeah. Okay. Two copies."

She could have brought the laptop into the kitchen, but she decided to stay in her little office. Better that Grant not see the look on her face right now. He didn't need to see her being silly, and that was exactly what she was being. Of course he had to leave. Tonight, and once this was over. He'd go back to California and his friends. That was that, and she just had to deal with it.

But she didn't want to. Right alongside fear, another ache was growing, adding to the butterflies and sense of impending doom. She didn't want him to leave. Not tonight. Maybe not ever. Maybe.

As she booted up her laptop and logged onto the server, she thought about the girl who'd wanted to do weather on TV and study hurricanes. The girl who'd wanted to be insanely rich and happily married. That girl had been a fool on every count. And apparently still was.

If parents were fair, Trish thought, they'd teach their kids to hope for being ordinary. Survive adolescence and get educated enough to get a decent enough job to make ends meet if you were careful. Maybe you'd meet someone special, and maybe you wouldn't. If you did, maybe it would work out and maybe it wouldn't. Either way, remember that most people's lives were…ordinary. The universe reached down to touch you with extraordinary gifts, or it didn't. And for Trish, it hadn't. Now, if she was going to be on TV, it was likely to be as a murder victim, a breathlessly told tale of corporate intrigue in which hers was merely a stock role: dead body on floor.

No fan mail. No high-level research. No wealth.

And no Mr. Perfect.

Except that Mr. Perfect was in her kitchen right now, she thought as she scrolled through her files and started the print job. He was in there making magic with food, just as he had made magic with her body before. He had played her most exquisite nerve endings as skillfully as he handled a chef's knife, as if it was the most natural thing in the world. On the Saffir-Simpson Hurricane Scale, Grant was a Category Five: *breaks down even the sturdiest walls.*

And like a Category Five hurricane, he was going to leave wreckage in his wake. Dreams and hopes long buried, picked up and life breathed into them, passions driven like flotsam on a storm surge, needs she had spent years denying not just watered but flooded. All that was missing was some reporter from the Weather Channel on her front porch, leaning into the wind-driven rain to report: *You can see the storm is really picking up. And as I stand here with power lines falling and tree limbs flying past my head, I should once again warn everyone to not be where I am doing what I'm doing.*

She would have laughed at herself except that a message popped up on her screen.

Account locked. Contact Administrator.

The last moments of happiness, the last wisps of hope, dissipated instantly.

"Grant? Grant!"

He nearly ran. Well, as much as he could with his bad hip, but the tenor of her voice had changed so much that he no longer heard it in tones of plum, but now in a sharp, biting blue.

He reached the door of the office, his hip shrieking now. "What? What?" All he could think was, thank God, she looked all right. In one piece. No blood.

"Look at this." She pointed to her screen and he limped over to her, three short steps that felt as if shards of sharp glass were grinding in his hip.

He bent over and swore. When he saw that her hands were shaking beside the keyboard, he took one and squeezed it.

"Hank's involved," she whispered.

"Maybe. Maybe not. Maybe everything is locked down for the auditor." But he didn't believe it because the instant he touched her hand, the darkness that had been edging his mind since the visions began to grow.

She looked up from the screen, meeting his gaze, and he could tell she didn't believe it, either, not even enough to clutch at the slender straw she offered.

He forced himself to concentrate on the practical. "You said you downloaded the files."

"Some of them. The latest ones that I had verified."

"Is it enough? Along with your e-mails to Hank?"

She closed her eyes a moment, as if steadying herself. "Yes," she said quietly. "I think so."

"Then make the copies of what you have. On CD, on paper. I'll take one set to Gage on my way back to the motel."

"Okay." She started to turn back to her computer, but Grant let go of her hand and gripped her shoulder. When she looked up again, he kissed her with warmth and passion.

"There *will* be a later," he said against her lips, lips still a little swollen from their earlier lovemaking.

Forcing himself to pull back proved harder than he

would have expected, but this was no time to grab her and curl up with her in the back of the darkest hole they could find. No time. He had to feed her so she'd have energy, and then he had to leave, because he didn't dare risk changing one little thing.

"Come get dinner as soon as you're done," he said, forcing a smile he didn't feel.

The meal that he had hoped would be special enough to extend the beautiful experience they had shared earlier, had hoped might leave her with a good memory of him, might as well have been sawdust. Oh, she complimented it, and once she tasted the chicken she even seemed to savor it.

But the darkness was crowding in, both outside and inside. He wanted to say something to leaven the moment, to ease her fear, to do *anything* that might make her feel better, but there wasn't a word or an act that could do that.

She tried, too, smiling at him, talking about how she hadn't expected to like the maple-vinegar sauce, and what a pleasant surprise it had turned out to be.

"I'm glad," he said. "I'll make it for you again." A mention of a future that might never happen. He felt as if he'd dropped an anvil into the middle of the table.

Neither of them ate as much as they might have otherwise, but as soon as they cleared the table, they filled cups with coffee and went to the living room.

And finally he had to say it. "I have to leave soon."

"I know. I can drive you back."

He hesitated. Would that affect anything? Probably

not. "Sure. If you want, just drop me at the square. It's not that far from the sheriff's office to the motel."

"Far enough. You think I can't see you're hurting?"

"It'll pass. I'll be fine." With respect to that, anyway.

She looked down at the cup she held in her lap. "It can't be much longer."

He didn't have to ask what she meant.

"If they've locked me out of the server, I don't think it's for an audit. I would have been contacted first."

"Usually." He wanted to argue with her, but couldn't.

"You said we were operating with a short fuse if Hank was involved."

"Unfortunately."

She turned her head with a pained grimace and looked hollowly at him. "I'll be glad when this is all over."

Yeah, and probably be glad to see the last of him, too, he thought. What had he brought her except terror? In her mind he was probably all wrapped up in the threat she faced.

At that moment he happened to glance at the clock on the box atop her TV. "It's after nine," he said, startled. "God, I've got to be going."

"But..." Her protest died before she voiced it. She put the back of her hand to her mouth, closed her eyes and took a moment. "Let me get the files," she said finally when she opened her eyes again. "And one thing. You said you saw me in my bedroom."

He nodded, feeling his heart jerk uncomfortably.

"Then that's where I'll be," she said.

He was amazed to see resolve in her gaze. As if she had crossed some internal bridge and left fear behind.

She went to her office and returned with two thick manila envelopes. "One for you, one for Gage. They're sealed for security reasons. I'm probably breaking a law just by putting these in your hands."

"Not if they're coded," he said. "I *do* know something about handling classified information."

"They're coded. I guess you're right. I could probably put most of this on the front page of the newspaper. The company would be furious, but nothing classified would be revealed."

"Then don't even worry about it. I expect both these envelopes will be in the feds' hands soon, and they can break the code."

She nodded, watching as he picked up his jacket, tucked the envelopes inside and zipped up.

"I'll drive you," she said again. "You need to give your hip a break so you can get back here tonight."

He hesitated, bothered in some way, but couldn't put his finger on it. The killer wouldn't come until after midnight, and if he was out there somewhere, watching, all he'd discover was that Trish was going to be alone.

So what was bothering him? The driving? He felt around in his head. No, he didn't get a bad feeling about her driving him. But something else…

"I don't know why," he said, "but bring your shotgun. You might want to check the house out when you get back. Top to bottom."

"But I've got watchers, right?"

"Yeah."

"Besides," she said, "the killer leaves the bar just before 1:00 a.m."

Reminding him of his own vision. She was incredible, and equally incredible was the determination he saw in her now.

"I can't take the gun. If the killer is watching, I don't want him to know I have it or that I'm concerned."

Irrefutable logic. He hated it, but couldn't argue with it.

So she drove him back to the motel, a five-minute trip. She had insisted he rest, that he could leave the envelope with the sheriff on his way back to Mahoney's. More logic, in a place where logic was all they had.

Before he climbed out, he had to reach for her, hold her close, kiss her as if his life depended on it.

"I'll be there," he said.

She almost smiled. "I know you will." She cupped his cheek and whispered, "It's almost over. Tonight. Tomorrow night. I can feel it."

"Yeah." His voice was hoarse. "Yeah." And pulling away from her felt about as painful as pulling off his own skin, but he made himself do it.

Because he had no choice. Because if he blew it this time, he was going to jump off a bridge.

Tad was drowsy, and she had to encourage him to take his nighttime walk in the backyard. He yawned a few times, but managed to do his business. Then he came back inside, not prancing as usual, but rather sedate.

She squatted down as she took the leash off inside the kitchen and rubbed his ears. He yawned. "I guess the tension gets to you, too, huh?"

He yawned again, then found a corner where he walked his usual circle, flattening grass that wasn't there. When he dropped it was with an almost comical thud.

"I wish I felt that sleepy," she told him. He opened one eye briefly, then let it droop closed.

"Some watchdog." Although, there was nothing to disturb him right now, no reason for him to bounce and bark. If someone tried to break in, though, he'd probably be true to his species.

She walked the entire downstairs, checking to be sure everything was locked up tight. No reason she had to make it easy on this guy, even though if Grant was right, he was going to get in, anyway.

Shotgun in hand, she finally headed upstairs with a cup of hot cocoa. Glancing at the clock, she saw she still had time. Time to get in her flannel nightshirt, time to read for a while and try to distract herself. Given the clarity of Grant's timetable, she didn't have to turn off the light until around twelve-thirty, which was good, because she didn't think she could stand being alone in the dark for long.

Not after finding out her account at work had been locked. If she'd had a remaining shred of doubt that she might be in danger, that had erased it.

She had become two loose ends without a middle.

The room still held the aromas of their recent love-making. She put her cocoa on the nightstand, gave up all hope of reading and, instead, rolled over to hug the pillow beside her. It still smelled of Grant, still smelled of *them*.

The scent comforted her as she watched the hands of the clock tick slowly forward.

Across town in the motel, Grant couldn't sleep, either. He tried to watch TV and gave up. Instead, he lay on the bed, knowing he needed to rest his hip if he was going to be anything more than utterly useless tonight.

Tonight. Why he felt so certain he couldn't say. He didn't have another vision or anything, just a feeling. Seeing that Trish had been locked out of her account had been an emotional Big Bang, and while he knew logically that it could have been nothing but a move by an auditor to preserve the records, he didn't believe it.

No, the cover-up had begun. Forces had been put into motion to protect someone or something. Maybe the FBI had called Hank, Trish's CFO, to set up a meeting tomorrow. Who knew? No way to know.

All he could say for sure was that something had shifted, because just yesterday she had been able to access her work account to get her e-mail.

Tonight.

The agony of anticipation and terror held him in thrall. No way out.

Tonight.

Chapter 11

A little after midnight, Grant rose and pulled on his boots and jacket. Just as he had every night before, he stuffed his room key in his pocket, turned out the light and stepped out into the brisk night air.

His hip had eased up some after the rest, so the walk to Mahoney's wasn't the grinding impossibility it might have become. Indeed, he was surprised when he glanced at his watch. He'd made it in record time. Five minutes early. He took in the scents of the night and the way the town had quieted at this late hour. It was almost as if the world had frozen into suspended animation, to be awakened only by the warmth of the rising sun.

"Evenin'," Mahoney said, sliding Grant a bowl of pretzels and his now customary shot of rye, neat.

"Evenin' and thanks," Grant replied. He sipped his drink, watching nearby seats, waiting to see a man leave. Then he realized that Mahoney had not only made him feel like a welcome regular, but seemed to have given him more than a single shot. Grant put a ten on the table. "It's perfect."

Mahoney nodded and grinned as he picked up the bill. "So's this."

"Yup," Grant said, forcing himself to make small talk. "I left the counterfeit ones back at the hotel."

"Thank God," Mahoney said. "They've been getting mixed in with the ones I print up in the back, and that's killing my quality control standards."

"Life is tough."

"True that, as my grandkid would say."

Grant usually enjoyed their repartee, but tonight was not the night for it. He smiled and nodded in a way that said *thanks, I'm done,* and sipped his drink again. Mahoney returned the nod and moved down the bar. Apparently not much slipped past him. It was a knack shared by most good bartenders. *Tonight,* Grant thought, looking down the bar at the empty stool two seats away. He'll come tonight. He'll order a drink, a shot of liquid courage, then he'll glance up at the clock. At ten before one, he'll leave. And Grant would follow him and then…?

Well, that was the big question, wasn't it?

And one for which Grant had no ready answer. He had to follow the guy, just to be sure it wasn't someone who happened to wander into a bar for a nightcap, having not the slightest intention of harming Trish. But once he'd done that, and once he was sure…what? It's not as if Grant was a trained bodyguard or even a former soldier. Even if he had been, he was a cripple. And unarmed. And the other guy would be a trained killer, a pro, doubtless carrying a weapon he knew how to use.

It was, Grant thought, a recipe for disaster. But it was the only recipe he had. And as he'd learned back in college, sometimes you just take a recipe and riff until something good comes out. *E pluribus wing it.*

It struck him, as he glanced at the empty stool again, that there was a lot of truth to Einstein's quip when asked to explain time being relative: "A two-second kiss is much shorter than two seconds with your hand on a hot stove." The hours he'd spent with Trish today had flown by. The few minutes he'd spent here at Mahoney's tonight were crawling.

He glanced up at the clock over the bar: 12:50 a.m. Anytime now. The scientist in him could almost track the up-tick in adrenaline. His fingers did not quite quiver, but he realized his palm felt slick against the glass. He knew it was the opening of pores, releasing sweat, part of the fight-or-flight response, a cascading of set physiological adjustments crafted by millennia of evolution to optimize physical performance in dire danger. It had happened on the plane in those awful moments after he realized he and his family, and the rest of the passengers, were locked in the death spiral of his vision. Then he had been unable to do anything. But tonight, once he saw the man, he could at least *try.*

The man should be here now. He should already have walked up and sat down, ordered his drink. It had to be tonight. Grant could feel it. But where was he? Grant looked at the empty stool again, and again at the clock over the bar: 12:50 a.m.

The clock's second hand wasn't moving.

"Oh, God," Mahoney said, apparently having seen Grant stiffen as he looked from his watch to the clock. "Oh, God. The clock stopped this afternoon. He left before you got here."

"Who left?" Grant asked, looking at his watch—12:52 a.m.

"The guy you've been looking for," Mahoney said. "Sat in that stool, the one you always look at. Scotch neat. Big sumbuck, too. He left not five minutes before you got here."

"But he's supposed to come at ten to one…" Grant said, his voice trailing away.

Then it clicked. In his vision, he'd been seeing Mahoney's stopped clock.

"Go," Mahoney said, smacking a key ring on the bar. "My bike's out front. I'll call Gage. Go."

"Thanks," Grant said, scooping up the keys. "Tell Gage to meet me at Trish Devlin's place. And tell him to get his UC team over there now. He'll know what I mean."

"The couple from Laramie staying next door?"

"Does everyone in this town know everything about everyone?" Grant asked as he made for the door.

"Yeah, they do," Mahoney said. "But your big sumbuck ain't from this town. Now go."

A single creak as the screen door opened.

The sound was almost too quiet to hear, but to Trish's ears it might have been a boom of thunder. Her eyes shot open, and her body stiffened. She looked at the clock. 12:53 a.m. It wouldn't be Grant. He wouldn't be here yet. And Grant would knock. There wasn't even a whine or a bark from the dog sleeping downstairs. Had she misheard?

She held her breath, listening, and heard a different sound, like some thuds. Was that a groan? But it was outside somewhere…and then another creak of the screen door. Her heart slammed.

Trish forced herself to take a long, slow breath, exhaling through her nose, as her father had taught her to do before squeezing a trigger. It quieted the mind, as well as the body. And she needed both right now. Then she slid first one leg and then the other off the bed, crouching on the floor as her hand grasped the stock of the shotgun. She lifted it as a mother might a sleeping baby, carefully so as not to wake it. Or, so as not to make a sound.

Why wasn't Tad barking?

Might it be Grant, after all? Even if it was, Tad would let out his usual happy yelps of delight. There was not a sound from him. Only the slow, measured, near silent steps of someone moving through the living room. Had her senses not been so attuned, had the sounds not been in her own home whose sounds she knew so well, she wouldn't have heard them. But she did. And Grant could not move with that stealth.

The killer was in her house.

Killer, singular? Trish asked herself. She'd always assumed so, because Grant's vision had but one actor. But she remained still, clutching the shotgun, closing her eyes, quieting her breath, and forced herself to listen.

Step.

Pause.

Step.

Pause.

Step.

It had to be one man. In her mind's eye, Trish could see him. Cautious step. Look around, testing shadow and silence. Then another cautious step.

Grant was right. They'd sent a pro.

He'd have a pistol, Trish reasoned. A rifle or shotgun would attract too much attention as he entered the house and later made his escape. She had only her shotgun. It was not a fair fight, not in close quarters. She would need longer to swing the shotgun's barrel, sight and squeeze the trigger. He would get off the first shot. And he wouldn't miss.

Unless she could make him pause. That meant not being where he expected her to be.

But he had already cleared the living room, she could tell, and the kitchen. He was in her office now. Then he would come to her bedroom. There was no time to open a window. And nowhere else to run.

Except the closet.

Yes, the closet.

Grant hadn't ridden a motorcycle in years, and then only once with a friend. He overleaned, oversteered and over-everything-else'd for the first few moments, until he learned to trust the gyroscopic effect of rotational energy in the wheels. It was like riding a bicycle without the pedaling. That he could manage.

As for the rest, he still had no idea.

The vision had been so clear. The killer would come into Mahoney's at ten to one and order a drink, then go over to Trish's. Crystal clear, but for a stopped clock. Now Grant was playing catch-up, racing someone who was better trained and better armed.

But not better motivated.

In the distance, across the city square and down the block, at the sheriff's office, he heard an engine rev. Mahoney had made the call and someone else was already on the move. And the couple from Laramie should be there, too.

Reason said they were better trained to handle the situation. And better armed.

But not better motivated.

Love and guilt, terror and a soul's aching need for redemption. They drove him relentlessly as he shifted the bike and twisted the throttle.

Cold air bit his face and whipped his hair, but it

didn't matter. Getting to Trish's mattered. And getting there quickly mattered more. Getting there only in time to see more bloody debris of broken dreams would not do. And it would not happen. Not again.

As he swerved onto Trish's street, he throttled the bike down, briefly considering the fastest way to get off that did not include a sprawling tumble onto asphalt. He would get inside no quicker and do Trish no good if he was even more crippled. That meant no heroic and foolish vault from a moving motorcycle.

The black SUV was parked two doors down and across the street. The vehicle a killer had driven. A man who intended to kill the woman Grant loved.

It.

Would.

Not.

Happen.

The bike slewed as he pulled into Trish's driveway, and for a fleeting instant he felt the back wheel begin to give way to centripetal acceleration. He squeezed the brakes and blinked as rubber and asphalt made peace. The bike stayed upright and he kicked down the stand.

Now without the roar of the bike's engine, his ears joined the sensory assault on his reasoning. His eyes swept the scene. The door was open. Near the garage, a tiny glint of metal caught his eye. It was copper. Phone cable. Cut. Just like in his vision. Impossibly, a line from Sherlock Holmes popped into his mind: *the dog that didn't bark.* Where was Tad?

* * *

Where was Tad? Trish wondered as she eased the louvered closet door closed, lifting as best she could with fingertips in the slats, to muffle the sound as its rollers slid in their tracks. There was hardly any sound to muffle. Good home maintenance paid off, she realized with a moment of black humor. She had vacuumed and sprinkled silicone lubricant in the tracks only last week. Or was that another example of Grant's theory of precognition?

There was no time to ponder metaphysics. The closet was not deep enough for her to stand with the shotgun at her shoulder. Instead, she dropped to one knee and braced the butt against the inside of her foot, left hand aiming the barrel up toward the door, right hand upside down on the stock, right thumb on the trigger. It was hardly the classic shooting position, but it would have to do.

It also had the advantage of making her a smaller target if the killer did fire through the door. She hoped he would make the mistake of firing at chest level, on the mistaken assumption she was standing. If so, the bullet would pass well over her head. The birdshot, by contrast, would take a nasty chunk out of his midsection.

But only if he was near the door. She could not depress the barrel far enough to hit him if he was more than a few feet back. If he stood across the room and peppered the door with rounds, sooner or later one would hit her. And there wouldn't be a damn thing she could do about it.

For that entirely sane reason, she dismissed the

thought as soon as it entered her mind. There was nothing to be gained by enumerating the hopeless possibilities. She had to focus on what she could do and let the rest take care of itself.

She heard the bedroom door open and eased the safety switch off. *Come on in, you bastard. Come on in.*

Grant almost tripped over the two bodies on the lawn. They must be, he realized, Gage's friends from Laramie. He squatted for a moment and pressed his fingertips to their throats. To his surprise, both were alive, despite the bloody mess at the center of their faces. They hadn't been shot, he realized. Instead, the killer had crushed their noses with punches, kicks or the butt end of a pistol. The woman let out a low moan, and Grant put a fingertip to her lips.

He lowered his face to her ear and more breathed than whispered, "I'm Grant Wolfe. Trish's friend. He's in the house, isn't he?"

The woman nodded. "S-sorry."

"Don't be," Grant whispered. "I need your gun."

She nodded again, though her hand seemed to wander vaguely over a belt holster that wasn't there. She was too disoriented to help, Grant realized. And as an undercover she'd have been wearing a shoulder rig.

"I'm sorry," he said as he reached inside her jacket, fumbling across her breast for the pistol.

"Ssss'okay," she murmured. "S-snap."

His fingertips found the retaining snap as she said the word, and he flicked it open and slid the pistol out. It was heavier than he expected. And he'd never fired a gun in his life.

"Thumb s-safety," she stammered weakly, looking at him. "Point. S-squeeze. T-two sh-shots. C-center mass."

It wasn't much of a gun-safety course, but it was all he was going to get. He nodded and rose, entering the house, moving toward Trish's bedroom as lightly as he could.

It wasn't light at all. And he knew it.

Grant! Trish recognized him from his very first step. Part of her heart leaped at the realization that he was here. And part of her heart cringed. If she could hear him, so could the killer.

The killer who was, even at that moment, standing near the end of her bed. Her empty bed. The wheels would be turning, she realized. Had she gone out for the night? Had he made some mistake, and she had slipped out of the house? Did he have the wrong address? He would quickly rule out those options and come to the logical answer. She was in the closet. But how quickly? Would his thoughts be loud enough to deafen the sound of Grant's movements?

For that she could only hope and keep the barrel of the shotgun trained on the spot where she knew he must stand if she was to have any chance at all.

But she could do more than that, she realized. She could let the killer know where she was. Or where she almost was.

She braced the barrel against her knee, reached up with her left hand and, as quietly as she could, slid a hanger an inch across the closet rod. It was so quiet she wasn't sure he would hear it. But that was the point. A helpless woman in hiding would be quiet. If she made any obvious sound, his combat-trained senses would pick up on it. But if he heard nothing…

She was about to move the hanger again and froze.

Step.

Pause.

Step.

Trish smiled. *That's right. A little closer. Just another step or two. Come on….*

Grant heard the sharp intake of breath from the bedroom. The killer knew she was in there somewhere. But not where he expected. She hadn't shot him as he stepped into the room. She'd hidden. That complicated things, he realized, for he had no idea where she was hiding, either.

But he knew her bedroom, and the options were few. One, really. The closet. She would be in the closet. The scenario played out in his mind. She couldn't hold the shotgun normally. The barrel was too long for the shallow closet. She would crouch and aim it like a mortar. The killer would probably have to get right up to the closet door. She would realize it. She would make some subtle sound to lure him closer. Indeed, she just had. Thus his intake of breath.

Seconds collapsed into instants.

* * *

Come on, Trish almost spoke aloud. If there were telepathy to go with precognition, surely the killer must have heard that thought. *One more step and you're mine.*

But he didn't take the step. Instead, she saw the shadows in the louvers shift as he lifted his arm. She heard the muffled spit an instant before the wood above her head splintered. Bits of drywall fluttered down as the bullet bored into the wall behind her, followed a moment later by the tinkle of a brass cartridge landing and bouncing on her floor.

Step closer, dammit!

Instead, there was another spit, another splinter of wood, another snowfall of drywall, another delicate ring of brass on hardwood. And this time the hole was lower. He was doing exactly what she had feared he would. Firing through the door, knowing that sooner or later he'd hit his target, without ever having to get close enough to expose himself to danger.

The unenumerated possibility about which she could do nothing. Or could she?

She let out an audible grunt and thumped her knee against the floor. *You hit me. You're done. Mission accomplished. Come check and see.*

Grant had seen the flashbulb pops of the shots, and he heard Trish grunt and slump to the floor. His heart slammed in his chest. The killer had shot her through the closet door. Grant had failed.

No!

Not this time. Not again.

He held the gun out in front of him, trying to mimic what he'd seen in cop movies, hoping it was accurate or at least close enough. This man had hurt Trish. This man would die. It was a simple equation.

Grant moved through the doorway, no longer worrying about noise. Mahoney had been right. The killer was a big sumbuck, with a sick half smile that made Grant's blood boil in black rage. The killer had lowered his weapon, one hand reaching for the closet door. Grant swung the woman's pistol up and began squeezing the trigger.

"No, you don't," Grant hissed, squeezing again.

And again. But there was no crack. No recoil. The safety! She'd said it was thumb-operated. He felt for it blindly, holding the weapon on the man, knowing he would not have enough time. For the killer had pivoted with predatory grace and was already sighting his weapon on Grant's face.

And the hole in the end of the silencer looked impossibly huge.

Then the closet door exploded.

The boom was impossibly loud in the closet. Trish worked the slide to chamber a fresh round as she kicked at the door. The killer had been turning to shoot Grant, and she was taking no chances. With a quick, popping grind of metal on metal, the doors rollers wrenched the track open and popped off. She kicked at the door again as it began to fall inward on her, rising from her crouch with the butt of the shotgun seated against her hip.

The killer had taken a step back when the first round hit, stunned but not down. In milliseconds she watched him weigh the threat of Grant in the doorway with a pistol he had not yet fired and Trish emerging from the closet with a shotgun that had already sent rivers of pain arcing across his synapses. He was turning to her. But he was slowed by pain and she was pushed by rage.

She didn't raise the weapon to her shoulder. She didn't take time to sight. She pointed at his midsection and squeezed.

The closet door tumbled across the barrel in the instant before the shotgun boomed and kicked again.

She had missed.

Or not.

With a howl like a wounded animal, he sank to the floor, the pistol falling from his hand as he clutched at his groin and a puddle of blood began to spread. Trish used the barrel of the shotgun to sling the door away and chambered another round, stepping closer, raising the butt to her shoulder, sighting on his face.

"Trish!" Grant called. "He's down. He's done."

Maybe so, Trish thought. But she wanted it over. She wanted to make damn sure this man would not get up. Ever. Except in a bag. She squeezed again.

This time it was Grant's hand, not the closet door, that deflected the barrel. Just enough that Trish saw the hardwood floor beside the man's head splinter.

"Trish, no!" Grant said, gripping the barrel, stepping in front of her. "He's down. He's done. And dead men can't talk."

She finally met Grant's eyes. She nodded. "You're right. Dead men can't talk." She looked down at the man on the floor. "And that's the only reason you get to live. So start talking. Before I change my mind."

At that instant, she heard her front door bang open with cries of "Police!" At the same instant, adrenaline deserted her and she began to shake and shake hard. She couldn't fight when Grant took the shotgun from her, and then she couldn't stand, as her legs turned to rubber.

Grant slipped his arm under her shoulder, holding her up.

"Up here," he shouted.

Helpless in the wake of shock, she could feel only more shock as Grant tossed her gun onto the bed and then a pistol. He kicked the assassin's weapon across the room.

"No," she said, feeling another surge of adrenaline, struggling to escape his grip so she could get her shotgun back. That man could still do something.

"Shh," Grant said, wrapping both arms around her. "Shh. You don't want to be holding a gun when the cops burst in."

At some level she recognized he was right, but she was shaking so hard, and terrified now that the adrenaline that had supported her had abandoned her. "Oh, God," she said, her voice taut with terror.

Her bedroom door was open, and a horde of cops poured through it.

"Down! Down!" they shouted pointing gun barrels and flashlights in every direction.

Grant started to ease down with Trish in his arms, but then a voice stopped it all.

"I think," Gage said from the doorway, "that our bad guy is already down."

He was answered by an agonized groan from the floor.

Chapter 12

Red, blue and white stobe lights filled the usually quiet street in front of Trish's house. With a blanket around her shoulders and Grant supporting her, she stepped out into a swirl of activity that must have attracted attention for several blocks. And she hadn't known the county had four ambulances.

But there they were, lined up at the curb, taking on two injured police officers and the man she had shot.

I shot a man. She couldn't absorb the thought and wondered if she ever would. *I wanted to kill that man.* Ugliness she had never before found in herself.

One of the ambulances was apparently for her, and no one heeded her protests that she was just fine. "Just go," Grant said. "This is going to hit you harder than you think, and probably very soon."

He would certainly know about life-altering events, she thought a bit hazily.

So she let them put her on a stretcher and wrap her in even more blankets. When she didn't want to let go of Grant's hand, they let him climb aboard, too.

She clung to his hand, annoying the medics who were trying to get readings. "You saved me," she said.

"You saved yourself."

"No." She shook her head and tried to raise it.

The EMT tut-tutted and pushed her back down. "Stop fighting," he said.

But she was focused on Grant. Completely and totally. "You believed the impossible, and you saved me. Remind me to tell you what a miracle that is."

"I think you just did."

The EMT elevated her feet just as the world swam out of view and darkness caught up.

Gage had to step in. The FBI had arrived, along with some even more serious-looking guys who were from the Defense Department, and none of them wanted to let Trish out of the hospital bed until she'd answered all their questions. Not even the doc could persuade them to wait, nor could Grant, who tried to make himself a human wall between her and the invaders.

It was Gage, wearing his uniform for once, who turned the tide. "Look," he said, "I've got an envelope of information on my desk for you guys from Ms.

Devlin. You can spend the night looking over that. Meanwhile, she's just been through hell and needs a little time. I'm sure she'll talk to you tomorrow. Go bother the guy she shot."

As he shooed the last of them away, he turned to Trish. "I've got a deputy standing by to take you wherever you want to go as soon as you're released."

"Thanks." She was feeling so drained now that she could hardly move. "What about the killer? Is he talking?"

"Let's just say that he doesn't have medical insurance. Apparently it doesn't come with his job."

"So?"

"So I told him that if he ever wanted to be in any condition to father children, he'd have to rely on the county to pay his medical expenses. Fast. And I'd only authorize that if he talked. Otherwise he could settle for basic emergency treatment before he got transported to my jail."

A snort escaped Grant, but Trish wasn't laughing. None of it felt laughable. "So he's talking?"

"He's singing. You may not have meant to hit him there, but good job!"

She was discharged after only a couple of hours. When they were in the patrol car, Grant instructed the deputy to take them to the motel.

"But I want to go home," Trish said.

"No. You don't. Not until I get someone in there to clean up the mess and make repairs."

Oh, God. Oh, God. She felt another tremor pass through her. "Tad…"

"Tad's at the vet's. He's okay, but he must have been drugged."

She looked at him, feeling the breath sucked out of her. "That means…that means…"

"That the guy got into your house when you drove me to the motel. Very likely. How he got past those cops I don't know."

"Maybe they didn't feel they had to watch as closely when I was out."

"Maybe. We'll find out. We'll figure out everything."

With that, she sighed and let him pull her head onto his shoulder. She couldn't sort through all this now. No way. It was going to take time. For now she was just going to let herself enjoy the comfort of Grant's nearness. She had years ahead of her to deal with what had happened tonight, what she had done tonight.

At the motel he tucked her under the covers to keep her warm, since she was still in her flannel nightshirt. He lay on top of the covers fully clothed and drew her into the circle of his strength, holding her close.

"Thank you," she said.

"Don't thank me."

"But you saved my life."

His answer was simple. "You saved mine."

"You would have gotten that safety off…"

"I wasn't talking about that."

"Oh." Hazily, she realized he was talking about the whole thing. His grief, his guilt. He had atoned. That made her feel better and she snuggled closer, loving the smell of him, the softness of his flannel shirt, the power she could feel in his chest.

"But if you want to talk about tonight..." He squeezed her. "I think I saw a lioness protecting her pride. But for you, he'd probably have managed to shoot me."

"I wasn't going to let him do that."

"No kidding. You erupted out of that closet like a Valkyrie."

"I'm not exactly proud of what I did."

"I understand. Sometimes, though, we *have* to do things we'd never want to do under ordinary circumstances. There was a killer in your bedroom and he'd already shot at you. You don't have to feel good about what you did, but you shouldn't beat yourself up, either."

"No...." Oddly, her eyes were growing heavy.

"Sleep now," he said quietly. "You need some rest. I'll be right here."

And she did exactly that.

She awoke with a start to the brilliant light of morning. It took a full half minute for her to realize where she was and that there was no longer any reason to be afraid. She heard Grant speaking and turned to see him on the telephone, talking quietly. When he saw her looking at him, he smiled and waved.

She waited patiently while he talked, not paying attention to what he said, just glad to look at him and be grateful that he hadn't vanished along with the nightmare.

He hung up and crossed to sit on the bed beside her.

Reaching out, he first stroked her tousled hair, then clasped her hand. "Do you want the update?"

"Sure." She clung to his fingers, wanting never to let go.

"The two deputies who were guarding you are going to be okay. Battered and a little broken, but otherwise good. How he got past them when you drove me back here..." He shrugged. "Lori thinks it was because they simply weren't being attentive enough, having been told the attack would come between midnight and two. As she said, they were watching from inside the neighboring house at that point, and it would have been easier for him to slip by."

Trish nodded. "I don't blame them. I'm just glad they're going to be okay."

Grant nodded agreement. "Gage is sending one of his deputies over to get you some clothes, so you won't be trapped in my clutches wearing only your nightgown forever."

"I like being trapped in your clutches."

A smile softened his face. "I'm thrilled to hear it. Second item—I have someone coming in today to clean up your house. The mess will be gone by this evening, but the repairs won't likely be done until tomorrow."

"I can deal with a broken closet door."

"It's more than broken. Splinters everywhere. But regardless, you also need a new front door lock. Closet door and front door tomorrow morning."

"Okay."

"Tad is doing well. The guy may be a hit man, but he

doesn't hurt animals. So your dog will be back in your arms as soon as we get over there. If you still want him?" He seemed almost hesitant. "I *did* force him on you."

"I'm glad you did. I'd keep him if for no other reason, but actually I'm getting very fond of him."

His smile deepened. "And as soon as we get your clothes, we're wanted over at the sheriff's department."

At that she closed her eyes and sighed heavily. "I know I have to, but I don't want to." Right now she didn't want to relive the horrible night or the events leading up to it. She wanted to pretend it had never happened.

Well, except for meeting Grant. That opened her eyes again. She looked at him, wondering if he was going to turn into another regret, but she didn't want to ask. Didn't dare to ask.

"I know," he said when she remained silent, "that I promised I'd be here with you all night. But I have a confession to make."

Her heart jumped uneasily.

"I trotted across to the truck stop to get us something to eat. It's just some rolls, but I didn't want anything that would spoil before you awoke."

"Coffee?" she asked hopefully.

"You bet."

With that, she discovered that she had some willpower left, some energy, though not much, and a suddenly huge appetite. She pushed herself up against the pillows and headboard and banished all unhappy thoughts, determined to keep them tucked away until she had to deal with them later during questioning.

She even managed a smile. "Bring it on, please. I'm hungry."

But instead of going to get the food, he bent over her and kissed her long and deep. Within seconds she was clinging to his broad shoulders and he was slipping his arms beneath her. The heat she felt seemed to burn everything else away.

Then he pulled back with a groan. "Not now," he said hoarsely. "Not now. The deputy will be here any minute." He dropped a quick kiss on her nose, then with an obvious reluctance that put a bandage over at least one of her fears, he rose to get the coffee and the rolls.

Their conversation while they ate rambled aimlessly, avoiding touchy subjects entirely. He told her about his friends. She told him about hers. They even spoke briefly about their parents and discovered they were both orphans now.

It was a conversation so ordinary that Trish felt herself becoming steadily tethered in the real world again, shaking free of the surreal events of the past days.

By the time Deputy Sara Ironheart arrived with a suitcase full of clothes, Trish had even started believing that life could be ordinary again.

And that seemed like the most amazingly beautiful thing in the world.

The meeting at the sheriff's office was awful. Grant wasn't allowed to come with her into the interrogation room where four federal agents waited for her with tape recorders, notepads and not-quite-friendly looks. The only comfort she had was Gage, who had dragged his office chair in so he could ease his habitual pain by sitting.

And it was Gage who drew the lines. "Okay," he said after introducing everyone, "I want some understandings before we proceed."

All of the agents frowned at him. One spoke. "You know we don't have to agree to that."

"No," Gage said amiably, "you don't. But if you don't, Ms. Devlin is going to get lawyered up before you ask a single question. And if she gets lawyered up, it's going to be with one of the country's most famous attorneys who happens to live not too far from here and is a personal friend of mine."

The agents exchanged looks, then the one who had spoken—Tom Feeney, if Trish had them all sorted correctly—said, "Look, Sheriff, this is an issue of national security of the highest importance. We need Ms. Devlin's full cooperation to find out what happened."

"Ms. Devlin actually knows very little," Gage replied, still amiable. "Most of it's in that envelope I gave you."

"Then what concerns you?"

"That you might try to imply something that just ain't so." Gage smiled, but it wasn't exactly friendly. "Kindly keep in mind that I used to be DEA. I know how interrogations can run. This is *not* an interrogation, and certainly not an interrogation of a hostile witness. Got it?"

Trish was becoming increasingly nervous by the second. "I didn't do anything wrong!"

"Of course you didn't," Gage said. "Which is my point, and the point we're going to get clear before we go any further. And the same rules will hold for the questioning of Mr. Wolfe."

"Now wait—"

"No, you wait. You wouldn't have even learned of this without these two. So I want absolutely *no* suggestion that either of them have done *anything* except help uncover a crime. Clear?"

One of the other men spoke. "We can take them to our office for questioning. Or to the U.S. Attorney's office."

Trish's heart slammed.

"No," said Feeney. "No. We're not going that route. There's absolutely no evidence that this woman or Mr. Wolfe engaged in any crime."

"Exactly," Gage said. "Which is why you're going to question them as witnesses to help your case, not as co-conspirators *even if you have other questions.*"

Trish waited, her heart in her throat, realizing that Gage was trying to make certain that no one questioned how she had discovered what kind of chips were stolen. So that no one even suggested that she or Grant or anyone else had gone to places they shouldn't have gone.

She managed a grateful look at Gage, realizing he was saving them.

Feeney nodded. "The point of this is to catch the bad guys, not implicate the people who tried to stop this."

"Then we're agreed," Gage said. He leaned forward, wincing a little. "So we'll start at the basics. Ms. Devlin noticed an inventory discrepancy and reported it to her CFO. She became concerned because she is aware that the plant produces classified chips. She became further concerned when her boyfriend, Grant Wolfe, immediately saw the threat inherent in her discovery *if* the missing chips were highly classified."

Feeney nodded. "I can go with that."

"It's true!" The words burst out of Trish. "It was his scientific background that gave me enough information to realize how dangerous this might be. And then when I found myself locked out of my work account..." She trailed off.

Gage spoke. "She promptly reported it to me and I called you. And once I called you, I knew that if what she suspected was true, she might be in serious danger."

After that things went smoothly. An hour later she was out of there. Grant was next and she waited impatiently outside. Finally he emerged, looking unruffled and completely calm. Gage followed him.

She looked up. "Is it over?"

Gage sat beside her on a plastic chair while Grant squatted in front of her and took her hands. "Mostly," he said. "Mostly. What's left is nothing to worry about."

"Most definitely not," Gage said. "You'll probably have to make a statement under oath about how you discovered and reported the discrepancy, and what happened after that. Just what you said in there. And you'll probably have to testify at trial to exactly the same information."

She nodded. "I can do that."

"So in that sense, it's over," Grant said, squeezing her hands. Then he grimaced and flopped into the chair on the other side of Trish. He leaned forward and looked at Gage. "We make some pair, you and I."

Gage shook his head and laughed. "The halt and the lame, that's us." He turned his attention to Trish. "Your CFO was named by the hit man. They'll probably be chasing connections for months to find out how many people were involved and where those chips might have gone. But one thing I'm certain of now."

"What's that?"

"You did the right thing and now you're safe. Your testimony won't even be critical at a trial, thanks to the hit man. Nothing more to worry about, Trish."

Nothing? she wondered as she rode back to the motel with Grant in the car he had rented. *Nothing?*

Just little stuff like learning to live with herself again and dealing with the fact that she'd shot a man and had wanted to kill him, and probably watching Grant walk off into the sunset—literally since his home was in California.

Once back in the room, however, a lot of that melted away as he drew her down onto the bed with him and hugged her, just hugged her. She didn't want to lose him. She couldn't bear that thought.

But outspoken though she usually was, there were questions she couldn't force past her lips. They simply wouldn't emerge.

After a bit he was the one who broke the silence. "I talked to Dex and Jerry while you were in with the cops."

Her heart squeezed. "I bet they can't wait for you to come back."

"Apparently."

"So when will you go?" It hurt to even ask.

"Well, that's what I want to talk to you about."

She tilted her face, trying to read his expression. He looked somber, she thought, and that couldn't possibly mean anything good.

"I like this town," he said. "I like the people I've met. I'm even getting used to Maude. And without Mahoney last night, I never would have gotten to your place as quickly as I did. The man hardly knows me from Adam, but he gave me the keys to his Harley. So I like this place and the people."

"Well, we have our share of prunes, if you know what I mean."

One corner of his mouth lifted. "Everywhere does. But people here seem to be focused differently. And I like it. So here's the thing—I want to come back."

So he *was* leaving. And wanting to come back didn't exactly sound like a promise. "I hope you do." And she hoped the tightening in her throat wasn't audible.

"The thing is, I'm going to need at least a couple of months back in California. To catch up on what's been going on with the business and the research. And to get my hip worked on some more. I shouldn't have let it go this long."

"No, you shouldn't have," she agreed, this time with her whole heart. "You were punishing yourself, weren't you?"

"You know me too well. So, anyway, I'm going to need a couple of months, maybe a little longer before I can come back."

She managed a nod. Now her heart was climbing into her throat.

"But I don't want to leave you."

She caught her breath, and things inside her began to unfurl with wonder. "Grant?"

He gave a little shake of his head. "I'm doing a lousy job of this, so let me just blurt it all out, okay?"

"Okay."

"I want you to come with me. I want us to get to know each other better, and then I want to come back here with you. I can telecommute with only a few trips to California each year. Can you handle that?"

A smile was beginning to grow on her face. "I think so."

He blew out a short breath, as if releasing tension of some kind, then came another rush of words. "I'm going to marry you. I know it. But I want you to be sure, too. I'm already in love with you. I want you to be in love with me."

She was smiling ear to ear now, and a tear of happiness slipped free. "I think I'm already there. How can you be so sure? Did you have another vision?"

He gave a little shrug. "Well, I *did* see a little boy with your gorgeous eyes."

Her heart soared then, and her future opened up at last into a wonderful place she thought she'd never find. She tightened her arms around him and said simply, "I love you, Grant Wolfe."

He smiled, a smile like the sun rising on a dreary day. "I love you, too, Trish Devlin."

Fate? Destiny? Or just a random probability?

They neither knew nor cared.

Love was enough.

* * * * *

INTRIGUE...

2-IN-1 ANTHOLOGY

COLD CASE AFFAIR

by Loreth Anne White

When pregnant Muirinn returns to her Alaska home town, she slams right into the past she's tried so hard to forget. But now rugged Jett could be her only hope of survival.

HER HERO IN HIDING

by Rachel Lee

After finding Kay injured and pregnant on a deserted country road, gorgeous rancher Clint swears to protect her—even if she is being hunted by a serial killer...

•••

SINGLE TITLE

SMOKIN' SIX-SHOOTER

by BJ Daniels

Although her new neighbour is all gorgeous cowboy, Dulcie isn't looking for love. She needs to solve a murder. But when she digs too deep Russell could be her saviour.

On sale from 17th December 2010
Don't miss out!

Available at WHSmith, Tesco, ASDA, Eason
and all good bookshops

www.millsandboon.co.uk

1210/46b

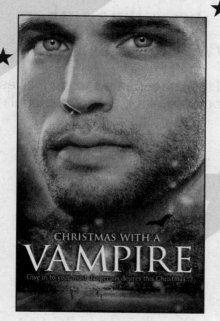